*She was laughing . . . lovely . . .
unmistakably*

Claude

"You do remember me, Mr. Vallon, don't you? Up
on the terrace."

She took a step toward him, breathless that he
would suddenly go, that they would all scatter like
a pack of cards tossed in the air. . . .

He was even handsomer than she remembered.

Suddenly his eyes met hers, deep, lingering, the
gray irises so light as to be almost hypnotic. It was
a look such as she had never received. Her knees
felt rubbery, her skin hot, then cold, her face flushed.

She found it impossible to look away. . . .

Claude
A radiant novel of young passion

Claude

THE
ROUNDTREE WOMEN
Book II

Margaret Lewerth

A DELL BOOK

All of the characters in this book are fictitious, and any resemblance to actual persons, either living or dead, is purely coincidental.

Published by
Dell Publishing Co., Inc.
1 Dag Hammarskjold Plaza
New York, New York 10017

Copyright © 1979 by Margaret Lewerth

All rights reserved. No part of this book may be reproduced or transmitted in any form or by any means, electronic or mechanical, including photocopying, recording or by any information storage and retrieval system, without the written permission of the Publisher, except where permitted by law.

Dell ® TM 681510, Dell Publishing Co., Inc.

ISBN: 0-440-11255-9

Printed in the United States of America

First printing—June 1979

There is a star, the sailors call it true,
Hung fixed above this planet through its night.
By day unseen, but to the heart in view,
Like love unsaid, until the need for light.

Think on it when you turn your face away,
Look back, my love, and share with me one day.

—HENRIETTA ROUNDTREE, 1899

Part One

Thatcher—1897

Once a year the Devil set foot in Thatcher.

In the tranquil shimmer of a late July day, doors were flung wide, curtains fluttered, and duty was abandoned as the citizens poured out in welcome. Trumpet, trombone, two cornets, a piccolo, and a base drum burst on to Main Street. This was followed by a row of blazered dandies, strutting, twirling straw hats, and ogling the susceptible girls. Last, on a flat-top wagon drawn by two muscled gray horses, a covey of hip-rolling belles blew kisses, a young man in white and silver flourished a mandolin, and a flame-haired, not-so-young spangled lady rattled a tambourine and spun a brief satin skirt to reveal purple tights.

Kelly's Traveling Troupe had arrived.

Wet-lipped, hot-eyed, the young pursued it out the Pike Road and up to Preacher Hill. Later the middle-aged would succumb, riding sedately in an assortment of vehicles to sit on hard benches under a rickety tent and sate themselves.

It was as futile to contain the town as to fence water. Kelly's Troupe stayed a heady week. Every evening its raucous splendor paraded down Main Street. In the Roundtree house this coincided with supper grace.

Isaac Roundtree looked over the bowed heads of his brood and raised his voice in defiance. "'And the Lord shall smite down the harlot, Babylon, and clasp the white lamb of purity to His bosom.'"

Young Chastity turned a sudden pink. The boys nudged. Henrietta Roundtree, at the far end of the table, sighed soundlessly. She was no longer sure where Holy Writ ended and her husband began. She saw Cassie's quick flush. The girl was growing up. No, she was full blown now. With a familiar tug at her heart, Henrietta realized that the number at her table was dwindling.

There had been ten children. Now there were five. Three lay in Cemetery Hill. Mary Patience had taken her gentle determination into a dubious marriage in Chicago. Simon, the wild one, had gone west with a shadow over his head. Henrietta's own tempestuous New Orleans blood flowed through them all and seemed more kindled than cooled by Isaac's fervor. She loved her children with the intensity she brought to everything in her life. With them she would have liked to run after Kelly's Traveling Troupe to the summit of the hill.

Isaac finished. They ate in silence until Chastity set down her fork.

"May I go now?"

"Where?" Isaac looked sharply at his too-pretty daughter.

"To the show."

"I would have thought twice was enough."

"This is the last night, Father."

"Everyone will be there, Isaac." Henrietta knew it was a plea for herself. And a mistake.

Isaac stood up, a gaunt, gray-faced man, lifted by unbending work into the eminence of town councilman and senior elder. "I can only pray for righteousness when the whole town has gone mad." They heard the study door close. In another moment the room was empty. Henrietta caught her daughter at the door.

"How are you getting there, Cassie?"

"With Joel. In Mr. Putnam's wagon."

"You'll be all right?"

"Why shouldn't I be?" She kissed her mother and slid from her.

It was not an answer. No more of an answer than Henrietta herself had given on another summer night, how many years ago? How little life changed or passions altered. Inevitable as time, youth would love and err and love again. Unless—the single dimple in her left cheek flickered. Unless they were Roundtrees. In which case they would love and err and do penance. Or die.

Henrietta, slight, tall, supple as a girl, stood another moment looking into the washed-green light of evening. Then she closed the door against the new night.

It was nearly midnight when the final revelry ended on Preacher Hill. The town, its giddiness spent, slept. The Roundtree house lay in darkness, illuminated fitfully by summer heat-lightning. In the shadow of the rear door, Cassie waited. She had only to cross the kitchen garden, gain the darkness of the maples, then run into the meadow beyond, over the stone wall, through a field of shoulder-high corn, and she would be in the custody of the benign woods. Beyond lay the wagon road to the foot of Thatcher

Ridge. There she could take her time. It would not do
to arrive early.

But she must not be late. She waited for another
sheet of lightning to pass and began to run. She
reached the open meadow when the lightning trapped
her. An angular figure detached itself from a hickory
tree.

"Cassie!"

"Joel! What are you doing here?"

"Where you going?"

"Isn't that my business?"

"I thought it was mine since we're getting married."

"I never said I'd marry you, Joel. Never."

His fingers gripped her arm.

"We talked about it. I wrote you a letter, didn't I?"

"Let go of me."

She twisted free but she knew that would not end
it. She would have to come to terms with Joel first,
then and there, or everything would be ruined. She
lifted her face, fragile as a moonflower, and let her
hood slip from her pale hair.

"Letter? Joe, when you really care about somebody,
you don't put it in a letter. You come and speak up. It
was a very nice letter, the writing and all. And the
lines were so even. But a girl wouldn't call that pro-
posing. Of course we talked about marriage. But I
talk about marriage and things to a lot of boys. It's
about all you can do in Thatcher in the summer, isn't
it?" Her voice dropped to a melting whisper. "Joel,
can you keep a secret?"

The lanky young man shifted. Chastity Roundtree
was all he loved and wanted in life. He would die for
her. He would cross the continent for her. He would
build her the finest house she could want, someday.
But he already had reason to suspect that the Round-

tree mischief ran as hot in her as in the rest of them. The suspicion had led him to this moment and this spot.

"I don't want to know any secrets. I want to know where you're going. And when you're going to say yes to me."

"That is my secret, Joel. I'm not going to say yes to you or anybody. I'm not going to get married."

Relief eased into him. But only a little. "What else would you do?"

She stood on tiptoe and whispered into his ear. "I'm going to be famous, Joel. And when you come back from California all rich and prosperous, I'll invite you to come and see me. I'll never forget my old friends."

To her dismay his big arms locked around her. "No, Cassie, you're not! I know all about that. I saw you sitting on the front bench up there on Preacher Hill, making eyes at the fella up on that platform, and him singing and winking and blowing kisses at you. I didn't say anything then but I'm going to say it now. You're not going with him. You're a good, decent girl, and I'm going to marry you and give you every-thing . . ."

With a gasp he dropped his arm. She had sunk her small teeth through his shirt to the flesh.

"Just because you proposed, Joel Barker, you don't own me. I'm not going to be bought and paid for and settled like all the silly girls in this town. I've got tal-ent. Arnie says so. And I'm going to make a splash on my own! You can tell anybody you want but you're not going to stop me!"

She broke from him and ran. She stumbled once. Then she was on her feet racing into the dark with the lightness of a deer and the purpose of a hawk.

She was breathless when she reached the foot of

Bluestone Ridge. Another flare of lightning revealed a man, a hack, and a horse.

"You really meant it, Arnie!"

"What else did you think?" He kissed her and was surprised at the intensity of her young mouth.

In the closeness of the hired carriage his arm went around her. Arnold Hapgood, late song-and-dance man of Kelly's Traveling Troupe at last had what he wanted. Other girls had pretty faces, neat ankles, passable voices, and eagerness. Cassie Roundtree had class. He wondered when he could cup her breast or let his hand drift across her thigh. He suspected she would not resist too much. But he did not want to confuse the issue. Not yet.

In the swaying lantern light he flashed her his impudent grin.

"Hapgood and Cassie! How about it, baby?"

Her eyes widened with anticipation. The mischief glinted. "Cassie and Hapgood," she murmured.

He tightened his arm and slapped the reins.

They were taking the milk train from Bollington. To New York City.

Joel Barker knew before he reached home that he had nothing to tell. When the news broke of Cassie's elopement, for that was all he was willing to believe, Thatcher would be titillated, pleasantly shocked, but not surprised. Heads would nod knowingly at the Roundtree house. The old stories, the dark hints about Henrietta's hot New Orleans blood would be dusted off and relished for a while. Then it would be over.

So it might have been, had not the Reverend Obediah Starke made one of his surreptitious visits to New York, the better to guide his congregation with a closer knowledge of sin. On his return he confided to

Mrs. Starke, whose duty it was to spread the Reverend Starke's words, that he had something to report. He had seen Chastity Roundtree. In the flesh. Very much in the flesh. There was no mistake. In black and pink tights, hair frizzed, mouth scarlet, there was Cassie standing up on a stage in front of a line of similarly unclad young women, swaying her hips and singing. The Reverend was clear on this point. He had taken notes. She was singing "He knew just what to do and he was doing it." The Reverend explained delicately that the song referred to a young man repairing a torn bathing suit with a safety pin. But, as Mrs. Starke discovered, everybody knew exactly what was meant. So much so, that for weeks afterwards any Thatcher cutup, catching sight of the Reverend Starke from a safe side of the street, would mumble under his breath, "He knew just what to do. . . ."

What the Reverend Starke did not report was that Cassie's slenderness had become bone-skinny, her eyes haunted, and the sweet, wavering voice she brought to the forlorn banality of her act was met on Saturday nights with guffaws. So eager was the Reverend to pursue the path of salvation that he had not even remained long enough to see the star attraction, the sensational song-and-dance team, Hapgood and Dollie-Belle.

Isaac Roundtree went to New York to find her. He returned alone. For two days he shut himself in his study with his Bible, searching his soul to learn what he had done to earn such disgrace. Then, accusation boiling through him like hot pitch, he went upstairs where Henrietta sat in her bed in her lace peignoir, her dark hair rippling below her shoulders. The sight of her released the demons with which Isaac Roundtree was cursed. He savagely possessed her, clawing the white flesh as if it were destroying him. Then he rode out to the valley that held his farm. On a bleak winter field in the moonless night, he flagellated his naked body with a halter shank and prayed for deliverance.

After that Isaac Roundtree walked as usual, in frock-coated dignity, to his duties, and Thatcher poured out its respectful, silent sympathy. Without naming names, the Reverend Starke preached from his pulpit that a good man was the noblest work of God, and as the lesson for the day read the Parable of the Foolish Virgins.

Chastity came home at last. The shades of her room remained drawn. Those who did see her marveled at a gray, unearthly beauty that lay like a cobweb on her face. She took to walking the lonely Ridge. One March day she was found lying at the base, broken but lovely in death, her eyes fixed on the wind-cleansed sky. Accident or remorse? Thatcher did not know. God in His way took care of His own.

Henrietta, who never saw sin in a loving heart, poured her pain into her diary. "Chastity, my darling, my darling! I understand. I do! Perhaps . . ." the word was scratched out. She began again. "Surely, I might have done the same thing. If he had been a laughing, dancing, kindly man . . . if. . . ."

As so often happened, Henrietta's impulsive words broke off. Confession hardly begun had ended.

Chastity was left in peace. Not a wisp of ghostliness clung to her, not the grace note of a single portrait. Isaac, in self-punishment, saw to that. A small headstone at last materialized.

CHASTITY
1878–1900

The name Roundtree was omitted.

The decades passed; Thatcher forgot why. Other faces came and went, other voices, other loves and anguish flowed through the Roundtree house on West Street.

But blood is more durable than stone. Our immortality may lie in our genes. Like it or not, all our ancestors ride within us.

Those who believe that, might see Cassie three quarters of a century later, in a girl in blue jeans, pedaling her bicycle furiously out of Thatcher. On a May afternoon her face is a mask of innocence, her mind a web of unnamed desires, her destination lonely and deserted Thatcher Ridge. Her name is Claude Roundtree.

Part Two

Thatcher—1972
June

Chapter One

The girl pushed her bicycle up the dirt road to the barred metal gate and stopped. It was hot for early June, and the last fifty yards of her climb had taken her directly into the afternoon sun. She swept the long light hair from her forehead, wiped the moisture away with the back of her hand, and glanced quickly around.

With practiced ease, she turned her bicycle off the road and laid it behind a clump of massed rhododendron. It was safely hidden although the precaution hardly seemed necessary. No one came up to Bluestone Ridge these days except the caretakers, and they went into town together every Thursday. She had made sure of that.

Beyond the gate rose a cluster of tall cool pines, pierced by a wide and curving gravel drive. Looking up, she could just glimpse a jutting angle of the great flanked house of glass and granite that spread its two dark, outrageous wings above her and the town. The sight sent a tingle of expectancy through her. It was not Claude Roundtree's first visit to the stark and lonely house on the Ridge.

Named Blue Rocks by its owners and the Fortress by the less reverent, the house was known generally as the Orlini place. It was considered an affront to every white-clapboard, green-shuttered, time-settled house in the Connecticut town of Thatcher. For two years now it had stood unused, although it was said to be kept in what Thatcher called "apple-pie" order, as if the Orlinis would return at any hour. Perhaps they did, these odd outsiders, coming and going like birds of night passage. But if so, the caretakers never told. Observing Si Barker's new car and Effie Haskell Barker's new winter coat, Thatcher decided they were rewarded for their silence and labeled it disloyal.

But tongues no longer wagged. The Orlinis had paid for their arrogance on Bluestone Ridge. The oldest citizen could have warned them of that. The Ridge, a rocky spine wall part of the long valley west of the town, was once a legendary place of towering trees and deep ledges that the setting sun turned an eerie blue. The Indians long ago had considered it a place to be left alone. A force, a power, dwelt there, the legend went, that resented intrusion. The Orlinis had intruded with the cruelty of bulldozer and chain saw. The Ridge had struck back. With more satisfaction than charity, Thatcher waited for the next bolt to strike and, hopefully, for the house to vanish.

Neither of which had happened. Neither of which even faintly clouded the anticipation in young Claude Roundtree's mind on this June afternoon with its promise of summer. Even the thought of summer she had banished, the long, deadly summer that lay ahead. For a few hours in this deserted splendor she could live with her dreams. Claude's dreams were her only reality.

She slid quickly under the heavy iron chain that anchored the gate posts. Half walking, half running on the pine needles that bordered the gravel she followed the drive up the last steep incline, failing to note a small change that had taken place since her last surreptitious visit. The No TRESPASSING sign had been replaced. The new sign read: TRESPASSING STRICTLY FORBIDDEN. UNDER PENALTY OF THE LAW.

Once out of sight of the gate, Claude slowed her pace to savor every step of her approach. A jet trail streaked the blue mist of the new sky. She followed it for an instant with serious eyes. Something rustled in the underbrush. A small rabbit ran confidently across the gravel. Otherwise there were only the stillness and her own light footsteps. The drive curved at last out of the pines, swept around a boulder and onto a commanding gravel circle rimmed with carefully constrained yew.

Claude drew a deep breath. This was the moment she lived for, the moment when she ceased to be Claude Roundtree. She could put no name to it. But it always happened when the shining magnificence of the house burst on her and touched her with distance. Here she was free. The word skipped through her mind. "Free to be me. No. Not me. Free to be somebody else. Somebody I've never been before." At home, in the centuries-old Roundtree house on West Street, the world was a prison. Up here it was a promise.

She stood an instant longer in the shadow of the yew trees gazing at the house. It was not stark. It was not ugly. It was lofty and soaring. It was radiance locked prismlike in the dark strength of granite. And for a few unchallenged hours it was hers.

She made the round of check points. There were no wheel marks on the gravel drive. The Barkers' pickup truck was gone from the lower garage. The three tennis courts bore no footprint or ball mark. The stables that had never held horses were pristine. And the long swimming pool, guarded by eight female marble figures, reflected their abundant nudity with mirrorlike accuracy.

The statues had bothered Claude at first. They were too life-sized, too near. She wondered what kind of people ever sat on the terrace looking at them. Art was appreciated in Thatcher but at a distance. But now she had become used to them. One day she had stripped off her jeans, her sweater, and briefs, and plunged into the pool. The distant sound of a car had sent her scurrying to safety. It had proved a false alarm but she never tried the pool again, even though the statues seemed to invite it. Perhaps that was their purpose. It was part of the magic of the place. Everything was forbidden, yet everything, for a few stolen hours, was hers.

From the red-tile terrace she could look to the far end of the pool where a marble nymph was caught, not unwillingly, in the arms of an inscrutable satyr. As the light from the water played on the stone, the nymph seemed both to struggle and yield. Conquest and surrender, terror and delight, lust and innocence. It filled Claude with an uneasiness she could not define.

Yet was not that the essence of these visits? No explanation, no definition, no awkwardness to be suffered. She could people this emptiness with her imagination, and her silent guests could be dismissed in a breath.

She passed a fat, head-tall, red Etruscan vase and peered through the glass wall into the living room. The heavy white curtains, half drawn against the sun, revealed a long expanse of deep white rug, an ebony-black grand piano, and at the far end, the curving, wrought-iron staircase down which she saw herself move step by step to an admiring throng. Faceless, to be sure, but she could hear its applause.

But it was not applause. It was something else she heard now. Something real. And approaching. A quick rhythmic crunch of footsteps on gravel. She spun around. Nothing moved in the afternoon stillness. The steps had ceased. Then she heard them again, coming from the left where the lawn sloped to the gravel paths of a formal garden. She glanced wildly around. There was no place she could go. The entire terrace was in full view of anyone coming from the garden. And there she was peering into the house like an interloper. Or a thief. She ducked behind the enormous red vase and held her breath.

She saw the shadow before she saw the man.

He came into view, stripped to trunks and wearing the striped shoes of a runner. He was slender, of average height, his hair crisp and graying, his face bronzed and as lean as the conquering satyr. He threw himself into a lounge chair beside the pool, shaded his eyes, and looked up to the terrace.

"If you have any good reason for hiding behind that vase, you'd better give it to me!" His voice was elegant and thin with anger. It also bore a faint, tantalizing accent.

Claude felt her knees weaken, her face burn. She might have guessed. She had not been hidden at all. He could see her reflection with the vase in the glass behind her.

"Now!" He had risen and was coming up the stone steps. "Or shall I . . ."

She slipped from behind the vase. "You don't have to call the police." As usual with Claude, fear gave way almost at once to indignation that dimmed any lingering sense of guilt. "I haven't stolen anything. I don't want anything. And I haven't done any harm. I was just looking and if I intruded, and if you are Mr. Orlini, I'm sorry. I'll go right away."

He looked at her for a long moment. "How old are you?"

She bridled. She didn't mind being accused, but if he was laughing at her. . . . "What has that to do with it?"

"I asked you a question."

"I know."

"I assume you're old enough to be responsible."

She understood. But she would rather be rude than let this stranger with his mocking voice consider himself so superior. She was not a child.

"Okay. If you want to call the police, Mr. Orlini." Claude was achingly aware of her torn jeans, her scuffed loafers, and her sloppy T-shirt. She was also aware of the light gray eyes that focused on her face without blinking.

"I am not Mr. Orlini. My name is Marc Vallon." He bowed stiffly and made it seem natural. "I have no intention of calling the police. I am a guest in this house. Who are you?"

"Does it matter?" She was aching to get away.

"That's the second rude answer you've given me, young lady. You have something to learn about the art of conversation. I shall repeat my question."

It occurred to her that he was detaining her.

"My name is Claude Roundtree and I live in Thatcher. Down there."

"Ah, yes. Charming. Is that all?"

"What else is there? Look, I'm going, Mr.—Mr. . . ."

"Vallon. Marc Vallon. Don't you listen as well as talk?"

"Mr. Vallon, I've apologized. Now if you'll please excuse me. . . ."

"How do you propose to get down off this Ridge? Have you a car?"

"No, I haven't. I have a bicycle. It's good enough." She heard her own voice, young, impolite. It was not like her, but there was something about this man, his unwavering gaze, the suppleness of his tanned body, that disturbed her. She could not guess his age nor could she keep from glancing at his eyes. They were stern, though his thin lips twisted.

"I see. And where might it be?"

The questions, the endless, useless questions rooting her there. But she was no longer embarrassed. He was only a visitor. He would probably be gone soon. Didn't he ever blink his eyes?

"It's down in the bushes below the gate where I always . . ." she broke off.

"So you come here often." It was not a question.

"Only when I'm sure no one is around. I made a mistake today."

For the first time he smiled, a twisted half-smile. "You like the loneliness up here?"

"I like the view." She brushed her hair from her cheek. She had no idea of the flushed loveliness her intensity gave her.

"Is that all?"

"It's my power spot."

"Ah—so?" He apparently did not believe her.

"I mean . . ." she had talked too freely, yet she found herself unable to stop. "I mean, when I come up here I feel bigger than myself. I feel I can do a lot of things that I didn't think I could do. I can sort of put it all together."

"You are an unusual young woman, Miss Round-tree. It would be my pleasure to say that you are welcome here whenever you choose to come. Unfortunately, that is impossible."

It was on the tip of her tongue to fling out "I haven't asked, have I?" Instead she heard herself say quietly, "I understand. But thanks anyway. Good-bye, Mr.—Mr. Vallon."

She started toward the driveway and found him beside her, his eyes again disconcertingly direct.

"I would like to give you a little advice. When you reach the gate, there is a sign. Take time to read it. TRESPASSING STRICTLY FORBIDDEN. UNDER PENALTY OF THE LAW. I had it put there myself. Try to remember it. Good day, Miss Roundtree." He bowed stiffly and left her.

By the time Claude reached the gate, her anger had cooled. She would meet Marc Vallon again someday. She would be rich and famous and he, maybe, would be old and poor. She would listen to his apology in stony silence. And forgive him. It brought tears to her eyes.

She heard a car coming toward her up the hill. She steered her bicycle to the side of the narrow road and waited for a pickup truck to pass. The Barkers were coming back early. She saw Effie Barker's dumpling face swing around like an astonished moon as they passed. Claude did not wave. It did not matter what they thought anyhow.

On the terrace Marc Vallon slid the glass door open

and entered the living room. A young man came toward him with a sheaf of papers in his hand. He was stocky, blunt of chin, square of shoulder, and his eyes showed no awe of his employer.

"Who was that?"

"Just a local girl."

"What did she come up here for?"

"She said it was her 'power spot.' Whatever she means by that. It isn't any longer. I made that clear. Damn it, Hutch, that's your job. To keep the locals out. To keep everybody out. I want it done! We haven't much time and if we don't get a break in the weather soon, we'll be in trouble."

Davison L. Hutchins, aide-de-camp, detail manager, and bucket boy as he saw himself, was used to Marc Vallon's show of authority. He was also used to Marc's tendency to trifle with the truth where women were concerned. He liked what he saw of the girl on the terrace, her fresh-washed good looks, her long shining hair. Not a beauty but as pretty as she need be. And a certain elusive air that Hutch called quality.

Marc, at the foot of the stairs, flipped a hand. "Forget it, Hutch."

Hutch followed the confident, almost arrogant figure with narrowed eyes. He was not sure whether Marc Vallon intended to forget the papers he held. Or the girl. He hoped it was the girl.

Claude was in no hurry to reach home. She had too much on her mind. She never thought of herself as superstitious. But she had two abiding beliefs. One was in her lucky number, nine, which never failed her. But she saw nothing about this encounter that could add or subtract to nine.

Her other belief was in Destiny. Not Destiny as a

cosmic force like the fourth dimension, which she never would or wanted to understand. But Destiny as a private bolt of lightning that would strike her personally and lift her out of herself and Thatcher to set her down on some distant unimagined spot where her yearnings would be answered, her talents recognized. She was not sure what talents. Destiny would have to take care of that, too. But in the end she would be rewarded with fame, fortune, love, and marriage.

Sometimes she reversed the order. She was grown now. She had been through what her Uncle Willard called the slings and arrows of outrageous adolescence. Impatiently she told herself she should have settled whatever was left of that mystery long ago. Instead she found, late at night or early in the morning when her defenses were down, that she was blundering helplessly through a labyrinth of paths labeled variously love, sex, marriage. If she could find the single road through them, there would be no mystery. As it was, she could not think of sex without love, nor could she love anyone she would not be willing to marry. It was a box, and by the time she was twenty, it would be a bind.

She could see that now. But looking back she could see no missed opportunity.

There had been Rolf Quimby, the high school science teacher, older than any of the boys she knew, and tantalizing behind his beard. There had been three months of delicious unfulfilled trysts, hand touchings, and secret glances that had enlivened Biology I. There had been one mad icy night when his car rattled up Preacher Hill and stalled. Instead of sweeping her into his arms he told her he was leaving. He told her that undefiled love was the most beautiful of all. "We shall keep our secret forever." She had nodded, too moved to speak, seeing herself walking aloof and mysterious through life carrying the dark fire of tragic passion within her. Three weeks later the bulletin board carried a small newspaper clipping of the marriage of Mr. Rolf Quimby to Ms. Phoebe Plante, of Pawtucket, a student of applied psychology.

That was long ago. As she looked back, Rolf Quimby, among his dissected frogs and steamy test tubes, barely filled the outlines of hidden passion.

The clumsy years were behind her now. The prom nights and the football games, the parked cars and sweaty groping hands, repulsed by her own fastidiousness.

There was only Larry Higgins, as the pulsing spring headed into summer. Larry, the pharmacist's son she had known since childhood. When he was eight, up on snow-encrusted Preacher Hill, his sled rammed another, and the end of the runner had gone into Larry's eye. He had lost it and for a long time he had worn a black patch. Now he wore glasses, the right lens darkened. It had never bothered her. Larry was sweet, and she felt a deep compassion when other girls refused him. He had become a habit, then a shield, and, although Claude was too honest to want it, offered her a dogged, adoring faithfulness. Claude did not think of sex with Larry Higgins.

She pedaled slowly down West Street. For an instant the pedestaled birdbath in the Eltons' yard shimmered into marble. A marble nymph, an inscrutable satyr. She saw again the statue at the pool's end, the captured passion, so eloquent, so breathing, without beginning, and without climax. She felt the uneasy eagerness she could neither express nor define when she watched it from the terrace. Was not this the essence of those visits now so bluntly ended?

The Connecticut twilight had begun its slow drift through the maple trees when Claude reached home. She went up the steps to the porch, hardly aware of it. The fantasy of the afternoon still held her, the glimpse of something unknown, indefinable, the unblinking appraisal of those all-knowing gray eyes. Even the name was remote, foreign. Marc Vallon. She had never met a man like him. She wondered where he came from, what he did. Then telling herself it couldn't possibly interest her, she wondered whether she, Claude Roundtree, would ever get far enough from Thatcher to meet such a man again.

"Claude, dear!" Edythe Roundtree, warm and careful, looked closely at her fourth child, this blossoming daughter of so many moods. "Larry called you twice."

"He's going to pick you up at seven thirty for the movies." It was Kim, the youngest, from the living room. "I told him super."

"Thanks a bunch."

"Well, isn't it, Claudie? Super, I mean?"

"Sure. Why don't *you* go with him, butterball?" But there was no sting in Claude's voice. She loved them all. That was part of the trouble.

"It's not butter. It's muscles, and Miss Pritchey says I need every one of them if I'm going to win the broad jump. Besides, he didn't ask me."

Claude had forgotten the date, if she had ever really thought of it. Now the trap was closing. But not without a struggle. The pool, the figures, the sunlit, dream-filled elegance still floated in her mind.

"Claude!" Her mother's voice followed her. "I think it would be nice if we invited Larry for dinner some night."

"Mom, for heaven's sake! He's into health foods."

She closed the bedroom door. Marc Vallon's strange inscrutability was fading. She reached for it and her mind played her a trick. He became the satyr at the end of the pool.

Chapter Two

The second-story, plate-glass window on Main Street that bore the letters ROUNDTREE AND ROUNDTREE, ATTORNEYS AT LAW was shaded against the sun, muffling the afternoon traffic. The building that housed it was a remnant of Thatcher's Victorian heyday. But, old-fashioned as it was, every cupola and scallop gleamed with fresh paint. Leo's cobbler shop still occupied one side of the first floor, and the barbershop the other. Things did not change that much nor did anyone want them to, but the stairs were newly railed, and the hallway's smell of resin and hair tonic, to which Martin Roundtree had grown so accustomed, had lost some of its assault.

Within the offices of Roundtree and Roundtree, dignity, permanence, and time prevailed. The deep, brown-leather chairs offered ease, the rows of legal books confidence, and the fine but threadbare oriental rug stability. It was a place where for decades Thatcher brought its trust as well as its problems.

On this afternoon John Roundtree, the other half of

Roundtree and Roundtree, sat in his father's desk chair. Not by choice but because he knew his visitors expected it. John, in his midtwenties, had grown accustomed to doing what was expected, and now that his father had fallen into the habit of leaving early, what was expected had locked a pattern. John would not label it, even to himself, a burden.

He was a tall, gaunt young man with features that would some day be craggy. His dark eyes were serious (too serious, some said), but his manner gentle. And that seriousness was what the delegation filling the leather chairs and overflowing onto the tufted-leather sofa wanted.

John looked them over. There was Duncan Phelps, married to his cousin Ariel, the startling beauty of the Roundtrees; Duncan, trying now for two years to meld tradition and new purpose in his ministry at St. Mark's church. His dark jacket showed ragged edges; he looked tired. There was Big Moon Wright, a large-muscled man and a force for order, proprietor of Big Moon's Diner in seedy Juno's Landing, two miles down river. Cliff Simmons, son-in-law of the *Standard's* publisher and editor. Cliff was in the process of divorce. He looked nervous and insecure. There was Freddie Slater, heir to Slater's Stationery store. And Pete, in dirty sneakers, long tangled hair, and ragged, tawny beard. If Pete had a last name no one knew it. He was the owner of Pete's Rock, a shabby, throbbing discotheque, in the heart of Juno's Landing, which under its somewhat sacrilegious name offered Thatcher's young temptation and, it was hinted, worse. But Pete was a friend. That was why he was slouching at this moment in one of the Roundtree office chairs.

There were others, all young, all friends, and what they had to say to John was preposterous.

John scanned the group. "Why me?"

"Because. . . ." Big Moon was the spokesman. "If anybody's going to get this town off its ass, it's gotta be you."

"I'm not a public speaker. I'm not a glad-hander. And I hate politics."

"Nobody likes 'em, baby," said Pete softly. "But there's no other way. Somebody's got to get us a new road up here, and maybe a few roofs fixed down in shantytown."

"And a new bridge. The old one's not going to last out many more rough winters." Freddie Slater traveled it every day for the Bollington afternoon paper.

It seemed remote, with the June sunshine sliding under the window blind. John felt the silence.

"I know something about growing trees, a little about law, and not a damned thing about running for office."

"You know more than Harlan Phelps, begging your pardon, Reverend."

Duncan grinned but the pain was in his eyes. "I don't take offense, Pete. I don't think my father should be running for office. He's not in condition." It was a politeness accepted by all. They liked Duncan. He turned to John. "That's why I'm here today. I can't give you open support because—well, he is my father. But I won't make any waves. Ariel and I would both like to see you do it."

"So it's settled." Big Moon stood up. "John Roundtree for Congress from the Thatcher County district next fall."

"Wait a minute, all of you. Sit down, Moon." John was always surprised when he did take command. "I don't say you're crazy. You're good guys. My friends."

There was a laugh. "God almighty, you sound like a politician already, Johnnie," Pete roared.

"Yeah, but I meant it. Now shut up and listen and try to think. Even if I wanted to do this, there are too many minuses. First, my name's Roundtree. That hasn't always been lily-pure in this town. There are a few items here and there people might like to dig up."

"Oh, come on, John . . . you got a name. That's what . . ."

"And the second minus," John lashed through the rising voices. "The second minus is money. My family's got some land and an old house, but what you guys are talking about takes money. I understand Orlini is putting money behind Harlan Phelps. Sorry, Duncan. But I guess you'll have to sit still for this."

"I'm sitting still, John. Very still. Go on."

"I'm not afraid of Orlini. And he won't be around much."

"You know what's going on up at the Orlini house?" It was Cliff. "I understand some people are staying up there but the gate's chained."

"Some friends of Orlini, I suppose. Nothing to do with Thatcher." John would not satisfy Cliff's abundant curiosity. His eyes swept the circle of faces. "So that's about it. I'm grateful to you. And thanks. But I don't see how . . ."

"That does it, guys! That settles it!" Moon was on his feet again. "He's accepted. We're running John Roundtree for Congress in the September primary and then . . ."

Cheers broke loose. Somebody pulled John out of his chair and hoisted him on shoulders. He was paraded around the staid old office as the floor shook.

"You're out of your minds!" he gasped.

"Right. That's why we'll get the job done!" Voices

crisscrossed. "Money? What's that? Fishfood! Who needs it? We'll get everybody under thirty working for us, free. We'll get that good-looking kid sister of yours, John . . . that's what you need. A pretty girl up there beside you. Claude knows a lot of other girls. We'll get 'em hats. We'll put 'em on street corners and on the phone. We'll get Pete's band. . . . All you have to do, John-boy, is show up. And talk!"

"What would I say?" John was laughing but inside his stomach tightened.

"That's the beauty of politics. You don't have to say anything. Just look honest. The opposition can't do that. Sorry, Duncan."

"It's okay. I told you that."

They left at last. All but Duncan. John sat in one of the leather chairs and looked at something he couldn't see. The future. A future that had thrust itself on him.

"I think you ought to do it, John." Duncan's voice was sober.

"How do I know I *can*?"

"You'll have to find that out. We all do. They think you can. So do I. That's a few votes right there."

"I wonder about Dad." John wished he hadn't said that. It revealed too much. "But I don't want to involve the family. If I do this, I'll do it myself."

"You can't. That's not the ball game. It's people all the way, and don't overlook Claude. She's grown up now. And she's stifled. She just might be the biggest asset you have."

John walked slowly home. People he passed seemed especially friendly. He tried to imagine asking for their votes. It was not what he wanted to do. Once he had wanted only the silence of the big trees, the closeness of earth and sky. But maybe this was bigger even than what he had wanted for himself.

He passed the post office and noticed the chipping paint. He thought of the weakening bridge.

But at a deeper and more probing level, maybe this was his escape.

He'd talk to his father after dinner. And Claude . . . he grinned to himself . . . when he caught up with her.

The evening started badly. Claude had seen the movie. Larry, sensing her restlessness and his own stirring to the sorcery of the night, suggested a drive. Claude opted for Pete's Rock.

"Claude, your dad isn't going to like that idea."

She gave him a small part of that thousand-watt smile that made her almost beautiful.

"Are you taking Dad or me?"

Pete's Rock was open three nights of the week for business. The other three days Pete worked at Cal's Fix-It car lot. Sunday he kept for himself and his friends, and all day and night a blood-raising beat was likely to shatter the Sabbath calm. But it could not be heard two miles up river in Thatcher, and the inhabitants of Juno's Landing did not mind. It was Pete's home, and Pete was known by his neighbors as a good guy.

Larry swung the car down Wharf Street that ran along the river, turned up past the long-abandoned factory that thrust into the sky like a dead tooth, and parked in a dark, vacant lot. Across the street a seedy clapboard house glowed with a running neon sign, PETE'S ROCK. Claude's eyes sparkled.

They crossed a sagging porch.

"The guy ought to fix this place up."

"Maybe he likes it this way. All hanging loose. That's for me. You're so uptight, Larry." She slid

ahead of him through the door and found a platter-
size table near the band. Talk would obviously be impossible. He followed wondering what was possessing
Claude tonight.

It was early and the place was not half filled. Larry
ordered a ginger ale, Claude a Scotch and soda. Pete
strolled over.

"You know better than that, Claude. You're a minor
and you'd be getting me into trouble."

Claude giggled. "What's wrong with trying?"

"Not in my place, little girl."

"I adore strong men. Let's dance, Larry."

The rock group was heating up. Cool as a sliver of
jet, in the clinging black dress her mother had eyed
without comment, Claude swayed languidly around
the room, a good foot-and-a-half from Larry, her long,
spun-silver hair swinging, her fingers snapping, her
eyes half closed. Strangers flowed between them. She
seemed hardly aware of it. Whenever she passed the
band she gave a sweet little smile to one or another of
the shaggy-haired group. The guitarist thrust a micro-
phone at her.

"Come on up here, baby, and give out."

Pete materialized again. "Cut it, Hank. No mixing it
with the customers."

With a shrug, Claude made her way to the table.
Pete followed and sighed. The girl had style, the
Roundtree style. He could guess her age, but she
looked about sixteen and that was the way she had
been brought up. Untouchable as hell, and as vulnerable. She'd cause somebody a lot of trouble some day
not very far off but it wasn't going to be in Pete's
Rock. He pulled up a chair between Larry and
Claude. The music had come to a brief halt.

Claude eyed him, decided to ignore him, and then eyed him again.

"What was I doing so wrong?"

"Nothing. Except why don't you go up to the Grist Mill where it's nice and refined and do it there? It's girls like you that give this place a bad name."

"I told you, Claude."

"You stay out of this, Larry. If we're not wanted here, we better know it right now. There's such a thing as rights."

"There sure is. You gonna be around this summer, Claude?"

"I didn't know you cared, Pete."

"The whole town cares." He picked up the ticket beside the glasses. "The drinks are on me, kids. And there's people waiting. See you." He nodded; the lights went out. The rock group broke loose. A few strobe lights needled the darkness and from somewhere a faceless couple slid toward the table.

In the darkness of the empty lot Claude swung around furiously. "Why didn't you speak up, Larry? Just letting us get pushed around. Who does he think he is? I hate the crummy old place anyway. But I've got as much right to be there as anyone else."

Larry said the wrong thing. "No, you haven't, Claude."

"Why not?"

"Because you're Claude Roundtree and you stand for something. Couldn't you smell the pot?"

"Sure I did. Like somebody spilled raspberry jam. What's that got to do with it?"

He did not answer. In the deeper darkness of the car, in the light of a passing car, his one clear eyeglass glinted. He was looking at her humbly, imploringly. She felt a sudden twist of compassion.

"It's okay, Larry. I'm sorry. Honestly. I don't know what got into me. I hate that yucky place. I just haven't put it all together yet. Like the summer and what I'm going to do next and . . ."

Larry caught her in his arms, burrowed his face into her neck and pushed awkwardly at the shoulder of her sleeveless dress. She twisted free, cold with astonishment.

"Larry! Have you lost your mind?"

He slid back in the seat.

"I couldn't help it, Claude. Watching you dance and seeing you sort of far away like that. I thought about you all day. And all last night too. And for a long time."

She rearranged her dress. "I thought we were friends."

"We are, but gosh, Claude, you don't know what it's like. I'm going away to pharmacy college. And, well, I'm going to be around all summer too, and we ought to have a meaningful relationship. Not just sort of go along."

She wanted to touch his hand. She wanted to take the hurt from his face. He was a friend, and she had used him and she felt ashamed. But how could she explain that her whole soul was crying out for something beyond the stars, an elegance with a satyr's smile.

"I'm sorry. I just don't feel that way."

"You don't have to make up your mind now. It'll still be meaningful."

"Let's go home."

Under the porch light her mother always left on for her, he kissed her lightly, diffidently. It was part of the ritual. But she knew he had accepted defeat. Why did you have to hurt people just to be free?

"It was really cool, Larry. Honestly." She heard
fondness betray her. "I wouldn't have had half as
good a time with anyone else."

The door closed behind her and with it a chapter in
her life. She barely felt it pass, no more than a whisper of first youth. In its place, the flickering of an
ancient wisdom and an emptiness.

The light was on in her father's study. She sighed.
When would he learn it was no longer necessary to
wait up? But her father, thin, graying, proud, was an
ailing man. It was kinder to let him believe in his
duty. Lies were often kinder, she had found that
night. It was only the truth that made trouble.

It was not her father who looked up from the old
carved desk, but John, his face an eerie green in the
light of the desk lamp.

"Well, well—the duchess herself. How was the
movie?"

"We didn't go to the movies."

"Oh?"

"We went to Pete's Rock." She said it defiantly. If
she expected a reaction, she was disappointed. "And
Pete was obnoxious. He bought me ginger ale and
then practically threw us out."

"The laws of this state make it illegal for anyone
under twenty-one to buy liquor in public bars. It's illegal to smoke pot anywhere, and Pete draws the
roughest crowd on this side of the river. What else is
new?"

Claude kicked off her shoes, curled into the rusty
black leather chair curved to her father's shape. John
was nearly seven years older than herself. She had always thought him stiff and reserved, but when he
came to Thatcher to study law and take Michael's
place in their father's office, she had felt sorry for

him. It did not seem fair. Michael had disappeared so
long ago and now here was John, who had always
talked about raising sheep or growing trees, sitting at
her father's desk, tall and thin and turning green under the old lamp. Only in the last few days had the
somber look in his face lightened. But she was cau-
tious. Experience and some prolonged thinking had
brought Claude to the conclusion that you could not
really depend on any member of your family to be a
friend. Just when you did, they'd rear back and refuse
to understand. If she was going to do anything with
her life she would have to do it herself. She saw again
the pool and the light-gray, unblinking eyes fixed on
hers.

"Read this," said John unexpectedly. He handed her
a sheet of yellow legal paper covered with his decisive
writing.

"What am I looking at?"

"I forgot. You're the generation with the limited attention span."

"I could spend a year on those chicken tracks of
yours and never know what they meant."

It was the kind of banter he liked, and she saw his
face break into a smile. "Then you'd better begin to
learn, glamor puss. It's the announcement of my candidacy for the congressional seat from this district."

"Congressional! You mean Congress? You mean
Washington?"

"You got it. I had a talk with Dad tonight. He's
gung ho."

Claude jumped and threw her arms around her
brother. "I'm so proud of you, John! It's marvelous.
Senator John . . ."

"Representative."

"What does that matter? You'll be famous and important and . . ."

"I haven't won the election yet. Or even the nomination. I'm opening campaign headquarters in the old grain and feed store next to Higgins's pharmacy. Mr. Higgins owns it and he's letting me use it. For free. He believes in me. That's where you'll be."

Claude sat down abruptly. "Me?"

"You'll help me, won't you?"

"Sure. Sure, John. I'll do everything I can. Anything." She meant it, but a premonition, a deep-rooted instinct foreshadowed the words. He sensed it.

"I better tell you. There's no pay. I don't know how many hours you'll be working. But I certainly could use you, Claude. I have only one man to beat. Harlan Phelps. And he's got Orlini's money behind him. Are you listening?"

"Of course I'm listening. You mean Mr. Orlini—up there?" She nodded vaguely.

"I mean Ben Orlini who built that lousy dam too far upriver, who'd cut down every tree in Thatcher if he could put up a building, and who owns that monstrosity up on the Ridge."

"I don't think it's a monstrosity."

"How would you know?"

She didn't answer.

"You know how everybody feels about Orlini. Speculator, wheeler-dealer. Now he's moving up into big finance; he wants his own man in Congress. He thinks this town is soft enough to give it to him. I'm going to show him we're not. If we run this campaign right, we can knock his man Phelps out of the ball park. Right?"

She had not followed. She was looking across mirrorlike water to twisting marble shapes.

"We can talk tomorrow, Claude."

"No, no. I'm fascinated." She came back with an effort. "But the Orlinis don't live up there now. They say."

"He'll be back when the campaign heats up. Right now some fancy movie director is using the place."

"Movie director?" She barely heard her own voice.

"Don't widen your eyes at me, glamor puss. He's got the place chained off like San Quentin."

"Is he—I mean, whoever he is—really making a movie?"

"I don't know what he's doing. I've never seen him. All I know is that some guy came down to the office and wanted to get the right to use the old saltpeter swamp with all the briar and cattails at the north side of Uncle Will's land. Uncle Will said okay if they could get into it."

Claude managed to simulate a yawn. John looked at her closely, unsmiling. "Don't get any silly ideas, Sis. You might get into something very unpleasant. I need you for this campaign. You'd be a great help. But it's up to you."

"I will help, John. I promise." But how could she promise when Destiny had just struck?

Her mother's door was open as she passed.

"Claude?" the voice was as musical as a girl's.

"Yes, Mom?" She saw her father's thin form on the other side of the double bed. Still and sleeping. Did they ever—any more?

"Nice evening?"

"Super, Mom."

"I'm so glad. Close the door, will you?" The request came sleepily. Another ritual over.

* * *

Claude stood at her darkened window, looking out
into the stillness, the old maples, the stars entangled
in their branches. And the silence. The utter, utter silence of Thatcher at night. Somewhere there were
bright lights and bright sounds and bright laughter
and people falling in love. How often she had seen it
in her mind. But now she no longer had to dream it.
Destiny had forked out of the sky and touched her.
She had only to know what to do next.

Marc Vallon was a movie director. He had taken
time to talk to her. He had looked at her searchingly.
At her or at some undiscovered talent she might possess? And in the end, although he had forbidden her
to return, he had seemed almost reluctant to see her
go. Of course she had built fantasies about being in
the movies. But if you lived in a town like Thatcher—
she would not think about Thatcher tonight. She
would think about Chastity, her fourth or fifth cousin
long ago, who had been on the stage. Probably famous. Talent was in the blood. She had never considered it before. Except the time she had gone to Boston
to stay with Aunt Grace and had slipped away to a
modeling agency. The man had wanted to see her
legs, then he had wanted her to take off her blouse,
and she had run out flushed and furious.

But this was different.

This was unsought, unasked for. This was Destiny.
If it was true you could be anything you really
wanted to be, Claude had found her future. She
would no longer have to agonize between business
school or state college, neither of which she wanted.
They had already faded into the distant yesterday.

Without turning on a light she let her clothes drop
to the floor. The mirror reflected her body, silver-
pale. Her figure was too thin, her breasts too small,

her face not beautiful yet. But with the right makeup. . . . The trouble was she did not feel beautiful and that was important.

What Claude did not see in that face was its intensity. Nor was she aware of the conflicting forces deep within her that had set Roundtree women apart for decades, confining them to a stage much too small to hold them. Passion and suppression, in the same emotional flood, love and hate so close they became one, a yearning for the unattainable with its toll of pain far beyond the expected limits of the human heart.

This was Claude's inheritance. Whatever dark stirrings she sensed of this she had covered with a happy banter that made her seem almost childishly young. She charmed, even as she unwittingly deceived, until the steely glint of purpose flashed.

But until tonight she had had no fixed purpose. She had drifted. That was over. She would see Marc Vallon. She had only to figure out how. After that everything would fall into place.

She climbed into bed into the delicious feeling of clean sheets on her body. She lay sleepless, staring into the dark. She remembered Marc Vallon's eyes, with their light, black-rimmed pupils, sliding over her like water. She was aware of new sensations pulsing through her, confusing her. She threw back the coverlet and let the spring night play across her.

She would be famous. She would travel the world. She would know love—suddenly the enormity of this unknown Destiny frightened her. Chilled, she pulled the familiar old quilt over her and burrowed deep. Sleep came at last. She dreamed she was running up the Ridge to someone, a dark shaft of a man who was calling, calling her. And she could not stop.

*   *   *

Willard Roundtree surveyed his caller and sighed. Not that he had any objection to the young man. He was solid: solidly built, solidly spoken. His hair was cut reasonably short. He was clean shaven and he stood squarely on his feet until Willard asked him to sit down. His name was a little fancy but it had a solid ring. Davison Hutchins. Willard wondered what part of the country he came from; his speech was American but neither Yankee nor Western, and better than one usually heard from the young of today.

Willard banished that thought at once. After seven decades he decided to accept the world as he found it. He could remember his grandfather telling him that in *his* day a young man had been thrown into a Boston jail for wearing a beard. That was only a century and a half ago, and Willard solemnly hoped that enlightenment would bring tolerance. Searching his own mind, he doubted it. Do what he could, he saw this young man as one of the Intruders. Yet he liked him.

"Scotch, bourbon, applejack? The applejack, I should advise you, is homemade. I also have a dry Madeira, an excellent aperitif."

Davison Hutchins felt the muscles in his shoulders slacken. He had not looked forward to this visit. He had heard all he wanted to, about the Roundtree starchiness. The old man was proud as an eagle. But it was good public relations and that was what Marc Vallon paid him for. Good, if whitewashed, public relations. He sat back in the chintz-covered, ladder-back rocking chair and wondered if he had ever seen one like it before.

"I didn't know anyone still drank Madeira, Mr. Roundtree. I'd enjoy it." That should mollify the old man.

Willard returned with a mahogany tray, a ship's decanter filled with golden liquid, and two fine, lead-crystal glasses.

"I do my own housekeeping, Mr. Hutchins. When I can keep the women out."

Hutch felt a grin easing his face. "So do I, sir." He lifted his glass. "To your courtesy, Mr. Roundtree. I hope we'll deserve it."

The young man had manners. He also had flare. Willard distrusted that. Nonetheless, he had committed himself.

"So you start—uh—shooting you call it, tomorrow?"

"We have some shooting to do up at the house, but if the weather's right, we'll start down in your swamp."

"The wind's swinging east. That means overcast by morning."

"That's what we want."

"How long is this going to take?"

"Not more than three weeks. Probably less. Mr. Vallon works very fast, once he starts. And very privately. This is what you might call an intimate picture. No crowd scenes. And Mr. Vallon forbids any outsiders, any onlookers. That's what we want you to understand. You won't know we're there."

"That ought to please a family of beavers and a pair of romantic wildcats in that part of the valley. There's also an elderly gray fox who would be obliged to be left alone. And a snowy owl, if he decided to return this summer." Willard's eyes sharpened. "What's an intimate picture?"

"You've got me, Mr. Roundtree. It's Mr. Vallon's term. Something to do with the soul."

"Hmph." Willard met the stranger's eyes, and both men grinned. "They'll be glad to know it around here. Well, I've got my June plantin' to get in. And I'm late now. Winter beets. Butternut squash." Willard's eyes twinkled.

Davison Hutchins rose. He was not fooled. The old man could retreat into Yankee farmer if it amused him, but Marc Vallon would find a shrewd adversary if he abused the privilege of Willard Roundtree's land.

"We're very grateful to you, sir."

"Always glad to help culture, young man. By the way, northwest of the swamp, about five hundred yards, you'll find the remains of an old root cellar. Three centuries ago, all that land was farmed. You can see that from the stone walls running through the woods. They marked out the pastures. The trees are all second growth now, grown right over the old foundations. But the root cellar will give you some kind of shelter if it rains. And if you don't mind snakes."

"Thanks, Mr. Roundtree." Was the old man pulling his leg?

The telephone rang. Willard gestured to his guest to wait and picked up the old-fashioned receiver.

". . . Claude, my dear. . . . No, you're not interrupting. You couldn't. . . . You're quite welcome. . . . Of course I enjoyed it. You were the prettiest graduate on the platform. . . . My dear, it's your graduation present. Spend it any way you like. . . . Yes, right away if you like. . . . Yes, I intend to be here tomorrow. . . . Why, I'd be flattered. It's a long time since you've paid me a visit. . . . Thank you, my dear. I return your sentiments."

Willard returned to his guest, his face warm with an inner emotion. "What do you say when a beautiful young girl tells you she's dying to see you and she loves you and will you be home?"

"Exactly what you said, sir."

Willard accompanied his caller to the car and stood

looking down the long valley as the sound of the engine faded in the night. The stars were veiled, the sky thickening, but Willard could see the outline of the valley as clearly as if it were filled with moonlight. His land. The Roundtree land. He had held it against all threats, all comers. It was his until he died but he would see to it that it remained Roundtree land forever. If that word meant anything. He had begun negotiations to turn the land into a conservancy, a retreat for all living things that he loved. It would leave the Roundtrees no richer; they were land-poor now. But there was a pride in being land poor. It was like a backbone. Not visible but keeping the head high.

He looked up at the Ridge where a few lights shone, a garish epitaph for the three-hundred-year-old oak tree that had been cut down to make room for the house. His pain was still there. Yet in all fairness he could not hold his grudge against this young man who came from that brasher, changing world. Still, his was another foot in the door. Another shadow of intrusion. "Once more into the breach . . . once more. . . ."

He could fling the words like a standard into the valley but who would hear? Who even read Shakespeare now? Or would understand, if they did?

Willard smiled at his own slightly absurd image and returned to his living room. He opened the decanter of Madeira and poured himself a second drink. Excellent, indeed! He had given the young man a choice Sercial Madeira. To test his over-confident judgment? To evoke an argument? Or to teach youth there was a thing or two still to be learned? Yet Willard had enjoyed his caller. It had been pleasant to have a strong-faced, no-nonsense young man in his living room. The world belonged to the young. Hadn't he himself claimed it fifty years ago? He thought of Claude, and the image warmed him. A beguiling little witch if there ever was one. He wondered what she really wanted of him. Or had those ever-sharp female antennae guessed there was a young man here, a quite possible young man.

Willard told himself, not for the first time, he was an old fool. Whistling for Clancy, his big red setter, he sauntered toward the barn and found Charlie Redwing leaning against the fence, gazing at nothing in particular.

Charlie Redwing was a full-blooded Algonquin Indian, the last of the ancient tribe in the area. He occupied a cottage separated from Willard's farmhouse by a copse of trees. He was Willard's right-hand man. Together they worked the soil, respected the land, and were kindred to whatever creatures lived in the valley. Thatcher looked on Charlie Redwing as a handy man lucky to have met up with Willard Roundtree. Willard never forgot that the proud Algonquin, son and grandson of chieftains, descended from a people who had counted the valley a small part of their vast holdings and who had carried into the past a knowledge of it that no white man would ever acquire.

When Charlie stood gazing at nothing, he was seeing a great deal.

Willard leaned on the fence.

"We have visitors, Charlie."

There was no answer. Willard expected none. He drew his pipe from his pocket. "They mean no harm."

Charlie shifted his gaze toward the Ridge.

"There is great silence."

"The gods will tell us when they're ready, eh?"

"Too much silence. The winds have gone."

When Charlie was most enigmatical, he was on the scent of truth. Whatever his ancient and unique perceptiveness saw now, Willard preferred not to know. Charlie, like his own gods, would speak when the time came. Willard lit his pipe.

In silence, with the great dog settled between them, the two men surveyed the land, which to each, in his own way, was the heart of the matter.

At the fork of the road Davison Hutchins turned his rented coupe toward Thatcher. If the rains were coming, he had no wish to submerge himself in the brew of closeted temperament and impatient genius that would begin to churn the Ridge.

He had worked for Marc Vallon nearly three years now. He was beginning to wonder why. In fact, if he looked back, his whole life was beginning to take the shape of a gigantic and uneasy question mark. Money had been the primary need, but as a motive when you could see thirty nearer than twenty, it was not good enough.

He had always compromised with it, even in his earliest boyhood days. Money was something you had to earn, so you could get on with living. After his father, a railroading man on the Union Pacific, died in a freight accident (as his mother always knew he would, though Hutch had never understood how she knew), Hutch became what his mother called the "man of the family." At thirteen, Hutch thought this was a large order but it was only verbal. Erna Hutchins, swinging between domination and self-pity, rarely let loose the reins, bringing up two children if not forthrightly, at least emotionally. When she married again, to everyone's surprise, it was not in Pipestone but to the owner of a Sacramento car agency. No one knew how Erna, living in eastern Nevada, got as far as Sacramento for her romance, but there it was.

Erna, it appeared, was a railroading kind of woman.

So Hutch was free at last to pursue the only thing he really wanted. He learned to fly. He flew anything that could get off the ground. He hired out as mechanic, bush pilot, ferry pilot, and stunt man, and found the money going out faster than it was coming in. When he could no longer send his sister Margie a helpful check, he knew something had to change.

The Air Force caught up with him. He announced he would not bomb civilians in Cambodia, Laos, or any other tortured spot on this planet, so they put him into a medical helicopter. He hopped hedges, bucked monsoon rains, dodged jungle fires, and was downed three times. In the army, that was it.

Hutch came home.

He preferred not to think about the next years. A fly bum they called him, and women found it irresistible. Eager bodies but the same faces. He could and did forget them all. Except occasionally Janette. Janette, the Flower Person. He could not remember how he met her except that almost at once she offered him a skinny, impersonal, and incandescent body. She made no demands. She never asked him if he loved her. She would disappear and return without explanation. Unaccountably one summer twilight he stood in a field beside her. One hand held a tiger lily, the other clutched his sleeve, birdlike. Her lips were parted on the tiny white teeth which always reminded him of doll heads.

"I, Janette, take you, Hutch, as my life companion, as long as we both love."

"I, Hutch, take you, Janette. . . ."

He supposed it was marriage. Janette and her scarves and her iron-shod fragility moved into his one-room flat without disturbing its untidiness. Five months later she drifted out, selling what furniture he had for cash flow. "It is better this way," she wrote. "Possession is the mortal sin." He agreed.

She left no forwarding address, and he heard nothing more. On rare occasions the smell of mown hay or a glimpse of a roadside tiger lily would bring a fragment of compassion, and he would wonder in what other field she might be standing, if she bothered to stand at all. Such instants would pass. Girls made themselves as expendable as they were available.

Soon after, he went to Europe. Because it was there, he told himself. And because an air-freight line offered him the stability of a desk job. But he could never stay grounded. At a gliding field not too far from Paris, strapped into the fragile, long-winged craft that became an extension of his own body, he spent most of his leisure hours and all of his paycheck. In silent communion with air currents and clouds Hutch found the true ambience of the loner, and a kind of peace.

Then he met Marc Vallon.

An auto horn barked behind him. The light had turned green. Hutch waved a conciliatory hand and let the thin current of afternoon traffic carry him past a neat sign, THATCHER, 1741.

1741. Did people measure time by centuries here? For him, yesterday was already forgotten and tomorrow rushing toward him. The Hutchins's restless foot. His mother would say it came straight down from his great-grandfather Lemuel who had set out with one pack-mule and a mighty thirst to conquer the whole of Nevada. "And damned near did," his father would add.

Hutch slowed his car on Main Street and came to a

small, parklike area. FLAGPOLE GREEN, 1748. God, did
they date everything in this town? Dates could fence a
man in tighter than prison bars. With history as jailer.
He parked the car, crossed the Green, glanced at the
inevitable monument, cannon and cannon balls, and
saw a solid fieldstone structure ahead. THATCHER LI-
BRARY, 1892. He knew finally what he would do with
the next hour.

Mrs. Haskell at the desk glanced up with pleasur-
able surprise. She couldn't place the young man, but
his broad shoulders and square-faced grin reminded
her of somebody. Maybe in the movies, though he did
not look that type. Topographical maps? Certainly. She would bring them if he would just sit at
that table. Of course he couldn't take them out. When
Mrs. Haskell's brisk hands and hovering competence
had faded, Hutch looked around.

He looked again. Through the doorway labeled
ROUNDTREE READING ROOM he saw the girl. He could
not be wrong. The fall of silver-blond hair, the small
tipped nose, the straight back even as she sat and
read. She was the girl Marc Vallon had found on the
terrace and whose name he had carefully not revealed. That was an omission Hutch felt obligated to
correct. He waited.

Unexpectedly, the girl shut her book and jumped
up. She caught his eyes on her, flashed a radiant if
self-absorbed smile, and was gone. Hutch drew a long
breath, counted to twenty, and ambled to Mrs. Haskell's desk.

"Everything all right?"

"Oh, yes, I found what I wanted. Now I'd like a
book. The book the young lady was reading."

Mrs. Haskell walked into the trap.

"Oh! *Methods of Acting*. I'm afraid that's the only

copy we have and Claude's taken it. But if you are
interested in the subject we have a new one. Let me
see, yes. *Theories of Body Use in Drama.*"

He had his own theories of body use in drama,
proven and unproven. He returned to his chair.

Claude. That was a beginning. *Methods of Acting.*
So she knew. Power spot, indeed. He suspected from
the rigidity of her back that she intended to lay siege.
He stared, without seeing, at the wavy lines of
Thatcher's glacial deposits and came to a conclusion.
It was his duty to disabuse the mind and intent of this
young thing and to thwart at any cost her further in-
vasion of Marc Vallon's turf. She would be catnip.

He rolled up the maps he was nonreading, gave the
librarian his politest smile and went into the graying
day. He wondered why it mattered to him. Yet
Thatcher had suddenly become a more interesting
town.

Mrs. Haskell sighed. Might as well try to make water run uphill as change a Roundtree. Claude was not
only becoming a rather startling beauty, but there it
was, that strange mercurial thread, deep-hidden then
suddenly, unpredictably flashing into evidence. The
Roundtree wildness, the town called it. Summer lightning to Hazel Haskell who had a fondness for poetry.
A book on playacting "for a friend" indeed! Whatever
the strain was, it had begun with Henrietta who long
ago had turned the town upside down with scandal.
Chastity, Henrietta's daughter, had ruined her own
young life with her giddy notions. And only a few
years ago, Ariel, the French-bred Roundtree cousin,
now a minister's wife, had split the town with gossip.
Here was Claude, concealing nothing, though she
tried.

Mrs. Haskell found herself wishing her sister-in-law did not confide so much in her. Effie had told her in strictest confidence of seeing Claude come down from the Ridge one afternoon; and Effie Barker would go to the stake for the truth. More than that, Effie had not minced words. A young girl had no business up there, what with the goings-on at the place these days.

Hazel Haskell would keep the confidence. Effie and Si needed their jobs, and Hazel had seen too much of hardship to deny that need. And it was certainly not Hazel's place to make trouble for the Roundtrees. Thin, aristocratic Martin Roundtree, even if he was a little distant nowadays with his failing health, and Edythe, his lovely, gracious wife—why, they were Thatcher. They set its standards. They lived its example of family life. And now with young John going into politics against old Harlan Phelps and the talk of his drink and other things—no, Hazel Haskell was not the one to make trouble. Still she was uneasy.

She glanced at Claude, sitting motionless, intent. One elbow rested beside the book, fingers clenched. Suddenly the young hand flung out, wild and strong, to an invisible audience. Defiance? Or triumph?

Mrs. Haskell could not tell.

Chapter Three

The rain came sooner than Willard had predicted. For
the next three days the valley lay shrouded in clouds,
under a steady downpour.

Claude seethed with impatience. Once she believed
in something, her imagination forged it into fact. Now
her future had come and time was wasting. But she
would be ready. She spent long hours into the night
reading the book on acting. It did not sound difficult
once she understood it. But between the lines, she
found herself remembering the young man who had
watched her from the table at the library. At another
time that candid directness would have intrigued her.
Even now she wondered who he was. But only fleet-
ingly. Acting was total dedication the book said.
Nothing must come between the actress and her goal.

She sighed and closed the book. Total dedication
sounded more like total selfishness. She needed someone to talk to, someone who had been outside
Thatcher and known that vague and shimmering life
of make-believe to which she was inexorably headed.

On the second day of rain Claude took action. At
nine o'clock in the morning she sloshed up Carriage
Lane, the narrow dirt road that had once borne
Thatcher's well-to-do to their Victorian river outings.
At the end of the lane, a gray cottage, converted from
an ancient barn, bore an embellished green-and-white
sign BELLE BLAKE: DRAMA AND DANCE.

Miss Blake was something of a phenomenon in
Thatcher. Besides presiding at high school theatricals
and coaching private pupils in her small house, she
taught Awareness in the basement of Duncan Phelps's
church and was eagerly available for all civic and
public functions. Small, lithe, and intense, Belle
flaunted a mass of frizzy blond hair, eyes furry with
mascara and sharply propped and prominent little
breasts. The town forgave these eccentricities or pre-
tended to, because Miss Blake had once been on the
stage and Thatcher considered itself lucky to have so
experienced a teacher of the arts for its children.

While no one was quite sure why Miss Blake had
elected to settle in Thatcher, her bouncy willingness
and the aura of her career were now woven seamlessly
into Thatcher's life. There were some who hinted that
Miss Blake had had not so much a career as a past.
Miss Blake ignored them and pursued her path of endless, good-natured energy.

The front door of the cottage opened cautiously.

"My goodness, Claude Roundtree! I haven't seen
you since high school and here I am hardly dressed.
Come in, shut the door. I'll just finish my makeup and
then we'll talk. Sit down. I'll move those theater maga-
zines or maybe you'd like to look at them. I simply
can't live without my little contacts with the theater.
My, what a day! But the better the day, the better the
deed, right? If you want to limber up, use the barre,

but take off those dreary loafers. No support for the arches. Bare feet better."

Miss Blake was not displeased. She considered that she performed miracles for Thatcher's wholly average children, but the Roundtrees had not been among them. It was a prominent feather Belle Blake sorely missed in her pert little cap. Now with young John running for politics against Harlan Phelps, it would be useful to know them better.

Claude waited, reality displacing enthusiasm. She saw that whatever she found to talk about, she could never confide to Miss Belle Blake what had happened to her or even mention Marc Vallon's name. She also had the uneasy feeling that if she talked at all about her career, Miss Blake would ferret the truth.

Miss Blake returned, makeup completed and kimono replaced by a tight little sweater and skirt.

"Now, let's talk. I must have overslept. My evenings are as busy as my days what with—never mind that. You're interested in lessons?"

Claude sat back in relief. Lessons. She had not thought of that. Yet it might help to show Marc Vallon how serious she was. There was, of course, the problem of money. She had no idea what Miss Blake charged.

"When would you like to begin? It's in dance, of course?"

"No. The theater. I mean—drama lessons."

"Well! Are you thinking of a career on the stage?"

"No. Not really. I don't know whether I have any talent."

"My dear girl. Each one of us has something of the divine spark. Maybe as infinitesimal as a speck of dust. But it is there. Waiting to be kindled." Miss Blake swept a dramatic arm to the universe. "It is simply a matter of bringing it out. Of finding someone who knows how. I assure you. I can kindle that spark, no matter how deeply hidden."

It was not exactly encouraging but it was persuasive. Claude found herself enveloped in a professional haze that brought reality a step nearer to the promise of the Ridge. If she could only believe this.

"So let's see. Stand up!"

Claude mechanically obeyed.

"Now move your body. You're a blade of grass, a leaf, a tree! You're a running brook! A wave of the sea! You're the wind! Move! Move! Think beautiful. Loosen up! More oomph!"

To Claude's astonishment Belle was flinging herself around the room in short, excited leaps, urging Claude to follow. It was heady and exhausting.

Belle came to a stop.

Claude sat down, feeling self-conscious and foolish.

"That's where it begins. In the soul, in the spirit, in motion and change. The words can come later." She surveyed Claude. "You're inhibited, Claude. You have to learn to give! Give! Give! Free the body and GIVE! It's the divine in you, the sex in you."

It was more than Claude had bargained for, and yet she sensed a truth. It was a whole side of life she had only explored in secret. She did not relish Belle Blake's blatancy. Yet she was irritated at herself. Here she was hesitating when the door was opening.

Miss Blake regained her breath. "I do get carried away. But I do so believe that freedom is the basis of all art. I teach all my pupils that. When shall we begin?" She paused. "If it's a matter of price, we won't talk about that just yet. I'm interested only in talent."

Claude made up her mind. "Tomorrow, Miss Blake?"

"Oh, dear. I'm going to be away for a few days. However, if it's important. . . ."

The last thing Claude wanted was to draw attention to her urgency. Yet it was disappointing. She had no idea when the whole ephemeral company on the Ridge might vanish. However, secrecy was the lesser of two evils.

"That will be all right. When you come back."

"I'll call you the very minute . . ."

"I'll call you, Miss Blake. I'd rather." To Miss Blake's unconcealed curiosity she added, "I'd like to sort of keep it between us. Surprise everyone."

Belle Blake could not guess what this young Roundtree girl might be up to, but she knew the blood. And Miss Blake found all such threads of information absorbing and useful.

"We'll arrange whatever suits you."

Claude escaped, conscious that she had accomplished nothing. She had only drawn the mesh of Thatcher tighter around her.

On Main Street, with a lingering sense of aloneness, Claude paused at the old feed and grain store next to Higgins Pharmacy. She stopped in astonishment. Overnight a large plate-glass window had replaced the smaller panes. The cavernous rear, dusty from long-forgotten bales and sacks, had been shut off by a new partition that matched the new beaver-board walls of a workable office. Inside she could see half a dozen people milling around. She opened the door.

John's delight was obvious. So was his surprise.

"Sis! How do you like it? Look what the kids have done!" She had never seen him so exhilarated.

Bonnie Smith, round and glowing, her oldest friend from high school, waved a paint brush. Cynthia, another of the old crowd, her brown hair in long braids, her ever-present guitar on a nearby chair, signaled with a screwdriver. Pete hailed her from the top of the ladder, and plump Phyllis, made remote by divorce, nodded briefly over curtain material stretched on a pair of boards.

Something seemed to have slipped away from Claude.

"John, I had no idea. What can I do?"

"Anything your little heart desires, glamor puss." She wished he wouldn't call her that, not in front of everybody. It set her apart, and she felt that way already.

"Bonnie . . ." John called. "Got an extra paint brush?"

"No, but we've got a roller. Claude can work on the walls. If she wants."

"Right. You show her. And when Gus comes in with that rug remnant he promised, tell him where to stack it. No use putting it down until the painting's done. And, oh . . ." John was on his way out, "Bonnie, could you stay here through lunch in case the telephone man comes?"

"Don't worry about a thing. Congressman." Bonnie threw a fist into the air. There was a scattering of applause.

John grinned. "Aw, cut it out." He stopped at the door. "Thanks for coming, Sis." He patted her cheek.

Bonnie thrust a pan of cream-colored paint and a roller into her hands. "All you have to remember, Claude, is to rub the roller on the edge before you paint, so it doesn't drip."

"I *know*." But Bonnie had already turned away. Ginnie had arrived with the first batch of posters. She was met with squeals of delight. Ginnie was very,

very good at posters. She had made them all in high school. She held up one.

JOHN ROUNDTREE, YOUR MAN IN CONGRESS. HE'S THE ONE.

"I like it!" shouted Cynthia. She reached for her guitar. "John Roundtree, he's the ONE. He'll get things started and make things HUM. He's the man who'll get it DONE. Send our John to WashingTON."

It wasn't very good but it was young and bright and enthusiastic. Claude began rolling paint on the wall. She had never thought of John as having so many friends. He had always been quiet, almost taciturn around the house. She had guessed it was because of his secret unhappiness over the narrowness of his life in Thatcher. His life did not look narrow now.

She painted silently, efficiently, until the whistle blew. Noon signaled lunch in Thatcher wherever you were.

"Lunch break!" called Bonnie.

"I'll finish this wall, Bonnie."

"You can't, Claude. John's rule. I'm staying for the phone man but everybody else has to keep regular hours. Okay, everybody. Back at one!"

By five the walls were finished. In a hubbub of tomorrow's planning Claude slipped out. She had left a warm room in her life, perhaps never to return. John was embarked on the biggest event the family had known. By her own choice she would not be a part of it.

Why did you have to hurt to win?

Late that night a pallid half moon drifted from a cloud. The sky was beginning to clear. It was an omen.

Claude picked up her book and slid into bed.

"Acting begins with a projection of self away from

*the familiar and into the unknown, the place of the
imagination."*

She wished she could forget the probing curiosity in
Belle Blake's sharp eyes.

Chapter Four

Davison Hutchins stopped his rented coupe at the barred gate on Bluestone Ridge and swore softly. The rain had stopped in the night, the sun emerged with the morning, and June's perversity had turned the afternoon into soaring, steaming heat. He fished for the key in his pocket, unlocked the heavy chain, and drove his car to the other side. Then the process had to be done all over again. Marc Vallon's insistence on privacy was becoming obsessive. But as a large part of his job was to humor those obsessions, Hutch performed the ritual with care. He had no intention of losing his job, at least not until Marc paid him all the back salary he was owed. Yet he liked the Ridge, the clean cut of the ancient rock, the openness of the hills, the vault of the sky where a man could breathe.

He parked his car on the gravel drive and followed the brick path around to the terrace. The great, wide-winged house glittered like sheet metal in the afternoon sun.

The woman lying face downward on the edge of

the pool lifted her head from her arms and watched him approach. She made no gesture. Except for sunglasses, a white towel wrapped around her head, and the white caftan on which she lay with one edge falling across her ankles, Solveg Traner was nude. He turned toward the terrace steps.

"Davey!"

He disliked the name Davey. It was another item from that deep, cool veranda he preferred to forget. And it could bring him to a stop, as she knew.

"Where in God's name have you been?" Her voice with its husky sheen carried a knife edge of self-indulgence.

"You know where I've been, Soli. Holed up in something called Rampart Inn with the rest of the hired help, waiting for a sign from the great man. Where is he?"

"Jogging. Where else? I've told him it won't do any good but he goes right on. He thinks it makes him look virile."

He picked up a jade-green beach towel and tossed it at her.

"The help in this house, Soli, are local. No use making them think any worse of us than they do."

She sat up, wrapping the towel around her. Like everything that touched Solveg Traner, it was chosen for display. The color turned her skin a breathing gold.

"Sometimes you are tiresome, darling. But at least you are here. To relieve your mind I do wear the bottom of my bikini in the pool." Her laughter was light, exquisitely trained. "Even then, poor Mrs. Barker's face was stark white at the upper window this morning. Well, I can't give up all my pleasures. Now that you're here I don't have to. Come on in for a swim. You need it. You're simply dripping with perspiration,

Hutch darling. But with your muscles I really don't mind."

"Where's Leonard?"

"Oh, he won't mind either, I assure you. He's upstairs meditating. He always does before a day's filming. And since he's learned the lotus position, he never gets off it. I've told him it will give him an absolutely square derriere but there's no communicating with him in this mood."

With one graceful movement, she was on her feet and had somehow tied on her hips the two brown satin triangles that for her complied with convention. She stood poised at the edge of the pool, her limbs long and straight, her shoulders strong, her breasts full and ripe, her head superbly balanced on a slender neck. She might have been one of the statue goddesses on the rim of the pool except for her golden bronze skin and the mahogany rich hair tumbling to her shoulders.

Magnificent, as he had to admit again. In whatever role he saw her. Magnificent and man-eating. And part of his job. She was Marc Vallon's leading woman, and without her Marc would collapse like a man of straw. Everything Marc had staked on this last gamble depended on Solveg. She knew it, Hutch reflected. God, how she knew it. She knew all she needed to know about Marc, about Leonard upstairs in his lotus position, about any man. She could make Hutch himself feel like a schoolboy if he let her.

"Come on, darling, get out of your clothes and come in. It's divine!"

"Later."

In a swift splashless arc she was in the pool, swimming with long clean strokes, her head buried in the glistening water, her hair a dark shadow on her back.

She emerged at the deep end, hoisted herself onto the pool's edge until her breasts were visible, and smiled at him.

"Afraid?"

"Of what?"

"You are exasperating, darling. But you like watching me, don't you? Bring me a drink."

"Nope. You're filming tomorrow."

She sprang up on the edge of the pool, her eyes glinting. Hazel gold. Cats' eyes, he thought them. "Bring me a drink, Hutch."

"I'll send one out. Lemonade and oatmeal cookies. Cool you off and fatten you up at the same time." He turned toward the steps. She was beside him, trailing her caftan.

"What am I supposed to do up here in this godforsaken place by myself?"

"As I remember, it was your idea. Your old school chum from Bayonne or some place. . . ." He knew it nettled her, this reminder of time and place.

"It was not my idea. Julia Orlini was not my old school chum. At her age? Our mothers knew each other. When we met in Paris she talked about this house. Standing empty, since her son's accident. I think it's foolish to link events and places. If I did, I'd never go anywhere. But poor Julia was always so involved with her feelings. When she said it would make a marvelous setting for a film, Marc jumped at it. For free. Poor Marc. He could never have afforded anything like it. You know that. All art and no sense of money. As if the box office held the tooth fairy."

To Hutch's relief Solveg drew her caftan around her. He could hear Silas Backer's lawn mower on the other side of the yew trees.

"So don't tell me this is my fault, darling. I'm enduring it. And so will you. It will be pleasanter as friends."

"I'll read the fine print in my contract, Soli."

Her laugh followed him up the terrace steps. It had the good nature of a poker player who holds four aces.

The great, vaulted living room was cool, empty, and seductive. Heavy white draperies half-drawn against the sun, deep white chairs, deep white rug, teak and ebony wherever wood was needed, and the whole aloof ambience punctuated by a few pieces of excellent wood sculpture. Hutch liked especially an elegant, elongated sitting cat, head high and disdainful, ears alert, eyes forever focused on an invisible quarry. Hutch liked cats. He saw women in them, with their unpredictable loyalties, the hidden cruelties of claws sheathed in softness, the sleek silky invitation to touch, and the equal sleekness of escape. The unknown sculptor of this cat knew his subject. And whoever had purchased it knew what he wanted. It was a man's purchase, not a woman's.

He had never met Ben Orlini, whose wealth had built this house. A little man, self-made, forever on the move, just departed or expected soon, names dropped like heavy gold coins—London, Tehran, Athens, Hong Kong, Munich, Rio. Ben Orlini was beginning to wrap the toga of legend around him, matching unguessed power with unguessed wealth. Hutch had little use for legend. In fact he dismissed the unknown Ben Orlini as something of a hoax, of trying too hard. Why would a man build the soaring magnificence of this house on an uncomfortable ridge overlooking a small New England town whose future was already behind it?

For Julia, his wife, obviously. Despite its dimen-

sions, this was a woman's house. Hutch had met Julia
Orlini only once, in Paris, on one of the rare occasions
he was willing to escort Solveg alone. A prestigious
affair, the opening of an art exhibition, followed by a
reception for all the Paris haut monde, with a satisfying sprinkling of titles and oil sheiks. Mrs. Benjamin
Orlini was listed as a patroness, and through devious
and hidden pressures, Solveg Traner, distinguished
world-famous actress, was to be guest of honor. Nature had failed to be impressed, and Marc Vallon's
plane had been grounded in Rome. His voice on the
telephone had assumed near hysteria.

"Solveg cannot go alone."

"Not part of my work rules, Marc."

"I make your work rules, Hutchins."

"I'll fall over the ambassador's feet. Or on the ambassador's wife."

"What?"

"Joke, Mr. Vallon."

"I am not in a humorous mood. If you cannot see
the importance of this to my work, then you may see
its importance to your job."

Marc Vallon always took longer to say "or else" than
anybody. But once said, Hutch knew he meant it. And
as his contract was in French, he had never read it
through.

"Gotcha, Mr. Vallon."

"I want Solveg there ten minutes after the ambassador—and not one second later."

"That might require a little more time."

"What?"

"The impossible always does. Not to worry, Marc."

He delivered Solveg not more than forty-five minutes late and saw her safely fluttering her accent between a Hindu ex-potentate and an Austrian ex-duke.

Both vanishing species, he reflected. He would do better later. He took up his official position three paces to the rear and one to the right. A moment later Solveg flung her splendid arms past duke and ex-potentate to a skeletally tall, graying, thin woman in silvery silk without a jewel. A slight hesitation, then Julia Orlini's glance swept Solveg, turbanned and full-bodied in poppy velvet; Solveg mentally computerized the silver gray silk. The two women embraced.

"Darling, you look marvelous!"

"So do you!"

"My oldest friend!" Julia smiled at no one in particular.

"Not quite." Solveg's accent was enchanting. "You haven't changed a bit, Julia. So chic!"

But the two women obviously understood each other. For the next two weeks Marc Vallon escorted them around Paris. One evening Hutch was told to assemble a small camera crew, makeup would also handle wardrobe, extras would not be needed. Oh, and notify Leonard.

"Your leading man doesn't like orders from me."

Marc distractedly agreed. Leonard Ross was belatedly told that the last part of the new Marc Vallon film would be shot in authentic American background, in Connecticut near a town named Thatcher.

"We're so fortunate," Solveg bubbled. She, like Marc, was apt to forget even the necessity for a leading man. "You'll adore it, darling. Julia's shown us pictures. A simply gorgeous location. So rugged, so desolate, with this fabulous house. So right for the final takes. Poor Julia. Ben built the house for her and now she never goes back to it. Not since Nick, that's her son, drove his car off the Ridge in a thunderstorm. So sad. He wasn't killed. It might have been better. Julia doesn't talk but there's something strange about it, I gather. Of course I don't ask questions. She spends most of her time with him. Almost in mourning. She doesn't even wear jewels when she goes out. You saw her at the reception, Davey darling."

Hutch couldn't help it. "I thought she looked great."

"Of course. If she wasn't so painfully thin. And when a woman owns the most famous emeralds in Paris, you would think . . ."

"She could do as she liked," he finished for her. Solveg eyed him coldly, the accent gone.

"Davey, sometimes I think you have a peasant mentality."

"Yep. Us kids always trod out the taters for Pappy's moonshine."

Solveg blew him a kiss and laughed. That was the trouble with Solveg. She was virtually unconquerable. Strong-willed as a racehorse, she could take and she could give. Her attitude toward defeat was as steely as it was simple. She never recognized it.

Two days later they had flown to New York, Marc and Solveg, and at Hutch's insistence, Leonard, all first class. The rest of the group were in "economy," a word that bore no relationship to Marc's working vocabulary. The location was free, Marc saw in it genius unfettered.

Now, on this June day, pulsing with unexpected heat, most of the work had been done. Hutch need only set up the final outdoor scenes, delayed by the rain. And Marc was out jogging, Leonard meditating, and Solveg sunning her legendary body in this nirvana of unreality.

He could sit and wait. He could drive back to the inn. Or he could get into bathing trunks and cool off in the pool. But that meant Solveg. She possessed it like an oracle. He glanced at his soiled working pants, and at the pristine softness of the white chairs. He sank into one and let the cool silence of the house envelop him.

He awoke rumpled, refreshed, and startled to see Leonard, his long legs stretched out in the chair opposite.

"You look like hell asleep, old boy."

Hutch rarely permitted himself chagrin but Leonard, so help him, was wearing a white dinner jacket. The man had a certain bearing, lost on the others, that merited respect. He had played with the best. He had accepted the humiliations of this present employment with a certain thin pride. Hutch felt the beginning of chin stubble and grinned.

"There are those who tell me I don't look much better awake. But then some women lack understanding."

"Most," said Leonard.

Hutch wondered if the fading actor really knew but that didn't concern him. Any man could and should live his own life. And any woman, with a few possible exceptions.

"Where's our peerless leader?"

"It's only three minutes to six."

They sat in silence.

Promptly at six o'clock Marc Vallon appeared on the balcony above the glass-walled living room. In knife-creased, pearl-gray trousers, impeccable navy blazer, and foulard silk scarf, Marc was as aware of his casual elegance as of the two faces turned up to him. He surveyed them for an instant then, ignoring the iron-grill railing, he came down the wide curving stairs, lightly, swiftly, on the balls of his feet.

As if the bastard hadn't a care, thought Hutch. Not a care. He raised a hand in mock salute.

Marc took in the open sport shirt and rumpled chinos. "Staying for dinner, Hutch?"

"You know damn well I'm not. I came for shooting orders . . . two hours ago."

"I didn't have them two hours ago. But I've got them now. I've been all over the ground. There's a slight incline above the swamp that will be dry enough for Soli to fall on. You'll have to come through the marsh, Lennie."

"Oh, my God. Leeches, I suppose?"

"Tell the crew, Hutch, we start shooting at five."

"A.M. or P.M.?"

"You know the answer to that."

"I want the order in your own commanding tones."

"Five A.M. Crew on hand at four."

Leonard started to protest, thought better of it. He was no longer young. The classic nose, the cleft chin were still good but there were certain undeniable folds, certain weaknesses surfacing under a strong light. Leonard disliked the role and its subordination to Solveg Traner but he needed it. It was said that if any director could revitalize an actor, Marc Vallon could. Besides there was a good makeup woman.

"Why the dawn, Marc?"

"Because I want the mists. I've been over the place half-a-dozen times now, and it's right when that first light of day breaks through. A melancholy light that a woman would understand when she's gotten everything she wanted and finds it as cold and comfortless as silver."

"Marvelous!"

With a little laugh, Solveg was standing in one open glass panel to the terrace, her hair was caught up,

Grecian style, in three gilt bands, above a chiffon robe in flowing shades of salmon. She was a woman of the sunset. She waited an instant for the effect to take hold, then entered the room.

Hutch rose as he knew she expected. Leonard pushed himself to his feet. The lotus position might ease his soul, but at this moment it was playing hell with his thighs.

"I adore the dawn, Marc. It gives me a vibrancy, a sense of oneness that lifts me into a new vision of myself and the universe." She swept them with a gracious smile. The slight accent, enchantment to millions, vanished abruptly. "At least it will keep the damned rustics away. You promised me that, Marc."

"I leave that to Hutch."

"No way, Soli, for anyone to pry. You've got the Ridge behind you, six hundred feet of it, the swamp in front, and a whole mess of catbrier and marsh grass and rocks beyond. Besides, this whole valley is private. Anyone who was curious would have to fly in and hang in a tree. You've got nothing to worry about except . . ." he was tempted to say snakes, but at this point it would do nothing for anyone. On the day before filming, Solie's temperament had to be guarded like a newly bathed poodle.

"Except what, darling?" Her large eyes brooded on him.

"Except your ardent admirers." Marc sounded bored. "And that, my love, is up to you. As always."

Solveg drifted toward the open glass pane. "There's a new moon, Leonard, come see it."

Leonard rose stiffly but obediently. Hutch watched them on to the terrace. He wondered at what exact hour in life you became a has-been. You had to be something first. He had not reached even that point. He wasn't likely to find it in this direction.

"Have a drink, Hutch?"

Hutch sensed the reluctance of the offer. Marc demanded a certain formalizing of life. Hutch looked at his own hard-worn sneakers and grinned. "After sitting on my tail here half the afternoon, what do you think?"

"I think, Hutch, if you weren't the most useful man on my staff, I'd fire you. Either keep Soli happy—and I don't care how—or don't hang around. She gets restless, and what have we got? One week of outdoor shooting, the whole climax, and I want the best performance from Soli that she's ever given. So you keep your over-grown muscles out of here." Marc thrust a glass of whiskey into Hutch's hand.

"Suits me, boss." He waited for Marc to fill his own glass. "I've been doing a little look-see in the library. You've got yourself quite a piece of real estate to play with here. The Indians called this Ridge 'Place of Anger.'"

"What does that mean, if anything?"

"Very ancient rock, pre-Cambrian, ferrous. Attracts lightning. Makes things happen. Mind of its own. If it likes you, you're in. If it doesn't . . ."

"You might say a power spot?" Marc flashed strong white teeth. So he had not forgotten the girl. Which would make it more difficult if she decided to return. Hutch was very sure, after the encounter in the library, that she had made just that decision.

Marc had not filled his glass. "It's an interesting idea. I'd like to put it to a test someday. Hutch, your instant research bores me. But if you can rig up an honest-to-goodness major thunderstorm, I'll get the whole company out and we'll start shooting. That's what I'm looking for. Primal forces in conflict, man and nature."

He set the unused glass back on the teak bar. "Everything I have is riding on this film. Everything. It'll be my masterpiece. But nothing's going to get in the way. Not you. Or Soli. Or Ross. You're here for my use. Until the job is finished."

He went out. Hutch watched him go down the terrace, past the pool with its overblown statuary, in the opposite direction from Soli and Leonard.

He felt suddenly stifled. It was happening increasingly since that day when Marc Vallon stood on the glider field, outside Paris, shielding his eyes, watching him glide in. When he had landed, Marc Vallon made him an offer. He needed a stunt man for a crash landing. It was a dizzying offer, and Hutch was nearly broke. He had done the job easily and he had showed an understanding of Marc's work, an ability to get things done, an indifference to hours. Marc offered him a contract—staff assistant, public relations, cleanup man, general factotum. Hutch had no name for his job but he knew early on that Marc leaned on him. Hutch lacked both temperament and awe, and he could keep machinery revved up and on schedule.

But now Marc was leaning too heavily. Hutch saw something in the finely chiseled face in this overbright twilight he had never seen before. Fear. Marc Vallon for the first time was afraid of failing. When a man had that fear, he could become ruthless.

Hutch let himself quietly out the front door. As he drove down the road, he thought again of the silver-haired girl in the library. She had a freshness he had forgotten. Clean, like the sky he had forfeited. But a book on acting? Marc could do that to people. But for this girl? No way, he told himself. No way.

* * *

Claude was lying flat in the deep grass, elbows propped, eyes fixed to a pair of oversized binoculars, when she heard the sound. She glanced cautiously around. A faint breeze fingered the grass. The shadow of a solitary cloud drifted across the hill behind her. Otherwise nothing moved. Nothing anywhere in the whole length of the valley. The morning had the transparency of glass. The sound was not repeated.

A squirrel, she told herself, or a pheasant or a woodcock in the underbrush. Even a curious young deer at the edge of the woods behind her. Yet it had seemed so near. Time was passing. She was growing jumpy. She had been lucky so far. Uncle Willard had not even asked her why she wanted his binoculars. Her father had let her take the car. But now, for more than two hours, she had been lying here, watching, waiting. She had seen nothing.

"You are too late."

Claude sat bolt upright. Up the rise on a rock perched a man in a battered straw hat chewing a blade of grass.

"Charlie Redwing! That's the meanest thing I ever heard of! How long have you been there?"

The Indian looked skyward. "It is noon. Time of peace. Time to sit."

"That isn't what I asked you."

Charlie rose and came down the slope toward her. "What did you ask me, Miss Claude?"

"I asked you—" She looked up at his emotionless face. "Are you spying on me?"

"Spying?" Charlie made his usual retreat. "What does that mean?"

"You know as well as I do, Charlie Redwing. How did you find me up here?"

"Oh, it is never hard. The valley tells me what I should know. That is why I say you are too late."

"They've gone?" Claude jumped to her feet, dismay routing caution.

The Indian shook his head. "The day before yesterday you come at noon. Yesterday you come at two o'clock. This morning at ten. Always too late."

"Then you've seen them! You know where they are!"

Patience, Uncle Willard had said. You must be very patient when you talk with Charlie Redwing. Claude waited. In a minute or two he came to her side, took the binoculars gently from her, drew a clean red handkerchief from his back pocket, and began carefully to wipe the lenses.

"They're all right, Charlie! I can see okay. Just tell me where to look!" Every passing moment was a loss.

"There is nowhere to look now. I said you are too late."

"They've gone?"

He nodded and continued to clean the binoculars. He inspected them, held them up to his eyes, and silently swept the valley. Then he handed them to her.

"You will see more now."

"But if they've gone . . . ?" How could anyone live so slowly? Her whole future was slipping away. "Charlie, have they gone for good?"

He nodded. "There is no goodness there. But when they go it will be good. Good for the Ridge and the valley."

"I mean—do you know if they are coming back?"

He nodded. "Oh, yes. They go with the light of the morning."

"Charlie, I have to find them! It's the most important

thing in my whole life! It's my only chance!" The last
word quivered.

Charlie Redwing gazed broodingly down the long
valley, silent and still in the light of the coming summer. Yet it was neither silent nor still. Overhead a
hawk coasted, deceptively idle. A flock of crows rose
in caucus over the young corn. Nearby a woodpecker
jackhammered the gray corpse of an ancient elm.
Charlie smiled a greeting and pointed upward. But
Claude saw nothing. How could this strange, knowing
man understand her anguish? Yet without him she
might never see Marc Vallon again.

His gaze returned to the Ridge and lingered for a
moment on the crest where shards of sunlight glanced
off a barely visible glass wing of the house.

"They have come as strangers. They will leave as
strangers. But they have wisdom. They know the
power of the spirit is greatest at the sun's rising. They
work at dawn."

"Dawn! Have you seen them?"

"I watch them. So does the Ridge."

"Charlie, could you show me where?" She had no
fear that Charlie would reveal her secret. He talked of
winds and clouds, the movements of the stars, and the
mysteries of soil and seasons. But human secrets he
kept to himself.

He looked at her solemnly for a long instant. Not so
much at her as through her, to something he could see
on the other side of her being.

"I do not think you will find what you want. But
when the will is so great, it is like flowing water. It
will find its way."

He walked quickly from her, down the slope, looking back only once. She took it as a signal and followed him. No twig snapped, no pebble rolled as he

entered the woods bordering the fields. Her own loafers scuffed the dry leaves as if to waken the valley.
She would never learn to walk like an Indian. But she
could try. She stepped more carefully, and he glanced
back in approval.

Finally he stopped. They were in a stand of tulip
trees, straight and tall as ships' masts. Between two of
the trees was a clearing; beyond the trees the clearing
narrowed. Charlie Redwing gestured. "That's the
path. You see it?" Claude thought she did. "It will
take you to a boulder. Go right and you will find another path leading down to the swamp. Halfway is a
ledge. You can see them from there. You will be safe.
The valley protects its own."

It was an odd thing to say. She did not know how
to answer. She hesitated too long. As lightly as it had
appeared, Charlie Redwing's solid shape blended into
the woods and was gone.

"Thanks, Charlie. Thanks a lot!" she called. The
words fell into emptiness. He had not told her when
they might be there again or how she would find the
way in the dawn. But that would be up to her.

Claude slept little that night. She pored over her
borrowed library book on acting. Psychic harmony,
that's what she must think of. And something
called public solitude. How in the world could
you be solitary in public? Then there was the
emotion of truth. She wouldn't tackle that yet. She
had trouble enough with plain, everyday truth. She
got up once, balanced the book on her head, and es-
sayed unsteadily to cross the room. The book crashed.
She jumped back into bed. Her mother, who could
sleep tranquilly through a thunderstorm, reacted to
every unusual squeak. Claude lay in the dark wonder-

ing what she would wear and imagining tomorrow's confrontation. She would not remind Marc Vallon that they had ever met. She would walk slowly and gracefully toward him letting her long silvery hair swing, a gracious half-smile on her lips, perhaps just a little forgiving. He would be struck by her poise, by her wild primitive beauty—or maybe her delicate, pure loveliness. He would see the glow of dedication in her dark eyes, realize the fire of temperament within her panting breast. Or should she stand still, simple, exquisite while he approached, humbled by the proud lift of her imperious head, aware only of her spellbinding beauty? Claude fell asleep.

She awoke with the light full in her face, a whitened light. She had overslept. There was only time to pull on jeans, a T-shirt, her old loafers and creep down the back stairs. The dew lay thick, and the seat of her bicycle was wet but there was no help for that. It was a quarter to six, and she had four miles to pedal to the dirt road that led into the valley.

Charlie Redwing had been exact in his instructions. But he had not told her what to do when the valley lay swathed in milk-white mist, from which only the tops of the trees emerged. A Japanese landscape in which the known had become the unknown, and the unknown a surrealist nightmare. Claude laid her bicycle against a large rock and walked helplessly along the edge of the woods. Somewhere within them were the tulip trees, somewhere a path. It would be futile to search. She could only continue on the pasture land where she could see where she was going. She came finally to a small rise. The stubble was rough and damp, the land uneven with rocks. And the mist everywhere. She was as hopelessly isolated from everything she had planned and

dreamed, as if she had been swept to another planet.
She sat down, and the tears of frustration came. But
not for long. She irritably wiped them away, leaving
soil marks on her face. The white mist may have engulfed her life, her dreams, her future. It had not engulfed her appetite. She was ravenously hungry. Willard's farmhouse lay to the right. All she had to do
was to follow the crumbling stone wall across the pasture land.

Suddenly she stood stock still. Out of the mists below her came voices. A man, then another man. A
woman, rather husky and sharp. Then a third man.
She listened, straining. The third man had a foreign
twist to his speech. She could not distinguish the
words. She had lost her sense of distance. They could
be immediately below her or half a field away. She
sat down noiselessly. The mist must be lifting or they
would not have come.

"This is madness!" Solveg in a long gray wig stead-
ied herself angrily against a stunted tree.

"Exactly! Precisely what I want. You are inside your
own mind, my dear. It is slipping from you. The
power you have reached for is gone. Gone. There is
nothing, nothing but milky mists swirling around you
as you grope for what you have lost. Use that stunted
tree, just as you're doing. Splendid. Splendid." Marc
was apt to speak in duplicates when he was working
well. And it was going well now, better than he could
have expected. "Cameras ready! Hutch, where the hell
are you?"

"Here." Hutch in a half slicker, the bottoms of his
trouser legs stained with mud, emerged from the
mist. "You'll have to stay on the edge of the pasture.
You could break a leg in this fog in the swamp."

"I'm not concerned with that."

"Of course not. It won't be your leg."

"All right, all right. Leonard, as you come from the swamp, watch those rocks!"

"You have another problem," Hutch added quietly.

"What?"

"There's somebody up on the rise."

"Who?"

"How do I know?"

"Get rid of him. Solveg will go to pieces if anyone watches her when she looks like this. And the mist is beginning to rise already. Now stay out of the way. Cameras, take one!"

Seated on the incline, Claude held her breath. It was Marc Vallon, his voice as clear as the day she had met him. The others had no meaning. She wondered who "my dear" was, but obviously there had to be a female part. Claude thought about the woman. She sounded old. Too old to act much longer, maybe. He would need someone new. The mist was thinning. She leaned forward.

Silently, as silently as it had filled the valley, the fog lifted. The tops of the trees were lost, then reappeared. Strands of mist lingered between the trunks and in low places. But the scene below Claude emerged as clear as if washed in pallid light. There was Marc Vallon, exactly as she remembered him except that he had exchanged running shorts for neat white ducks and a white turtleneck sweater. Supine on the ground lay a woman in a long dark dress, her gray hair streaming behind her. Gray. Claude glanced twice to make sure. And then a third time again, startled.

A young man was climbing toward her, out of the mist. He was tweedy, broad shouldered, and serious.

She recognized him at once. It was the man who watched her in the library.

"Oh. Hi." she said uncertainly.

"Hi. Ms. Claude."

"How do you know my name?"

"One of my many talents." He grinned. "Besides I've been expecting you. You remember me?"

"Oh, sort of. Not very well."

"I'll refresh your memory. We met or, rather, we didn't meet in the library."

"I know."

She looked incredibly young. Hutch discovered he had made another mistake about her. She was not the usual fresh-faced pretty girl, who hung around film locations. Her eyes were dark with their own secrets, her face dirt-streaked and luminous, her features small and fine and proud. Quality, he thought, out of deep soil. The sign THATCHER, 1741, suddenly made sense. She was a creature of the mist and light of this valley. And he guessed she could be as stubborn as hell.

"How you do look at people!"

"I'm wondering how to tell you to leave."

"Leave?" She settled herself deeper and winced on the sharp stubble. She saw his amusement.

"You can't be very comfortable."

"I'm very comfortable, thank you. I have no intention of leaving." Her gaze was fixed on a distant white figure, revealed through the last of the mist. "Besides, if you know my name then you ought to know I have every right to be here. This is my uncle's land. So is that, down there where the swamp is."

Hutch sighed. He might have expected this. Usually he could put two and two together and get five. He had an urge to pick up all arrogant hundred pounds of her and spank her. But he had to admit he was enjoying himself. She was looking past him as if he did not exist.

"Miss Roundtree, I presume."

"What? Oh, yes." She did not turn her head.

"I am Davison L.—L. for Lemuel, if you believe it— Hutchins. My friends, who are legion, I assure you, call me Hutch. I'm quite sure the pleasure is all mine."

"Right."

"It is my unfortunate duty, Miss Roundtree, to evacuate you, uncle or no. Orders. My boss takes a dim view of my ignoring him. My work, little as I like it sometimes, is not indispensable."

"Oh! They're doing a scene!" Claude jumped to her feet. "I can see him now!"

"See who? Whom, as they probably say in Thatcher."

"Mr. Vallon, of course!"

"Now wait a minute, honeybundle!" Hutch made the mistake of seizing her arm. His grip was viselike.

"Let me go! Or I'll have you arrested for assault and impairing a—a major! I happen to know Mr. Vallon and I intend to see him!" She twisted free with the help of a well-aimed kick at his ankle. "And I am not your honeybundle!"

"You're right about that, Miss Roundtree." Only pride kept him from bending over to soothe his smarting bone. "But let's go over that once more, with less feeling. You know Marc Vallon?"

"Of course I know him. Why would I be waiting up here if I didn't?"

"For a screen test. Like all the others."

"What others?" But she didn't say it aloud. It would give him too much satisfaction.

"That's the last thing on my mind!" Lies didn't count with someone as rude as this. "I wish to renew an acquaintance." She lifted her head imperiously, the gesture of defiance, the book said.

"Mud on your face."

"What?"

"I don't think you've been crying. A girl like you couldn't. It just looks as if you had. Your face is dirty."

Claude rubbed her cheeks red with embarrassment. He was impossible. You could not feel indifference toward a man like this. You could just—she groped for the word—hate him. She noticed that behind his tortoise-rimmed glasses his eyes were deeply blue. Worse, they seemed to be mocking her.

"Thank you," she said stiffly. "I stumbled against a tree."

"My sympathies." He bowed. "To the tree."

It was easier to laugh than to quarrel. Besides she could not help herself. His mouth, strong and thin-lipped, twitched at the corners, but he did not join her.

"Miss Roundtree, as my feeble efforts have failed before your devastating charm—and footwork—I'd like to give you a piece of advice. If you do know Mr. Vallon, you ought to know that he wouldn't talk to his own mother after filming a scene."

"Why would he want to talk to his mother? But thank you just the same, Mr.—Hutchinson, is it?"

"It'll do," Hutch murmured.

She gave him a small one-thousand-watt smile and hurried down the incline. Hutch watched her glumly. She was bad news, she had a kick like country moonshine and she was walking as surely to the guillotine as if she had been a younger Marie Antoinette. Single-minded and prettier—and damn the metaphors. He followed her slowly toward disaster.

* * *

Marc Vallon stood with one foot on a tree stump, a clipboard on his knee, making notes. If he saw Claude coming, he gave no indication. A cameraman nudged his assistant; two of the sound crew halted their packing up. Solveg, seated on her log, turned her head ever so slightly, then fixed her eyes on the distance. The girl was young, undeniably lovely, and undeniably naive. It was the old story.

Claude hesitated, stopped, and waited. He must finish writing sometime. At least come to the end of the page. She stretched her neck and saw that he wasn't writing at all. He was tapping his pen and that meant he was thinking, which was worse.

"Good morning, Mr. Vallon."

"Didn't my assistant tell you we do not allow visitors?" He did not look up, which meant that he had seen her coming.

"I'm not a visitor. And I'm not a stranger. I met you, remember. Up on the Ridge. At the house. And you said if it was up to you, you'd let me stay but unfortunately you were not able to do that. So I didn't think you'd mind now if I asked you something. I mean you have finished the scene and all, haven't you?"

He raised his head, looking not so much at her as through her, dusted his knee, and tucked the clipboard under his arm.

"You do remember me, Mr. Vallon, don't you? Up on the terrace. I was behind the vase . . ." She took a step toward him, breathless that he would suddenly go, that they would all dissolve into a pack of cards tossed in the air. He was even handsomer than she remembered.

Suddenly his eyes met hers, deep, unblinking, the gray irises so light as to be almost hypnotic, rimmed in black, as black as the heavy lashes that shadowed them. It was a look such as she had never received. It slid over her like water on her bare body, like hands. Her knees felt rubbery, her skin hot, then cold, her face flushed. She found it impossible to look away.

Then as suddenly his eyes shifted, the handsome face settled into its mask of remote concentration.

"Yes, I remember you. Hutch!" he called. "Show this young lady off location and make sure she understands she is not to return." He turned his back. "That's all for today. Tomorrow at three. On the Ridge."

"Darling!" The older woman's voice was as rich as it was commanding. "You know I will not begin work at three. Two or four. Three is my low hour."

There was an instant of silence. "Crew at three. Miss Traner at three forty-five."

That might have been the end. Except at that moment Miss Traner screamed, a piercing howl of terror that echoed against the rocks behind her. A five-foot blacksnake was slithering from under the log and pouring its supple folds past her feet. Claude saw the cameraman lift a rock.

"No! No!" she yelled. "Don't kill it!"

She plunged across the marshy soil, leaving one loafer caught in the mud. "He won't hurt you! He's not poisonous or anything!" She shoved the cameraman off balance and heard the rock clatter to the ground. Miss Traner, for all her grayness, had leaped to the other side of the log. Claude picked up a broken branch from the ground and held it toward the snake. The snake began to coil itself around the end.

"See!" she cried furiously. "He's only a harmless blacksnake. He wouldn't hurt a flea! He wouldn't even have come out if you weren't here to bother him.

He has as much right here as you have! More! And all he hopes is that you'll go away and leave him alone!" She flung the words at all of them, and it felt good.

With the snake dangling in loops from the end of the branch, Claude marched up to a fringe of woods where a long-unused stone wall was succumbing to neglect. She lowered the branch and the snake slid gratefully onto the rocks, found a place the sun was beginning to warm, and slipped into it. Claude did not look back. She hated them all. Marc Vallon's rudeness, the old woman's panic, the grinning men—and whatever his name was, who had treated her like a child. But most of all she wanted to forget that look, as if she ever could. The thought of it weakened her and brought a warmth to her face.

She walked into the woods with as much dignity as she could manage with one shoeless foot. She would come out beyond the swamp. It would take only a little longer to cross the pastureland to Willard's farm.

Instead she winced and sat abruptly. The cut on her foot was small but it was bleeding. She reached for a handkerchief, found none, set her foot on the cool wet grass and wanted to cry. But that would be the second time this morning, and nothing was worth that. She wondered if she would die of starvation or bleed to death first. Not that it mattered. Not that anything mattered now. She lifted her face to the morning sun and closed her eyes. She opened them to a shadow falling across her.

Davison Hutchins was standing above her, holding her loafer wiped clean and dry.

"How did you find me?"

"I never lost you. Here."

"Thanks. But it wasn't necessary."

He looked down on her, angry, muddy, and clawing

as a wet kitten. "I didn't think it was. Still, I have an incurable urge to return lost articles. Cub Scouts will do it to you every time. Where did you learn the snake trick?"

"It wasn't a trick. Anybody knows blacksnakes are harmless. And they like to climb trees."

"Oh." He lowered the loafer. "Shall I put it on?"

"I can do it, thank you."

It was then he saw her bloodied foot. "Hey, let's have a look."

"It's all right."

"I expect it is. But let's look anyway." Before she could answer, he had taken the foot so gently she barely felt it. He tore a strip from a clean handkerchief and used the rest to wipe away the blood.

"You don't have to do all that."

"That's right."

"It's fine. Honestly. Dew and cobwebs."

"How's that?"

"I said dew and cobwebs."

"That's what I thought you said."

"It will always fix a cut or anything. That's in my great-grandmother's diary. Morning dew and old cobwebs."

"Sure. Well, there you are." He slipped the loafer over the bandage and gave the foot a needless pat.

She scrambled up. "I suppose I should say I'm sorry for kicking your ankle."

"You should have said it thirty minutes ago. But I don't think you will."

"If you're going to be nasty again . . ."

He grinned. "My dear pussycat. The milk of kindness has never yet curdled in me."

Was he mocking her again?

"Or if you ever dare say I told you so about—about

what happened back there, I'll never speak to you again."

That was not what he had in mind. He saw again the luminous youth in her face and told himself he was a damn fool. But she had been hurt, and for that he would make Marc Vallon pay. Someday. Somehow.

"I guess that's everything I can do . . . except take you home."

"No, thanks. I've got a bike."

He didn't ask where. There was no use pushing his luck. Or losing his head.

"Right."

"So I'll be going." But she didn't go. She lingered. "Have you anything to eat?"

This time he concealed a smile. He drew from his pocket a very small, very battered, box of raisins.

"Oh, yuk. But thanks." She took it.

From the other pocket he pulled a plastic bag. It held the ruin of half a doughnut. Her eyes lit up.

"Oh, terrific!" She not so much ate the doughnut as annihilated it, wiping flecks of powdered sugar from her mouth. "That was really great, Mr. Hutchinson. Thanks."

"No problem."

She slipped through the woods, a nymph, half substance, half light, the sun dappling her extraordinary hair. He had never met anyone so innocently confident, so vulnerable. She should marry the local boy whoever he might be and live safely ever after in this time-forgotten town. Yet he found himself hoping there was no local boy. He heard Marc Vallon call him. They would be gone soon. Not soon enough. He had seen Marc deliberately turn on the voltage.

* * *

Marc Vallon sat working late at the long teakwood table in his borrowed bedroom. The ubiquitous white draperies, half-drawn, revealed the night's emptiness beyond the glass wall. The few pinpricks of stars were gone. Thunderstorms were forecast for tomorrow. That suited him—a threatening sky for the monumental final scene. If Leonard showed his usual timidity, he would keep the cameras on Solveg. He was tired of temperament. That incident with the snake this morning exasperated him. It might even have embarrassed him had he permitted it. She was not much more than a schoolgirl, this impudent sprite who had thrust herself into his consciousness, first on the terrace, then yesterday, her eyes dancing then blazing as she held that ridiculous branch with the dangling creature, a young dryad, virginity not yet eroded by the ancient mysteries. He wondered. Whatever she was, she had made them all look like fools.

He was weary, with the drained weariness that always accompanied the ending of a film. Yet tonight his weariness held something indefinably deeper. *Weltschmerz*, his Viennese grandmother would have called it. World weariness, weariness of the soul. This house, that had at first delighted him with the calm of its creams and whites and black and browns, had become a chilling carapace. Like a blinded man he longed for color, as he longed for some new wellspring of energy he could not name. He had given more to this work than any other in his life. It was to be his masterpiece. It must succeed. It was too late for failure.

He heard the door open. Solveg, wrapped to her throat in night purple, glided wordlessly across the rug and stood beside him. Still without speaking, she opened her robe, took his hand, and drew it down her bare body. His hand fell back on the table. She dropped into the white depths of a chair and stretched out her thin, perfect feet.

"My God, it's quiet!"

He nodded. He wished for an instant he could respond to her but that was long ago.

"How much longer, Marc?"

"That depends on you and Leonard."

"It may depend on Lennie and the cameramen and anyone else in this godforsaken place. It does not depend on me. I have given everything I have to every crappy scene in this picture, on schedule and without a flaw. Not a retake. Don't tell me anything depends on me."

It was true. No one could have done more, but her language nettled him.

"You've lost faith in it?"

She was out of her chair and on her knees beside him. "No, darling! no. Not for a minute! It's going to be a magnificent triumph. Your greatest! Marc Vallon—and Solveg Traner. Together—at the top! Then let them come to us! We'll spit on them all, darling!" She half rose, drew his head between her breasts. Her scent was musky, stifling. She stroked the thick graying hair then released him. "But I want to go home."

"So do I."

"Do you, Marc? Really?"

"When the job is finished. I can't seem to block out the final scene the way I want it. To get the desolation of this place, this Ridge, the brooding eternity of the land and the sky. . . ." He picked up his pen.

She smiled. "Who is she, Marc?"

He knew of course whom she meant. "Who?"

She drew the folds of her robe around her.

"You know perfectly well who. She came up to you like a bitch in first heat."

"I wouldn't say so."

"You never do, darling. Where did you meet her?"

"She was up here at the house one afternoon. I found her on the terrace when I came back from running."

"And you sent her away, of course?"

He was tired of her now, but he could not afford to antagonize her. She must give him her finest performance tomorrow, and some danger was involved.

"At once. But as she happens to be a Miss Round-tree, I cannot keep her out of the valley. Her uncle owns most of it."

"And tomorrow, when she shows up?"

"She won't."

Solveg laughed, a full-throated ripple. "Darling, you may be the most brilliant filmmaker in Europe but you are a child about women. Especially the very young. She will be back tomorrow. Fifty dollars on it. She'll want a screen test."

He rose. "Why would I want a paper doll when I have the *de Milo*?" He would lie with her tonight, the warmth, the richness of her skin, the heady scents, the empty play. It would soothe them both. Perhaps he would sleep. Sleep. That was what he really sought. He slid the robe from her strong body and half lifted her to the wide, white bed. As she moved against him, he was reminded for a fleeting instant of the voluptuous blacksnake, writhing in folds from its hiding place.

An hour later, an unfulfilled, weighted hour, she gave a small laugh. "Darling, I have a marvelous idea. When little nature girl shows up tomorrow, tell her

you will see her. In Paris. In August. At three o'clock
in the afternoon. But she must be prompt!" The laugh
had the brittleness of dissatisfaction. "She'll get the
message. I'm going to bed, darling. You know I loathe
waking up with anybody."

Her scent lingered, cloying, possessive, reminding
Marc of the youth he had lost to her. And how little
he needed her now. His nearly finished work held all
that mattered, his final hope.

When sleep finally came, the sky was young with
silver. Like a young dryad's hair, he thought, as his
eyes closed against it—a young dryad's hair in the
mist.

Chapter Five

"Warm, humid. Thunderstorms forecast for this afternoon. . . ." Edythe Roundtree snapped off the kitchen radio and went to the pantry door to listen. Martin had not yet started his slow journey downstairs. But it was sixteen minutes before eight, and she could see him in her mind, a last glance in his mirror at his immaculate linen, his smoothly shaved face, the meticulous knot in his tie, the care he took in his appearance that always delighted her.

She set a saucepan of milk to warm on the back of the stove. It was one of the many small civilities she had brought to their thirty-year marriage that had pleased him. Warmed milk for hot coffee. Civilized, he had called it. But then everything about young Edythe Templeton had been civilized when Martin met and married her. He swept her from the settled comforts of a New York City home and a budding career as a singer into his own uncertain future, anchored at last in this two-hundred-year-old-family homestead in the improbable town of Thatcher. Thatcher County, north and northwest of all Edythe had known and accepted.

Edythe had brought her amenities with her, lifted her silvery voice in Thatcher's Presbyterian Church one innocent Sunday, discovered that the Roundtrees were three-generation Episcopalians, and thereafter sang anywhere she was asked. By trial and error, by never making the same mistake twice, she became a Roundtree, as she understood it. One could make one's own terms, Edythe learned, if one just didn't talk about them. She molded the rambling old house to her own graciousness. She produced five children. And she set Thatcher a gratifying example of refinement, stamina, and endurance—a combination Thatcher not only admired in women but expected. Edythe Roundtree's tears, when she shed them, were as private as her compromises.

She swung open the pantry door to the dining room. John, her second son, (her only son now, although she had never accepted the finality of Michael's disappearance) was finishing his breakfast.

"Dad's on his way down," John announced.

Not that she needed to be told, Edythe reflected. She knew and listened for every creaking board in the house, as she had ever since that black night seven years ago when Martin had been found on the floor of his study, two hours after their eldest son walked out of the house, never to return. Jim Cartwright had diagnosed Martin's collapse as a stroke, enough to doom a man as slight as Martin Roundtree. But the Roundtree obstinacy had prevailed. Martin had fought back.

"Why doesn't he use his cane, Mom? He'd make much better time." John lowered his voice as he laid his napkin aside.

"He does when he needs it." Edythe did not add

that Martin had given up the cane almost entirely since his second son had come with a reluctant law degree to practice in Thatcher. The proud new letters on the Main Street office now read ROUNDTREE AND ROUNDTREE, ATTORNEYS AT LAW. Martin walked straighter and surer ever since. John did not need another reminder of the responsibility he had assumed.

The steps were in the hall now.

John rose. Edythe stood at her place.

"Stay and have a cup of coffee with him," she whispered.

John's eyes, her own light-blue eyes, clouded. Then he smiled. The smile came more frequently these days, she noted. Politics might agree with John. The resolution to his pruned and stunted life.

"Good morning, my dear. Lovely day. Good morning, John. I see you're prompt. Or is my watch slow?"

"I'm early, sir. I plan to be at my headquarters at eight. That should make sure everybody gets there by eight-thirty."

"Well, well. Rush, rush. But that's the modern world, isn't it? I would think the republic would stand while a man breakfasts with his son, but these are changing times."

John resigned himself. "I'll have a cup of coffee with you, Dad."

"Go along, if you must. When you set yourself a schedule, stick to it. If you don't when you're young, you may not be able to when you're my age."

"Yes, sir." John wondered again how his father, not yet sixty, could so often sound as if he were talking for posterity. What did Michael call it? "The Poor Roundtree Almanac of Aggravating Advice." John remembered his older brother less vividly now, except

for Michael's flair for rapid-fire words which John so
notably lacked.

"Which reminds me," Martin continued blandly. "If
you have set yourself this Spartan schedule, I hope
you will apply it to Claude, since she's working for
you."

"Anything Claude wants to do is fine with me. But
she's her own boss, Dad."

"She has entirely too much time on her hands."

"Martin," Edythe broke in, in spite of herself, "it
isn't Claude's fault that she finished high school in
February, instead of last June. And she was a great
deal of help to me after Kim's accident. . . ."

Martin waved it aside. He liked order, and when his
youngest child had fallen from a maple tree in stubborn pursuit of a cat quite capable of coming down
by itself, disorder had reigned. As well as anguish. He
did not want to be reminded how deeply he loved his
children.

Edythe was still talking. ". . . and Claude has
filled her time with odd jobs. This will be her last free
summer before she goes to college. Or wherever." She
finished limply. There was no use in pouring old concern on to this morning's fresh breakfast. Claude had
always been their most unpredictable child, swinging
from radiance to secretiveness, forever glancing into
mirrors to be reassured. Of what? She was lovely. She
would be lovelier. Lately she had been going to her
room after dinner too early; her light remained on too
late.

Yet Claude was no longer a child. They had kept
her too young, perhaps. The besetting sin of families,
Edythe thought wryly. Walled in by love until in desperation the young ran off into marriage or whatever
else offered the quickest freedom. To this day she had

never known what drove Michael from the house.
Martin had shut that door in stubborn pride and shut
it had remained. Edythe would make sure that although Claude might leave, she would never be
driven. If she could make sure.

"I'll start your egg, dear." Egg precisely three-and-
a-half minutes. A warmed pitcher with warmed milk
for the coffee. One day at a time. One steadying day
at a time.

The thunder rolled closer. Edythe shivered. She had
never conquered her fear of Thatcher's thunderstorms.
They came down the valley with the tread of angered
gods, to the roll of demon drums and whiplashes of
lightning that crackled off the rocks, splintered the
trees, raged at the land until sated; only to circle, return, and rage again.

She heard Martin's voice.

"Where are you speaking today, John?"

"At Baxter Grove. And Juno's Landing this afternoon. Pine Hills tonight. I'll be in the office this
morning, sir."

Edythe set the egg timer. Time, it seemed, must be
watched carefully if one were not to lose control.

She wondered whether Claude had eaten breakfast
when she left the house so early.

"Juno's Landing? Going after that vote, eh?"

"If I can get it. I'm running for the people, sir. And
with them. All the people, I hope."

Martin's face grew thoughtful, the sharply intelligent face masking a mind respected for its dispassion
and its judgment. John found himself resenting that
long-ago reputation. Yet it was as much a part of his
inheritance as his father's fine features, which had become his own.

"I'm glad you know your own mind, John. I applaud you. Although I don't entirely agree with you. The Greeks believed that the wisest government was by those best suited to govern. They proved it. However, you'll need every vote you can get if you're going to beat Harlan Phelps."

John shifted impatiently. His father had a way of twisting his thoughts then sliding away leaving John in mental quicksand. But he would not argue. Not now, here, this morning. He had his father's support because the Roundtrees supported each other. Anything else was unthinkable. He hoped the day would never come when he would have to hurt the old man.

He grinned. "I'll get every vote Ben Orlini's money hasn't bought for Phelps. And maybe a few that it has."

"Then you won't need Juno's Landing, John."

Martin had the last word as usual. Edythe, still posed at the pantry door, watched her tall son stride from the room. John had his father's seriousness, the Roundtree obstinacy of purpose, and more than his young share of self-sacrifice. But he had something else—an awareness of coming change beyond the control of any man. Martin would never admit to that. Perhaps he would never have to.

She returned to the kitchen and turned on the radio. The ten-minute interval brought a repeat, ". . . thunderstorms by late afternoon. . . ." Edythe shivered. She would stay home this afternoon, draw the curtains, and admit to no one how much she longed to draw her family home, safe against the savagery.

"Hi, Mom."

It was Claude at the bottom of the back stairs. She looked pale but extraordinarily lovely, her eyes unusually bright. Edythe glanced at her sharply then

away. Nearly eighteen. Claude had grown to woman-
hood it seemed, when none of them was looking.

"Has Dad finished yet?"

"Not quite."

"I haven't time to go in. I'll grab a doughnut and
run. I told John I'd be there at eight. And I can't be
too late because I'm only working half a day. Plant
you now, dig you later!"

At the door, Claude turned. "Mom?"

"Yes, dear?"

"Why did you look at me like that?"

"Like what?"

"I don't know. Sort of funny. Because I'm late
again?"

"Well, you are, you know."

"I *know*, Mom." The door banged.

The egg-timer sand had run out. The egg would be
overcooked. Edythe poured the warmed milk into the
warmed pitcher and headed for the dining room.

Time, it seemed, must be watched carefully if one
were not to lose control of it.

Claude glanced at her graduation watch again,
jumped from the green wicker chair at the repainted
desk, and ran to the plate-glass window of John's
small, improvised political headquarters. Just for once,
she thought, her co-worker, Bonnie Smith could come
back from lunch on time. Or John might be early. She
could only hope as she searched Thatcher's busy Main
Street. At ten minutes to one, she could see at least
half a dozen passersby she knew. But she did not
wave. The last thing she would do at this moment was
to encourage anyone to come in. She would have to
leave by one at the latest to reach the Ridge before
two-thirty. If she were to have any chance to see Marc

Vallon again, it would have to be before he started work. She learned that much yesterday.

A night's broken sleep had brought Claude to a resolution. Mr. Vallon had been excessively rude to her. But he was a genius. She had blundered into the middle of his work. And added insult to injury by losing her temper like a schoolgirl over that silly, harmless snake. She would go back today and apologize. He would see in her a new dignity, the sincerity in her deep, anguished eyes, a face that must be filmed. Claude caught her own image in the plate-glass window and a little of her confidence slid away. Her mouth was too wide, her forehead too high. But a man like Marc Vallon would see beyond that. Especially if she were sincere. She would be very sincere.

The bell over the door jangled.

A slight, dark-haired girl came in with a smile and a scent as elusive as the single dimple in her left cheek. Scent was not worn in the daytime in Thatcher, but Ariel defied the town on that, as she had defied Thatcher when she married Duncan Phelps. Duncan was to marry Lowell Roundtree until Ariel had arrived. No one knew exactly what had happened but the talk had burned like a grass fire. Scandal still clung to Ariel in little eddies of bridge parties and afternoon teas. Claude had overcome her disappointment in losing Duncan as a brother-in-law by finding in Ariel an unexpected friend. Now the whole sorry story seemed a part of her childhood. She caught up with Ariel; they were equals. Except that Ariel was married, and Claude—at moments like this Claude felt the burden of her virginity. Looking at Ariel now, the slight thickening of that slim body, Claude tried to guess how it felt to be pregnant. She wondered for the millionth time how a girl like Ariel, Paris-raised, different in so many ways, could have settled in Thatcher as a clergyman's wife. Claude felt a rush of pity. Her own future suddenly stretched ahead as dazzling as it was veiled.

Ariel plunked a long, oblong object on the desk.

"A present for John," she announced.

"He'll be in any minute." Claude looked into the street. If she could only ask Ariel to take over for her until John or Bonnie came. But John was opposing Harlan Phelps in the election. Harlan was Ariel's father-in-law. Claude had no idea how Ariel or Duncan felt about it. Duncan and his father were anything but close—but she would not embarrass Ariel now. That was the trouble with a small town. All knots and hurt feelings. She, Claude, would be far away from it someday. Maybe sooner. Which brought Claude back to her immediate problem.

"Ariel, where are you going when you leave here?"

"No place. Home. Want to come? We haven't had a good talk for a long time. I miss you, Claude."

"Me, too. Maybe another time. I wondered—could you drop me out on Uncle Willard's road on your way home?"

"He isn't there, *chérie*. He's with Duncan in the church basement. Some of the pipes are rusting badly. . . ."

Rusted pipes. Late lunch hours. Silly presents. Nagging thorns, Claude thought, all conspiring to hold her from the shining secret her day held.

"Would you drop me out there anyway, Ariel?"

Ariel smiled but her answer was lost as the door was flung open. John towered in the small office.

"Ariel!" The warmth in his voice might have surprised Claude had she been listening.

"I can't stay, John, but I've brought you a little present for your headquarters." Ariel tore the plastic loose and held up a framed picture. At least it looked like a picture, except that it was cloth with embroidery on it.

John looked puzzled.

Ariel laughed. "I made it. It's the Roundtree coat of arms."

"It's beautiful. It's really great. I didn't know we had one." John was looking at Ariel, not at the embroidery.

"I invented it. See, the *R* here in the left quadrant. The oak leaves there. That's for strength. The wild swans there. That's for fidelity." Her eyes met John's for an instant. She pointed to the fourth quadrant. "That's a gauntlet. For honor. I looked it up. It's old French, and our ancestor Henrietta Roundtree came from New Orleans so—*voilà!*"

John took the escutcheon and found his voice. "I'll hang it right there over the desk. It'll hit everybody in the eye the minute they walk in. Integrity, fidelity, honor." He looked at her gravely. "Thanks, Ariel."

"If everybody likes it, I'll do it in needlepoint for Uncle Martin. Now I must go. I've promised to drive Claude out to Uncle Willard's. . . ."

Claude winced inwardly. How stupid to have asked Ariel. Now it would be a family hassle.

"Not staying this afternoon, princess?"

"I told you, John."

"Sure, sure. You're still on your week's vacation." His brooding, serious eyes were on Ariel. "Thanks, Ariel. For coming by. It means a lot."

The drive out was done in near silence. Claude longed to talk. Anticipation had mounted to wirelike tension. She felt that somehow she must tell her hid-

den excitement or it would burst from her. Ariel was
the only one of them all in whom she could confide.
Yet at the moment she felt a jolting sense of betrayal,
as if Ariel had gone over to the other side. The talk in
the office had been entirely between Ariel and John,
as if she, Claude, had not been there. So there was no
one, really, she could trust. She would have to do this
herself, whatever was to be done. And yet—she
glanced sidelong at Ariel's arresting face, thinned
down now, cheekbones prominent, the ivory skin too
pale, the hint of shadows under the deep-set eyes. She
is beautiful, Claude thought, she is Roundtree, but
she never will be Thatcher, no matter how hard she
tries. If there was anyone she could talk to—the car
was slowing. Willard's dirt road lay ahead.

"Ariel . . ." she hesitated.

"What, *chérie*?"

"Ariel, did you ever want something so badly—I
mean more than anything in the world—that it just
sort of choked you? But you couldn't tell anybody
about it?"

"Yes. Of course."

The lightness of the answer startled Claude. "I
mean something so, so big that it would change your
whole life?"

"Yes." The car stopped.

Claude hesitated. "What did you do? Did you finally tell anybody?"

"Only my mother."

That did it. If it was something you could tell your
mother. . . . Some of the desperation drained from
Claude's voice.

"What happened then?"

"I haven't seen my mother since."

That was what could happen when you confided in

your parents. It was a sacrifice Claude did not want
to think about, yet.

"Did you finally give up what you wanted so
badly?"

A fleeting smile lit Ariel's lovely face. The solitary
dimple in her left cheek came and went. She doesn't
look any older than I am, Claude thought. It was marriage that set Ariel apart.

"Oh, no, I didn't give up. I got it."

Claude sighed. They were obviously talking about
two different things. Ariel could not have wanted anything as deeply as Claude did or she wouldn't speak
of it now so matter-of-factly. And she wouldn't have
ended up here in Thatcher, a minister's wife. Stuck, as
Claude saw it.

"Thanks for the lift, Ariel."

"A pleasure. Come and see me when you can. I stay
home quite a bit these days."

"I will, really. Promise!"

Claude waited on the dirt road until the car was out
of sight. Then she cut across a meadow, skirted two
plowed fields greening with young corn, and headed
toward the Ridge. Twenty minutes later she found the
long-unused path Charlie Redwing had shown her,
the path that led her unseen to the crest.

Marc Vallon surveyed the area with satisfaction.
The Ridge rose at this point to a startling emptiness.
A rock slide sheared an abrupt thirty feet on the right
to meet the gentler slope. The camera would turn it
into a thousand-foot drop. He had marked the safety
spot clearly where Solveg would plunge, and tested
carefully the trampolinelike structure the property
men had rigged to catch her. He had no fears for Solveg. She was as surefooted as a mountain goat and

confident as a lioness. She would make no mistake.

Ahead, a grove of black fir cut a saw-toothed silhouette against the graying sky. The camera would give it the vast distance of a forsaken world. Nearer, the site, rough with stubble and the faded stumps of fallen trees, had the desolation of the Apocalypse. It was exactly what Marc Vallon wanted. He might have searched the world and found no such location. Ben Orlini must have cleared this site for a purpose when he was building his curious, ego-driven house. But whatever the purpose it was not fulfilled. Only stubble grew. An old road was nearly obliterated. The new road twisted away.

Marc studied the sky. Even the heavens were cooperating. Westward, dark cumulus clouds were beginning to billow from the empty horizon. He saw Solveg against them, her full breasts lifted, her shoulders strong, her wild gray-black hair blown backward like her full black skirt. Woman triumphant, contemptuous of the man she was destroying, supreme in her conquest. She would fling out to poor Leonard her final, devastating revelation, step backward—one step too far. With the scream of a harpie she would plunge from the edge of the rock slide, consumed at last by the winds and the fury of the elements that had nurtured her. No actress in the world could play the scene like Solveg. Perhaps she was right. They would be at the top. Again. But never together. That was past.

He looked at the western sky. The thunderheads were rising faster than he had anticipated. He wished he had not indulged Solveg. They should begin the shooting now. But he knew better than to knock at that silent bedroom door. It had been bad enough to find Lennie in his lotus position with a bottle of

Scotch at his side. Marc had taken it gently away. He knew Lennie needed the Scotch to get him out into the coming storm. But he wanted that fear, that slavering weakness on Leonard's face in the final scene. It would make Solveg a more hated woman in the end. The audience would want that. They would want to see her punishment. Or was it Marc himself who wanted to see her brought down? His forehead was wet with sweat. He brushed it away with a fresh handkerchief. He always became a part of his work, totally, emotionally involved until there was no other reality, until he was defenseless against success or failure. He wiped his forehead again. Where the devil was everybody? Hutch, the cameramen, the grips? He would get Solveg out of her bed, Lennie off his backside; he would . . .

A branch snapped; he heard the shuffle of dry leaves. A little below him, above the darkness of a rock, he saw the glint of pale hair.

He should be furious. It was against his clearly stated orders. How many times would he have to dispatch this defiant, spoiled, arrogant young—dryad, he thought helplessly. She had come from behind the rock. Against the dulling sky her hair was a fall of quicksilver.

"Mr. Vallon, it's early, so I know I'm not intruding. I came back to apologize." The words ran together.

"Did you indeed, Miss Roundtree? It isn't early, and you are intruding. So whatever you have to apologize for, state it. Then for the last time, I will ask you to leave."

He stood, rapier thin, immaculately clean in white trousers and turtleneck. And even handsomer, Claude thought, in this odd, fading light. He was looking at her now with unblinking, brooding eyes. Claude drew in her breath.

It was the way he had looked at her yesterday, the look that had slid over her like water, soothing, yet exciting. She had thought of it last night in her tossing sleeplessness, her body tingling, her face hot, invisible thistledown fingers playing on her. No invention of apology had brought her back today. It was that look, something she knew but could never express, nor would ever reveal. She felt her cheeks warm. She must fight it. She had her career to think about.

"I came to apologize for what I said," she began stiffly.

"What did you say?"

"If you don't remember . . ."

He had shifted his gaze. "Miss Roundtree, I have a great deal to do. I don't remember. If that's all . . ."

"I said some rude things when I was holding the snake and I'm sorry. And that is all." It wasn't coming out the way she intended.

"You said what you thought, I presume."

"I did—then."

"Then don't apologize. Apology is a form of surrender. I'm sure you don't intend that."

"I guess not."

"Then if you'll excuse me . . ."

He was turning away. She would never see him again.

"Mr. Vallon, when are you going to start—what do you call it, shooting?"

He looked at the thin, expensive watch on his wrist. She noticed how prominent the wrist bones were, lean, skeletal.

"In twenty-eight minutes."

"Would you mind awfully if I watched? I'll hide behind that rock. No one would even see me!"

"Would it make any difference if I did mind?"

She hesitated and felt her lip tremble. Everything had gone wrong. Pretense was futile. "No. Except I'd find another place."

There was an instant of awful silence. Then unexpectedly, like a slit through a bolted door, Marc smiled.

"You're a difficult young woman."

Something inside Claude eased. "I don't mean to be, honestly. But don't you see? This is my only chance. Or I'll never get out of Thatcher. If I could only talk to you when you weren't so busy. I—I think I could be something great, like a star or something if you could only tell me what to do. . . ." Her voice drained away. She had caught a glimpse of someone coming along the rise from the direction of the house. She recognized the blunt figure, the forward thrust of shoulders. The last person she wanted to see at this moment was Davison L. Hutchins. "I wouldn't take much time, honestly, Mr. Vallon."

"In that case I couldn't do much for you. Everything worthwhile takes time. I prefer candor. What are you after? A screen test?"

The dark-rimmed, light gray eyes stared through her as if she were glass. She looked down at the stubble under her feet, at her absurd, blunt shoes that yesterday had seemed so sharp. Why did he have to ask, if he could read her every thought? It would be easier to turn and run, pretend this had never happened, go home and marry Larry Higgins and live out her life in Thatcher, growing dull and frumpy, her beauty wasted, her hair gray, her hands rough and worn from washing dishes. The dire saga passed in a split instant through Claude's active brain, brought a lump of self-pity to her throat, and made her realize Marc was waiting for an answer. A screen test? Hadn't that been in the back of her mind from the beginning.

She swallowed hard. "Yes."

"Yes? Yes, what?"

"Yes, Mr. Vallon."

"For the love of God, I'm not trying to improve your manners. Though somebody should. You want a screen test. You want me to give you one."

"I want you to tell me if you thought—I mean, if my face is all right. I mean—I could learn all the rest about being an actress."

"Could you indeed?" He was studying her, that look again, a mysterious invisible sheath of silk sliding over her body. Her face flushed.

"I guess I shouldn't have bothered you."

"That's correct. But you have, so I shall say two things. The first, Miss Roundtree, is that you talk too much. The second is that I will think about your request."

"You mean . . ." The sentence was never finished.

Marc's voice cracked like a whip. "On condition that I do not catch sight of you again. Until my work is finished."

"I promise! Honestly!" She vanished down the path and behind the rock so completely, Marc wondered if she had planned it that way.

Hutch was coming toward him. His usual easy smile gone. He had missed nothing.

"Playing games, boss?"

"Get rid of her, if you can. I can't. Call Soli. Tell her we're starting fifteen minutes early."

"You've got to be kidding."

"Then I'll tell her. Someday I may discover that I don't need you at all, Hutch."

Marc strode toward the house, wondering at his own irritability. In a way he could not define, his sense of command had weakened. He could not tolerate that, from anyone.

Claude fitted her body against a hollow of the rock and waited. Nothing had happened. Her watch had stopped at three ten, so she had no way of knowing how long she had crouched there. Marc had not returned from the house, and Hutch had disappeared in the opposite direction. Against a darkening western sky now the color of old iron, the stubbled clearing with its fringe of ragged tree stumps appeared as desolate as a devastated plant. Only the slow surge of thunderheads above it told her that time was passing.

Claude shivered and thought of the ancient malignity of the Ridge. She knew where she was now, at the edge of the clearing where once the best blueberries in Thatcher County were to be found. As children, they had made their way up here through the woods with wrapped sandwiches and empty pails for long, lazy summer afternoons in the August sun. It had all ended when Billy Haskell slipped off the edge of the rock slide and broke his arm. They had been forbidden to return. Claude had sneaked back once with her friend Bonnie, but it had been no fun. Bonnie was scared. The next year they had outgrown blueberry picking, replacing it with tree houses. How childish it had all been, how little it had all mattered.

Claude, in her new-found maturity, gave a small satisfied sigh. That was all behind her now; ahead lay a new life, glittering with promise. A faint rumble, barely audible, from the somber cloud mass, re-

minded her of the present. She would have chosen a
less-gloomy site to begin her adventure, but perhaps
this was to be her next test. She had come this far, she
would not leave.

The thunder died. The silence was complete. Even
the bird calls had ceased. Suppose no one came. By
the time the storm came and went it might be dark,
too dark to find her way down.

She thought of Chastity, the other "actress" in the
family. Chastity Roundtree, her name in spidery writing in the brassbound Bible at Uncle Willard's. And
again, in granite on a small rose-carved headstone in
the Roundtree plot in Thatcher's cemetery.

CHASTITY,
1878–1900

At eighteen Chastity had run off to New York with a
faith healer and gone on the stage. She must have
been talented for there were a few yellowed programs
with her name in them among Uncle Willard's papers.
Then inexplicably she had come home and the following summer met with an "accident" on the Ridge. Nobody would talk about that, and until this moment
Claude had never cared. It was enough to know that
she herself had inherited Chastity's beautiful silver-
blond hair and, she hoped, her talent. But now as the
sunlight was departing the Ridge, she wondered.
What kind of accident? What had happened to
CHASTITY, 1878–1900?

She was growing stiff. She stood up, risking visibility. But the movement brought a shuffling of dry
leaves. She had promised to stay out of sight and that
meant out of hearing. She crouched again. The rus-
tling of leaves was repeated. And again. Footsteps.

Someone was coming up the Ridge from behind her. She'd hear voices in another moment, and the site would be filled with people, cameras, orders, and Marc Vallon, quick as a white flame among them, a magician, directing, controlling, commanding, and suddenly finding time to look for her and at her. With that look.

"Well—had enough?"

With an exasperating grin, Davison Hutchins stood between two saplings.

Claude slid to the base of the rock and stretched out her two aching knees. She did not smile.

"No."

"I didn't think so. But you'd better go along now."

"Mr. Vallon said I could stay."

"Quite possibly. But there's not going to be anything to stay for."

"You mean they're not going to film anything?"

Hutch came the last few feet up the rise and stood looking down at her. If she had been willing to look up, she would have seen concern in his eyes. But she stared stonily past him.

"One hour and twenty-two minutes. Miss Roundtree, may I call you Claude? You are tough, determined, crazy, or all three. But the party's over."

"They're not going to make the picture?"

"Not today. According to our prima donna. Now can I help you anywhere?"

Claude settled herself. "No, thank you."

"Right on. It's your turf."

Suddenly, angry as she was, Claude did not want to lose sight of him. "How did you know I've been here an hour and twenty minutes?"

"Twenty-two minutes. I saw you talking to our peerless leader. I must congratulate you. Most ambi-

tious young women are reduced to sheer terror—
before they fall on their backs."

"I don't know what that means."

"Good. Shall we go?" He stretched out a hand.

"What's the picture called?" She did not see his grin
return.

"*La Troisième Manon*."

"What?"

"Do you know any French?"

"I took it in high school. Like everybody."

"In that case, I'll translate. *La Troisième Manon*
means The Third Manon."

"I don't get that. What's Manon?"

"Do you read?"

She glanced at him, saw his mouth twitch. He was
putting her on but it wasn't unpleasant, talking to this
superior-sounding man she never wanted to see anyway. She giggled. "Of course I read."

He found the giggle enchanting. He slid down the
rock and sat beside her. "*Manon Lescaut* is the name
of a book by the Abbé Prévost. It is French. Two op-
eras have been made from the story. One in French
by Massenet, one in Italian by Puccini."

"I've never seen an opera. I wanted to know about
the movie Mr. Vallon is making."

"Corrected. Do you always take the shortest line between two points?"

"I don't like being laughed at."

"On the contrary. My respect for you grows.
Manon is a girl who led two lives—the first innocent.
She fell in love. Instead of going to the convent where
her parents rightly thought she belonged, she went
with her young man. He had no money so she didn't
marry him; she lived with him." He was aware of the
intensity of her young eyes, of her young body.

"Go on."

"She got tired of that, as any ambitious young girl would, so she left him to live with a rich old man."

"She never saw the young man again?"

"Oh, yes, she did. That's where the trouble came in. She took the old man's jewels, started off with her young lover, and got caught. For her punishment she was exiled to America and died on a desert."

"Where was the young man?"

"He was with her."

"That's silly. Why would she die?"

"That's what our peerless leader said. So he is making this picture about the third Manon. The first as innocent, the second as evil, the third as the real woman. All power and revenge."

But she was not listening. She was scrambling to her feet.

"What did you mean before, 'the show's over'?" she demanded. "Look!"

The open site was suddenly filling with people, voices, and paraphernalia. The air had become electric with excitement. Marc Vallon was walking down the slight incline beside the woman Claude had seen the day before, in the same long black dress, her gray-streaked hair falling nearly to her waist. Behind them walked the man she heard called Lennie, the leading man. He came, slowly, woodenly. Halfway down the rise, he stopped as if waiting for a command. The woman glanced back and said something Claude could not hear. Marc shook his head angrily and left her.

"See! They're going to make the picture, just like Mr. Vallon said. Why did you say they wouldn't?"

But she did not wait for an answer. To her astonishment, Vallon had crossed the clearing and was coming directly toward her. Hutch moved in front of her.

"You're not going to shoot, chief?"

"He says he's all right. He's willing. I can't afford to wait. I may never get a sky like this again." His glance slid off Claude. "I thought I told you to get rid of her."

"As you discovered, sir, it isn't easy."

Whether it was that infuriating grin or Marc Vallon's calculated rudeness, Claude could not tell. She pushed past Hutch, her head high.

"Mr. Vallon, if you wanted to get rid of me all you had to do was say so. Not send *him*. You told me you would give me an appointment if I stayed out of sight. And that's all I was doing. I wasn't bothering anybody. But if you didn't want me around, why didn't you say so? Why did you tell me I could stay? If I'm going into the movies, I ought to see how it works, shouldn't I? I'm not one of those girls who are so scared of you they fall backwards . . ."

Hutch coughed. Marc stared at her. She drew another breath. "I thought I had the word of a gentleman but if I haven't, just say so, Mr. Vallon, and you won't have to ask anybody to get rid of me. Especially *him*." She flung the last word like a stone.

From a long distance somebody called Marc Vallon. He bowed stiffly to Claude.

"You have the word of a gentleman, Miss Roundtree. Here is my card." He wrote rapidly on the back of it. "My address and the day and hour when I can see you. Please be prompt."

With another slight bow, he left her. She held the card unsteadily, not daring to look at it. She wanted to flash her triumph in front of Hutch, but something in his face stopped her. Something she could not read.

Something oddly sad. Without a word he turned and went out on the site.

Marc, from the center of the clearing, was giving orders. "Soli, you'll come down the rise to the edge of the cliff. Stop when you come to that cross of white paint. That's where you'll stand. Against the sky. Len, you'll come toward her from this direction. Stay about six feet from the ledge. Do you understand, Len?"

Leonard, still motionless on the rise, nodded.

"We have only a few minutes before the storm breaks. That's what we're here for. To get that storm. So we'll shoot at once. No mistakes!"

Lightning feathered the distant thunderheads, answered by a low growl. Claude glanced at the writing on the card. Angular, foreign, difficult to read. Except the number nine. Nine! Her lucky number! It was a portent. She would make out the rest later.

She thrust the card into her bra between her small breasts and slid back behind the rock. She would not miss a second of what was happening. Not with her own career half begun. The card pricked her deliciously as she leaned forward to watch the black-gowned woman move across the stubble.

She's old, Claude thought. Old. He'll find a younger part for me. Like the young, the innocent . . . what was her name?

Claude gave herself up to fantasy.

Marc Vallon was not an easily satisfied man. Some called it his perfectionism, others his insecurity. Marc himself saw it as his genius for detail and mood. He grew with his work. As scene followed scene, he found new depths in his own vision.

Maybe. But as the thunderclouds roiled closer, a nervousness ran through crew and actors. Solveg stood at the edge of the drop on the faint cross mark of white paint, her head high, her body stiffened. Her silence was as ominous as the sky. Leonard, on the slight rise, visibly flinched at every nearing crack of lightning.

"This better be the last take, chief." Hutch had his eyes on the boulder at the edge of the woods. The little idiot concealed behind it would not leave until the last cat was hung. He wished he could stop worrying about her.

"Magnificent!" said Marc. "Look at Soli against that sky! I want the darker clouds moving in, a flash of lightning if I can get it. And I think I can. And *voilà!* No words. No score. Nothing. A woman of fury and vengeance, flaunting the very elements and, at the moment of her triumph—destroyed!"

Hutch had heard the words before. There was no appealing to Marc in this mood. He stepped back and wondered how he could get Claude to his car before the storm burst. Marc blew on the ever-present silver whistle that hung on a white cord around his neck.

"All right, everybody! Soli, hold just as you are. Superb! Lennie, come down slowly, powerfully, nearer the drop. We want to suspect that it's her love for you, not her vengeance, that sends Soli to her death. . . ."

"Take three!"

A thin wind whistled across the stubble, bending the bushes, tearing at Soli's black skirt and black hair. She was, Hutch had to admit, magnificent, unafraid, undaunted, contemptuous only of weakness. Leonard walked slowly down the rise. The man had guts, Hutch told himself. Courage was not absence of fear. It was overcoming fear. Len walked, as if drained of all emotion, toward the woman who had ruined him, taller than he had ever looked. It could quite possibly

be his finest performance, matching Soli's, even—
Hutch smiled inwardly—snatching the film's climax
from her.

But where was the man going? He should have
turned to her. The flash of lightning Marc wanted
crackled almost above them. Len paused only a second at the drop. Then, like a man in a dream, he
stepped over the edge. A high-pitched scream came
from behind the boulder.

"Cut!"

A blur of running figures and voices drowned out
Marc's voice. Hutch was first to reach the drop. Lennie Ross lay at the bottom. Even the bushes that
might have broken his fall failed him. His neck was
twisted oddly. His handsome, weak face turned upward, eyes staring, mouth open, as if waiting for the
applause he would never hear. Crewmen and cameramen were taking what routes they could to where
Lennie lay. Marc stood frozen, incapacitated. Soli
stared downward, an aged harpy, broken phrases
coming hoarsely from her. "The fool! The fool! Didn't
he see! He was drunk! Drunk! *You* . . ." She flung
herself toward Marc but he drew back, seeking the
only refuge he knew, his isolation.

Hutch passed them both, a terrible thought lacing
his mind. What tragedy had played itself out among
these three? Was Solveg's fury directed at Marc for his
part in the horror, or deeper, at Leonard for his ultimate, irrevocable triumph in the final moments of the
scene?

He found Claude huddled behind the boulder,
shaking.

"What happened, Hutch?"

"An accident. Come on. I'm taking you home."

He slid his arm around her. She seemed willing enough to let him lead her.

"But what happened? Will he be all right?"

He did not answer. There would be time enough to tell her when he had taken her safely away from the questions, the probing, the publicity that would follow. Heavy drops of rain began to spatter the leaves. The storm would burst any moment. He wished he had a jacket to wrap around her, then he wondered if she would accept it. She had begun to walk, rapidly, independently of him. And to talk.

"I saw it all! He just kept walking. Walking. With his eyes wide open. Staring. He must have seen the edge. But he didn't stop! Didn't he know it was there? Didn't anybody tell him? I saw him fall. All the way. But I couldn't see the bottom. Hutch, what happened? He looked like a blind man."

"Stop thinking about it, Claude. It was an accident."

"He's dead. Isn't he?"

"Yes. My car's up there just ahead of us on the road. You can tell me the quickest way to your house. There's no reason for you to be any part of this or even to think about it."

"No reason? No reason!" She turned on him, furious. "No reason! I *am* a part of it. I was there, and it was horrible. And there's no way you can tell me not to think about it! I feel so sorry for that poor man and if you don't care about him, I do!" Her eyes filled.

"I care. I care a lot. That's my business but it's not yours. And at this minute there are priorities."

"What priorities? If you mean me, I can get home alone." Her voice shook. Anger was holding back hysteria, he thought. They reached the car.

"Which way?"

She got in, meekly enough. "I'm not going home.

I'm going to Uncle Willard's. That's the farm down there. You take this road back to the fork. That's where they—they think I am."

She wasn't much more than a kid at times. Somewhere between fourteen and twenty. Thirty, he amended, as he caught her stony look. He swung the car around. To his relief he saw her eyes bright with tears. It would at least end any hysteria. To his greater relief they did not spill over. He felt helpless at women's tears. He did not want to feel helpless with Claude Roundtree.

He patted her hand. "Heavy stuff. But you'll be all right."

"Of course I'll be all right. But that poor man won't! Hutch, he wasn't told to walk over the cliff, was he?"

He sighed. She was going to dwell on it, no matter what. That could be troublesome, if not dangerous.

"Of course not. I told you it was an accident."

"Then why were his eyes wide open and staring? Why didn't he even cry out? He just walked. As if he were drugged. Or hypnotized or . . . or . . ."

"Okay. Do you want to go back and ask Vallon?"

"It wasn't his fault!"

"Of course not," he said too quickly. But he was irritated by her quick defense of Marc.

A driving rain hit the windshield. They reached the farmhouse in silence.

"Better run for it."

"Thanks, Hutch. I guess I'm not very grateful."

"That's right."

"But I am sorry. Terribly sorry about what happened."

He saw the gleam of tears again. "Thanks. Lennie would have been glad to know."

He watched her enter the house and wondered if he

would ever see her again. As the door closed behind her, the storm struck. He sat for a moment in the car, windshield wipers useless against the downpour. Fire-white lightning split the sky and crackled against the Ridge. Thunder rolled into the valley, palpable as a wall.

He thought of Lennie, lying face upward. He hoped they had taken him out of the ravine by this time. Weak as he was, with all his stored-up fears, Lennie had flaunted them all in the end—Marc, Soli, death itself—with a certain flare. He deserved at least that simply decency from them.

Hutch swung his car into the storm, finding a kind of relief in the combat. He was surprised at the depth of his own feelings. Not grief for a burned-out actor. He was no strange witness to despair. It was nearer outrage, in the shape of the little white card he had seen Marc Vallon hand Claude and about which she had said nothing. He could guess what was written on it. He saw again her intensity, wild-willed as a filly.

And there lay his frustration. He had no way of reaching her. She would no more listen to him about Marc than she had listened about Lennie's bleak exit. Instead, she had instantly gone to Marc's defense.

He skidded the car savagely around a muddy turn. Claude had seen too much and knew too little.

He would give a lot to be able to protect her from herself.

Chapter Six

The *Thatcher Standard* gave Leonard Ross's death headlines and a front-page column. The next day it reported that the coroner had confirmed the death as accidental. The following day a lower left-hand box, page two, reported that the actor's body had been sent to his birthplace, Scranton, Pennsylvania, for cremation. Marc Vallon was mentioned once as producer-director of the foreign film *La Troisième Manon* and Solveg Traner twice as Ross's "leading lady." Davison Hutchins hoped fervently that Soli would never see the articles.

There was little likelihood. Solveg shut herself in her room, refusing to see anyone. Marc remained in the house, willing to talk only to the coroner. Everything else he left to Hutch. Marc was a stunned man but he was not shattered.

"I never expected anything like this, Hutch. I gave Len every opportunity. He was a fool. He drank himself into walking off that cliff. But by God, he gave a performance! His greatest. I'll see the rushes in Paris but I know already what they are. It changes the ending. We can't go beyond that. But he took it right away from old Soli, didn't he? Though I'll kill any man who tells her that."

Marc hesitated, as if there was something more he should say but he was not sure what. "I'm sorry about Len. But a man couldn't wish for anything more than to die doing his best work. He proved I was right, didn't he? He had talent. He couldn't handle it."

Not after Soli had shredded it to bits. But Hutch kept this thought to himself.

"Do you want to make any statement?"

"That's your job, Hutch. You know what to say. That's what I pay you for. Say nothing here in this dead town. I want to get out of it as soon as we can. Something dignified for *The New York Times,* mostly about the picture. And all you can get into the Paris papers."

Yet Hutch felt compassion for this man. Marc Vallon had been wounded. Not so much by the immediate accident as by another evidence of the perversity of fate, an inexplicable animosity that had dogged him too long. His masterpiece at its very climax was flawed, though he would not use the word. The great finale had been taken out of his hands. It might be improved but it was no longer his own intense vision. His ego would have to accept the fact that the improvement was not his. In the empty aftermath of his work Marc Vallon might find room to mourn his friend. But not yet. The lean gray face settled into lines as ascetic as those on a Goya saint. His light eyes showed the burden of defeated purpose, coupled with an oddly boyish bewilderment. Marc in his secret hours was facing pain.

Solveg left in the morning. Marc waited only for the

coroner's verdict in the afternoon to follow her. Hutch saw to the tidying up, paid the Barkers well for their trouble and their silence. He had taken two annoyed calls from Julia Orlini in Paris, deploring the publicity, and one excited call from Ben, fearing scandal. Hutch had reassured them both. It was a simple accident, everything had been handled with dignity, Marc and Solveg were on their way to Paris now. The Orlinis, Hutch told himself, were strictly Soli's bailiwick. She could manage their grace and favor in her own way.

At Rampart Inn the next day he stood in his low-ceilinged bedroom watching cameramen and crew below. They were departing with the noisy confusion of a flock of daws. He still had details to finish. After that he wondered what excuse he could have for staying on in Thatcher. At least he had been able to keep the story at a minimum. And her name out of it. Not, he thought, that the little vixen had earned his solicitude. It came in spite of his better judgment. Like the sound of her giggle and the image of her face. She would not thank him for any of it. But he could not help wondering how she had stood up to things.

Very well, he thought dryly, as he watched the camera truck depart. Most girls, Hutch presumed from a lifelong habit of avoiding female analyses, would chatter hysterically, blow the whole episode out of proportion, and make a nuisance of themselves. Claude had had her tearful moment of involvement, her self-drama. She was probably coolly sitting it out, plotting her next move. He would call her when he was free. He owed her that. He was free now, he reminded himself.

The driveway was empty at last. The sweet, cleansing peace of June lay everywhere. The hills melted gently into the blue mist of the horizon as if a storm had never clawed its fury across them. He liked this strong, green country. Three hundred years of history had poured westward from it. Its rock-toughened muscle, its staunch ideas of self-dignity, veined the land. His own people, long ago, had come from just such country. This town, rooted in its proud valley, could shrug off with ease the shabby little tragedies of ego and ambition, played out for a brief moment on its rocks.

Hutch felt something uncoil with him, a slow letting go of tension, of the bravura he held like a shield against his emotions. A man could be himself in this place when he was sure of what that self was. Here, perhaps, he could even learn. He stood looking a moment at the benign blend of hills and sky. He was at last ready to make the call he had been postponing.

Instead, his own phone sprang suddenly to life. He was not entirely surprised by the voice at the other end. Only chagrined. He should have known better. He had counted on Marc to do this necessary courtesy. It was the least the great man could have done. Marc had failed even in that. Now the failure had become omission, the omission in the long view, quite possibly a mistake. At the moment, Hutch was taking a very long, very personal, view.

Willard Roundtree was brief, with a nettling tone of command. Hutch hastened downstairs, found his rented car in the rear parking lot, and through the deceptively soft day headed for the second time within the week to the valley below the ridge.

Claude sat in the afternoon stillness of her brother John's makeshift campaign office and considered her problem. In the three days since the front-page tragedy burst onto Thatcher breakfast tables, Claude had displayed a remarkable devotion to John's political career. She discovered that here at least she could sit at the desk or stand at the window and escape the deluge of gossip that Thatcher could produce when it was both curious and disapproving.

Not that Thatcher had ever heard of Leonard Ross. Few had even been aware that a motion picture was being filmed up on the Ridge. When it was learned that the picture was French, the younger people lost interest, the older pursed their lips. In Thatcher, French movies had a suggestive recall of furtively read French novels and baudy postcards, still found occasionally in the attic of some former sporting gallant, now lying in a shroud of respectability on Cemetery Hill.

It was not the dramatis personae that concerned Thatcher. It was the ever-recurrent speculation of the vengeful Ridge and the disasters attendant on its invasion. Had not the Orlinis' own son, Nick, skidded over that same ledge in a storm? It was rumored that there were bruises on his body that the accident could not have caused. And nearly seventy years ago one of the Roundtrees themselves, young Chastity, had plunged from it—pregnant, it was whispered. The talk bubbled, and the fault circled again and again to the outsiders, the Orlinis. They had desecrated the Ridge by felling Thatcher's revered three-hundred-year-old oak tree. Now this. Who but the Orlinis would think of turning one's own home over for a movie? The sooner the matter died down the better, Thatcher concluded, savoring the morsels through tight lips.

At the Roundtree table Martin made short work of it.

"This kind of publicity is not wanted in Thatcher. We'll drop the subject."

Claude, in the refuge of John's headquarters, had
read every printed word. In one way she was relieved
that her name was not mentioned. It would have
brought the whole matter to light much too soon and
forced a crisis. But deeper, she would like all
Thatcher to know. "Miss Claude Roundtree was at the
site of the tragedy because of her friendship with the
famous director Marc Vallon, who is planning a
screen test for her. Mr. Vallon already sees Claude
Roundtree as a promising young actress, a rising
star . . ."

They would, someday. Claude had read and reread
the card that now lay wrapped in tissue paper in her
wallet. "MARC VALLON, 213 Rue Dauphine, Paris."
Not even "France." In the world of Marc Vallon, no
other word was needed. PARIS!

On the back the angular writing was now clear to
her. And vivid. "August 9. 3:00. Prompt." She liked
the underscoring. That made it real. And important.
She would be there, of course. Prompt. No one, nothing, could prevent that. The tragedy on the Ridge had
blurred to a mirage. The storm, the old woman in
black, the man falling, all fragments of a play she
might have seen. Like the gallows scene in *The Prince
and the Pauper* she had seen once in a summer-stock
company. The horror had haunted her that night. It
had gone with the day.

She held the card tenderly. She would have to earn
the money. She had already searched the papers for
air fares. She could ask Angie Welles who ran a local
travel service but she was not ready to trust anyone
yet. She would have to tell John she could not help
him. And the family—that would be the worst. But
martyrs had gone to the stake for less. Rue Dauphine,

August 9 . . . she felt Marc Vallon's eyes deep on her and shivered.

The bell on the door jangled. Claude thrust the card and wallet with one quick movement into her tote. Martin Roundtree entered.

He smiled down at her. "Surprise you, kitten?"

"Oh—no, Dad."

"You jumped like a cat on a hot stove."

"I—I guess I just feel jumpy." She rose and kissed her father.

"I had begun to think that you might be. John called me. His speech at Birchville went very well. They want him to stay and talk to the local committee and the Grange group. He's doing better than even I anticipated. I think it surprised even him. But he's a Roundtree and people don't forget that." He glanced at Ariel's embroidered heraldry framed on the wall. 'Integrity. Fidelity. Honor.' Ariel did a fine thing when she made that. I'd have liked my father to see it."

He sat down in a wicker chair and fanned himself. He looked better than he had for some time. More like the way she remembered him, kindly, a little distant, seriously courteous, and always ready to read to her when she climbed into his lap in the black leather chair before supper. He chose the book. She did not always understand it. But she loved the sound of his fine, careful voice and the safety of his arm around her.

Maybe this was the time to tell him, to blurt it all out, her secret dream, her great chance, the future that had suddenly burst open with firework brilliance. He would understand. He might even help. He would be proud of her.

"Dad . . ."

"You need a little sunshine, Claude. You're too pale these days. Loyalty to John's future is fine. We're all in it. But work and no play makes even the prettiest girl glum. So I thought I'd walk over here this afternoon and serve as a replacement. Go on out and enjoy yourself."

If he expected a whoop of joy, he was disappointed. She stood uncertainly. He thought he knew why.

"I know what's bothering you. You've let this mess up at Orlini's place upset you. It's upset a lot of people. I want you to forget about it. Movie people—they're a depraved lot."

"How do you know?" Her chance was gone, if there had ever been a chance. The wall was back, the curious, invisible barrier built of time and blindness between them.

"I wasn't born yesterday, Claude. I know a great deal about the world that I hope you will never find out. And if I hadn't, Si Barker would have set me straight."

"Si? What did he tell you?"

"Si's grandfather, whom you would not remember, was coachman to our family long ago. Those are ties a man doesn't forget. He and his wife are caretakers up at the Orlinis' now."

"You mean he spied on those people?" She wondered what else Si had seen up there. And told.

"Spying is a pretty harsh word, Claude."

"What would you call it?"

"He told me what he thought I should know."

About her own visits up there? "What was that?"

"Are you defending those people, Claude?"

"I don't think you should call them depraved just because old Si Barker gossips."

"That will do! I don't listen to gossip!" Martin was

angered by his helplessness. If he could have sent her
from the room, denied her a pleasure, or done any of
the tried-and-true expedients that had kept his hand
firmly in control—but she was grown now. And she
had slipped from him. Like the others.

"When a woman swims in the nude, when she lives
with two men in one house, I call that depravity. If
you have any other words for it, you might tell me."

Martin opened his newspaper.

Claude had made a mistake. She had wanted her
father to understand. She sensed now that it would be
impossible. He had shrunk into the wicker chair as if
he were fading from her. She noticed how sparse his
graying hair had become, how thin and spotted his
hand.

She bent her head to his. "I'm sorry, Dad. I just
think fair is fair."

"So do I, Claude." He laid her hand against his
cheek. "And right is right."

Outside the building she picked up her bicycle and
found herself swallowing hard. She would have to
hurt him. She knew that now.

She despised Si's gossip, as she rebelled against the
narrowness that fostered it. Swimming in the nude?
She had done that herself and in that very pool. As for
the woman, the aging woman with the long gray-
black hair, living with anybody? That meant love, and
love was for the young.

The word itself brought a rush of physical warmth
through her. She imagined herself living with Marc
Vallon up on the Ridge. She imagined the pool at
midnight. They would both be swimming. Nude, of
course. He would wrap her in her robe, lead her into
the house, take her robe from her . . .

She shivered, caught up in fantasy.

She would not go home. She would not even go to see Ariel as she had promised. The Ridge would be abandoned now. She would push from her mind the horror she had seen there. She felt the great empty house draw her, on this shimmering afternoon, with the magnetism of a perverse fate.

"She was up there when it happened." Willard Roundtree stated it flatly without question.

Hutch knew better than to deny it, explain, or even try to protect Claude. He had wanted to do that since the first exasperating moment he had encountered her near the swamp. It had proven increasingly difficult. He nodded.

"So she saw it all," Willard continued.

"Not the bottom of the drop. I got her out right away."

"I'm not sure it would have bothered her. Claude may have the face of an angel but underneath she's her great-grandmother to the last fiber. And that's steel. All imagination; the rest determination. It played hell with Henrietta's life and everybody else's. That's her picture over there."

Hutch dutifully inspected the faded sepia in the oval frame. "Claude doesn't look like her."

"Not a bit. She just behaves like her. I'm glad it's over. If it is." Willard looked sharply at the young man.

"A lot of girls get movie struck when they see a film being made." He wondered what the old man was getting at. Surely Willard Roundtree had not asked him out here for this kind of empty talk.

"I thought so at first when she came out here one day to borrow my binoculars. To watch birds," he chortled. "I should warn you Claude hasn't what you might call a reverence for truth. Birds! That young one hasn't the patience to look at a setting hen. But when she didn't come to borrow the binoculars, I began to wonder. But Charlie Redwing was keeping an eye on her."

That sounded like spying. Hutch resented it. Surely they didn't subject Claude to that? After all she was— "What?" he thought helplessly. She was young, stubborn, unpredictable, and would cause him endless trouble, but he wouldn't stand still for spying. He knew what a family could do to you that way. He sipped at the whiskey that the old man had offered and gave himself some silent advice. Cool it. Roundtree hadn't played the Madeira bit this time. He had greeted him like an equal and brought out the bourbon.

"Who is Charlie Redwing?"

"Full-blooded Algonquin Indian, grandson of a chief. His people once owned this valley and a lot more besides. Still do, by blood and instinct. Charlie knows every footfall in the valley, the good from the bad. Know anything about Indians?"

"A little." Hutch felt himself moving cautiously. "There are Paiutes where I come from."

"Where's that?"

"Nevada. A place called Pipestone."

"Don't know as I know Pipestone. But then it's a pretty big state."

"It's southwest of Winnemucca, east of Carson City."

Willard chuckled. He liked the young man better and better. "Sounds like silver country."

"It was. For some."

"So they told me."

"You've been to Nevada?" Hutch found it hard to keep the surprise from his voice.

"A while ago now. I've managed to see a bit of the world now and then when crops were good. About as much as one man needs to, I reckon. 'Rich eyes, poor hands,' as Shakespeare said. But I never regretted a single pine tree shilling I spent getting around. Silver, eh?"

Hutch should have recognized Willard Roundtree's folksiness for the smoke screen it was. But he was only aware of being categorized. Yet his resentment was fading. The old man had a larger-than-life quality, incongruous in this low-ceilinged farmhouse with its pine walls, faded maps and pictures, leather chest, oversized spinning wheel, and black square piano that must be nearly a century old. He glanced at the old-fashioned oak stand, holding what must be the brass-bound family Bible. The room and the man shared a quality, a defiance of time and trivia, of whatever sapped the human spirit. Now at odds with that young, flashing-eyed defiance he could not erase from his mind.

Genes, inheritance, seeds of the land? He was aware he had not answered Willard.

"My great-grandfather thought he'd struck it. Silver. Up north of the Comstock." Hutch grinned. "Everybody in the family was named Davison Hutchins after him. In case the inheritance came through."

"Did it?"

"Not up to the time I left home. I've never been back to find out."

It was more than Hutch intended to say. He rose.

"I'm sorry, sir, that Mr. Vallon didn't come here to thank you himself for the use of your land. He was pretty badly shaken up."

"I didn't expect him to."

"If you'll accept my thanks instead."

"I don't want thanks. Land is to be used, if it isn't hurt. I can't see that your people did any damage." Willard's sharp eyes twinkled. "Except to my reputation as a custodian of public morals." He paused. "How did you happen to get into the filmmaking business?"

"I was hungry."

"Best reason in the world, Mr. Hutchins."

"Hutch, sir. I'm not trying to please grandpappy."

Willard gave his dry, short chuckle. His guest was beginning to show signs of restlessness. The old had no business delaying the young.

"How long do you expect to be in Thatcher?"

"I'm not sure, sir. There are a few more things to be done." Hutch could not have named one. "Mr. Vallon doesn't like loose ends. So it depends," he finished limply.

Willard nodded and walked with him to the door.

"If you find time, drop around again. I think you'd enjoy talking to Charlie Redwing. Sees farther through a millstone than any of us."

On the porch stood the largest Irish setter Hutch had ever seen, a genial red giant of a dog who waved a great plumed tail. Willard eyed him severely.

"So you're back, Clancy? Hutch, this is Clancy. Lives here—when it suits him. He knows as much about good and bad in this valley as Charlie. Clancy, this is a friend."

The big dog plumped a shaggy paw on Hutch's foot, wagged his red-gold tail, and leaned. Hutch stroked the silken head. This place was full of astonishing superlatives. From the size and weight of the dog, he was glad to be identified as a friend.

"All right, Clancy. You've made your point."

"He's magnificent, Mr. Roundtree."

"And well aware of it. But he is a gentleman."

They stood for a moment on the rough-wood porch. The view down the sun-filled valley was superb. The Ridge rose soft and green, a benign protector. Hutch found it hard to think of the dark-souled tragedy that had stalked here. Willard's eyes were fixed on a distant spot where a reflection of glass glittered through the leaves. Beside the glitter was an indentation like a missing tooth.

"That's where the land was hurt." Willard's face had gone grim. "Up near where the Orlini house is built, there was an oak tree. It was a mighty tree, more than thirty feet around at the base. Its lowest branches, like tree trunks themselves, extended over fifty feet, and the roots maybe triple that. It was more than three hundred years old. Do you know what that means? It was here when Charlie Redwing's people still hunted in this valley. It saw the first colonists settle farms and build those dry-stone walls that still run through the second growth of trees. Ever try to build a dry-stone wall? It stood there when militiamen pulled cannon through this valley on the way to Boston and Bunker Hill. And it saw the women making Yankee gunpowder down at the saltpeter swamp. It was old when the first railroad came to Thatcher. And it was waiting when the doughboys came back from The Great War. Some of them marched up the Ridge and cried."

Willard Roundtree paused, as if waiting for the anger within him to subside.

"A few years ago when part of the Ridge was up for sale, they tried to raise money to save the oak. But times weren't good here in Thatcher. We did what we

could. We thought we were winning." He paused
again and cleared his throat. "The man who bought
the land cut that tree down to make a driveway. A
driveway! People as far away as Juno's Landing said
they could hear the chain saw. Well, I'm an old man
and probably an old fool, but I should know one
thing. The only thing you can count on any day of
your life is change. But let me tell you something.
They cut down that tree to ground level. They found
what was left, the base and the roots, was too strong
to be pulled out without blasting part of the Ridge
away. So there it is now, under the gravel, thirty feet
round, its roots reaching into the earth no one knows
how far. Charlie Redwing will tell you that no man in
his right mind should sleep on the Ridge now."

They had reached the car. Hutch had had a glimpse
into an old man's heart and wished he hadn't. He was
relieved when Willard chuckled.

"But I've been keeping you. I get to talking with
young people and forget that it isn't the years between us, it's the perspective. Tell me something." His
voice lightened deceptively. "If a girl was foolish
enough to think she could get into moving pictures,
how would she go about it?"

So this was the core of it. Not only Charlie Redwing
knew every footfall in the valley. The old man knew
and worried. Hutch would like to set his mind at ease,
but you didn't go soft with Willard Roundtree, not if
you wanted his respect. Hutch could not have explained even to himself why that had become important. He looked directly at Willard.

"Someone would have to take an interest in her."

"Not very likely?"

"She's an attractive girl!"

The older man nodded. Hutch climbed into his

rented car. Willard raised his hand in salute. The meeting was over.

Hutch turned his car up toward the Ridge. He would go through the chillingly empty house once more and make sure that every evidence of Marc Vallon's presence was gone.

Then he would call Claude Roundtree.

With the great dog at his side, Willard walked thoughtfully toward the barn, wondering whether he could trust any man.

Claude sat at the edge of the Orlini swimming pool, clutching her knees and watching a silver jet trail lance a flawless sky. The sun was hot on her back. She felt curiously at peace. The worst—and the best—had happened. Her father had stated his case. She knew where she stood. Ahead lay a future radiant as the day. August 9. She saw the date hanging like a charm from the vapor trail. One day, not very distant, she would be up there, winging to her destiny.

The snipping of shears returned her to earth. Si Barker, on his knees, was trimming the grass, grown unusually ragged along the marble edge of the pool. He had done his worst, too, but he had not given her away.

"Is that hard to do, Si?"

"Trimming? Nothing to it. Provided it don't get ahead of you. But what with all that rain—and Euphie . . ."

Euphamie, of course, his wife.

"Is she supposed to do it?"

"Lord love a duck, no. But she got plumb firm about my working around the pool while they were here. She said I'd have it trimmed down to bare earth

afore I'd quit." He scratched his head and emitted a
dry bark of a laugh. "She was right, too." His gnarled
features tightened. "Miss Claude, I got no right to let
you stay here."

"But you can't help it, can you, Si, because I am
here."

"I got orders."

"Whose orders?"

"That young feller with Mr. Vallon. Nice enough
feller but he knew what he wanted. Sort of bossed
things."

Claude laughed lightly, the kind of laugh she would
practice for her screen test. A light ripple of amusement that would speak volumes.

"Oh, you don't have to pay any attention to *him,* Si.
He just worked for Mr. Vallon. He wasn't anybody at
all. Besides, they've all gone now. Haven't they?"

"Yep. Effie's up vacuuming and hanging out rugs
and curtains like there'd been some sort of plague."

So he had gone without even calling her to say
good-bye. It was just as well. He'd have done something awful like finding out her plans and spoiling
them. She was free now to concentrate on August 9.
And how to get the money.

She stretched out her long fine legs that were
tanning nicely already. Just the same, he might
have called. She would not have gone out with
Davison Hutchins but she would like to have had the
satisfaction of saying, with an airy smile, "See you in
Paris!" Without telling him anything more. Besides,
after that silliness the day he brought her down from
the Ridge in the rain—kissing her hair as if she didn't
know. He really owed her some sort of good-bye.
Maybe she would run into him in Paris after her suc-

cessful screen test. She would be sure not to remember his name.

Another jet began its splendid span of the sky. Si sat back on his haunches and rubbed his knees.

"How much do you get for that kind of work, Si? Cutting grass and trimming and all?"

"Depends where you do it. Out at old Mrs. Plummer's I got regular but no lunch and I had to figure on gas. Your dad always paid above regular but not steady. On the other hand your ma always set a good lunch and beer. They pay best out at the cemetery, because it ain't always easy to get workers. Lot of us got folks up there, and it don't seem right running the mower over them," he wiped his forehead.

"Let me try it!"

"No ma'am, miss. I ain't about to have Mr. Orlini's good shears scratching up that marble edge."

"I wouldn't do that."

"Maybe. Maybe not." He went down on his knees again and began to work away from her.

Her eyes narrowed. "Si, why did you tell Dad about what went on up here—while they were here?"

He sat upright, like a startled rabbit. "How did you know that?"

"Dad tells me everything. We're very close. It wasn't very honorable, was it? But you didn't tell him about me, did you? Even after you saw me coming down the road that day you and Effie passed me in the car."

Si Barker sighed. He did not understand any of this but somehow it constituted a kind of threat. He felt caught like a bird in a mesh. He could not see any danger, yet he could find no way out. "Miss Claude, if I told everything I saw and heard about the young folks in this town, I wouldn't have time to make a dollar."

"I know, Si! You're a loyal, wonderful man, and we all appreciate it. That's why when I want to give you a hand, you shouldn't be so uppity."

She had not only confused him, she had lost him. She jumped up, crossed the marble flagging and was on her knees beside him.

"Besides, maybe I could get a job out at the cemetery if you showed me how."

"*You?*"

"Why not?"

She had already asked herself that. There weren't many summer jobs available in Thatcher. Baby-sitting would never get her to Paris, and she had never been sensible like Lowell and learned to type. Besides, she'd hate to sit cooped in an office all summer. There was the cemetery or the car wash. She took the shears from him.

"Like this?"

"No, no. Keep the points under the grass. Tilt the outside of the blade against the marble. See."

It was not as easy as it looked. The shears were heavy, and the angle hurt her wrists.

"You make me fidgety, Si. Just go away, won't you? And let me try. Get a beer or something."

He would not get a beer. Effie would come down on him like a dump truck. But he could use the shade. He hesitated.

"Look, if I'm not doing it right it will grow back, won't it?"

It would. There wasn't much damage she could do if she kept clear of the marble. Her smile warmed him like new milk. The prettiest of the Roundtrees, he thought. But a handful. He shuffled off between the yews and did not hear the faint sound of a car.

Claude did. She bent to her work. It would be obvious to anyone that she had a right to be here.

Hutch crossed the drive. Only the scrape of his shoes on gravel and a rhythmic clicking he could not identify broke the new quiet. He thought of the great base of the dismembered tree that lay beneath. He could almost feel the mound. He wondered idly if some vital end of the massive roots could ever break from its tomb and push its way to life. He brushed the image away. He was a realist. What had been done was not of his doing nor his time. His world lay ahead. If the old had to succumb with the years, wasn't that the course of all history? Yet deeper he was aware that Willard Roundtree had impinged deeply and enduringly on his mind. Willard had, in effect, demanded understanding, and Hutch had yielded. It was a tie not easily severed. He was glad to leave the gravel for the neat brick path.

He circled the wing of the house to the terrace. And stopped. The blue-jeaned figure upended alongside the pool might be anyone, except for the fall of silver blond hair that concealed her face and widened into a shining fan on the marble edge.

"Well, well, well."

Claude pushed her hair back and sat up. She had seen him coming. She would not be surprised.

"Is that the only thing you can say when you see a person?"

"Not at all. I have a rather well-rounded vocabulary suitable to most occasions." He took the steps two at a time and stood looking down at her. "Enjoying your work?"

"As a matter of fact, I am. I thought you had gone."

"Which saddened you so much you sought refuge in hard labor."

"Oh, stop talking like that. You don't sound like anybody I ever knew."

"I must be making progress."

"What did you come back here for?"

"Why did you?"

"I don't have to explain."

He grinned. "Neither do I. But we might have a try at it. Would you like an ice-cream soda?"

"What?"

"You know. Ice cream. Fizz water. Through a straw. I'll even buy separate sodas."

She sat back, laid down the shears. "Where?"

"Well, there's a local emporium I saw at the shopping center. The Candy Stick?"

"That's for kids."

"Oh, sorry, Miss Roundtree. What would you think of a dim bar in a palace of sin I saw called the Grist Mill."

She got up. She was hot and sticky and her mirror lay in her tote beside the bicycle. Bicycle! She'd have to leave that to Si.

"I'll buy you a Shirley Temple, double cherries."

"You think I'm just a kid, don't you? Mr. Hutchins . . ."

"Hutch."

"I don't like being with you very much. You make me uncomfortable. And I have a lot on my mind. And I don't like being with people I don't like . . ."

"That's redundant."

". . . but you were very considerate that—that day of the accident, and you did drive me home, so I owe you something."

"Exactly."

"I don't think you know much about girls. I loathe Shirley Temples."

"So do I. Let's go, Miss Roundtree."

"And whatever you might think, I am not a kid."

"That's what worries me."

She rose and walked slightly ahead of him. He called her.

"Just a minute."

She looked back.

"You don't leave shears lying open, Miss Roundtree. Didn't you know that?"

The Grist Mill Hutch mentally labeled Instant Quaint. A rounded half-wall embracing a bar and a group of dime-sized wooden tables, opened to a dining area. An old millstone beside the door bore the irrelevancy of potted ivy. Red-checked curtains, red-checked table cloths, a juke box, and an area cleared for dancing completed the staples. Over the bar hung crossed wooden hay rakes. The windows were made even narrower by a wall decor of yellowed bills, coach timetables, an occasional well-stained flour sack, and a framed announcement of the services of the Ferryboat Juno. A flowing red-and-green neon tube advertised beer to the whiney assertion of a transistor radio, now mute.

"Let's sit in the bar," said Claude.

Hutch wondered again how old she was, but as the place was empty, the light dim, and there didn't seem to be much demarcation anyway, he led her to one of the little round tables, deeply penknifed with initials.

"That's me, there—C.R."

"Do you come here often?"

"Sometimes. When I'm not busy." She flung her

long hair back, a bewitching and not infrequent gesture. "When you called this place a palace of sin I thought that was pretty silly."

"So did I. You have lovely hair, Miss Roundtree."

"Thanks. I might cut it off. But I'll keep a pony tail so Dad won't know. He'd die." She fished in her tote, jumped up, and in another instant was back in her seat. The juke box grumbled and blared.

"Look here, if you want to play that thing, I've got a quarter."

"I know. But I didn't need it. Anyhow, that's male chauvinism, isn't it?"

The box drooped to a low moan and Hutch found that they might, after all, be able to talk. She swayed slightly to the music, pink lips parted, snapping her slender fingers. She had fine hands. Everything about her was delicate. In appearance, he added silently. Only in appearance. He wanted to take that fragile hand. He was aware of the light, impersonal touch of her knee as she moved. And, as he told himself, he was on the verge of becoming a damn fool.

"You know, it's funny being here with you, Hutch."

"Why funny?"

"Oh, I don't know. You're part of something else, some other thing that happened, and I can't put it all together. It's like you don't belong here."

"I'll try to do better."

"And besides, you're so superior all the time."

"Who, me? I'm just a simple country boy, from the West."

She stared at him. The disappointment was obvious.

"I thought you came from abroad. I mean, like Paris."

"I live where I work. Just now I'm working for Marc Vallon. As you know."

The color came and went in her face. "You don't work for Mr. Vallon all the time?"

"Not if I can help it. I'm a fly bum by instinct and choice. Ah, the place is inhabited after all."

The door next to the bar swung open. A gangling young man in spectacles, emerged, still buttoning a gray busboy vest. He ambled toward them.

"Hi, Claude."

"Larry! Golly."

"Sort of surprised you, didn't I? I started work yesterday. I work at the drugstore all day, then at four I come over here. Four to ten. It's a breeze. Good tips. Oh, sorry—" he took Hutch in. "I didn't mean it was necessary. Or anything. I just came on duty. That's how come I kept you waiting. Well, what do you know! My first customers today." He gave Hutch a longer look.

Claude had obviously no intention of making introductions. Hutch stood up. "Hutch Hutchins. You're . . . ? He held out his hand.

"Larry Higgins. An old friend of Claude's. Higgins Pharmacy right next to John's headquarters. You know—Claude's brother, running for Congress. My dad lent him the place. Right, Claude? Everybody says if John keeps his nose clean and goes on the way he is he'll win big. Right, Claude?" He slid a bony hand to Hutch. The left lens in his eyeglasses was darkened. His handshake frail. "So what'll it be? I might even join you. The boss doesn't mind when the place is empty."

Claude had stopped snapping her fingers. The juke box had whirred off. The silence was immense.

Hutch said gravely. "Anything you like—Miss Roundtree?"

"She can't have anything. I mean we don't serve hard liquor to . . ."

Claude's eyes glittered. "For Pete's sake, Larry. Hutch knows all that. I guess I'm old enough to know what I want."

"You could have a Cold Horse. You like that."

Claude stiffened in her chair.

"A Cold Horse?" Hutch was beginning to enjoy himself. Claude looked enchanting when she was angry, and she had shifted nearer to him. "I guess I haven't traveled enough."

"Oh, it's for kids. . . ." she shrugged.

"Claude invented it, Hutch. It's like a Horse's Neck. You know, ginger ale and a lemon rind, only Claude plops strawberry ice cream into it."

"I did. Once. A long time ago. Don't you ever forget anything, Larry? I'll have iced coffee."

"Make it two, Larry."

Larry vanished. Claude's hands clenched the table.

"What's wrong, Claude?"

"Everything gets spoiled, doesn't it? You can't go anywhere around here without somebody knowing you all your life as if you'd always be just that way. And never any different."

"Now, look. You don't get thrown off by meeting a boyfriend. He looks like a nice guy."

"He is a nice guy. But he's not my boyfriend. He's somebody I've grown up with. Do you know what that means? To go out with somebody who knew you when you had braces. But I go out with him because—oh, it doesn't matter, does it? You can sit there and think I'm just small town and—"

"I'm not thinking anything like that, Claude."

"It's okay. But I'm not always going to be." She heard a rattle of ice and glasses. Larry returned with the iced coffee. He might have sat down with them except that Claude was studying the table.

"How long you going to be around, Hutch?"

"I don't know."

"Be seeing you again, maybe?" The good eye showed friendship and the need for it. Larry would be all right, Hutch thought. He wondered what had gone on between Claude and this boy. Probably not much. He felt uncomfortably old and spent.

Claude had stashed her bicycle at the Orlini gate on the Ridge. They would have to go back for it. She was quiet in the car. They drove in silence up the Ridge road. When he got out to unlock the chain, she remained in the car as if lost in abstraction.

"Would you like to drive to the top? For a last look?"

He wondered why he had added that. She would probably be coming up here with her head full of notions all the rest of the summer. He would at least like to know that she was safely off to college or wherever girls in Thatcher went until they married somebody.

He parked the car in the drive. She led him familiarly around the house to the terrace and the pool. She slipped ahead as if she were alone.

The late afternoon sun cast a spell of gilded silence. Nothing moved. No leaf stirred, no branch creaked. Even the summer winds seemed to have deserted the place. The pool was a motionless sheet of metallic light, the statues reflected cold and exact. She sat down on a marble bench alongside the pool. He sat beside her, though she seemed hardly aware of it.

"It's so beautiful, isn't it?" Claude finally said.

"What is?"

"All this."

"I think it's pretty awful."

"Why?"

"It's overdone, pretentious, and all that blown-up statuary would be ridiculous if it weren't so vulgar. It proves one thing. How wrong money can be."

"That's your opinion."

"Right." But he did not want to argue. Actually, he could not have cared less what Orlini had built himself up here but it relieved his emotions to disagree.

"Would you like to know what I think, Hutch?"

"Sure. If I don't know already."

"I think you're just against things. I think you want to be different so people will pay some attention to you because you're not a genius like . . ."

"Like Marc?" he finished.

"Well, I wasn't going to say that."

"The hell you weren't. But you know," he glanced sideways at her, "you might just be on to something. Want to continue the analysis?"

"No. I just want to sit here."

"Your power spot?"

"Who told you that?"

"Word gets around."

She let it go. It was as if she were separating herself from him by simple willpower.

"Maybe I can understand that," he said finally. "A power spot. Would you like to know what mine is?" He did not wait for an answer. "It's up there, three thousand feet, riding a current of air like the birds. Nothing but beautiful quiet motion."

"You're a flyer?"

"Yes. But this isn't flying. It's soaring. You know what gliding is: Flying in a motorless plane that moves like a kite. Soaring is that, only better. You look for the cumulus clouds. That's where you find the thermals. The rising currents of warm air that carry you up and up and up. The birds know all about that. There's nothing like it. I'd like to take you soaring someday."

She was silent. "I'm sorry I said what I did, Hutch. About wanting people to pay attention to you and all."

"Oh, come on. Don't let me down now. I count on you, Miss Roundtree, for the absolute truth. I probably am an antisocial son of a bitch. I'm a loner. They say you can't be a loner and like to soar. You depend on too many other people. But up there I feel like a loner. Builds my ego. So we're friends?" He grinned at her, met her eyes, and felt his smile fade.

The golden light deepened. An early swallow dipped across the pool. The silence was no longer silence. The bright air pulsed with invisible stirrings.

Claude sat stiffly telling herself that it did not matter what Hutch said. She would probably never see him again. If she did, she would be already launched on her future. She hated him for making her feel inadequate. Yet his talk of clouds and sky and birds and being alone made her want to cry.

She was aware of his closeness, bound to him against reason in a sorcery of light and stillness. She was aware of his coat sleeve against her bare arm, of his masculinity that shut out all past and future. She would leave. She would flee this luminous conspiracy that threatened everything she wanted. Instead she sat overwhelmed with such inexplicable longing that she shut her eyes and felt the coat sleeve rougher against her. She wanted him to touch her and she wanted to escape.

He felt the tremor and looked down at her. He remembered a luna moth he had once seen, long ago, its three-inch, pale green wings quivering as it alighted and clung to a porch railing. A thing of mist and moonlight, of such phosphorescent beauty that he had reached for it, his hand brushing its body. It fluttered, tottered, then spiralling into the darkness, it disappeared. He never knew how much he had bruised it. He never saw another.

Claude, small, tense beside him was staring into space. The moment had come to take her in his arms. He wanted her with a surge of youthful desire he thought he had lost. She was untouched, he was sure. She would make of love the mystery, the newness that he longed for in a world where sex had become a trinket as easily won as forgotten. Even to touch her would be a rite; to possess her would be a wellspring of renewal. He could believe again in the loveliness of passion, the luna moth, waiting, quivering, exquisite beyond a man's imagination.

She caught his look.

"Let's go," he said bluntly.

She followed him silently. Nothing had happened. Nothing but the witchery of the hour and the light. Yet, *something* had happened. Something disorienting. Something that had changed the neat, manageable balance between them.

He walked with her in silence down to the gate. She pulled her bicycle from the rhododendron bushes. He did not offer to help. She wondered what to say that was final and kind. She knew she could only order her own life if she put distance between them.

"Hutch, I think I should tell you something."

"No shoulds, Claude."

"I have an appointment to see Mr. Vallon. He gave me his card."

He had seen it happen. He had guessed the mes-

sage. The memory infuriated him again. The danger
was over.

"Too bad he couldn't keep it."

"What does that mean?"

"He's gone back to Paris."

"I know. That's where I have the appointment. His
address is on the card."

He stared at her. She could not have believed Vallon! She could not really delude herself that he had
any interest in her except as another pretty, untal-
ented, but accessible camp follower? But he would
keep it light.

"Claude, you're too bright . . ."

"I knew you'd talk like that! I knew you'd make fun
of me. But I have the card and . . ."

"Claude, listen to me."

"No, I don't want to."

"But by God, you will!"

"I'm sorry I told you. I just wanted you to know."

"And I want you to know something." All the exasperation she had caused him was clotting into anger.
"Up there by the pool I wanted to make love to you.
I'm a normal male and you're a bewitching young
female, as you're damn well aware. But I didn't. And I
have no regrets . . . "

She caught her breath, but her emotions were too intense.

". . . because you don't need a lover. You need a
keeper."

He heard her gasp. Their quarrel was rising to the
intensity of lovemaking. He should walk off and wait
for her but the issue was too serious.

"Now listen to me! You're young and you're a little
silly—shut up and listen—but I know Marc Vallon. He
has no intention of putting you into his films."

"He said he'd see me. I can handle the rest."

"You bet you can't. Vallon could dash off a dozen cards like that and forget them just as fast. Right now all he wants is to forget everything about Thatcher. He's been through a bad time here. A man died up on the Ridge."

"That wasn't his fault!"

He felt a shade of relief. Her innocence had protected her at least from that.

"Claude, try to believe me, will you? Tear up that card or keep it for what it is. A souvenir. That's all he meant it to be. How in hell would he expect you to get to Paris?"

"Then why did he write 'prompt' on the card?"

She saw his hesitation. "If you could give me one teeny proof that Mr. Vallon didn't mean what he wrote, maybe—maybe I'd listen. Can you? Can you?"

"Claude, the man is—"

"Is what? Mr. Vallon was kind and serious and—and a gentleman. And I believe him. A lot more than I do you! And I'm going to be there, no matter what! If you do one little thing to spoil it, I'll pay you back for keeps!"

A few minutes ago beside the pool he had thought her too young for passion. Now he saw the cold vendetta of a harpy.

She had pushed her bicycle onto the road. She turned, her eyes suddenly glistening with tears. "Can't you see, Hutch? I must do this! You don't know what it's like to live in Thatcher all your life. Never being able to do what you really want. Always pretending to be somebody you aren't, just because your ancestors were somebody once. Or thought they were. I'd leave forever only I can't do that to them. Not now. This is where I'll live and this is where I'll die unless something happens. And it has! I have a chance! Not just for me, but for Mom and Dad and John and Lowell and Kim. And being somebody myself, somebody I've never been. Somebody new! Do you know what that would mean, Hutch? This is the only chance I'll ever have! Can't you understand that at all?"

She brushed the tears with the back of her hand.

He felt his own helplessness, threaded with self-doubt. But he could not let her go. Not without trying once more. Very gently he said, "I might, if you'd explain it to me."

"But I've been explaining!"

"I'm a slow study." He managed a half-grin. "Would you try again? Say, at dinner tomorrow night?"

"No. I don't think so. Thank you."

"Then dinner and we'll talk about something else. I'll pick you up at six."

"It wouldn't do any good. You'd just mix me up."

"If I promise not to? I'm leaving in a few days."

She brushed at her eyes once more, her face turned from him.

"I don't know. I just don't. I'll think about it. That's the best I can say. But don't pick me up. If I decide to, I'll be at the library steps. If I decide."

He watched her ride down the road, her back soldier-straight, her pale hair streaming, the distance between them widening with every determined turn of the pedals, until the fading light swept her away.

Where? he wondered. He looked up at the stark house grown chillier in the dusk. Where?

A low insistent knocking at the door woke Hutch. He rolled over heavily and looked at his watch. Two twenty. The knocking continued. He wondered how long it had been going on.

His landlady stood at the door. In the dimness of the hall light he could see only pink—pink curlers, pink face, pink wrapper. She looked frightened.

"I'm so sorry to disturb you, Mr. Hutchins. There's a phone call. Our switchboard closes at this time of night so you'll have to take it in my sitting room . . ." she seemed to turn pinker ". . . if you don't mind. It's from Paris."

"Thanks, Mrs. Weller. I'll be right there."

"We don't have calls from Paris very often. I hope it's not bad news."

"I'm sure it isn't. It's morning over there now."

She gave him a dumpling smile, kind with relief. "I never thought of that."

She turned up the hall lights fully. Hutch trotted down the stairs, tightening his robe belt with exasperation. Of course it was bad news. Marc Vallon at this point in his life could only be bad news. And at this hour. Marc made it a ritual never to talk on the telephone before eleven in the morning. Brain vibrations are not stabilized before that, he would explain. Hutch entered the little parlor Mrs. Weller called her own and wondered what the hell Marc could possibly have to say with unstabilized vibrations.

"That you, Hutch?"

"Sure it's me. Do you know what time it is here?"

"Never mind that. I want you here on the first plane in the morning."

Claude's face took shape over the phone.

"Can't possibly, Marc. Next week at the earliest."

"Next week?" Marc's voice rose and splintered. As always when he was excited the slight accent of his Viennese ancestry edged through his careful English. "Hutch, listen to me and for God's sake don't talk. I know you've worked hard, I know you need a few days off but you can have that later. You must come tomorrow." There was a slight pause. It seemed to Hutch that the thin distant voice shook. "It's Soli."

"What's the matter with her?"

"She's hysterical."

"Oh, for Christ sake, Marc." He glanced around. Mrs. Weller had vanished, and the door to her bedroom was securely shut. "Look, I've had all of that overheated broad I can take for a while. Give her a pill. You've got enough around. Or get a doctor."

"Hutch, she's threatening to jump into the Seine or run naked through the streets. I've got her locked in my room but . . ."

Hutch tried to imagine the scene. Soli was quite capable of carrying out both threats. She could swim like a fish. She enjoyed nudity like a second skin. She'd survive both, but the publicity would be disastrous, as she well knew, he thought wryly.

"Hutch, are you there?"

"Yeah, I'm here."

"Don't you see? It would ruin me. Ruin the opening of the picture, ruin. . . ."

And make the Thatcher headlines again, ruining his own unadmitted cause, if not making it impossible.

"What ticked her off, Marc?"

There was a slight pause. The voice came with effort. "She accuses me of wanting Lennie dead."

Hutch stared over the telephone at Claude's fading face.

"Hutch . . . ?"

"I'll get the first plane I can out of Hartford in the morning. The best I can do will be a night flight for Paris."

"Thank you, Hutch. You're the only one who can handle her when she gets . . ."

"Shove that, Marc. You pay me. I'll do what I can."

Hutch tossed in the darkness of his bed, struggled with his images and tossed some more. In the faint gray of dawn, he at last fell asleep. He awoke like a man taking a blow. Five minutes past ten. Half the morning already gone. He had to make arrangements, drive to Hartford, but above all he had to find her. Where or how at this hour he had no idea. The thought of leaving without seeing her was unbearable. The image of her sitting on the library steps with no word from him, her back stiffening, her face set against an unsuspected hurt—he would find her and see her once more if he had to knock on every door in Thatcher. But as for her "appointment" with Marc in Paris, he would see that Marc wrote her an honest letter. Marc would owe him at least that much now. Even if it meant losing her.

As he dressed, Hutch toyed with treachery. Let her come to Paris if she was that stubborn. Marc would not be there. But he himself would be waiting. They would have long, gentle days together, walking in the sun-filled parks, sitting under the awnings of little unchic cafés he knew so well, lingering at the quay-side bookstalls. He would show her his Paris, the great twisting river that parted the city with its two-thousand-year-old burden of history, only to bind it together with the fairy-blown links of thirty or more bridges flung chainlike across the flowing brown-gray water. He would drive her out to the gliding field and take her into the world he loved best: The vast, clean, shining space where a cloud or a current would sweep them upward, silent as birds. She would not be afraid. He had never met a girl as free of fear. They would have supper at a riverside inn and return to his flat.

Treachery. Would anything he could do outweigh

the scalding hurt of her disappointment? Claude belonged here. He would force Marc to write that letter if he had to choke it from him. If, in the end, he lost her, let her stay in Thatcher. Marry that druggist boy with the bad eye, Larry.

Hutch banged his suitcase closed and faced an unsteadying fact. He would not use the word *love*. That was a girl's word, light as a broken promise. What he felt for Claude Roundtree was the kind of overwhelming tenderness he had spent a lifetime deriding. He wondered whether he would ever be able to tell her.

Larry Higgins looked up from arranging a counter stand of combs and curlers, without surprise.

"Oh, hi."

"Hello, Larry." Hutch disliked his role. "I wonder if you could do me a favor."

"Sure. Anything, Hutch."

"I have to leave town unexpectedly. I wanted to say good-bye."

"That's mighty nice." Larry thrust out a hand. Hutch shook it and continued.

"I mean to Claude too."

"Sure. To Claude. I understand that."

Hutch wondered if there was anything that happened in this town that Larry Higgins did not understand.

"I called her at home but there was no answer. I looked in on the campaign headquarters next door but I didn't know the girl there."

"That's Bonnie Smith, Claude's best friend. She takes over when Claude takes time off. Of course it isn't like John's own sister being there but . . ."

"I understand," Hutch interrupted hastily. "Will you see Claude when she comes back?"

"Sure, I see her come and go. I keep an eye on her. My good one." Larry pointed and grinned.

You had to like the boy, Hutch thought. He had an amiable pride. "Would you give her this note, Larry?"

"Sure. Sorry you have to leave. I guess you got important things to do for Mr. Vallon."

Hutch glanced at him, "How did you know I work for him, Larry?"

"I saw you up at the Orlini house one time. I knew you soon as you walked into the Mill yesterday. Only I didn't say so in front of Claude after all that happened up there. I delivered a prescription one evening and I saw you through the glass, sitting with the actress, I guess she was. I never met an actress. I never saw a real live one in the flesh before. Wow." Larry whistled. "I could've stood there looking at her all night. That red hair. That low-down dress. She was something man, something!"

"When did you deliver a prescription?" Hutch asked blandly.

"It was—let's see—the night before the accident. Sure, it comes back to me. Dad doesn't like to fill that kind, but it was legal and all. I can't tell you what. That's unprofessional and, as Dad said, movie people are different anyhow. So that's when I saw you. You were having a drink. Boy, I hope whoever needed that prescription didn't have a drink. Mr. Vallon gave me five dollars for bringing it up. I sort of hoped he'd let me watch the picture being made, but he said nobody was allowed to do that. On account of the actress. But I sure am going to watch for it. Oh, hi, Mrs. Elton."

Another customer had come in. Hutch signaled a good-bye and left. As he crossed the street to his parked car, he would have given all he possessed for one glimpse of Claude, one last sight of her flying hair, one last sound of her giggle. Now he could only carry it all somewhere between his heart and his viscera.

When you made a pact with the Devil, you danced to his tune.

He had a great deal to think about.

Chapter Seven

Thatcher's day from long habit started early. Nearly the entire town could be counted on to hear the seven-thirty A.M. local news from radio station WBOL, Bollington. The announcer was as crisp as he was cheerful.

"John Roundtree, contender for the Congressional seat from the Bollington District, has stirred enthusiastic interest by his revival of an old American political custom. He has challenged his opponent, veteran lawyer Harlan Phelps, to an open debate on the Fourth of July. The time: Three o'clock. The place: Flagpole Green in Thatcher, Roundtree's hometown. Roundtree supporters predict that this will be the hottest debate since Douglas met Lincoln. We think it looks more like David challenging Goliath. Well, you remember what happened to the old giant. Roundtree is the youngest candidate for a Congressional seat in the history of Thatcher County and a member of one of the county's oldest families. We wish him luck. So bring your picnic baskets, folks, for a real old-fashioned, no-holds-barred, political hoedown."

Edythe Roundtree snapped off the kitchen radio and found her eyes misting. John was doing it, her tall, thin, too-quiet son with the thoughtful eyes and the infrequent laugh. John, who had always been shy. People liked him and trusted him. He was coming out of that long moroseness that had baffled them all. She suspected Claude had a lot to do with his new ease of manner. If prayers could help John win, she herself would be on her knees until Election Day. But the Lord had a way of being dispassionate in these matters. She would have to think of something more practical.

She swung open the pantry door to the dining room. John had already breakfasted and gone or she would have flung her arms around him. And regretted it. Edythe had long ago resolved not to be that kind of mother. She listened but heard nothing from Claude's room. The child looked too pale these days. It would be like her to overwork for John's sake. Martin would not be down for another ten minutes though he had, of course, heard the announcement upstairs. Not that he needed to. John, she was sure, had confided his plans to his father long before making them public. Increasingly he sought Martin's advice and she had left them often sitting late in the den, heads together, poring over papers beneath the green-shaded lamp. Her family was growing closer. One of the invisible, unforeseen rewards of a thirty-year marriage.

She returned to the kitchen humming in the silvery voice that had been once an ambition, now a time-dimmed pleasantry. She turned her mind to picnic baskets.

She would be the proudest woman on Flagpole Green at three o'clock on the Fourth of July.

In an egg-yellow clapboard house, half a block down from the Episcopal Chruch which Duncan Phelps had renamed Church of Hope, Ariel stretched out her arm to shut off the radio and sank back into bed. She hated this dizzying surge of helplessness in the morning, when the room spun and the world waited out there bristling with duties, and she lay here unable to cope. It would pass, of course, this helplessness, and she, Ariel, would give birth to a child. For a few seconds the enormity of its wonder possessed her. Then her mind returned to the day.

John. She would have liked to help him. She sensed he needed someone, a woman, a softness outside the closeness of that house on West Street. He had never spoken of a girl nor had she ever met one in his company. She had been aware of his dark, deep-set eyes on her, and it made her uncomfortable. He responded too quickly to her smile, her words. Still she would give a lot to help him. But that was impossible.

Duncan, her beloved husband, was Harlan Phelps's only son. They had met not more than once or twice in the last three years. Harlan Phelps lived now in a huge, politically expedient house outside Bollington. He had never forgiven Duncan for going into the ministry. Duncan had borne in silence the pain of his deepening contempt for his father. But he had been explicit on the election campaign. Whatever they believed privately, he and Ariel must remain completely neutral. Ariel agreed.

The dizziness passed. She felt better. The day lay gloriously new outside. She would like to be a part of it. But her role was limited. She loved Duncan as much as the day she married him. But she was a wife now and French enough to understand the binding domesticity of that word. A wife for nearly three years, watching Duncan fight for what he wanted. He had brought his youth, his eagerness, the newness of his ideas to the two-century-old stone church and they had fallen on hard ground. Many of the older people were turning their backs. Many more had joined other congregations. Only the young were loud in their support and their presence. The young did not pay the bills.

Duncan would not admit discouragement. But at night, in the warmth of the scented double bed, when she cradled his head against her breasts, she sensed his bewilderment.

"We don't have to stay, *chérie*."

"You mean walk out? On the kids who need me? Would you want that, Ariel?"

"Darling, no!" She kissed him and knew a momentary chill of fear.

She lay longer in the sunniness of the plain bedroom. She would make a French picnic basket for the Fourth of July. Without wine, of course. And a wedge of Brie would look too extravagant. Probably enough ham sandwiches to fill a large paper bag plus a gallon jug of lemonade. She would be expected to bring extras.

The dimple in her left cheek flashed once, the Roundtree dimple. Someday she and Duncan would have a real French picnic. A proper basket, in a field of flowers. She would wear a wide-brimmed hat with long blue ribbons, and a flowing dress. There would be just the two of them. No, not two! Three. *Three* now. And forever. She wanted this child. It was a child of love that she and Duncan had made.

She dozed smiling, only to dream badly. John Round-

tree was calling her. Harlan Phelps was standing between her and her child.

She woke to the faded, sprinkled wallpaper she
hated, and the egg-yellow house they could not afford
to repaint. She thought of the day ahead, a meeting of
the Ladies' Altar Guild, a sewing class for the Brown-
ies. She and Duncan had promised to dine with the
Roundtrees. She could escape it all in her condition.
But it would not disappear.

She longed for the reassurance of Duncan's presence but he had left early. She rose heavily, wondering what she had ever done with her life that she had
somehow lost her way.

Harlan Phelps sat on the edge of the motel bed,
snapped the radio off, and dropped his head in his
hands. The window drapes were still drawn but the
dim light only accented the dreary facelessness of the
room. A nearly empty whiskey bottle, two glasses, one
lipstick-stained, and a scattering of face-cream jars
and cigarette stubs added to the stifling sleaziness.
That was the trouble with these goddamned motels,
he thought. No air. He turned up the air conditioning.
It responded with a rattle and a moan.

"What's wrong, lover boy?" Belle Blake slid a thin
arm over the covers.

"Come on, get up. I've got a lot to do."

"All *right* already. You needn't snap my head off."

He went to the bed. She was right, of course. He
had enjoyed their sex, as he always did. For a small,
bony woman she was as hot as wire, and she knew all
she needed to know to satisfy him. He had needed Belle
last night, as he had for the last—what was it—five
years now. But he hated the mornings. Her fuzzy red
hair, her blanched face shorn of makeup. He would

not tell her yet but this would soon be over. He was running for public office. When he reached Washington, he would find someone classier, somebody who knew the way around.

She reached out a hand, curled it, and drew him to her.

"Harlan, baby," she murmured.

He let her have her way for a while. Then abruptly pushed her away.

"Let's get going, doll."

She pouted. She had reached that age where a woman takes comfort in little-girl mannerisms.

"You're no fun this morning, Harry."

"I have a lot to do. And a hundred-and-twenty-mile drive to Thatcher."

"What about me?"

"For Christ's sake, Belle—what about you? I'll take you as far as the East Danville bus station. There's a two o'clock bus for Bollington. Your car's there?"

"Yes."

"Well, is this any different?"

"Yes, it is." She slid from the bed. The movement brought color to her face, and the transparent black shortie helped him to forget his morning distaste. Last night she had worn it with black tights and patent-leather dancing boots. She had done high kicks and grinds and lifted his middle-aged inertia into a frenzy of desire. Belle Blake knew how to please a man. He would miss her. Sometimes.

She thrust her incredibly thin feet into mules and pulled her silky, orange robe tight.

"I wish Emily would die." It was a little girl's voice, lightened by petulance. But Harlan resented it. He never wanted to think of Emily on mornings like this. When he did, he saw her as vividly as life, a round, smiling little woman, scented with lavender, comfortable as a currant bun, quite adequate in sex when they were young. Now when they no longer shared a bedroom, Emily was a flitting, but warming, presence in the big house, as essential to his well-being as the night-blooming savagery of Belle Blake.

"I wouldn't count on it, Belle."

"What does that mean?"

"It means Emily is what she is and no part of us."

"But she has a heart condition."

"For Christ's sweet sake, everybody has a heart condition or something. Emily is Scottish-born, she lives on oatmeal and tea, and she'll outlive us both."

"That's not the way you used to talk."

He went to his traveling bag and took out his last clean shirt. The final word seemed suddenly necessary.

"Are we going to fight, Belle? You knew I had a wife when we first started this. I still have one. And will for a long time. I don't believe in divorce, too much time and trouble. So if you don't like the way it is, say so."

He had hurt her and he felt better. It might just be the beginning of a way out. They dressed in silence. He glanced at her once or twice. She was bone-thin, but still good-looking. She might have been somebody once. Hardship had refined her face, and pride had given it a certain arrogance. Before she slipped on her dress, she decided to make peace.

"What's happened, lover? I was half-awake. I heard the radio. Something about John Roundtree, wasn't it?"

He could talk to her as he could never talk to Emily. That was one of Belle's holds on him, a shrewd, biting intelligence, quick as a cornered squirrel. Quicker than his own intelligence and he valued it.

"That young damned fool. . . ."

"John Roundtree?"

"That's who we're talking about, isn't it?"

He was in a foul temper. She knew him well enough to begin to understand.

"What's John done?"

"I'll tell you what he's done. According to the radio he's challenging me—*me*, old enough to be his father—to a debate on the Fourth of July in Thatcher. Bring your picnic, folks. God almighty, doesn't he know that went out with the last barber pole? It'll be the laugh of the summer. If that kid wants to make an idiot of himself, okay. But as for me . . ."

"What are you going to do about it?"

"I'm going back to Thatcher and raise hell. Martin Roundtree isn't going to stand by either and watch the boy make a jackass of himself. After all, I was a law partner of Martin's for nearly ten years. I can beat the kid seven days to Sunday but I don't want to break him. Why didn't he come to me first? He owed me that."

"Maybe he has. You've been away for the last four days."

She could always relieve his worry. He went to her, slid his hands over her body, and released her. It was a gesture of easy and loveless possession.

"It was worth it, doll."

Over breakfast Belle asked the question she had been storing. She asked it carefully.

"You feel pretty sure of winning the election, don't you, Harry?"

"Sure I do. That kid's still wet behind the ears. He

can't talk on his feet, much less think." His glance was sharp. "Why did you ask that?"

"John's not stupid, Harlan. In fact quite a few people think he's pretty smart."

"What are you trying to say, Belle?"

"I'm trying to tell you what I hear. I live and work in Thatcher. I talk to people. You're out of the town now. You don't."

"So that's what they're saying. The Roundtree kid's smart. Okay. But he'll have to prove it. I've practiced law for thirty years in this state. Everybody knows me."

"You also drink a lot, and what you don't drink you toss out on a poker table."

His face reddened but he knew she was right. "Go on."

"John Roundtree's the young knight, Harry. You better face up to it. Clean as wash and his name isn't bad, either."

Harlan laughed. It was short and grating. "Come on, doll. The Roundtrees have got every sin in the book buried somewhere. If they want to rattle skeletons. . . ."

"They don't. That's just the point. Nobody seems to care about the past. What they see is the fair-haired boy taking on . . ." she hesitated.

"Yeah. Goliath, that jerk of a radio announcer said."

Her breakfast was cooling. Belle ignored it. She both loved and hated Harlan Phelps. She knew his weaknesses and his cruelties. Instinct told her he would push her aside like cold coffee when it suited him. And it would suit him soon. But not yet. She was not ready to lose him. She liked a winner. Whatever she had of this man, she wanted it winning.

"When is Mr. Orlini coming back?"

The "mister" nettled him. "For Christ's sake, why the respect? He's nothing but a little guy who's made it big."

"Very big. Bigger than anybody else on your side, lover."

"Maybe. But I can be very useful to little-shoes Orlini when I get to D.C. He knows it."

"Have you talked to him since the accident, or whatever they want to call it, up on the Ridge?"

"Once. He came back to New York. He's all shook up. He doesn't go for that kind of publicity."

Belle smiled. There were times when she felt superior to both Harlan Phelps and Ben Orlini. "It might be very useful to you, Harry."

"What might?"

"That whole story. Nobody knows whether that actor who went over the ledge was drunk, drugged, or he committed suicide. They've certainly tried to hush it up. But I don't think we've heard the end of it. If it turns messy, it could be embarrassing for anyone who happened to be around at that time."

"Like whom?"

"Well—like innocent little Claude Roundtree, for instance."

He stared at her. "Claude—hanging around that crew?"

Belle shrugged and nibbled a piece of cold toast with her small teeth. As in everything she did, Belle strove for daintiness.

"How the hell did you find that out?" His heavy face went slack when he was surprised. In the relentless light of morning, Belle noted, he was beginning to look bloated.

"I keep my ears open and my mouth shut, lover

boy. All for you. I knew all about Marc Vallon during my own career. Ten years ago."

More like twenty, Harlan thought to himself.

"I know Marc's reputation. I put two and two together and got five the day Claude came to me and said she wanted acting lessons."

Harlan gave a low whistle. "Little Claude a movie actress? You're kidding. That'd kill the old man."

"We start the day after my vacation is over."

"Tomorrow?"

Belle dipped the last of the toast into her cold coffee and swallowed it.

"If I feel like it."

"You'll feel like it, doll." He smiled. "I like it. I like it very much."

Belle repaired her red mouth. "I'll certainly do my best to help her. Who knows? John Roundtree's pure little sister may have quite a career."

On the long drive back to Thatcher Harlan Phelps let solitude pour cool water over him. He paid, as usual, for the few hours of youth Belle gave him with an increasing awareness of middle age. Today he felt heavy and sated. And frustrated. He had not said to Belle what he intended. He had not ended it then and there. She had given him no chance. Rather she had shaped the talk into a lance that probed his own confidence, exposing his dependence on her. Clever. Too clever by a damn sight. But then he had never been attracted to stupid women.

He had his mother to thank for that. Marry smart, Harry, she would say. A dumb woman can't help you. He thought of the gray-frame building near the Thatcher railroad tracks where he had been born. He had dreamed of riding those luring rails like his flag-

man father, until the day those rails took his father's
life. His mother said he had to do something smarter.
Like the Roundtrees. Martin Roundtree was going to
be a lawyer. Harry Phelps could do anything Martin
could do. His mother envied the Roundtrees and
molded her dreams to them. Not much money any-
more, but they had a big house and respectability and
something indefinable that she called quality. Very
important to Thatcher and to her. It came from a long
time of living a certain way, with books and polished
silver, and knowing when to say please and thank you.
"You weren't born with quality, Harry." He could
hear his mother's firm voice. "But you can get it by
living right and having manners. Honesty's about the
finest quality a man can have. Without it he can't
have quality at all." He had not followed her tortuous
logic but he had worked hard.

By thirty-five he had become a partner in Roundtree and Roundtree, the most prestigious law firm in
Thatcher County. He had married pretty and compe-
tent little Emily Duncan from Boston and had a son.
A son. Harlan would not think of Duncan now. Instead he thought about the first big man in the state
to notice that Harlan Phelps was on his way, Caleb
Appleby, congressman for twenty-six years from
Thatcher County district. Cal had held his seat by the
simple process of never lifting his head onto the firing
line. He had never initiated a bill or voted against the
party. He had put party funds to sound use, utilizing
his seemingly endless goodwill in perpetual travel to
close party ranks and increase membership. It made a
decent fellow of good old Cal, and no enemies. A man
could become President that way, the old pols used to
say. Caleb would grin, backslap, and wink. He came
from Bollington, didn't he, once the harness-making

capital of the nation? Who knows but the horse might come back.

Caleb liked smart, up-and-coming Harlan Phelps. He liked the cut of his jib and found him pliant. He had welcomed Harry into the party organization and urged him to go into a law practice on his own. Harlan continued to prosper. When Cal Appleby died, in the thirty-first year of his incumbency, the party realized that Harlan Phelps would be a natural successor. Old Caleb had never lost an election or betrayed a party member. Harry Phelps would carry right on.

Harlan Phelps believed it until the day John Roundtree declared his candidacy. Martin's son, barely at the legal age limit of twenty-five, standing for a seat in Congress, and as his opponent! Harry laughed it off with bravado. But in a morning's low aftermath, such as this, uncertainty burned like a hidden canker. Was it the old sense of inferiority to the Roundtree name? Was it the suspicion that he, Harlan, lacked the knowing toughness of old Caleb Appleby? Or was it deeper? An echo of his mother's dim words—"the quality of honesty."

He slanted the windshield shade against the brilliance of the day. He knew where his torment lay. It was his need of youth. It was his son, Duncan. Harlan's pride had its foundation stone in the boy. It had grown as Duncan had grown into handsome, glowing young manhood, an athletic hero in his school days, his mind capable of any demand made of it. Harlan had seen him off to Vietnam with a flourish of mental trumpets. Duncan had returned, to announce he had only one direction to walk. He would become a minister. A son in petticoats, Harlan had sneered, then thundered. There was more but Duncan had held to his purpose. Emily continued to see her son and his

Roundtree wife, but the break between father and son
had been lasting.

Time might have narrowed it, but for one incident.
In the dim booth of a slatternly bar-café outside Bollington Belle had suddenly leaned across the table
and whispered to Harlan to sit back and not turn.
Then she held up the mirror of her compact. In it he
saw unbelievably the familiar, strong shoulders and
well-shaped head of his only son. Duncan, in a worn
tweed coat, was sitting at the bar alone. He had
downed his drink and left quickly. But Harlan did not
know whether Duncan had seen him cosy with Belle
or not. It was not the incident itself that burdened
him. It was the unknown. If he were sure Duncan had
seen them, he would almost have welcomed the opportunity to bare his soul, confess man-to-man and
meet his son on surer grounds than they had ever
shared. If Harlan were certain Duncan had not seen
them, he could continue the slight if tentative recon-
ciliation he had begun through Ariel. Either way
there would be a healing. Uncertainty alone had para-
lyzed him.

Yet at this moment, confronted by youth, challenged on his own ground, he would give half his
chance of success to have Duncan beside him. Elec-
tions were not won today by old pros walled up in
hotel rooms. They were won by pretty girls and plac-
ards, enthusiasm and, most of all, by the freshness of
open air and youth. He could face even the ridiculous
Fourth of July debate young John Roundtree had
flung at him, with Duncan and Ariel beside him. Why
shouldn't he have them, his own blood and kin? Why
shouldn't he gamble for once on uncertainty, as he
had gambled on his whole life?

The day was passing. He was nearing Thatcher. He

felt a dryness in his mouth, a staleness in his lungs, an emptiness where his feelings might have lodged. He would stop at Bantam Brady's Pub and think it over. A man had a right to make a claim on what was his.

He parked his car behind the pub and pushed open the door.

He had forgotten Belle Blake as completely as if she had never existed.

Claude crouched at the window, laid her cheek on her arms, and looked into the deepening twilight. From below came the buzz of summer insects. Somewhere among the aging maples and hickory trees was repeated the insistent shrilling of tree frogs. Above the darkening mass of leaves swung a lighted crescent of a moon echoing the brilliance of the single planet suspended over it. Venus? Jupiter? Dunkie used to tell her those names when he came calling on her sister Lowell. But that was long ago, before he became the Reverend Duncan Phelps, married to Ariel. He was no part of her life now nor were any of them. The hushed garden had become a prison walk, the great trees she had loved, barriers to the world that lay waiting. She had no need any longer to dream away the unspoken poignancy of the twilight. She knew. All that she needed now was to act, to put matters in motion.

She heard voices in the hall below and rose to her feet. She resolved to tell her mother and father and John her decision tonight. But not anyone else yet. She would have enough to do to stand up to her father. She would be patient, respectful, but she would close her ears to his arguments as she had closed them to the warning in Hutch's good-bye letter. Hutch disappointed her. She had felt an odd, new kind of con-

tentment with him. If he had only been on her side, it
would have been heaven. Instead . . .

> Claude,
> I'm going to write something I wanted to say if
> we could have had dinner. Forget Marc Vallon. I
> can guess what he said to you. He is an exceed-
> ingly distracted man. He is apt to do things with-
> out meaning them. You could find yourself very
> embarrassed. Put that mind of yours to something
> meaningful [he had crossed that out and replaced
> it with the word 'rewarding'], like, what you
> would think if I managed to get back to Thatcher
> soon? I intend to.
>
> Hutch

She had torn up the letter in fury. He had taken her
for a fool. It was not what Marc Vallon had said, it
was what he had *written*. And the long look he had
given her two different times. As if he saw into her
and understood who she really was. The thought of it
even now made her shiver.

To her dismay she heard voices in the downstairs
hall. She had forgotten they were having company.
Willard's laugh, Ariel's silvery greeting, Duncan's
deeper voice. They were all there, and she would die
before she made her announcement before them. She
would have to keep her secret locked painfully inside
her, like a swelling balloon, for one more day. And let
her family smother her one more night. But no longer.
Her fate waited bright as that planet over the trees.

The dinner table was as noisy as it was affection-
ate. Only Kim was absent. Kim, twelve now, sought
perpetual refuge from her elders with a friend named
Jimmie who owned a pony. Kim, thought Claude,

would have squirmed all the way through dinner, as
she herself wanted to squirm. The talk was continuous,
and the subject was entirely John. Still, it was a relief
that no one seemed to notice her silence or even her
presence for that matter.

"It was a shrewd move, John." Willard was speaking. "Whether Harlan accepts the debate or not—and I
think he will—you've made yourself highly visible."

"It's more than a matter of visibility, Will." Martin
spoke grandly from the head of the table. "Though
that's important, I grant you. It's our strength as a
family. A family is greater than the sum of its parts, as
I've always told you. A sound family. The Adamses
knew that two centuries ago. They set this country an
example of high principle. We have the same Yankee
heritage. I believe, John, that through you we will
show this country that those old-fashioned standards
of honor and integrity, truth and reason still exist in
the fiber of its people."

There was a small silence.

"Yes, Dad," said John.

Claude found herself looking above her father's
head to the oval-framed oil portrait of her great-
grandmother Henrietta, the passionate, legend-
surrounded New Orleans beauty who had married
Isaac Roundtree, progenitor of them all. The free flow
of dark curls, the black eyes that followed anyone
looking at her, the bewitching smile with its single
left-cheek dimple, bore no hint of Yankee severity. Indeed she seemed to be laughing at them all with a
secret too rich for telling. I'm part of her, thought
Claude. I don't look like her but I *feel* like her. I want
to live like her, in my own way. No matter what people say.

She caught John's eye. He winked at her, and she colored.

"What about you, angel puss? We haven't heard anything from you, and you're my chief of staff."

She came back.

"I'll be there, John. On the Fourth of July. Front row."

"Of course you will, Claude. We all shall. I hardly thought that needed to be said." Her father's rebuke was mild yet telling.

"I wasn't thinking about the debate, princess." Everyone was listening now. She wished John wasn't sitting opposite and so far away. "I'll need you at Pinesville on Tuesday to direct the kids who want to help us. And in Bollington on Thursday. We're holding a rally at Clarkstown the following Friday." He smiled warmly. "You're my secret weapon, Claude. My only one, since I can't persuade Ariel to join me." His smile faded for an instant.

"John . . ." began Edythe.

"John knows we're with him." Ariel reached for Duncan's hand.

"I don't think this should come up," Martin spoke severely. "Duncan has a loyalty to his father and to his wife. We ask no more than he sit with us as a friend here tonight."

The moment was uncomfortable. Claude fervently hoped that the talk was turning from her.

"So that leaves us, princess." John grinned at her. "But we'll do it, between us. By the way, I like that skirt you're wearing. I think it will look better than jeans on the road. I'll buy you a lunch at the Grist Mill tomorrow, and we'll get down to details, right? I want you to pick out a good campaign hat for the girls."

Claude clenched her hands under the table. It was here. The moment when she would have to declare herself. Not as she had imagined, privately in her father's study, but here, now, in front of them all. Unaccountably she found herself on her feet.

"I have something to say to you all." Her voice sounded thin, distant in her own ears.

"Hurray!" John clapped his hands in mock applause. "Another speechmaker in the family!"

"I am not making a speech. But I have something to tell you . . ." the words trembled. ". . . and I hope nobody will interrupt until I have finished." The table stretched endlessly, a hundred pairs of hostile eyes waited. "John, I am not going to be able to help you this summer. I want you to win more than anything. I will do everything I can that I have time for. But you see—you see, I won't have much time." She swallowed, and the words came childlike and simple. "I am going to have a screen test at three o'clock on August ninth in Paris."

"Claude!" Delight rang like a silver bell from Ariel. Then she was silent.

"I don't think I understand, Claude." Martin leaned forward.

"A screen test, dear? What for?" Edythe showed bewilderment. "You don't mean Paris, France?"

Why were they all being so dull-witted? It was so clear and could be so easy. She spoke carefully. At least her heart had stopped pounding.

"Mr. Marc Vallon, who is a very famous director, has given me an appointment on August ninth in his studio in Paris."

"You talked with Marc Vallon?" The name came out like an obscenity. "When?"

"One day while they were making the picture, Dad."

"You were up on the Ridge?" The duel was between herself and her father now.

"I wanted to watch. First I borrowed Uncle Will's binoculars. You didn't mind, Uncle Will?"

Willard shook his head, his face thoughtful.

"Then one day, Mr. Vallon told me I might watch from behind a rock if I didn't get in the way, and then he gave me the appointment and . . . look, I'll prove it!"

She dashed from the table, relief lightening her feet. Whatever happened, it was over. She returned and handed her father Marc Vallon's card. "Turn it over and see."

He must have read it, because he took so long. She dropped a hand on his shoulder. He seemed to stiffen under it.

"You know I forbid this, Claude."

"Yes, Dad. But I have to do it anyway. I've got myself two jobs to pay my fare. I'm going to mow grass and trim hedges up at the cemetery, and two afternoons a week I'll work at the gas station while Sam is off. . . ."

John seemed to be rubbing his face with his hands. But Martin was ashen. He dropped the card on the table, rose, brushed Claude aside, and walked stiffly from the room. A moment later they heard the door to his study close.

"You've hurt him, Claude."

"I know! And I didn't want to!" She turned on them all, a small animal who would not be cornered. "Didn't any of you ever want anything so badly that you'd just die for it? It's the only chance I'll ever have here in Thatcher to be anybody. Mr. Vallon isn't what

Dad thinks. He's kind and he's a genius and he's willing to help me, and all I have to do is get there. I'm going to pay for it myself. I'm not asking any favors! I'll even pay for my own acting lessons. Miss Blake said I have talent and . . ."

"Belle Blake?" Duncan's question cracked like a whip.

For an instant faces turned to him. Duncan remembered he was not supposed to know the town gossip. He was not supposed to remember he had seen his father with her. The bar. The quick guilt. "I mean, Claude, what could she do for you?"

"She's been on the stage. She knows what you have to learn. Why shouldn't I go to her, Dunkie? Uncle Will, are you against me, too?"

The old man looked up from studying the table cloth. "I don't think it would make any difference, honey. I don't think it should. Are you planning to go alone?"

Her mother stared at her. "Oh, no, Claude!"

It was at least a partial acceptance.

"Why not, Mom? There's nothing to it. I get on a plane and then I'm in Paris. I'll arrange it all. It's simple, isn't it, Ariel? You went back and forth by yourself. Unless you'd come with me?" It was easier to keep talking as if it were settled.

"I'd love it, Claude." Ariel's voice was soft with something left unsaid.

Duncan covered her hand with his. "But the doctor. . . ."

Edythe was on her way to the hall.

"Mom?"

Edythe turned, her expression unreadable. "I understand, Claude. Better than you think. I do believe you don't want to hurt us. But the tragedy occurs when so

much determination is spent on a goal so little understood. I am going to your father."

Claude picked up the precious white card from the
table. She was alone. She wished for an instant Hutch
meant what he said about coming back. But he would
be against her, too. He would be on their side. She
longed suddenly to rip the weeks from the calendar,
to be standing this moment, her hand on the bell of
that unknown door in the rue Dauphine behind which
a new Claude waited.

"I'm sorry, John. I really am. About the campaign."

"I'll make out, princess. I have girls by the dozens
all clamoring to work for me. And Ariel will pick out
that hat."

His kindness was too much. Claude fled, her eyes
brimming with tears. So she did not hear, nor did anyone else, because John said it silently.

"Go to it, Claude. Get what you want."

Part Three

Paris and Rome

August

Chapter Eight

The island of Capri, a rectangular lodestar in the blue shimmer of the Bay of Naples, has for uncounted centuries been a refuge for and from human excesses. Solveg Traner, lying on the tiled loggia of her secluded villa, was no exception to its pilgrims. Beyond the thin-soiled limestone, rock thrust upward another two hundred feet, there encrusted with the momentous ruins of one man's savagery and lusts. Below, the island dropped in a fall so sheer that from where she lay she could see beyond the closeness of flower borders only the pulsing distance of the sea.

She liked heights. She sensed their power. Her own bodily tides responded to the elemental conflict of open sky and the pull of earth and sea below. She could understand why a distraught emperor two thousand years ago had built several villas on Capri's four square miles, never finding what he sought and in his frenzies hurling builders and slaves, concubines, fawners and lovers into the sea futilely, to placate the gods that were his inner devils.

Tiberius had stained this island and thereby added immeasurably to its fascination. Lying in her hidden retreat, Solveg let the timeless winds and the ancient currents surge around her. Here she felt larger than life. And failure seemed petty.

Marc had given her this villa in the heyday of their success and their passion. For three years now he had not returned to it. The last man she had brought here had shut himself within the villa, made quick, timid love to her, and left. She had watched him go, her face lifted contemptuously to the wind, a furious goddess in apology to the elements for a man too thin of spirit to understand them. It was ironic that at the end that weakly handsome Leonard Ross had been betrayed by what he feared most—heights and storm.

Yet she missed Lennie. He had brought her solace and friendship when her body needed both. Now there was no one, no one but herself and Marc and the emptiness of the nights. But she would not age into one of those gaunt-eyed women, drifting through fashionable resorts, trailing the lure of silken shirts and foreign cars to young studs with hot hands. She was Solveg Traner. She demanded pursuit and homage, though the ultimate conquest would be hers.

She stirred restlessly in the fragmented shade of a mimosa tree. Alongside the villa's white wall a sun-browned old man in the perpetual stoop of a keeper of the soil bent over a bank of solid blooms. Each one, she knew, had its roots in a clay pot. When the old man was gone, she wondered who would follow him in the cherished mysteries of pot gardening. For his kind had banished death from the gardens of Capri. No sooner did one flower wither, then another in full bloom took its place. Small and enclosed as they were on their rocky escarpments, the gardens of Capri

glowed in perpetual flowering. No room for the fading, no place for the lingering sweetness of time.

Solveg banished the image and sat up abruptly.

"Giovanni!" She spoke in rapid Italian.

The old man shook his head and lifted a blunt soil-
stained thumb in the direction of the road behind the
villa.

So Hutch had not yet returned. He had accompanied her from Paris only on command. His reluctance
had confronted her like a wall from the moment he
had walked into the curtained Paris apartment where
she had lain, eyes and ears closed. Since she had not
plunged into the Seine nor run naked through the
streets, Hutch had stood looking down at her with
that devil's grin. She would have liked to have pulled
him on top of her and humbled him. Instead she had
abruptly laughed, announced she was exhausted to
the point of suicide, and was going to Capri. She had
enjoyed watching Hutch squirm and dodge as Marc
ordered him to accompany her. Solveg had been under great strain, she must be well before the film's
premiere, she must not be alone, someone must be near
on whom she can call, et cetera. She had not heard the
last of Marc's tirade. She did not know what final per-
suasion Marc had used. She had leaned wanly on
Hutch at the airport. Now she had been at the villa
for nearly a week. Hutch had dutifully checked in every afternoon and disappeared again. She had no idea
where. She suspected the hot tourist-ridden square
where the young girls paraded their lean tanned legs
and scantily covered breasts.

Youth. She thought again of the long-haired young
blonde who had fixed wide, adoring eyes on Marc
in—what was the place?—Thatcher. She would have
forgotten the girl as she had forgotten everything else

of that miserable time, except for the way Marc in turn had looked at her. That look. Solveg herself had felt its compulsion, how long ago?

She moved slowly from the chaise longue. The August heat was depressing her with waves of lassitude. She had not come to Capri to be bored. A bicycle bell and the clang of the grilled gate alerted her. She dismissed Giovanni and arranged herself picturesquely against the iron railing that secured the villa from the drop to the sea.

Hutch crossed the loggia in four long strides.

"Mail." He thrust out a handful of letters. She left such details to Marc. She indicated a marble table at the rear of the loggia. Hutch put the mail into his pocket but made no move. Defiant in everything, she thought. Yet she found herself liking it.

"Where have you been?"

"This morning? Up at Anacapri, talking to three goats and a very pretty girl."

"Why?"

He flung out his arms. "I suffer from claustrophobia. Or hadn't you noticed? Up there I can breathe."

"Carlotta says you have not slept in the villa since we arrived."

"That wasn't part of the orders."

"And if it had been?"

He looked hard at her. "Soli, I think you've recovered. I'll call Marc tonight and tell him . . ."

"You don't have to. I talked to him this morning. He expects us in Rome tomorrow."

"Okay, I'll make the arrangements. For you, Soli. Not for me."

She had been stung into argument with him before. He would submit to Marc's orders. Of that she was sure. But at this moment Marc and Rome and whatever else she must do lay lost in the summer haze. The empty loggia had the scented closeness of a boudoir, the man beside her the maleness of a gladiator. She moved, and the filmy caftan opened to her thigh.

"Did you enjoy yourself up at Anacapri?"

"I like goats. Good-natured and independent as hell."

She laughed. "And the girl?"

"The same. She gave me some goat's milk. Not bad. She had bare feet. Not bad, either. Sexier than a bikini. I might have developed a fetish if they had been washed." He glanced at her with a grin. He could only defeat Soli by meeting her on her own ground. "She invited me into an abandoned convent tower, out of the sun. But I began to think of all those nuns. And besides, it was time to get the mail."

She might have swept from him in disdain. Instead she returned his grin. The sun-bathed solitude was a dizzying presence. "You are so proud of your indifference, Davey. You really should grow up." She moved closer to him. The heavy scent she wore mingled with the heat. "There are no nuns here, Hutch." She slid her arms around his neck and linked them. She was a strong woman. He felt not only the irritation of the moment but the helpless absurdity. And something more, the heavy smothering of sex. This woman could devour a man. And had.

"Kiss me, Hutch."

"Very well." With his arms at his sides, he kissed her, savagely and without feeling, his mouth metal against her open lips. She dropped her arms and struck him once across the face. Then she walked quickly into the villa, her caftan flowing to the lines of her regal, demanding body.

He had made an enemy, implacable as she would be vengeful. Yet the knowledge brought relief. He had closed a door. He would return to Paris and confront Marc as he had failed to do earlier. Then he would take his contract losses and leave.

He would find Claude. Whatever she was up to in her crazy innocence, he would take her in charge, make her understand. With one impulsive, distasteful gesture he had freed himself. Somewhere on the other side of that invisible horizon, she would be waiting. That brought an inner smile. Waiting? Claude? Hell, no. She might even now be on her stubborn, headstrong way. But he would find her. Suddenly, for Hutch, the world widened into the sweetness of certainty.

Marc had remained in Paris, absorbed in the final cutting and editing of *La Troisième Manon*. There was not much to do. He was a precise director. He plotted every detail, every movement in advance of the cameras. His mind held frame after frame, already perfected, before he committed it to film. If the result lacked spontaneity, it was rich in the veneer and intensity for which Marc Vallon was famous. Until the entire project was finished, almost to the day of the premiere, Marc's concentration was total. All else was irrelevant.

Now Hutch had been in Paris two days, still without being able to see Marc. Then in the cherished privacy of his slope-ceilinged flat, the phone shattered the midnight quiet.

"Hutch?"

"For God's sake, chief!"

"I've been busy. What are you doing in Paris anyway? I gave orders . . ."

"Waiting to talk to you. I can come around now."

Hutch was not sure whether he heard or imagined an unidentifiable voice in the background.

"Impossible. But as long as you're here, I want you to see the final screening. Tomorrow at four."

"Look, Marc. There are a few things I have to say."

"There always are, dear boy. We have a great film. It could be my greatest. Four tomorrow. Be there. Good night."

It was the best Hutch could do. It was not going to be easy to break with Marc for the simple reason that Marc never listened to what he did not want to hear. It would be no different tomorrow. Hutch had been through these screenings with Marc before. Marc would sit, unapproachable, with lidded eyes, breathing heavily. As the film rolled, he would begin to sweat lightly. If at the end he was satisfied, he would order a vintage champagne he could not afford for everyone in the vicinity and he would get elegantly drunk, not on the wine but on the flattery. If he did not like what he saw, he would stalk in black silence through a side door and closet himself in his apartment until his genius led him out of the morass. In either case there would be no opportunity for talk of any kind. Hutch cursed the luck that had brought him back to Paris for the solemn rites of the Final Screening. Somehow he had to wring from Marc Vallon the date he had written on that fraudulent card to Claude.

As he rolled back into bed, Hutch realized with a sudden irrelevancy that the Fourth of July had come and gone. For the first time in his expatriated years he had failed to buy a lapel flag. He would never have done it at home, but here among foreigners the Fourth held a proud, rootless poignancy he would not have admitted to. He wondered what she had done with the day. Thatcher would have a parade, led inevitably by the fife and drum minutemen. How many summers had he himself tied a handkerchief around his stubbled head and thumped his junior-size drum with more fury than accuracy through the streets. He would like to tell her about that. He would like to buy her a double ice-cream cone and share homemade deviled eggs and chicken sandwiches in the summer sun. At night, he would take her dancing.

Hutch stared into the darkness, struggling with a new sensation. He was not only feeling sorry for himself, as he knew, but he was, for the first time in memory, homesick. Homesick for a place he had lived in only three weeks, and for a girl who never even answered his letter.

In the dark closeness of the screening room Marc was neither breathing heavily, nor sweating lightly. He was sitting stiffly, his lips pursed, his eyes fixed on the screen as though looking not at but through it.

The final scenes were rolling. The Ridge in Thatcher, the boulder behind which Claude was hidden. In Hutch's mind she was there now, a physical presence he wanted to reach out and seize. But aside from the huge rock nothing was familiar. Marc's inner vision had turned the place into a tormented landscape, brutal and desolate under the approaching storm. Solveg stood like a satanic priestess against the black rolling sky, watching Lennie as he came slowly down the slope. Hutch shut his eyes for an instant, sickened, then opened them to see Marc continue his cold, unreadable appraisal. The man was not inhuman. What, then, lay in his mind? Lennie advanced, as if drawn by a magnet. Hutch watched him fail to turn toward Soli. His paced walk dreadful in its deliberate-

ness, he went on to the cliff. As he stepped outward
the camera abruptly shifted to Soli. And Hutch saw
what Marc was waiting for. Soli's face was a mask of
living horror, spent as an ancient whore's at the death
of all passion. The flesh itself seemed to have greened
and sunk into the skeleton of her face. She was beyond the calculation of age.

Behind her, from the turbulence of darkening
space, came an eerie cry, thin-drawn as the shriek of a
dying species. The face was Soli's, but the cry Hutch
recognized. It had escaped, stifled, from Claude's
young anguish. Disembodied, it had become the
sound of eternity, transforming the final scene from
the triumph of a majestic woman to a glimpse into a
withered and private hell. The lights went up. Applause broke out involuntarily, dwindled in embarrassment. No one in the room was unaware.

"My God, Marc!" Hutch felt himself talking to a figure in stone.

Marc lifted his lidded eyes. "Tremendous, isn't it?"

"You can't keep that last scene!"

"Can you conceive of a better one? For once in my
life I am humbly grateful to Destiny."

People were moving about uncertainly. Some
stopped at Marc's seat offering uncomfortable con-
gratulations. The power of the final scene was ines-
capable. So was the tragedy.

"Champagne, Hutch. The usual."

Was the man still captive of his vision?

"Do you think anybody wants it after that?"

"We have produced a masterpiece. Do you think
there is anyone here who doesn't know that?"

By midnight Marc's euphoria reached its height. He
had been holding court since early evening at his spe-

cial table at the Café du Bouffon Triste, a Left Bank retreat he had made his own years ago when he first sampled Madame *la propriétaire*'s subtle blend of adulation and superb bouillabaisse. It was Madame's story, told by her grandmother, she claimed, that the dark-walled, smoke-grimed little bistro had received its unlikely name from no less a person than Toulouse Lautrec. But its patrons believed that Madame herself had named it for her wraith of a husband, known only as Jojo, who hopped nimbly among the tables when he was not secreted in the kitchen. However, it was Madame herself who bought and cooked the fish that made Le Bouffon Triste famous.

Tonight, as always after a Marc Vallon screening, the little café was jammed. Its pale-yellowish light from three hanging, brass-hooded features cast a waxy glow on the faces of out-of-work actors, seedy writers, and envious directors. There were enough achievers in the crowd to satisfy Marc. The rest he ignored. Madame, her ample folds encased in straining black satin, sat on a high stool behind the cash register ready to debar the unwanted. Jojo appeared only to pass napkin-wrapped bottles over heads to waiting hands. The noise was deafening.

Hutch, at the table next to Marc, watched soot-eyed, high-breasted nymphs circle into Marc's embrace, press an indifferently received kiss, and reluctantly circle out. Hutch refilled his glass. He might as well enjoy himself. Having made his decision he was freed of tomorrow's moment of truth and its head-splitting unpaid bills.

At last Marc stood up, to whistles and applause.

No one had seen his film, no one had reviewed it. Only those who made a living from Marc, or hoped to, were stamping and clapping.

"My dear, dear friends—" Marc looked magnificent, Hutch acknowledged, the eagle head thrown back, the long sensitive hands flung eloquently out, the impress of invisible laurel already on the pale, intellectual brow.

"My friends, you know I have never sought fame. *Le Bon Dieu* knows I don't want anything as troublesome thrust upon me. But I have sought perfection. This afternoon, at the final screening of *La Troisième Mamon*, I found it. There are few moments in any man's life when he reaches his ideal. Tonight I stand on that peak with you, my loyal friends, as witnesses. I am grateful to you all."

Marc sat down, wiped his forehead, and closed his eyes. The cheers rose.

Madame lowered the lights. The crowd took the hint. The party was over.

"Get me a cognac, will you, Hutch?"

"Sure, chief."

Hutch fetched two glasses and sat down at Marc's table.

"Great show."

"It's what they want. Cabbage heads, all of them. Hutch, where the hell did that scream come from at the end of the picture? When Lennie—" Hutch sensed that Marc's mind had turned back to the film.

"Don't you know?"

"It wasn't Soli. She couldn't get her voice up there if she were burning. Hutch, she's showing age, isn't she? What happened to her up there on that rock anyway?"

Hutch saw no need to answer.

"Hutch, who screamed? At the end there."

"God damn it, you know who screamed. You told her she could watch if she stayed out of sight. She did, behind that boulder, where she would see the whole rotten business, including Lennie's fall. Of course she screamed."

Marc seemed to be struggling with himself. "The girl. Of course. Now I remember. What was her name? Very young. Quite lovely. That scream. All emotion— all human frailty."

Hutch realized his glass was fragile and relaxed his fingers. "The girl, as you call her, Claude . . ." it was not easy even to mention her name to this man.

"That was it—Claude. Marvelous hair. And legs. Temper, too, I remember."

"Yeah, well, you gave that girl—who knows nothing about you or your business—"

"I am not in business, Hutchins. I am an artist."

"Yeah, okay, all right. You gave her your card with your Paris address on it and a date."

"Did I really?"

"She thinks she has an appointment with you."

"When?"

"That's what you're going to tell me."

Marc leaned back and smiled. He was quite drunk in his own Promethean way.

"Marc, what was the date you wrote on that card?"

"I haven't the faintest idea, dear boy. I was rather busy."

"She's coming to Paris. You're the only one who can stop her."

"Stop her? Why in the world would I stop her? I wouldn't stop anyone from coming to Paris. If I'm here, I might see her. I found her quite refreshing, as I remember."

"She thinks you are going to give her a screen test."

"They all do. But I think we could have a pleasant time without that."

"She isn't that kind of girl. She's young and innocent

and star-struck. In the name of decency will you write her a letter and . . ."

"Write!" Marc eyed him in something close to shock. "Write a girl who wants to see me? I have never done that in my life. One written word and you're involved. You're crazy, Hutch. The discussion is over."

"Not quite." Hutch hunched his bulky shoulders toward Marc. "You'll sober up tomorrow, chief, and the date you gave Claude will float up in what you call your creative mind. I'll be around in the morning to get it."

Marc might have fired him on the spot; instead he leaned back in his chair and laughed. What angered Hutch further was that the laugh was not sardonic or leering or any of the cheap gestures a man might make. At this moment genuine amusement livened Marc's features.

"Your language, dear boy, is as vivid as your American puritanism. So chivalry is not yet in rigor mortis. I detect that you have formed a certain attraction for the woodland sprite and you want to protect her, whether she wants it or not. She won't thank you for it. If she comes to Paris I shall see her. If I don't, she will certainly have other experiences here to reward her. It used to be said that one's first visit to Paris should be made before twenty or after forty. Between, it's mere bourgeois travel. Paris belongs to the young. I was eighteen when I first came to Paris. Straight from the labor camp. I met Soli in Paris. What a woman then! Born—where was it? New Jersey? Half Polish, half Italian. Polish women—most passionate in the world, Hutch. You don't know women until you've had a Polish one. Paris. To be young in Paris."

He was rambling. Madame was nodding over her cash register. Hutch had the taste of ashes in his

mouth. When a man gave up clean air, he became what he breathed, what someone else wanted him to breathe.

Marc stood up unsteadily. "She will do very well in Paris, that girl. She has *l'esprit*."

Hutch would walk home. He would drink in whatever freshness the humid hour offered in the fetid dampness rising from the Seine. The quays lay deserted, the closed bookstalls tombstones of the night. Hutch was sweating, his shirt soaked by the time he reached the rue Bonaparte.

He opened the door to his flat. The light struck an envelope that had been slid under it. It bore an airmail stamp. The envelope was yellow, with an orange border. On the back, hand-drawn, drooped a spray of bright pink, bell-like flowers over three feminine, block letters, U.S.A. Hutch did not have to see the Thatcher postmark.

He read the letter in alternating currents of exasperation and self-blame.

Dear Hutch,

I got your letter breaking our date from Larry, which was all right but don't leave any more letters that way because Larry makes remarks, and I've had enough of those. I went down to sit on the library steps anyway. I go there a lot because it's sort of quiet and I can think. Our house is not a good place to think in these days. It's my father mostly. He sounds like you about it all only he doesn't say so much. Just goes by sort of in the hall. Mom sides with him although I don't think she really does all that much. It's just being mar-

ried that makes her that way. I wouldn't side with anybody just because I happened to be married, if I were.

Anyhow it's more peaceful now that they've gotten used to the idea. Dad won't let anybody talk about it at the table. I have a job at the cemetery trimming edges and it's nice up there except when it rains and then I don't work. The gas-station job didn't pan out. I still hope it will because Angie Welles told me how much it costs to get to Paris and I was surprised. I haven't told anybody yet because I'd rather surprise them and be famous, than just tell them first and maybe not be as famous as I'd like.

I had to stop taking acting lessons with Miss Blake. I guess you didn't meet her but she has fuzzy red hair and bounces around a lot and she's been on the stage. But they cost an awful lot. And she kept asking questions I didn't care to answer. Besides, she was teaching me a method to let everything go and look sloppy as if I have to pay to learn *that*. So I'm reading a book, and I practice saying things in curves shooting upward. And I breathe a lot. But I've given up walking around with a book on my head. It won't stay, and if you ask me, people who can make it stay don't wash their hair enough. But Miss Blake didn't like my stopping. She says an actress needs new experiences. I think you have to use up the old ones first, don't you?

Please tell Mr. Vallon I will be prompt like he said. I know how busy he is because he is a genius, and tell him not to worry, I will wait any amount of time. That's all for now.

Love Claude.

P.S. Everyone says John won his debate on the Fourth of July hands down. Mr. Phelps got all red and hot, not from drinking as usual, but because he was so angry. But I was lucky. I found a dime and a penny on the Green and one from ten is nine and nine is my lucky number. Love C.

P.S.S. Please don't write back. Somebody will see the letter first, and the word Paris is just a red shirt in front of a bull in our house. Love C.

P.S.S.S. I hope you like droopy tulips. They're my signature, and if I'm famous I'll wear them in diamonds like old Mrs. Plummer wears her dead poodle. L.C.

It was obvious to Hutch on the second reading that Claude applied the word love to a letter as automatically as the stamp. And the value was the same. It was obvious on the third reading that her coming to Paris was as unstoppable as a flow of boiling lava.

He read the letter once more. He finally fell asleep leaving it crumpled on the floor and gnawing at his subconscious. When he woke to the familiar smell of fresh bread from the street, a solution stared at him. It would take thinking about, but what else had he to do? It was a not-impossible gamble, and that, for Hutch, had been the definition of his life.

Chapter Nine

Claude gave herself to the relentless schedule of her days and to an inner core of loneliness that by now had become habit. The faces at the dinner table seemed as impersonal as the names on the granite headstones around which she guided the grass clippers. Yet that very remoteness fortified her. There was no one to look at her too closely and see that beneath her determination lay a nameless uncertainty she would not admit to as fear. August 9. Only four days away.

She reached the end of the border and sat down in the shade. It was nearly noon. She longed for the whistle to fill the void. A car turned through the cemetery gates. She recognized the gray pickup. It was not the first time since she had been working in the cemetery that he had jolted up the gravel road to see her.

Willard Roundtree stopped the truck and came toward her, fanning his face with his wide-brimmed farmer's hat.

"Nice and cool up here."

"Hi, Uncle Will. I left the Roundtrees to the last. And now there isn't time to finish. But I shouldn't be the one to do them first."

"A very healthy attitude. A damn fool thing, anyhow. A plot stone that size just to say ROUNDTREE and all of 'em crowded around it when they wouldn't speak to each other alive. I have a better place for myself. Down there on the hill near that young maple tree. Planted it myself and got to like it so much I figured I'd enjoy it for company." Willard winked at her. "Don't you give me away. Time enough to let them have at me when I'm down there snug and comfortable and can't hear 'em."

"That's silly talk, Uncle Will." But her eyes were fixed on the distance and she smiled absently.

"I agree. Wrong end of the spectrum for today. I've come to invite you to lunch."

She turned a brightened face to him. "I accept!"

The noon whistle blew. It seemed to release an inner spring within her. They walked toward the car and she giggled. That giggle, he thought. It could break a man's heart. If there were such a man. "A girl's not supposed to accept just like that, is she?"

"Accept what?"

"Well, lunch like I did."

"She is, if she's hungry."

"That's not what I mean. I mean there's no mystery about it. A girl should keep a man dangling, sort of, not sure whether she will or won't. That's my trouble. If I want to do something I just say so and then I'm sort of obvious and a man loses interest. I mean, if you were younger, Uncle Will, and inviting a girl out you'd lose interest if she accepted just like that, right off the bat, wouldn't you?"

It was good to hear her talk. She had been too quiet these past weeks. He steered the truck through the gates.

"That would depend."

"On what?"

"On what the invitation was."

"Well, just say for lunch, like now."

"In that case it would depend on what time I had had breakfast, which happens to be six this morning."

She leaned back and let the truck's rattle lull her. How had he guessed that she did not want to be alone today?

Lunch, which consisted of Willard's special cold vegetable soup and a round loaf of coarse cornbread, was over too soon. Claude cleared the dishes and returned to the farmhouse parlor to find Willard sitting smoking his pipe.

"You don't need anybody, do you Uncle Will?"

"Where did you get that idea? I need everybody."

"I mean you cook all those wonderful things yourself."

"Matter of survival, my dear. You'll get better food in Paris."

Paris. He had said it as casually as he might say milk. No one mentioned the word at home. It was as if Paris was not a reality but an image she had somehow intruded into the sensible world. She seated herself on a three-legged stool that had done two centuries of service, and hugged her knees.

"Have you ever been to Paris, Uncle Will?"

"Certainly. The man who has Paris in his soul is fit for treasons, stratagems, and spoils. There's an inaccuracy there, but it will do you good to discover it for yourself."

She had never tried to follow Willard's circumlocutions. He knew more than any of them and he always left her feeling out of breath. She tossed back her hair. She could not stay much longer and yet she would like to remain in this room until the moment tomorrow when she stepped onto the plane. The thought sent a shiver of anticipation through her.

"When were you there, Uncle Will? Paris, I mean."

"Too long ago. Like everything else in my life." He eyed her closely through the pipesmoke, the eager young beauty of her face, set stiffly against hurt, her hands slender as wings, roughened and stained now by her unlikely labors. Her hair, her veil of hair. A wedding veil? Out of date, that idea. Yet it was not old-fashioned nor would it ever be for a man to want to shield innocence and protect fragility. It was in a man's genes, his testicles, Willard smiled to himself. Then he came back to reality. Claude was about as fragile as that flame of a little woman, her great-grandmother Henrietta, who could drive a four-in-hand with her small gloved hands while nodding her Paris hat to a tight-lipped neighbor. Henrietta would have understood and applauded this young, unvanquished descendant. In fact they were two of a kind, separated only by the triviality of a century.

As for innocence, it was a matter of definition. By her own faintly written words Henrietta had lost hers one southern summer night to a Yankee farmer named Isaac Roundtree. So began the widening legend, ROUNDTREE, that now was cut in granite over Thatcher—ROUNDTREE. Once again Willard was glad that he had never parted with that faded diary or revealed its contents.

He heard Claude's little giggle. "Why are you looking at me that way, Uncle Will?"

"I was not looking at you but through you, my dear. At someone else. Old men do these things."

"Who? Tell me. Who were you looking at? Was it Chastity?"

Chastity. Henrietta's last daughter who, like Henrietta, flung her happiness to the stars. But, unlike Henrietta, found life a spent and shabby trifle to be thrown away.

"What do you know about Chastity, Claude?"

"I know she ran away to New York. And she was an actress. So it's in the family."

"I can see the logic. If you want further genetic reassurance, your great-grandmother's own father, Phillipe Boulaire in New Orleans was a Shakespearean actor, of sorts, though his family was too high-born to tolerate it."

Claude had a myopic and happy disregard of history but she knew a reason when she heard it. "There, you see! My family isn't high-born or anything silly like that, so why should they be so mad at me now?"

"Wrong word, Claude."

"I know. If they were mad we could all fight it out. But they just won't." She jumped up. "Got to go!"

He rose and took her by the shoulders. "You're going to be all right, Claude." It was not a question.

"Sure I am."

"You have enough money?"

"Yep. Part of it's your graduation money and some of it is what John paid me though he didn't have to do that. I made the rest."

"And you're staying . . . ?"

"Hotel Maratte, if you want to know. It's on something called a Left Bank, and Mrs. Welles says she doesn't know how good it is, but I don't care. I won't be in it very much anyhow, after my screen test."

"Have you any plans to come home?"

"Oh, sure. But I don't know when. That depends on Mr. Vallon of course."

"But you have a round-trip ticket?"

Claude hesitated. "Sort of."

"What is a 'sort of' ticket?"

"Don't tell Dad or Mom. I have the money for it but I didn't want to buy it yet. It's sort of unlucky. Angie Wilson thinks I should."

"So do I."

Henrietta's brood. (Without Henrietta's grammar.) Innocence. He wanted to believe her body innocent but her mind, he told himself, had the ageless cunning of a sibyl. Discussion was obviously superfluous. He opened the ancient drop-leaf desk on a confusion of papers, letters, newspaper clippings, weather reports, soil samples, and other evidences of an unfinished life. From the clutter he drew a small package wrapped in tissue paper.

"A going-away present, my dear."

"For me? Oh, Uncle Will!" She heard the tremor in the last syllable and felt her eyelids sting. It was the unexpected, the kindly, that disrupted. She tore off the wrapper. Claude had never been one to savor, Willard thought. Not at Christmas, nor at birthdays, nor at surprises. When life presented itself, she reached for it.

It proved to be a small book, bound in soft butternut suede. There was no title. She opened it. The pages were blank.

"A diary?"

"No, Claude. Not a diary, nor an address book, nor a memo. Just blank pages. Charlie Redwing made the cover. I had it bound. Write whatever you want to or

write nothing. Every blank page can become what
you wish. But it will be there to talk to when you are
alone."

She understood but she was not ready to answer.

"There's writing on the last page."

"It's something I copied from Henrietta's diary. She
wrote it the last year of her life. Read it when you
come to it. If you come to it."

She was anxious to leave. The threads were tightening. She wrapped the tissue paper around the little
book and pushed it into her tote.

"Thanks, Uncle Will. For everything!"

"I'll drive you home."

"I'd rather bike. Honestly. I can get my wheels
down from the back of your truck, myself."

She was beating her wings.

"As you wish, my dear."

She flung her arms around his neck, pressed her
face against his rough cheek. "Wish me luck, Uncle
Will!"

He let her go. He wished her more than luck. Happiness, he might have said, but he knew that no one
could wish what he could not define, not across half a
century. He watched through the window as she lifted
her bicycle easily from the truck, chivalry thwarted.
He wondered if any man could hold that gossamer,
steel-ribbed spirit for very long. Or would she, like
Henrietta, fling herself at a man who for a lifetime
would never really see her. He wondered most of all
about the persuasive voice, the transparent detachment of Davison Hutchins. Yet he had a sense that the
young man was honest. He wished he had taken the
trouble to meet Marc Vallon. But then he might have

meddled. The old, he reflected, had a high nuisance value unless they were careful.

Claude thought of stopping to see Ariel. Ariel always brought Paris nearer. But Claude was past that need now. Ariel had pressed her mother's Paris address on her; Claude had dutifully written it down, determined to forget it. That would be another claim, another demand, another obligation. Her own life was opening into a miracle. She must handle it her way. Alone.

The house was cool and, thankfully, empty. In her room she stripped off her hot, dirt-stained clothes, showered, and threw herself on the bed. She jumped up once to take the tissue-wrapped white card from her wallet. Marc Vallon, 213 Rue Dauphine, August 9. 3:00. She read the numbers, and read them again. She added, subtracted, multiplied and divided, and marveled at the number of times her lucky number appeared. And tomorrow she would be eighteen. Eight and one . . . nine.

All her past, all that surrounded her, fell away in the face of that blossoming. She thought again of Marc Vallon's look. It had become companion to her secret hours. He had seen deeper into her than anyone in her life. He had understood that within her lay hidden talents that only needed to be set free. Or else why had he offered her this chance? She felt at this moment she could give her very being into his skilled hands and those talents would burst into life.

Such thoughts turned Claude's face quite pink. She rolled over and buried it in the cool pillow and let the moments pass, hot and secret, that were sweeping her toward Destiny.

But they were not yet ready to let her escape. Ed-

ythe produced a birthday cake and commented that
she looked rather pale. Kim asked her if she was
scared of flying. John announced, to her hesitant surprise, that he would drive her to the airport. There
were presents suitable for traveling. In the end the
strained, unstated offerings of their love beat back
her heady sense of flight. They were anxious. She
wanted to embrace them all. She was leaving a
wound. She wanted them to understand. She was very
near tears when her father asked her to come into the
study.

In the green lamplight he looked gaunt. The cords
in his neck showed. He studied her for a few seconds
without speaking. She thought suddenly of her long-
vanished brother Michael. He must have stood before
his father, on this same threadbare medallion of the
oriental rug, that night before he flung out of the
house never to return. She would never hurt her father like that. She would make him proud of her
someday.

"Sit down, Claude." Martin took his own black
leather chair. "I won't keep you long. You know what
I think. I know what you intend. We shall never agree.
But that is not a matter of parental discipline. It is a
matter of the generations. You will be eighteen tomorrow. Your mother and I have looked forward to that
day for . . ." he smiled, ". . . shall I say, eighteen
years? We did not anticipate that you would elect to
spend it so far from us."

"I couldn't help it, Dad. It just happened."

He brushed the interruption aside with a toss of his
hand. She realized that anything she might say had
been done with long ago. She returned to waiting silence.

"I understand circumstances even when I fail to understand motive. I believe with all my heart you are making a mistake. You are going among people and a way of life you know nothing about. But I believe you will go bravely and honorably." He seemed to be searching her, looking for something he knew was there. "You may be hurt. In all likelihood, you will be. But you are sound, Claude. You have been taught that. You will be all right. I believe that." His voice hinted at a tremor, but he smiled again. "I must believe that."

She clenched her hands and tried to swallow the thickening in her throat. Why? Why did he have to spell it out like this?

He reached into his inside pocket. "Angie Welles tells me your hotel is adequately clean and decent. I translate that to mean minimally. If this turns out to be the first of your disillusionments, I want you to have, what we called in the navy, an escape hatch." He handed her a long envelope. "Open it when you need to."

"Oh, Dad!" She was on her knees beside him, a child again beside that great authoritative black chair. He was stroking her hair, the envelope crushed against her chest. The silence pulsed in waves of green lamplight through the old room. How long? Martin thought—three, four, or was it five generations now that had come, flung their emotions to these darkly paneled walls, and gone, leaving nothing but the empty inevitability of time? As if in answer the hall clock struck.

Claude lifted her head and said the one small thing she was capable of. "I'd better finish packing, Dad."

He nodded. "John's giving up his day for you tomorrow. Don't be late."

She left him. Upstairs in her room, she thrust the

envelope into a drawer, sat on the bed, and let the tears break, the sweet, secure tears that came just before one was eighteen. And not yet alone.

Claude would remember in detail only two events of the flight to Paris. The first was when she sat with John at New York's Kennedy Airport. Because of John's usual thoroughness they had arrived two hours early. She barely noticed. She was too dazzled by the magnificent strings of lights the city flung against the fading sky, by the immensity of the airport, by the flow of humanity to the width of the world.

John bought her a lemonade and a paperback romance. She thanked him absently. Then he leaned forward and asked her a question that made her heart pound.

"Claude, how did you meet this man, Marc Vallon?"

She no longer feared the truth. "I went up on the Ridge and watched them making the movie."

"I know that. But when did you meet him?"

She sensed a trap but refusing to answer would not help. "I—I just spoke to him. He gave me his card and said he'd see me. And wrote the date."

"Was that the day of the accident?"

"I—I think so. Why?"

"I hoped you hadn't seen it."

She had almost forgotten it. It had become part of the film. Kind as he was, John was still being protective. She found herself watching the clock.

Airborne, she was for the first time in her life too excited to eat. She sat looking out into the night sky and a half-moon that made white pillows of the clouds. A stewardess leaned across her and snapped down the shade.

"We're going to show the movie now."

The lady seated next to her reading a book looked up and smiled.

"You don't have to let them pull the shade if you don't want to. You've paid for your seat. You're entitled to look out the window. It's one of their petty tyrannies."

Claude left the shade down and thought about Paris.

Her plans were exact. Angie Welles had showed her on a detailed map that the rue Dauphine was on an island in the middle of the Seine River and her hotel five walking-blocks away.

"When you're on the Île de la Cité," Angie said, "walk to the center of the square in front of Notre Dame. There is a medallion set in the paving. They call it the heart of Paris."

Claude told herself she would let the heart of Paris go. She would find her way on a test walk tomorrow to the rue Dauphine. The next day, August 9, she would spend the morning getting ready. At two she would walk leisurely and surely to number 213. If it rained she would take a cab. She would wear her new white dress that showed off her tan.

She must have slept, because without warning came the second unforgettable event. A voice.

"We shall arrive in Paris in thirty-five minutes."

The lady with the book was returning to her seat.

"If you want to use the facilities, my dear, you'd better get in line. Behind that fat gentleman in shirt sleeves. There is no ladies' room. It's quite barbarous."

Claude splashed cold water on her face, brushed her hair, and felt better.

She returned to her seat and looked out the window. The grayness had parted. They were over land.

She saw green fields, minuscule roofs, dark threads that must be roads, and a pearl-gray loop that could only be a river.

She fought a sudden queasiness.

Paris was rushing toward her.

Chapter Ten

The Place Dauphine, a triangle of bare soil and occasional shade trees, lies on the prow end on the Île de la Cité, that boat-shaped island that splits the Seine. It cradles twenty centuries of Paris history and thrusts itself, an impartial arm, between the Right and Left Banks.

The Place itself consists of two rows of tall, elegant houses, now converted to apartments, which have met time with dignity, changed with tolerance, and remained unobtrusively fashionable. It is a place where a man might ensure his self-image and grasp stability in a shifting world. A man like Marc Vallon.

On this August afternoon the Place Dauphine drowsed in its summer trance, blinds drawn, shaded trees abandoned, sidewalks empty except for a single girl.

A young man pushing an empty delivery cart stopped, leaned against a building, lit a cigarette, and followed the girl with his eyes. She was young. She had a free-swinging walk, good shoulders, but small breasts. Her legs were marvelous. He enjoyed good legs, slender American legs. Her pale, unretouched hair swung like a skein of silk; her skin was fresh cream. Truly an American. He watched her walk to the end of the row, turn and walk back, indifferent to the deserted street and seemingly unaware that the Place Dauphine was hardly what a *petite poulette* would choose for a walk on a hot afternoon in August.

Halfway down the block she turned again, glanced at number 213, and continued to the corner. The young man sauntered across the street. In an open ground-floor window a thin woman leaned on her elbows, the neck of her flowered-print dress pulled wide, revealing a creped chest to whatever breeze came from the river.

He jerked his head toward the girl and spoke to the woman. "Eh, Gabrielle, would you like to make a little bet?"

"I wish you luck." The woman drew her lips tighter. "She came yesterday and asked me if this was where Mr. Vallon lived. I would not tell her, of course. I know the type. She came back today and said she had an appointment. Imagine! An appointment at three o'clock in August! I do not know an August when Mr. Vallon has stayed in Paris. She showed me his card. She must have stolen it somewhere. Go on! If that is what she wants, I'm sure you can do as well." Her laugh was coarse. "If not better!"

The young man flipped his cigarette to the curb. Claude had turned back from the corner. He stepped in her path.

"Looking for someone?" His English was slow but adequate for such situations.

"No." Claude sidestepped. He moved quickly in front of her.

"Perhaps I help you?"

"I don't think so. I am not looking for anyone. I'm waiting for someone."

"In that case, I can help you." He felt in his pocket and reassured himself of a folded bill and a jingle of coins. "It is very hot. If you would like to wait, there is a little café around the corner. You could wait there, and I would come and find out. It is better than walking."

"No, thank you."

"But you are fortunate, mademoiselle. Everything in Paris is shut." He closed his hands. "Bang, like that, in August. It is only that madame at Le Café Vert has lost her husband, and it is better to make little money while you are grieving, yes?"

"Yes, I guess so. Thank you very much, but I'll wait here."

He did not move. "You are an American, no?"

"Yes."

"And you have not been to Paris before?" It was a guess but he had found it workable.

She looked past him. The woman had gone from the window. Now she would have to wait near the door and see for herself when Marc Vallon returned. It was understandable that a man as busy as that would be late. The woman might have let her into the building at least. But this was Paris, and nothing had been what she expected or imagined. Not from the moment she had stepped off the plane and discovered it was not nine o'clock in the morning but three in the afternoon. No one had told her that one whole precious day would be swept from her without a ripple. Confused, she had walked past the waiting faces in the stark, impersonal airport as if there would be one she might know. There was not, of course, and as she

stood waiting in line at customs, she told herself angrily that she had no right to expect anything like
that. She had made it all quite clear, hadn't she? She
did not exactly see Hutch waiting there. She saw a
space in the crowd where he might have stood.

But she was over that now. She would not think
about her hotel room either, so closed in that she had to
put her bag on the sagging iron bed. Or the common
bathroom with its missing floorboard and overpower-
ing smell of raw disinfectant. The hotel had no dining
room but she had found an eatery, not much more
than a counter, two blocks away. Le Hot Dog. Soggy
but affordable. She was surprised that a map of Paris
cost two dollars; at least the money that the news-
stand man had picked from her outstretched hand
came to two dollars.

But it did not matter. She was here. In Paris. 213
Rue Dauphine. August 9. And it was only twenty past
four. She did not like the nearness of this young man
in his sticky open shirt and too-tight jeans. But maybe
that was the way people talked to each other in Paris.
And he was only being friendly.

"So it is your first trip?" he repeated.

"Yes."

"I knew."

Something in his voice, a thread of amusement,
flicked her. Was there something about her, the way
she dressed or looked, that was wrong? She glanced
nervously at a window as she had done a half-dozen
times on her walk here. He was watching her, his eyes
impudent.

"You want to know how I knew that?"

"Yes." She said it reluctantly.

"You are charming, chic, beautiful." His eyes swept
her with each adjective. "But you do not know Paris.

Or you would not be walking up and down this block like a—a common girl . . ."

She flushed red and stared at him.

". . . because, my *petite*, he will not come."

"What do you know. . . ." She choked back her words. What would Mr. Vallon think if he came and found her quarreling on the street with this—this . . .

He was watching her closely. That flush! How long had it been since he found that *couleur* in any girl? "And do you know why your appointment will not come? Look up there." His arm swept upward toward the rows of glistening windows along the street. For the first time she noticed the shades were mostly drawn.

"I make deliveries in this street. I would not be here now if the skinny old bitch there would go out for her own bread and her food. But no. I must come. You want to see Mr. Vallon? Those are his windows. Fourth floor. Closed tight. Blinds down. Nobody stays here in August. Not on this street. So come on. We'll have a little Pernod. I will show you other things about Paris. I have a little room."

He had taken her elbow. She shook him off furiously.

"I don't believe you. If he wasn't here, she would have told me!"

He laughed. He liked girls who could flame.

"You do not know Gabrielle. Go, ask her. I will wait."

"Please don't. I don't want to see you. And I don't want to talk to you. And I won't go anywhere with you. Just go away and leave me alone!"

She ran to the door of the building and rang the bell. She heard it faintly in a distant corridor. She pressed the bell again and then leaned on it. At last she heard steps.

The gaunt woman held the door on a chain.

"What is it now, mademoiselle?"

"Mr. Vallon? He is in Paris, isn't he?"

"No."

"Why didn't you tell me? I've been waiting."

"I told you he was not here." The woman started to close the door. Claude slid her hand around it.

"Do you know when he is coming back?"

"No."

"Do you know where he's gone?"

"Mr. Vallon does not wish me to give any information at any time."

It seemed to Claude that the woman's cold eyes held triumph.

"If you please, mademoiselle. . . ."

Claude withdrew her hand. The door closed. She stood in the sunlight, for the first time feeling the heat of the pavement beneath her feet. The young man had gone. The woman had closed her window and shaded it. The street was empty.

Claude began to walk. Numbness would replace reality for a little while.

Hutch, sitting in the seedy lobby of the Hotel Maratte, looked at his watch as he had been doing at ten and fifteen minute intervals for the last four hours. He had made a mistake, a bad one. That, as he might have admitted if he ever permitted himself self-pity, had been the story of his life. Within hand's reach of what he wanted and then a mistake, a misjudgment, something carefully thought through and then not carefully enough. Twenty minutes to eleven. Where in hell was she?

He rose, for something to do, from the sagging, tu-
bular chair and bought a pack of cigarettes at the
vending machine. He had given up smoking two years
ago, but he had consumed one pack already tonight.
The night clerk had come on duty, an aging little man
in a soiled wing collar of ancient design, and a bow
tie hanging by one snap. His gray hair stood in tufts.
His vest was stained, his eyes weary. He had seen too
much of human nature, and there was nothing different about the case in point.

Hutch knew the answer before he asked the question. "Miss Roundtree has not called in, has she?"

"Not since I been on."

"There are no messages?"

"You expecting one?"

"No." Hutch's final question had been answered
bluntly by the day clerk. He would ask again. The old
man might not be so assuming.

"Would you give me her room number?"

"We don't do that in this hotel, young man."

"But you'd know if she checked out?"

"Key's hanging up there." He jerked his head to
three rows of hooks where an occasional key mutely
hung. Few of the denizens of the Hotel Maratte were
night prowlers it would seem, but which key was hers
was locked behind the bland hypocrisy of the night
clerk. He leaned across the desk.

"Listen, son." His eyes were wet. "If she stood you
up, I know a place. . . ."

Hutch went back to his chair. Anything might have
happened. She might have packed and left before he
arrived, the key still dangling there. She might be lost,
in which case she should have gone to the police, with
the attendant uproar *les flics* would cause. Or she
might have met someone. He tried not to think about

that. He had called Marc's apartment twice, futilely. It was an empty gesture, an excuse for action, like rising from his chair. He knew where Marc was.

He had been too clever. Willard Roundtree had not resented his transatlantic phone call two days ago. The old man had not unwillingly given the date of Claude's leaving and her hotel, but the warning had been unmistakable. "She's headstrong. She'll see this thing through, no matter what. Roundtree blood."

"I've met up with it, sir."

He heard the smile in Willard's voice. "I guess in your place I'd do the same thing. Take care of her, if you can."

He had failed that. Instead he had yielded to a second bright idea. He would let her arrive, find her own way, keep her nonexistent appointment and be waiting for her when she came back. He had watched her from the distance at the airport, telephoned the hotel to make sure she had arrived. If she ever learned of it, he could guess that she might despise him. On the other hand she might have learned a lesson.

Five minutes past eleven. He was alarmed now. The night clerk was watching him suspiciously. She would not stay out this late in a strange city with someone she did not know. She would not have let anyone pick her up. The thought sickened him. Alarm slowly iced into fear in his stomach. Any moment a call might come.

At nine minutes past eleven the heavy glass door swung open. Hutch hardly dared to look up. She came in slowly, her hair hanging limp and mussed, rain spots showing on her white dress, her face empty of expression.

"Claude!"

She stared at him. "Oh—hi . . ." she managed.

Then she was in his arms, her face against his jacket. Her body shook. He hoped she would cry, but only long dry sobs came. He held her close, his face against her hair, her body light as a wing; the sweetness became part of his agony.

Perhaps too close. She straightened, pushing him gently away. "Oh, Hutch, I'm glad to see you. I didn't think I could face this place. I'm being silly. I know it was a mistake. A terrible mistake. Mr. Vallon wasn't there. But I know he would never have . . ."

She could still defend Marc. And the night clerk's greedy eyes matched his ears.

"Where the hell have you been?" He had not meant to let his anger, born of love, show.

Her head came up like a young colt's. "What does that mean?"

"Don't you know that no girl runs around Paris by herself at this hour?"

"I wasn't by myself. I was . . ." She took an unsteady step toward a chair and sat down, her face as white as her dress.

"When have you eaten?"

"I had coffee and one of those half-curled rolls."

"When?"

"I don't remember." Her head dropped back against the chair.

"Okay. We eat." He whirled on the intently watching night clerk. "Will you for God's sake give me the key to this young lady's room so I can get her coat?"

The little man snapped his bow tie secure. It was not the way things usually went in the lobby of the Hotel Maratte, but then these were Americans. He handed Hutch the key.

He took her to one of the few good places he knew that stayed open all night. On the Champs Elysées, it catered to an after-theater crowd and remained open until August 15 for the rich tourist trade. It was elegant, expensive and the tables of hard-eyed, middle-aged sybarites looked up curiously at the pale girl in her raincoat and the grim-faced man. But the maître d' knew better.

"Certainly, Mr. Hutchins. Mr. Vallon's table is available."

Claude gnawed on a finger-sized hard roll. The color was coming back to her face.

"Mr. Vallon's table?"

"Not by choice. But we both need food. And it'll be all right here. I'm ordering you white wine and hot soup first. Drink both slowly."

She sat back in the secluded alcove, her eyes roaming the room, her lips parted. There was no doubt of her capacity for enjoyment. She reveled in each new experience.

"He really sits here?"

Hutch already regretted his choice. He waited until the wine and soup were served, ordered the remainder of the dinner, and leaned forward.

"Okay, what happened?"

"Well, it was awful. I just walked up and down and up and down, and that awful woman wouldn't tell me anything. Then I found out that Mr. Vallon was away, which she could have told me in a second, and so I left. But I know it was some kind of mistake so I'll write him a letter and . . ."

"I'm not talking about Vallon. And, if you're interested, I don't want to talk about Vallon. What happened between three o'clock and eleven . . . ?"

"How did you know when my appointment was?"

"A little bird told me."

"Mr. Vallon, I suppose. Did you know he was away?"

"I'm asking the questions, honeybundle."

"I'm not your honeybundle."

"If you can put that featherbrain of .yours into somebody else's mind for five seconds, you might realize that you scared the hell out of me and you owe me some kind of explanation."

"I don't see why." She gulped the remaining half glass of wine down in two swallows and giggled. "But I will. I like that stuff." She pointed to the bottle.

"Good." He moved it to the far side of the table. "So where were you?"

"At the movies."

"The movies!"

"Yep." She smiled enchantingly. "The *cinéma*. I've learned that much."

"Claude. Listen to me. Even in Paris, where everybody does too much of everything, you can't stay in a movie for eight hours."

"You can if you see it through twice. And a half." She giggled. "I didn't think all that much of it anyway."

He saw that he must proceed with care. He wanted to spank her, he wanted to take her to bed, and between both ideas, he wondered privately how he had gotten himself so involved. Another of his mistakes. So here he was, back at square one.

"What was the movie?"

"The Secret something or other. It was all in French so I really didn't understand much."

He saw the light. *Le Choix Secrete*. "The Secret Choice" produced, directed, and written by Marc Vallon. One of the great man's less notable efforts of several years ago. He wondered where on earth she had found it and tried not to think of the neighborhoods she must have wandered into. The picture had played the respectable houses so long ago.

"Anyhow, I thought it was pretty silly. It was about a woman, she was sort of old but beautiful, who was married to a man and in love with another man. Anyhow, when her husband decided to divorce her and go away, she didn't want the other man. Which didn't make much sense. But I stayed twice and a half to see Mr. Vallon's name and I thought when I called him I could say I had seen his picture which would help."

Mercifully, the waiter brought the poached sole.

Hutch waited until she had eaten her way through the final chocolate nut sundae with maple sauce and whipped cream, which was not on the menu but which was eventually produced with the aid of Marc Vallon's aura.

"Claude, when do you expect to call Vallon?"

"Oh, I'll keep calling until he gets back. He can't be away for long or he wouldn't have made the appointment. I can certainly understand how an important man could be detained and maybe . . ."

"Listen to me." He saw the startled look in her eyes and hated himself. But there was no other way. "Vallon is not coming back to Paris, not for a month anyway. He never stays in Paris in August. Never. Most people don't."

"Then . . . why?" Her mouth trembled. She bit it hard.

"Why did he write that date down? God only knows. He has all sorts of ways of getting rid of girls who pester him. He probably thought that was the easiest, that you would never take it seriously."

She sat so silent, so rock-still, so pale, that he was frightened. He groped for something consoling to say and found nothing. She was fighting some sort of battle within herself, beyond him. He thought if she would burst into tears, he would put his arm around her, make plans for the week that would bring a smile. A giggle. And it would be over. He waited. She spoke at last, her voice flat but sure.

"I don't believe you." She rose and picked up the raincoat she had kept around her shoulders. "If you will tell me where he is, I'll call him and prove you're wrong. If you won't, I'll find out and call him anyway. I don't believe Mr. Vallon would do what you said. And I don't think it was very nice of you to say so."

Watched by thirty pairs of curious eyes she nodded graciously to the waiter, the maître d', and the wine steward, and marched, head high, out of the restaurant. A murmur of talk ran among the tables, a few titters, a couple of drunken, bawdy laughs. Hutch scribbled his name on the bill and wished he'd had the wit to write Vallon's instead. He flung out to the street and saw her, small in the distance, walking rapidly down the black rain-polished avenue, the brilliant lights strobelike on her small, straight figure.

He caught up with her at a traffic intersection and whirled her around by the arm.

"Now you listen to me, Claude."

"Oh, stop saying that. I've listened to you all I want. You're worse than my brother. Now hear this, hear this—I told you what I think and that's all there is to it. I'll find out where Mr. Vallon is and don't think I won't, and then . . ."

He couldn't remember being so angered by any woman. Yet he loved her. He could feel the knot twisting in his viscera.

"All right. Be my guest. So you won't have to run around Paris like a bitch in heat asking for him, I'll tell you. He's in Rome." He wrote quickly in a pocket notebook, tore off the page, and thrust it at her. "There's his number. Call him in the morning, not before eight, and ask him. He won't remember who you are, but you can tell him. My God, how you can tell him! Just don't expect it to be pleasant. I'll be around in the afternoon. By that time you might have learned a thing or two. Then I'll move you out of that fleabag of a hotel and put you on the first plane that will take you back to where you belong!"

He hailed a passing cab, half pushed her into it, and gave the driver the address and a bill. He held the door open an instant longer and refused to see the whiteness of her face.

"And that, Miss Roundtree, will be that! This is one exercise in baby-sitting I won't charge for!" He banged the door shut.

The cab started. Hutch had already turned his back and walked away. Claude remembered to put Marc Vallon's telephone number in her bag. It was what she wanted, yet it had suddenly become a detail in the enormity of the night.

Chapter Eleven

To Marc Vallon insomnia was a way of life. He had long ago adjusted to the dark, measureless hours following midnight. He had learned to let his restless mind drift in their void, peopling it with fantasies and visions he would tell no man. Often in the ashy residue of the morning he would find the ember of an idea to be fired into a new work. Sometimes he believed that he owed the best of what he did to his sleeplessness.

But in the air-conditioned stillness of his studio, the heavy velvet drapes opened to the pale Roman night, Marc Vallon was not living with fantasies. He was living with ghosts. He had not yet been able to tell Soli of the momentous finale of the picture. She had been, on the three occasions when he saw her, charming, witty, elegant—the woman he had loved so desperately, once. She was eager and full of plans to play Anatole France's superb, debauched siren. She was intelligent enough to know that to play Thaïs fully, she must play her with cynicism. She would perform a

bare-breasted Thaïs, nude in the temptation scene.
Her body was still good. She had laughed. "As you
well know, my pet."

She never spoke of Lennie. Nor did she ask about
the screening. It was as if she had closeted her emotions with the past. It would be better if she were
never to see the picture, never see Lennie's deathlike
walk to oblivion, never see the drained and aging
truth of her face, that would remain her image. But
Soli never missed a premiere. He would have to tell
her soon. He would also have to tell her he had other
plans than Thaïs. But what under heaven they were,
he had no idea.

The ghost that walked through Marc's sleeplessness
robbed him of inspiration. Leonard Ross alive had
been a thorn in his flesh; Leonard Ross dead was an
accusation. It was futile to tell himself over a desper-
ate cigarette that Lennie brought himself to that moment, that he had a death wish, that he, Marc, had
given Lennie work long past the decay of his talent.
Given Lennie work? The phrase itself was a mockery.
Lennie was Soli's lover; she needed the frail actor in a
mothering sort of way. Marc accepted that and held
the untidy structure together for the sake of his vision.
Why not? One paid for genius as one paid for success.
The weakness in any link could destroy the chain. So
he had indulged weakness for a composite strength.

In the darkness of his studio, illumined only by the
pallor of the window, Marc rose, lit a cigarette as he
did so often, crushed it, lit another. As if in the re-
newed glow he would find signs of his own humanity.
He had coddled Lennie like a son. He saw him to
sleep on more than one of Lennie's fear-wracked
nights. He ordered the capsules when Lennie could
not work without them. And he had carried premoni-

tion like a time bomb within him. Lennie saw his failure in his diminished parts. What else would a man
do? It had been inevitable.

But not quite. When Lennie began his walk to the
cliff, Marc knew. It was in Lennie's face, in the slow,
unwavering steps. Marc had watched. *Watched.* He
had not lifted a hand. He was mesmerized by a new
vision, as Lennie walked . . . walked on. . . .

The telephone rang with a scream that brought
Marc from his chair. He lit a lamp needlessly.

"Yes?" he barked.

"Good evening, chief."

"Hutch! In the name of God . . . !" He took a
short, angry breath. "Do you know what time it is?"

"Two twenty A.M. Your favorite telephone hour.
Right? How are you?"

"I'm . . . have you lost your mind?"

"No. I need to know." Hutch's voice was as pleasant
as it was restrained. Marc knew the tone.

"What is it?"

"You have a problem."

"Take care of it. You woke me out of a sound
sleep."

"Sorry, boss." The voice conveyed disbelief. "But
anyhow, I can't handle this one. She's here."

"Who?"

"Claude Roundtree."

"Who?"

"The girl from Thatcher, Connecticut, U.S.A. You
remember Thatcher?"

Marc did not answer.

"You gave her an appointment, and she kept it. As I
told you she would. She's been walking up and down
outside your apartment here in Paris for two days, not

to your credit. So in the name of charity I gave her your telephone number in Rome . . ."

"Damn it, you didn't!"

". . . so she can call you and you can do the one decent thing in your life and tell her to go home. You don't intend to see her and you can't make an actress out of her."

"You tell her."

"I have. She doesn't believe me. She thinks you're a god. At least a gentleman."

There was a pause. "When is she going to call?"

"I told her in the morning. Marc, for once in your life, do a kind, humane thing. Talk to her and tell her. She came all the way to Paris on a shoestring. Worked for every cent of it—in a cemetery."

"What?"

"Skip it. I'll look out for her in Paris, get her on the plane home. But it's up to you to put her out of her misery. Break her heart if you have to. She's been hurt already. But tell her the truth. Tell her that card you wrote for her isn't worth the paper it cost and it was only a joke."

"I don't joke."

"That's right. But tell her anyway. Marc?"

"I'll talk to her."

"And you'll make it clear to her?"

"Very." Marc hung up.

At his end, Hutch put the receiver down slowly. He had done all he could. Claude would be hurt but she could handle the truth. She was that kind of girl. His own relation with her would be solved later. First things first. Yet as he sat staring blindly at the phone, he felt a nameless dissatisfaction. It grew from Marc's voice, as if Hutch had not taken everything into account.

In his apartment in Rome, Marc turned out the lamp, returned to his bedroom, and fell heavily asleep. She had long silvery hair, he remembered. Her eyes sparkled. Or did they flash? She was young.

As Marc Vallon fell into heavy sleep, Claude woke in her narrow hotel room with a start. As always in a strange place it took a moment to orient herself, to reestablish the pattern. She remembered and jumped from the bed. The hotel, the dirty-paned window that looked out on a wall, the rattle of ash cans—Paris! This was the morning she was to call Marc Vallon in Rome. Not before eight. She checked. The number was securely in her bag. The time was five thirty-three in the morning.

But there was no more sleep for her. She would dress, have coffee at Le Hot Dog when it opened, and then find a telephone. That might take some time but she would not call from the open phone in the lobby. Not where everybody could hear. The desk clerk had made her business his every time she came in or went out.

Le Hot Dog was closed but a slit of a cafeteria further down the street was open. She slid on the one remaining stool and cast an unfocused but radiant smile around the place. The working men, who had not taken their eyes off her, returned to their coffee, a few half-smiled and felt younger. The hulk of a man in blue denim overalls on the stool next to her moved to make room.

"Coffee and a croissant, please." She smiled at the counter woman. The woman pushed the cof-

fee at her with a thick arm, slopping some of it out
of the mug without bothering to wipe it up. It was
thick and bitter. But the croissant was delicious, fresh,
flaky, and still warm. How did they do it? Whatever
the Thatcher Bakery sold as croissants were not even
cousins to these. But she wouldn't tell poor Mr. Getll
that, not with his wife in a wheelchair from arthritis.

She ordered another and sat munching dreamily on
it. The day was pregnant with significance. She had
read the phrase once and wondered whether she
would ever have such a day. Here it was. But it was
not pregnant at all. It was the turning point of her
whole life. And she was beginning it at seven on a
beautiful morning in a Paris cafeteria, eating like everybody else, as if she really belonged. She might
have lingered on, but the woman snatched the empty
coffee mug and cleared her throat. People were waiting behind her.

At Le Hot Dog they had spoken English. Here
Claude did not understand the charge. She dug into
her bag and held out a bill. The woman took it and
returned a coin. There was a growl from the heavy
man beside her. The woman glared; Claude heard a
quick interchange, and the woman dropped two more
coins on the counter. Claude picked them up hesitantly; the man nodded encouragement. She gave him
a shy smile. He took off his cap and bowed. From the
door she waved and stepped into the sunshine. He slid
his cap back on his head, wiped his mustache, and
returned to his sausage. For an instant time had
stopped, golden and still.

There was in Paris at seven fifteen on a fine morning apparently no telephone. She entered the lobby of
what looked like a hotel and came out as quickly. A
man and woman were coming down the stairs, arm in

arm, smelling of liquor. The woman said something coarse but whether it was to her or about her, Claude could not tell.

She found at last a telephone booth outside a wine shop. The receiver hung dead at the end of the cord. She studied her map. She would have to find her way to a main boulevard or she would be lost. She would also be late. The call to Marc Vallon now loomed larger even than the appointment at the Place Dauphine. She would hear his voice. It was the moment of Destiny.

Ahead a girl or a woman, she could not tell, was sweeping the sidewalk. Dark, frizzy hair, a green mini-mini skirt, and sandals that revealed dirty toenails. But she was as lithe as a willow and she looked friendly.

"*Excusez-moi . . .*" Claude bogged down once more. If she had only had the wit to practice French up there on Cemetery Hill. "If you could tell me . . ."

"Sure, what do you want to know?" The voice was solid, American midwest.

Claude didn't believe in luck exactly, but she did believe in numbers. And sometimes in stars. This was the way things could happen on a pregnant day. She glanced at the house number. Twenty-six. This was her third day in Paris. Two times six was twelve, less three made nine.

"You're an American!"

"Yep." The girl was eyeing her dress.

"I have to make a phone call. It's very important. And I can't find a telephone."

"There's one inside the shop." For the first time Claude noticed the small boutique behind them. A few cheap dresses and some black-edged lingerie were shielded by yellow plastic. "You can use it. If it's local."

"It's—to Rome."

"Rome? Italy? Sorry. Only local calls."

"Do you know where there is a phone?"

"There's one around the corner at the tobacco shop."

"In a booth?"

The girl's look was openly curious. "Yeah. In a booth, sort of. He charges ten centimes to use it, but I guess you don't mind that."

"No. Which way do I go?"

"He doesn't open until eight. Look, I don't open the shop until nine but you can come in, if you like, and wait. It's going to get hot."

Seven twenty. Forty minutes to go. Claude smiled gratefully. "I'd like to. If it isn't too much trouble?"

"What's trouble?"

She led Claude into a small dim shop with a single counter and two stiff chairs.

"I don't have the things out yet but I'll hang a few so you can see."

A thin voice shrilled from somewhere upstairs. The girl disappeared through a curtain behind the counter. Claude heard a sharp interchange in brittle French, and the girl reappeared. "That's my mother-in-law. Reminding me when we open. I told her I knew. For six years I've known. Six years. God help me. I have a pot of coffee on. Want some?"

The coffee was excellent. They exchanged names. She was Patty Brant from Duluth, Minnesota. Now Patty Lejenne, Patti's Boutique, Paris. She hung up a few dresses. Too mini for Thatcher, Claude thought, but this is Paris. She liked the long-legged girl with the wide mouth, though Patty made her feel somehow immature. The girl dropped into the other chair.

"Would you mind telling me, before I die of curiosity, why a girl like you has to call Rome, Italy, at eight in the morning? Some guy? Because if he's run out, I say let him go, sister."

"He's—he's not a guy like that. I mean—" Claude hesitated.

"Oh. He's different?" The sarcasm was open.

Claude shook her head. "It isn't that way. He's a movie producer, and I have an appointment. I mean I had and . . ." suddenly Claude wanted to talk. All these months of bottling up what was deepest inside her, even last night with Hutch who was so smart about everything except her. She wanted to sit in this cool little place so far from everything she knew and talk. Talk. "He's a movie director. A very important one. He's going to give me a screen test. He made the appointment with me for yesterday at three and then he couldn't keep it. Some important emergency or something and he had to go to Rome, and I'm to call him this morning." She stopped. The words had, in spite of her desperation to believe them, a tinny sound, unreal, worn out, as if an old-fashioned movie were played through to a predictable ending. It wasn't that way at all. It had happened. His look had told her more than his voice or even that white card. There was a shining future that she could not put into words for anyone. Talk, as she discovered once again, was never much use when you needed it most.

For a few seconds the silence lay troubled between them. Then Patty's wide mouth twisted into a half-smile.

"Sure," she said gently. "Sure. It's a break, isn't it? I was going to be a dancer, back in Duluth. I went to

Chicago. I was pretty good." She jumped up from the chair and flung her leg high above her head. "I can still do it. If any big-shot movie director had said he'd even talk to me, I'd have followed him half around the world. There was one." She was lost for a passing instant in reverie. "But I met Jacques. Ver-rry Latin. French. He promised me the world. I settled for Paris. And got a mother-in-law and a flat over the boutique, and two years later Jacques got himself killed driving ninety miles an hour. I was twenty-six. In Paris twenty-six is too old to be anything. But what you are. I couldn't go back to Duluth. I figured in Paris I might get a second chance. Or meet someone. There are no second chances, kid. Take it while you've got it. When it's the end of the line, you know it." She picked up the coffee cups. "Only don't get married. Ever. If you care about yourself, body or soul. It's a one-way street—all the way."

When she returned, she had changed her dress. "I'll walk around with you to the tobacco shop. I don't suppose there's anything you'd care to try on?"

Claude came out of her spell. "Yes. That orange dress." It was not her color but it hung like temptation on the rack. And she wanted to buy something.

"You sure?"

"Yes. If you don't mind."

In the miniscule dressing room she gazed at herself. It was the shortest dress she had ever worn. It clung to her body. It gave a color to her skin and eyes she had never seen. But it spoke Paris, and her father's gift of new bills lay untouched in her bag. Would Marc Vallon like it?

"You need more eye makeup, but it does something, that's for sure." Patty handed her the package.

The telephone at the tobacco shop was curtained

off, but it was better than a wall phone. Patty
changed several of Claude's bills into what seemed
handfuls of coins. One obstacle remained. Claude had
no idea how to make the call, and the operator lost
patience.

"Here, let me. As soon as it starts ringing I'll give
you the receiver."

It took a long time. Claude, standing outside the
curtain, watched the street come to morning life. Finally Patty brushed back the curtain. "Your number
got through. It's ringing now." She handed Claude the
receiver. "Good luck, kid. Hope the orange dress
works. If it doesn't, come back, we'll try again." She
winked and with swinging hips left the shop.

Claude listened to the ringing and felt her heart
pound. Through the half-drawn curtain she saw Patty
move down the street. A black-haired young man
stopped her. They talked. Patty bumped her hips sideways, the young man slapped her backside lightly.
Patty moved on, looking back at him once with a grin.
Patty, at thirty-two, had made her own audience.
When it no longer mattered.

Suddenly, Claude felt her mouth go dry, her hands
cold. The ringing stopped. The phone had been
picked up. She heard a faint, unmistakable "Yes?"

"Mr. Vallon?"

"Yes?"

"This is Claude Roundtree. Do you remember
me . . . ?"

It took more strength of character than Hutch
thought he possessed to wait until noon to see Claude.
But he would give her time to shed her tears, accept
her hurt, and learn to live with her own lovely, dimin-

ished image, as Claude Roundtree, Thatcher. He
would take her to the best lunch Paris offered and
then an afternoon of whatever would restore that giggle. Sight-seeing, a bicycle ride in the Bois or maybe,
hopefully, his secret urge to take her soaring. She had
the courage for it. Up there in the blue silence, she
might regain her perspective, if not her common
sense.

He smiled ruefully as he picked up the scattered,
unread newspapers. Common sense was not the quality he loved her for, though he admitted to himself if
he ever found it, it would make their relationship easier. Relationship. He disliked the word. It was cheap
and evasive. And it certainly had no bearing on
Claude and himself. The simple fact of whatever, if
anything, lay between them was that he loved her and
she—she, whenever she did look at him, saw only an
obstacle. Hardly a basis, he thought as he hunted for
his jacket, for a relationship.

It was twelve twenty when he parked his dark
green sports car in front of the Hotel Maratte and
hoped nobody would indulge in that Parisian street
pastime of scratching a line along the body paint. But
even that would not disturb him today. He whistled
"Over the Rainbow" as he pushed open the heavy
glass door.

The lobby was deserted. So was the desk. Hutch
banged on the desk bell. He banged again. At last the
day clerk emerged from the rear, wiping his chin. He
was a young man in shirt sleeves who already presented the specter of the time when the vest would be
stained, the hair gone, and the weary shoulders
hunched over the same counter. He did not like
Hutch on sight.

"You wish something, M'sieu?"

"Yes. I'm meeting Miss Claude Roundtree. Would you send someone up to tell her I'm here?"

"Round Tree?" He glanced at the row of keyhooks, shuffled through papers behind the counter. "Round *Tree*? The American girl?"

"Yes."

"She has gone."

"Did she say when she would be back?"

"She has left. Checked out. Finis! Phuit."

Hutch did not believe him. Incompetence, bred to indifference, flourished like mold in this seedy structure. He had an urge to shake a better truth from the fellow.

"When did she go out?"

"Let's see. It was before the post. About ten thirty."

"With her bag?"

"I've already told you."

"Did she leave any message?"

"What's your name?"

"Davison Hutchins."

"Ahh." The clerk shook his head as if clearing it. "Ahh, yes. I wrote it down. We do not supply stationery to guests. Here." He picked up a slip of pad paper. "If Mr. Hutchins should call, please tell him thanks for everything. I have to make the afternoon plane for Rome."

Hutch snatched the slip of paper, read it, crumpled it into his pocket, and strode out of the lobby. He was stunned, but, like ice water, it brought him to his senses. He saw with a restored clarity what he should have foreseen. He had three choices—to go home and get very drunk, to find that girl he had seen at the Revue de Paris, or to drive straight to the airport.

He swung the fast little car out of the city and for

once saw the logic of a country without strict speed laws.

The airport had the dismal conformity of a hundred others on this August afternoon. It was thronged with people, waiting, milling, seated on their bags, leaning against stark walls, or wilted into seats behind the huge plate windows, watching without seeing the great multicolored birds of space. Most of them were tourists, adrift from their moorings, sent moving like schools of fish at the loudspeaker's dehumanized commands. Expectancy for them had by now been replaced by tired feet and sweating bodies. A show of hands might have revealed that a bathtub superseded the Coliseum. Few took any notice of the intense young American girl and the ardent young man standing close to a wall and closer to each other.

"Hutch, there's no use being angry. You told me what would happen. You said call Mr. Vallon and find out for yourself. And I did. He couldn't have been nicer. He knew me right away and apologized for missing my appointment and said it was unavoidable, and I could certainly understand that. And he said to come to Rome as soon as I wanted and call him from the airport when I arrived and he'd have somebody meet me and find me a place to stay. And he would make up for his discourtesy. So I decided to go right away and I was lucky to get a seat, and I wouldn't have except the woman ahead of me in line remembered she hadn't called her neighbors to take care of her parakeet, and I got her place. And if there's anything wrong with that, Hutch, you'd better tell me and stop just being annoyed about everything. You must have known it would happen this way when you gave me Mr. Vallon's phone number, didn't you? So what's wrong?" She looked lovely in a dark brown linen skirt and jacket. The pale blue scarf gave a blush to her face. He stepped back as if from a danger zone.

"Have you said everything?"

"I haven't anything to say. It's you."

"Oh. My turn now?"

"What time is it?"

"You'll make the plane. I'll guarantee that. I wouldn't be surprised if you piloted it. Claude . . ."

"Don't say it, Hutch!"

"I haven't said anything yet."

"Don't say 'listen to me.' Because I have. I've listened to every word you've ever said to me and it's always made me miserable."

"Try this." He took a slow breath. "I love you."

The pinkness faded from her face. Her mouth opened in a silent O. He waited for the giggle. It did not come.

"*Love* me? I mean right here—in the middle of all this?"

"It isn't the place I'd choose, and I have a limited vocabulary . . ."

"But you can't!" It was more of a wail than a denial.

"I tell myself that. In fact I've labeled the whole operation Mission Not Even Impossible. Just mad."

"But it isn't. I mean possible or impossible. You've gotten me all mixed up. But don't you see it spoils everything?"

"Yes. I can see that."

"I mean how could I—I mean love anybody and have my whole career ahead?"

"I wasn't thinking of the general public." He wanted to leave now. He had not intended to say what he did. It was an indication of weakness, and he had fought weakness of any sort all his life. "Better think about that plane, baby."

Her eyes were too bright. She seemed reluctant. "It's the nicest thing anybody ever said to me. I'll think about it a lot. All the way to Rome. But I've got to dedicate myself to my career, haven't I?"

"Dealer's choice. I wanted you to know. Now I advise you to forget it." He picked up her tote. "Time to go."

She walked beside him silently to the gate. She turned to him. "Hutch. . . ." She kissed him on the cheek and fled. Thistledown.

He did not watch the plane take off. Before the next week was out, Marc Vallon would summon him to Rome. He remembered the tremor in her voice. He wondered if he could endure it.

Chapter Twelve

Solveg dropped the telephone into its gilt cradle, glanced at her dressing table mirror and realized that she could no longer afford anger. It settled like a weight on her face. She forced a smile, pushed her cheeks upward, and walked impatiently past the glass from the room.

It was the third time within the week she had phoned Marc and received no answer. He would not leave Rome without telling her. She knew he was already thinking about their next picture and he liked to be left alone in these early, formative days. He had not even reported to her on the screening, which meant he was pleased with it. She would not call him again. He would come to her when he was ready, for the simple reason that he could find no other actress of her talents to play Anatole France's ravishing courtesan. Or at her fees. The film would depend on her. She could afford to wait.

Nonetheless she moved restlessly down the marble

stairs, across the shaded loggia, and into the privacy
of the small park enclosed within the villa's walls.

Solveg's villa was her enduring extravagance. Like
so many houses within the city its exterior revealed
nothing to passersby but a heavy door flush with the
street. An overhead lantern and inconspicuous black
doorbell were its only ornaments. A lion-headed
knocker had been removed during troubled times and
not restored. Once inside the outer door, opened by a
crippled war-veteran porter, the visitor crossed a dim
vestibule to a second door of carved oak. A bellpull
brought a heavy black-garbed woman who ushered
the visitor into a wide reception hall tiled in watery
shades of green. There he could gaze out through the
rear on the miracle of Rome's luxurious private life:
An inside park, lush with grass, sculptured yews, cy-
prus and acacia trees, dancing fountains, and an aqua-
marine teardrop of a pool at the center.

To Solveg this villa was the core of her life. Any
crass beginnings could be forgotten. Any failures, dis-
appointments, or reminders of time's passing were
banished. Here among the trees and walks, the
beauty, the exuberance, the passions of youth were
caught and imprisoned in marble.

Solveg could not now afford any of it. But as she
told the wet-lipped lawyer with the black beard who
called on her regularly, the day she lost her villa she
would kill herself. He assured her that Rome was too
proud of its American-born star to risk that. He would
call again. That had been the uneasy status quo for
several years.

What she needed was a new triumph, a personal
triumph.

And solace. She had already come to the conclusion
that she would forgive Hutch for the miserable yet

somehow titillating little episode in Capri and that suitable time had elapsed to allow him to regret it. She needed him as she had once needed Lennie. Handled skillfully, Hutch could be made to realize it. Even his rejection of her had had a primitive virility to which she responded.

They would soon be together for the filming of Thaïs. Marc talked about a site near ancient Alexandria. Hot days, torpid nights. The Alexandrian whore wore little. Solveg's mind ran like a mouse in a cage, seeking an exit.

What had happened, had happened. She would not even admit to a curiosity about the finished screening. A film finished was a year gone, and a year gone was a narrowing of life. She had long ago disciplined herself never to look back. Only by thinking a future, could there be one. It was a future that kept a woman young, never the past. However shocking the tragedy of the film's finale, Solveg Traner the actress, could harden herself to see it as her triumph. Late at night, in the secrecy of her room, she would mourn Lennie with abandon.

But it was not enough.

She made one circuit of her private park, and with it, one decision. She returned to her room. To her surprise her phone call was answered almost at once.

"Hutch, darling!" Men had found that throaty urgency irresistible.

A slight pause. "Hi, Soli."

The flatness dismayed her. She wanted to be casual.

"I wasn't sure I'd reach you in Paris. Marc hasn't called you yet?"

"Why should he?"

She had expected abruptness. It was part of the

challenge. But here was a quality she could not identify, an icy remoteness, an anger. "He will, of course.
He's already busy on the plans for the Thaïs film.
We're thinking of calling it *Cross of Desire*. How do
you like it? If you don't, say so. I'm giving a little
party to announce it. I do need your help. Do you
think you could come down, perhaps by tomorrow?"

Again the odd delay. "Have you seen him?"

"If you mean Marc, I told you he's working. I'm
resting. Please come, Hutch." The celebrated voice
carried a faint tremor of promise.

"I've been thinking about it."

"Marvelous, darling."

"Yep. Real dandy. Bye, Soli."

She heard the receiver's click. He had been so terse,
so noncommittal that she wondered if he had been
drinking. Maybe he had a girl with him. Maybe—her
smile was slow and lingering—maybe what that young
man needed most was a little capable understanding.

The heavy woman in the black dress stood in the
open doorway. "Signorina?"

"Not now, Rosa." This was the hour in which she
was never to be disturbed. But Solveg knew she could
never manage servants. She had worked too long and
too hard herself. She felt a kinship with them. At
times they gave her the only warmth she knew. "Well,
what is it?"

"There is a lady to see you."

"Tell her. . . ." She rarely had women callers. "Oh,
tell her anything."

"She is an American. She did not give me her name.
I showed her into the loggia."

"Must I, Rosa?"

The heavy eyes warmed. Rosa understood with
earthy common sense, the sudden retreats of this bril-

liant, tumultuous woman. A little girl left alone too
long.

"Brush your hair, *cara mia.*" She picked up a gold-
colored ribbon from the dressing table. "I will bring
tea out to the garden."

With her hair caught back, her feet in gold sandals,
her body free in a togalike sweep of natural linen, Solveg knew she looked well. She was not sorry.

Julia Orlini rose from a white wicker chair.

Marc Vallon kept his word.

With some help from an English-speaking attendant
in the large bustling Leonardo da Vinci airport
Claude called the number Marc had given her. He answered promptly. More than promptly. The rich courteous tones came over the wire heady as wine. He was
delighted to hear from her. He would send a car at
once. It should not take more than a half hour. She
was to sit near the entrance of the waiting area.

A half hour seemed barely time enough to calm the
nervous throbbing inside Claude. She tried to sit back
in the plastic chair, watch the crowds, and think
about nothing. But she discovered she had already become used to airports. She could think of nothing but
that voice. It somehow blended in her mind with the
look he had given her the day she first met him. Yet
what kept her heart pounding was the exquisite courtesy, as if she were already important, as if—her face
grew warm—as if she were already a star and he was
the beseecher. She would try to be cool and very calm
and dignified.

She was as sure as she was of the fate that had
brought her to this moment that all of them—Hutch,
her father, and the hinters in Thatcher—were wrong
about Marc Vallon. He was a genius and he was also a

gentleman. Even his voice had a nobility. She wondered if he came from some ancient, titled family, if he had to endure for the sake of his work what others did around him. She felt she could do and be anything under his guidance.

A man in livery bowed directly in front of her.

"Miss Roundtree?" His accent was thick. "I am Mr. Vallon's chauffeur." He pronounced it oddly. "The car is ready."

Claude nodded graciously and slung her tote over her shoulder. The car was not all that she had anticipated. She slid into the short, squat interior, and as she settled down she glanced at the rearview mirror, and met the eyes of the chauffeur. They were expressionless. In a way she could not explain they chilled her. She turned her face to the window and watched a strange new landscape take shape.

The long summer twilight was draining away as they approached the city. The remnant of light deepened the earth tones of the houses, the walls, the ancient buildings, but lingered on the new high rises. The chauffeur suddenly spoke, pointing a blunt thumb toward the horizon where a pale bubble hung. "San Pietro."

She understood. The dome of St. Peter's, the greatest of all basilicas, said to be able to contain within its walls any other cathedral in the world. She had read that much in the tourist literature on the plane before her thoughts had turned inward again. She wondered now if she would see any of this unreal, dusk-wrapped city. She would not expect it. She was not a tourist. She had come for one purpose. The idea in itself gave an edge to her excitement.

To her surprise the car stopped with a jolt of brakes in a narrow street, not much more than an alley at home. The chauffeur helped her out, swung her bag out of the trunk, and carried it to a doorway in a row of gray buildings. He pushed the door open, handed her a key, and bowed. "Mr. Vallon will call you tomorrow."

She heard the car depart. Ahead lay a small dim vestibule and a flight of narrow stairs. The tag on the key bore the number 2B. Not a sound reached her from anywhere in the building. Claude was not susceptible to panic but something unnerving fingered her throat. Move, she told herself, move. She picked up her bags and climbed the stairs. 2B was at the rear. She thrust the key into the door. It opened easily. She stepped into a studiolike room of whitewashed walls and modern metal furniture. A single lamp was lit and a white blind was drawn down against the single window. A table held a pottery bowl of fresh fruit.

Someone must have been living there. Someone must have set it in order. She discovered a closetlike bathroom with fresh towels, a gas range hidden behind a screen of slatted natural wood and a half-size refrigerator stocked with milk, eggs, cheese, and bread. The clothes closet was empty, as were the drawers of a chest. A double bookshelf was crammed with paperback editions. Italian, French, and a language she could not identify. No English. The baleful vacant eyes of a small TV set stared from a tripod. She turned a switch. It jumped dizzily to life in ripples of orange and green accompanied by an hysterical, foreign voice. She turned it off.

It was then that the silence engulfed her. It pulsed from the walls. It stifled all sense of time. It blotted out past and future and closeted her in a strange vacuum. She had an impulse to run down into the street. To knock on another apartment door. But she knew she would do neither. This is what Marc Vallon had arranged. If his intentions meant anything, it meant this, too. She would have to wait. But even as she listened, the silence swallowed his face and voice. She was alone.

She fought back a tremor of panic. She hung up her dresses, kicked off her shoes, and brushed her hair. None of it took long. She was not hungry. She had eaten on the plane. She would write home but there was no paper. At the bottom of her bag she came on the suede-bound booklet Willard had given her. "If you ever want to talk to anyone. . . ."

She carried it to a chair. Blank pages, one after another. Like the hours of this trip. She had done nothing yet. She had accomplished nothing. She had not one thing to write down. Paris. Rome. Names of soaring magic. She had not even seen them. Worse still she felt no different this moment than if she were sitting in her own room at home. Except that at home there would be sounds, quick steps, a door slamming, her mother calling.

She came to the last page and saw Willard's stiff old-fashioned writing. For an instant it was like an arm around her shoulders. She remembered. He had copied something for her from an old diary. Something written long ago. The words were as old-fashioned as the handwriting. But she read them.

When you have spent your silvered days in flight
And taken measure of the flowing tide,
When you have climbed the distant unguessed
    height,
And found the beckoning sky not yet too wide.

When you have known the sting of foreign wind
And crossed an ancient threshold with no door,

And longed to read a stranger's tongue and mind,
But unread travelled to a further shore.

There is a star, the sailors call it true,
Hung fixed above this planet through its night.
By day unseen, but to the heart in view,
Like love unsaid, until the need for light.

Think on it when you turn your face away,
Look back, my love, and share with me one day.

Below it Willard had written: "Henrietta Roundtree,
April 1899."

The book slid to the floor, leaving the silence unbroken. Claude shut her eyes against a sudden stinging. How dare they? How dare anyone reach into her like this, as if she were never to be free, never to find her own way? She snatched a pear from the bowl of fruit, bit it savagely, and had trouble swallowing. She loved them all. Wasn't that enough?

"I won't have it! I won't. I hate you for interfering, for not letting me . . ." But it was not at the little book or the firm, loving hand she raged. "You're spoiling everything, Hutch!"

The tears spilled, and she let them come. She would not admit even to herself the secret comfort of using his name.

Claude awakened next morning to a sense of panic. It was ten o'clock. No call had come. Sparse daylight found its way into the flat. When she lifted the blind on the blank wall she saw a steady rain falling. She found orange juice and coffee and a hard Italian roll. She heard a rattle of cans from the alley below, an occasional high-pitched bleat of a car horn, and once voices on the stairs. Then nothing. She would not give way to emotions. She would drip-dry her dresses, wash her hair, tidy the neat flat, think about her career, and wait. When the call came she would be ready, poised, calm, almost indifferent. She would tell Mr. Vallon she had spent the time concentrating.

At three o'clock the telephone rang. She leaped to it.

"Hi. How are you?"

Claude gasped. That voice, as if nothing had happened, as if . . .

"Hutch! What are you doing here?"

"Same thing you are, waiting for the master's voice."

"Hutch, I can't talk to you. I absolutely can't! I'm expecting Mr. Vallon's call . . . how did you know where I am?"

"Old hunting territory."

"What?"

"Nothing. This *is* Mr. Vallon's call. He wants to see you at three thirty. He is sending his car. Unless just possibly you prefer the pleasure of my much-in-demand company."

"How did you get to Rome so fast?"

"Ferry flight. I picked up a job. I'm a damn good pilot which you didn't know. Well, which is it?"

The ground was unsteady beneath her. She wanted to see him after all this loneliness. Yet he always upset her. He made her feel uncomfortable. She would arrive at Mr. Vallon's studio awkward, unsure, and then what? It could all be over if she took the wrong step. She thought of Patty sweeping the street in front of her store. She saw Ariel in her dull house in Thatcher. And she remembered her own anger last night.

"I prefer the car."

There was a slight pause. "Right." The words came from a distance, chill, impersonal. "The car will be there in ten minutes. Mr. Vallon does not like to be kept waiting." He hung up.

She sensed the finality of a decision.

When the car arrived she was on the sidewalk waiting. She avoided the lingering, expressionless glance of the chauffeur. She nodded a quick "Hi" and settled into the corner to watch the strange streets go by. Her flat must have been very close to Mr. Vallon's, for in a matter of minutes, the car drew up to a tall ornate building overlooking a park. The rain had stopped. A lemon sunlight filtered through the clouds. It was a good omen.

Marc Vallon himself opened the door of the fourth-floor apartment. He wore a dark blazer, and a knotted silk scarf of pale blue that heightened the lightness of his extraordinary eyes. He bowed over her hand, his rich voice encompassing her.

"How kind of you to come, Miss Roundtree. How patient you have been. You have dedication, the first mark of talent. We should work well together."

Claude stared at the velvet hangings, the white fur rugs, the couch with its fling of zebra pelt, and the narrow gilt columns on either side of a slightly raised platform at the end of the room. And found her voice.

"I'll work very hard, Mr. Vallon. I promise you."

The door closed softly behind her.

Whatever happened in the rest of her life, Claude told herself, she would never forget that first afternoon in Marc Vallon's studio. The dreamlike opulence, the faint musk fragrance, the lemon light that filled the room, brightened then faded to a spun-gold twilight. And the quiet. As if the walls had the thickness of eternity, separating her from everything she had been or known.

She sat stiffly on the edge of a deep white chair. He took an easy posture on a divan opposite her.

"You must tell me first, Miss Roundtree, what you know about acting."

"I don't know all that much, Mr. Vallon. I mean—well, I have read a book."

He smiled, his eyes fixed on her. "That's a beginning. What did you read?"

"I—I don't know really." She groped. Why hadn't she studied harder and remembered?

"Come. We must talk together if we are to work together."

"Well, I read about attitudes. I mean about practicing attitudes toward *things*. I did try. But I guess I wasn't very good at it. I really don't feel very strongly toward tables and chairs. A table is sort of there, don't you think? I just couldn't get mad at it."

She had said more than she intended, which was always her trouble. She had probably ruined her chances. She withdrew deeper into the chair. To her surprise he threw back his head and laughed. She had never imagined the great Marc Vallon laughing. Yet here he was, as if they were old friends.

"I quite agree with you, Miss Roundtree. I approach the same problem, rather differently. Let me explain."

The lemon light deepened. The sonorous voice flowed on around her, a river of images that she could barely snatch before they slid into something else. She found herself curled into the depth of the chair, her feet under her, her shoes dropped to the floor.

"And that is what I work for, Miss Roundtree. The complete freeing of the imagination. For that is the ultimate power of the human mind, the source of all its achievement. It alone distinguishes us from the lower forms. Perhaps a dog, a horse, even a plant can laugh or weep, if we could hear them. But the imagination, that is ours alone, to make of life anything we will. The supreme human gift that alone can create art."

He paused. The silence vibrated. His light eyes drifted over her.

"It is very simple," he continued. "No black magic. You learn to let go of yourself. You do not think of who you are, how you look, what you wear, or even your own body. You forget old rules and out-worn ideas. You let your imagination guide you. You learn to trust it. How you learn it is my job. So we shall try."

He smiled and rose. Claude found her shoes. She had not understood all that he had said. Not even half of it. But she felt alive, tingling, and nearer to Destiny than her life had ever brought her. The golden light was fading.

"I believe you want a screen test?"

Claude heard her own heart thudding. "Yes."

"I think it can be arranged but I should prefer to work with you first. I shall be leaving Rome at the end of the month. Before that I could arrange time—" He looked at her closely, almost fatherly, she thought. "Do you have funds to stay in Rome?"

"I think so." She would not burden him with that.

"Do you find the little flat comfortable?"

"Oh, yes."

"It is my guest room. I cannot abide to have people living with me. While you are here, the flat is yours."

"Oh, Mr. Vallon."

"Of course if you prefer a place of your own choice?"

"No, it's wonderful. I'm terribly grateful."

"Gratitude is a demeaning attitude, Miss Roundtree. And always difficult to define. We work together. Shall we say, two thirty on Saturday? I will send Carlo for you."

She barely heard her own thank-you or the door close. The old building boasted a gilded elevator but she sped down the granite steps as if they were new grass.

Carlo and the car were waiting. She discovered that the ride took only seven minutes. She would buy a street map and she would walk. Again she avoided the chauffeur's expressionless glance.

The flat, so strange this morning, had a warm familiarity on her return. She made two discoveries. She was very hungry. And she longed to tell somebody of the afternoon, the excitement flooding through her. She wanted to tell Hutch how wrong he had been, how right she had been. All along.

The telephone remained silent.

Marc Vallon pulled the thick drapes across the faded sky. Day's end could always bring him to depression. She was too young, virginal he guessed, an echo of a lost sweetness that would never come again. Seduction and its trappings were as stale as dust. This girl would not be seduced. She would respond like a flower and be as easily bruised. What did he want of her? Talent? He could find enough of that. He would be surprised if she showed even a glimmer.

He turned on a lamp and went out. Walking swiftly he entered the vast park that spread beyond Rome's cherished Pincio. He knew it as he knew his own hand. He walked here often and alone, through the pines, wrestling his demon. But it was too late even for that. He had known love and its imitations. He had known success and failure. There was time now only for success.

A girl passed him and smiled. He bowed with a courtesy that put distance between them. He saw Claude, curled tight and silvery, in his chair. Even as his demon mocked him, he knew he wanted to see her there again. He wondered when he could take her out to dinner—without frightening her.

Chapter Thirteen

Claude stood stiffly on the shallow platform in the softly lit studio. She wore a trailing mauve chiffon gown and her voice rose unsteadily. "You want to see me burn. But if I go through the fire with my heart . . ." she stopped. "I didn't get it right, did I, Mr. Vallon?"

"No, but go on, go on." He flipped an impatient hand. He was seated in a deep chair halfway across the room, elegant, remote, a mysterious figure who seemed to be guiding her with invisible strings.

"I can't."

"What does that mean?"

"It means I can't go on if I'm not getting it right. I just haven't got these lines straight. I've worked on them every morning but people don't talk like that. Not anybody I ever knew."

"That's a pity. All right, we'll start again. Now move a little. You're young, a little frightened. Perhaps you're thinking of a young man you loved once, far away at home."

She moved to the edge of the platform and caught her reflection in the tall Venetian mirror.

"I look silly." Actually she looked exquisite, more spirit than girl in the trailing bluish chiffon that clung to her like twilight smoke.

His face was stern. "You chose it, I didn't."

"But I'm supposed to be Joan of Arc talking to the bishops. Why couldn't I stay the way I was?"

"Because then you would have been Claude Roundtree talking to me. I gave you a choice of anything you saw in the closet."

"You told me to take something that didn't have anything to do with the part I was going to play. I did. But how can I act Joan when I know I look like this? It's silly, Mr. Vallon!"

No one had ever said quite that to Marc Vallon. He smiled.

"If you would remember to call me Marc instead of Mr. Vallon, you might not be so afraid of trying. But I think we've had enough for today."

"No. Please. I'll try once more."

He shook his head. "Come sit down here beside me. We'll talk."

She sat down on an ottoman opposite him, hugging her knees, dejectedly. Her hair fanned across her face almost within reach of his hand.

"Do you remember what I said to you, Claude, the first time you came here?"

"Yes." Would she ever forget one living second of these magic days?

"Do you remember what I said about imagination?" His fingers stiffened against an impulse to touch her hair.

"Of course I do." She swung around on the ottoman and leaned toward him. "You said imagination was ev-

erything. It was the—the power of life. And whatever
we imagined was more important than anything we
saw or heard around us."

"Good. Very good. And do you remember why I
asked you to change into something different every
time you came?"

"So I'd never feel like me. I'd forget all about me,
even the clothes I was wearing, because it had nothing to do with the part I was really playing in my
mind." She sighed. "I blew it, didn't I?"

"Not at all. It takes time to free yourself. You're
doing very well. In spite of your discomfort."

"I'm not uncomfortable. Honestly. I love it. And the
clothes are neat. I just have to learn to forget them as
if I weren't wearing anything, right?"

She was so guileless he wondered if she was mocking him. She was what? Seventeen, eighteen? His
years lay like a brand on his mind. What would she
say to forty? To forty-two?

He smiled. "Only if it suits you."

She giggled. She felt happier now. The strangeness
had evaporated. She did not want the hour to end.
"What should I wear the bikini for?"

"What would you say to Juliet?"

She burst into laughter artless and free. "I know
what Miss Blake would say. We did that at Thatcher
High, and Cynthia Wilson played Juliet. She certainly
would have looked better in a bikini than in the old
granny gown her mother dug up for her. When she
said 'Romeo, Romeo,' Buddy Jensen climbed up the
stepladder and it broke, and he grabbed her sleeve
and tore it, and her mother was furious because it was
a family heirloom or something."

"What did you play in that production?"

"In *Romeo and Juliet* I didn't. It was the senior

class, and I was only a sophomore. The next year Miss Blake wanted to give *Midsummer Night's Dream* so everybody could be in it—she thinks like that, sort of big . . ."

"What was your part in that?"

"A mustard seed or something. Miss Blake said I did it very well, even if I had only one line. But if you ask me, she gave me such a small part because a long time ago she had a crush on my brother John, and when he didn't pay any attention to her, she sort of cooled it. Imagine! He was still in college and she was over thirty. Thirty-five, some people said. But I went to her anyhow to take some acting lessons. After you gave me your card."

She met his eyes. They were so serious she wondered if she had offended him. She had talked too much.

"I guess it's time for me to go."

He rose. "I think so. Even imagination can be over-used. Are you hungry?"

"That's the first time you ever asked me that. I'm always hungry. Isn't that awful? I guess it's because my mother used to say I'd never get any flesh on my bones, so she'd feed me a lot. I never did, anyway."

"I wouldn't worry about it. I think your bones are quite admirable. I'm hungry, too. Suppose we do something about it?"

She caught her breath. Was he asking her out? This famous, distinguished man whose name was on movie screens and who had begun to fill her days like the hugeness of the moon she had once seen in a space picture.

"Would you have dinner with me, Miss Roundtree?"

"I'll change in a sec!"

She hardly noticed where the cab took them. She

was grateful that Carlo with his fixed eyes was not driving them. She sat stiffly in the cab hardly willing to believe that Marc Vallon sat beside her, handsome, courteous, as if she had been nobility, and real. As real as the magnetism of his look, his presence.

"Have you been to Trastevere, Claude?"

"What's that?"

"It's an area across the Tiber. Excellent small restaurants. Trattoria they're called. There's one I like in particular."

She was too quiet.

"Tell me, what have you seen of this marvelous city?"

"Nothing, really. In the morning I've studied my lines. And in the evening. In between, I've seen—you."

He looked at her for a long moment.

"I don't think I realized that." He paused, his voice deepened. "Rome must be seen. More than that, it must be imagined." Her face was turned toward him. He searched it. "It will be my pleasure."

Solveg tossed her gloves, handbag, and raincoat on the chair. She hated summer travel, and the flight back from Paris had been worse than usual. Tourists, crying babies at the airport, and every seat around her taken in first class. The man seated ahead had mistaken her for someone else. It was possible, of course, with her hair in a turban and her enormous sunglasses. Still—still she was glad to be home. Here she was safe, here she was Solveg Traner.

She had very little time now to change. She had called him from the airport. He would be here in less than half an hour. She had to look better than this.

Rosa picked up her things and stood waiting.

"Rosa, I am expecting a visitor at six. Tell Anina she may bring me a light supper in my room at eight."

Anina, Rosa's niece, a young untrained girl, giddy as a mite, was one of Solveg's small charities.

"I will bring it myself, Signorina."

"Where is Anina?"

"Out. Out. Every day this week that fool Carlos has been here, sniffing like a skinny little bull. Every day she goes off with him. I tell her he is no good. He will never be anything but a chauffeur with a hole in his pocket. For good money to pour through like dirty water. But I will see to her. Come. I will run your bath, *cara mia*. You are tired."

Did it show that much? She dismissed Rosa, bathed, and dressed quickly, nothing elaborate, just something soft, simple. She would be businesslike; she would not let him know the depth of the wound. Or that for her, survival was now the only issue.

And she would keep him waiting. That would be a slight return for the kiss she had begged for and received high above the sea at Capri. She could despise him now, and that in itself made it easier. He could be managed better with arrogance than gratitude.

She brushed her hair out full and applied a skilled makeup. She liked the result but she was ready ten minutes too early. Ten minutes to think about her trip to Paris. Ten minutes to remember what she had seen.

Instead she found herself thinking of the girl Anina. How simple life could be if one had only to toss one's head and run off to a night of dancing. Or love. The girl could not be more than sixteen. What did Carlos want? What did any man want? Youth. Forgetfulness. And another night. She had offered that herself once. Long ago. She would remember that. And not what she had seen in Paris.

* * *

Hutch sat at an outdoor table of the crowded street café on the Via Veneto and watched them pass, the fashionable and the unfashionable, the lovely, the lecherous, the curious, the indifferent, the staring, and the self-conscious—drawn like lemmings to this avenue of fashion and money, as if by breathing it they could share it. He rarely came here but he found himself, these days, seeking crowds. For body warmth? As a wall against himself? Or merely to postpone a very obvious decision?

He pushed the stale questions away, sipped a third Scotch, and considered motivation. He clearly lacked it. He had lacked it all his life. Or he would not be sitting here, intending to chuck the best job he had ever had and getting quietly drunk. He had not accomplished even that. He was as clear-minded and cold-eyed as a trout who had seen the hook in the bait.

Motivation. What the hell was it besides what a man wanted and couldn't have? Claude had motivation. God, did she! The motivation of a spitball the batter never saw. Marc had motivation. In one word. Marc. No problem there. It cleared away all scruples, all doubts. For Marc. But this was something else.

From his pocket Hutch pulled a crumpled piece of paper, the message he had found waiting earlier at his hotel. He had decided to ignore it. Good-bye to all that. Then he decided he would think about it. He smoothed the slip of paper. "Please come at six. I must talk to you. Soli." He finished the Scotch, pushed an extravagant tip under the plate, and hailed a cab.

Motivation. He wondered about hers.

Solveg greeted him as if she were conferring a favor, with no hint of the desperation he had read be-

tween the words of her message. She led him into the
small private sitting room that Marc had once labeled
the ossuary. It was crowded with mementos of Soli.
Pictures of Soli and Marc, Soli and Lennie, Soli, Marc
and Lennie, Soli in costume, Soli boarding a ship, Soli
debarking from a plane, Soli with the famous and not
so famous and innumerable, no-longer-identifiable
faces inscribed to Soli with love, to Soli in admiration
and, rashly, to Soli whom I shall never forget.

It was a room without windows. As Hutch knew,
one curtained wall led onto a stage that opened on the
long formal drawing room. Soli entertained lavishly
and when she did, her performers would come
through this room, out onto the stage, trailing clouds
of Soli's glory, he thought wryly. Tonight the drapes
were drawn shut. A bowl of fresh shell-pink roses
stood beneath a painting of Soli. The room became a
shrine.

"A drink, Hutch?"

"I assumed this was business."

Her laugh was forgiving. In the skillfully shaded
lamps she looked not much more than—he had long
ago given up rash judgments. He had to remember
she was a superb actress.

"I've been to Paris, Hutch."

He sensed rather than heard an ominous thread in
the meeting. Her voice continued, light, pleasant, a
beautiful and obedient instrument.

"Julia Orlini came to see me. Absolutely distraught
about her son, Nick. You remember. He was injured
when his car drove over . . ." she broke off with a
quick gesture. "Brain damage. Julia heard of a clinic
in Zurich and she took him there. The doctors said the
only way she could help him was to leave. You can
imagine, after two years of total devotion . . ."

It was not the point of the story, but Soli had her own methods. Hutch waited.

"So I thought she needed diversion. The fashion showings are on in Paris. The new things. St. Laurent. Balenciaga. Bohan. We were hopelessly extravagant, although Julia still orders everything in gray. With her jewels, I don't wonder. She's begun to wear them again." She hesitated. Hutch watched her but did nothing to prompt.

"Also for diversion I arranged a little party."

She was coming to the heart of the matter.

"For a screening. *La Troisième Manon*, starring Solveg Traner." Glass seemed to crack in her voice. "Why didn't you tell me, Hutch?"

He could only be kind. "You gave a great performance, Soli."

She brushed it aside. "Hutch, he kept the cameras going. He kept them on Lennie while Lennie walked on. Walked until . . . Marc never called out, never stopped him, he just kept the cameras going . . . it's all there!"

"Soli, Soli. We were all there. It happened too fast. No one could have known."

"Marc knew. He wanted it that way. He wanted it all. And my face! He wanted his proof!" She controlled her voice but not the whitened knuckles of her twisting hands. "I loved Leonard Ross. He was weak. Too handsome. Self-indulgent. But Lennie gave me what Marc never could. How would you understand that? But Marc understood. Marc begged me to do that picture. As he begged me to do every picture he ever made. It was Solveg Traner who made him great. But he couldn't forgive me for his own failure. It's all there when Lennie died! It's all there in that hideous face that isn't mine!"

It was role-playing, Hutch knew. Soli lived so intensely within her self-image that one could never be sure at what border she left reality. Yet he felt sorry for her. Marc had been a fool not to destroy the film's ending and to start somewhere, anywhere, again. But Hutch would not defend him. He had not come here to be wracked by thoughts of Marc Vallon.

Soli stared, unseeing, at a dim corner. But her hands lay still.

"Hutch, who screamed?"

She had taken him by surprise.

"It was not my voice. It was a child's! Who was there watching? When I had insisted that no one—no one—be allowed on the set. Who was it?"

"Does it matter, Soli?"

She smiled the twisted half-smile that chilled audiences. "You needn't protect her, darling. Because I know. It was that girl with the long light hair who talked to Marc—and dangled that snake at me."

"Not at you."

She smiled again as if he were a small, nagging boy. "I saw Marc's eyes on her. Is she with him now?"

"*No!*" He cursed himself for his own revealed anger.

"Always the gallant, aren't you, Hutch? Always safely straddling your fences?"

He rose abruptly. If he stayed he would say more than he intended.

"I may be a one-man audience, Soli, but I'm not your whipping boy. If you'll excuse me. . . ."

She went to him quickly. "Darling, it was petty of me to tease you. For all I know, you may be in love with her. But you see, I know. Julia's husband went back to Thatcher—that was the name of the place, wasn't it?—and heard that the Roundtree girl, Claude—that's it, isn't it?—had come to Paris. I pre-

sume Marc brought her to Rome." He started to
speak, thought better of it. "It doesn't really matter. I
knew he had someone here. He's been completely un-
available, or I wouldn't have thought of arranging
that screening without him. And then Carlo, Marc's
chauffeur, has been here bothering my little Anina.
It's always the sign that Marc is involved, when he
drives his own car." Her face was a mask. "It won't
last. It never does. The girl will get a screen test as a
reward. And be sent packing." To his astonishment
her eyes filled. "But whatever she wants, I shall never
forgive her for that scream. A child who had never
suffered, who couldn't understand suffering. To make
a mockery of everything that I felt! And the whole
world is to hear that! Hutch . . ."

She came so close her faint scent enveloped him.
"Hutch, that film must never be released. Marc and I
will make another. We already have plans. Julia Orlini
will lend us the money. She hated it as much as I did.
The Manon must be forgotten. I want you to help me
convince Marc of that."

He took a long breath. She had played out the
scene. She had come to her point. Her motivation—
survival. Had he ever doubted it? He shook his head.

"No way, Soli. Do you think he'd ever listen to me?"

"He'd have to. It must not be released!"

"If you mean it, then you're the only one who can
persuade him."

"That means you won't help me?"

"Soli, I'm leaving Marc Vallon's employ as soon as I
can find him to tell him."

"Oh no, Hutch! No!"

"Oh yes. In fact mentally I've already left. It's a
matter of picking up what he owes me."

"He won't let you go."

"He hasn't a choice. I can't fight a man with one arm shackled."

The stricken look in her eyes faded, leaving a metallic glitter. He had seen that expression before, a warning.

"It's the girl, isn't it?"

He forced a laugh. "You think too much, Soli. Sorry I can't help you. I wouldn't worry about the Manon. It might be the greatest scene you ever played."

"That's for me to decide, darling."

The visit was over. They were still enemies. Nothing had changed. And yet everything had. For now there was Claude.

A fine rain had begun to fall. Hutch turned up his collar and hurried through the dark, deserted street. Claude. Much as she had hurt him, he believed in her innocence because he had to. But for the first time he felt something bordering fear.

When he reached his hotel room, he called her.

There was no answer.

For Claude time had changed its shape and meaning. Dream-laden, mist-edged one day, blurred the next. Marc had taken charge of them, beginning with their first supper at the trattoria. Famous as he was, they had been left alone at a corner wooden table, lit only by a candle in a fat bowl. He had talked intimately, brilliantly, of places and people, names she had heard only dimly. Now he was making her a part of that distant, shimmering world. His light eyes left her only to refill his glass with the pale wine he called Lacrima Christi. Tears of Christ, he explained and smiled at her surprise. The vines grew where Christ had shed tears for the wickedness of Naples. She imagined telling them *that* in Thatcher. But she was learning rapidly how much of the world lay beyond Thatcher. He had not refilled her glass; he urged nothing on her. He seemed hardly to expect her to speak, merely grateful that she was sitting beside him, listening, in the circle of dim light. Within that circle she noticed how much younger he looked.

That night she had written home. ". . . and everything is marvelous. I'm working hard at learning lines. Mr. Vallon says I am to have my screen test very soon. Keep your fingers crossed. Love, Claude (the new movie actress!)"

Imperceptibly the change had come. He walked with her up the Pincio and found a pine tree under which they could sit while he heard her lines. He drove her, one fresh morning, to a place of sweeping lawns and sparkling fountains and, surprisingly, produced a hamper lunch. He sprawled beside her on the grass, his light eyes on her, as she struggled with her lines.

"I can get it right. But I think she's silly."

"Why?" He toyed with the ends of her long, silken hair.

"Because if she really hates him all that much why doesn't she just walk out?"

"She doesn't hate him. She hates the life he has put her into, like a doll in a dollhouse."

"Then why doesn't she tell him so? All this fuss over a silly letter, too. If I didn't like where I was, I'd just say so and go."

"I'm sure you would." He let her hair slide from him. "But then you wouldn't have a play, would you?" His laugh was boyish. "You'll understand Nora someday. But enough for today. Come!" He sprang to his feet, held out his hand. She took it. He pulled her up

toward him. It was the first time he had touched her.
It was as casual as a sigh. She was suddenly conscious of
herself and the flush in her face.

They walked slowly through the gardens, through
the maze of hedges and clipped trees. She had
no idea where she was or even of the gravel beneath her feet. She was aware only that he had gently
taken her hand again and her fingers were curled
around his. The blue arch of the sky was not wide
enough to contain the tremulous new pulse within
her.

The hour passed. In silence he drove her to her flat.
"Tomorrow at three," he said curtly. "As usual."

The elegant little black car was gone before she
reached the door. She climbed the stairs, heard a telephone ringing, realized it was behind her own door.
But she made no move to answer it.

It had nothing to do with her, really. That was for
Claude Roundtree. She had become someone else.

The next two days were unlike any Claude had yet
known. When she arrived at the studio, Marc greeted
her coldly, told her not to bother changing, and to recite any lines she could remember. He straddled a
stiff gilt chair, his voice as severe as his face.

"My dear girl, if you can't recite ordinary good
speech, how in the world can you make people believe you are an actress?"

"I'm trying to, but you interrupt me."

"All right. We'll start again. 'My Lords . . .'"

She was Joan again and she was miserable. She
could not believe that this was the man who had pic-
nicked with her in a garden, held her hand, looked at
her so deeply she felt her insides melt. Only two days
ago.

"I'd like to do something else."

"I'm sure you would. But this is the play we are studying. You came to work. I've seen none of it yet."

She was Joan. She was the martyred maid, she was among enemies, she was homesick, she was everything he had told her, but all that she could really believe was that she was Claude Roundtree and she was never going to be anyone else.

He dismissed her promptly at four and asked her if she wanted to return.

"Do you want me to?"

"Of course I want you to. But my darling girl, I can't hold your hand, feel you tremble, and make an actress of you. You must work. Work. And then—*then* there is a reason for everything else."

She fled so he would not see her burst into tears. She was confused, angry. She told herself that he meant nothing to her except a means to her career. She walked blindly through the dusty streets until, at last finding her way back to the flat, she threw herself on the strange bed and told herself she would die without him. In the darkening room she lay imagining how she would do it, and then she imagined he was already sorry, he would call her at any moment to apologize. They would go to the same trattoria. She lay tingling at the images that raced ahead of her thoughts.

When the phone rang, she leaped to it.

"I thought you might be hungry."

"Oh—Hutch!"

"Is that joy? Surprise? Dismay? Or your usual inscrutability? When can I pick you up? I want to talk to you."

"I can't, Hutch. Not now. Not this evening. I'm busy."

"Does that mean a date?"

"It means I'm busy. I have a great deal of work to do. Study. And other things. But thank you very much for calling."

"Thank *you*, Miss Roundtree, for answering. I had begun to think you had forgotten how. Good night."

She hung up, and the tears came. This time in floods. Why had she behaved like that? She wouldn't mind seeing him. She would have liked to go out and have dinner with him. He was solid and kind. And there, she knew, was the reason. She could not bear the reality of Hutch in her life now.

The next day Marc Vallon gave her a scene to read from something called *Lady Windermere's Fan*. It was easy and it made her laugh. He read with her. At the end of the hour he told her he would arrange a screen test for her.

The days passed in heady succession. Claude dutifully wrote home of the roles she was studying and how encouraging Mr. Vallon was. What she omitted was the magic that she could not define even to herself. One night after a supper of pasta and wine, how easily the word came to her now—not spaghetti or macaroni or ravioli but pasta—Marc had driven her to a street bordering the ancient Forum. He had stood beside her looking down on the awesome ruins. There was a moon. Swamp mist filtered among the sentinel columns and the fragmented walls, as it had since before the first stone had been set on the timeless hills. In the ghostly light it created a fantasy of shadows and shapes.

"You are looking at a crowded market place," Marc told her. "There is the road; the broken pavings mark it. Above, near those columns, the Senate, the great and noble of the city, is waiting. A victorious general is arriving. You can hear the wheels of the chariot, the hoofs of the horses. The cheers!" Marc had flung up his head as if he were the general. "He catches sight of a slave girl, watching from a corner of the temple porch. She is beautiful and she is young. Can you see her, Claude, standing on tiptoe to see the great general?" Claude found herself stretching to her toes.

"He must have her," Marc's rich voice continued. "He sends an aide who brings her to his palace. No man or woman can refuse the general anything today. He is mad with desire. He cannot marry her but he adores her. He dresses her in gold and jewels; he lavishes her with every treasure the world offers. He has her carried in a litter through these streets. He displays her at the Colosseum. He frees her by day and enslaves her by night." Marc was no longer looking out on the ruins. His light eyes were fixed on hers. "In the end he makes you a goddess. He has become the slave."

Claude shivered, drew her sweater closer. They stood in silence for unmeasured moments.

"Come. It's time to go."

She nodded. She felt she had to speak before she could make herself move.

"Are we going to walk down there?"

"Where?"

"Among the columns and things. To see it closer."

"You have seen it, my dear. You have lived it. What could you see that your imagination hasn't already told you?"

She sat silently beside him on the drive home, his arm against hers in the closeness of the car.

On another day there was San Stephano, a small fishing village on the crest, north of Rome. She sat beside him, high on a terrace looking down on the

paint-bright colors of the sea, the toy boats, and the
beach umbrellas. He made her laugh with his Italian-
ate English, as he tried to sell her an imaginary fish.

"But I don't like it with the hook in its mouth,
Marc!" The name came so easily.

"Then no hook." He waved his long slender hand.
"Presto. It is a very little fish, all gold, and it is swimming in a bowl. You take?"

"I take!" She giggled and held out her hands. He
took one hand and carried it, palm up, to his lips.

"I give." Again the slow sliding look of those light
eyes. And the little silences she was beginning to know.

One morning the telephone rang so early that she
jumped from bed in alarm. A Thatcher reaction. Nobody called in Thatcher at six in the morning unless
there was trouble.

"A perfect day for Pompeii, my dear. No work.
Wear your prettiest dress. I want to take some pictures." His voice came strong and vibrant. Her own
heart pounded with excitement. A whole day beside
him! She chose the tangerine dress from Paris. It made
her feel oddly unlike herself.

But in the powdery heat of Pompeii's excavated
streets it was too hot to walk. The ageless cobble-
stones gave off a heat that burned through her sandals. She sat down, breathless, at the base of an ancient well; he sat beside her.

"You are tired, Claude?"

"Oh, no. But my feet burn."

He slipped off her sandals. His hands were cool, his
fingers dexterous, as he stroked her feet and ankles.
His hands moved to the calves of her legs. Abruptly
he dropped them. And stood up.

"Better now?"

"Yes." The word sounded small and distant in her own ears. She told herself her dizziness came from the heat.

"Then I'll take some pictures. Your dress is marvelous against these stones."

He stood looking down at her with a smile. She was so often surprised by his height and his incredible handsomeness.

"A lovely town, isn't it?"

"It is?" It looked hot and gray and ashen to her.

"Of course it is. It's a resort, you know, for the Romans. You see the palm trees, the flowers, the cool houses with their painted walls and shaded courts." His magnetic voice began to cast its spell. "You are a Roman lady. Your husband has brought you here. But you have slipped out to meet me beneath the trees at this well. I'm a charioteer. We are lovers." He had ceased snapping pictures. "I find you here leaning over the well, looking into it. There, on that step."

She put her hand on the well wall and drew it back with a start. It fitted into a worn place that seemed to have been waiting for her. As if a hand had already been imprinted there. She heard him laugh.

"What's funny? It felt—it felt . . . I don't know. Spooky."

"It is. Lean there again." He was on the step beside her. "See. You have put your hand precisely where women for thousands of years have put their hands to draw water. Until those hands have worn the stone away. Now you have found it. You are a woman of Pompeii. Your imagination does the rest." He set his camera down. "Claude! Claude!"

"What?"

"Have you any idea how happy I am with you?"

"I'm happy with you, Marc."

"Not yet, perhaps. Not the way I want you to be. But you will be. I promise you that, Claude. I promise you happiness."

She did not know what to say because he had not really said anything, yet she was woman enough to know he had said everything. On the long drive back to Rome in the starlit night she felt she had reached the pinnacle of happiness. She would not try to guess or even to imagine what lay ahead. He drove fast and expertly. As the cool air flowed by, he turned once to look at her with a smile. "*Che sarà, sarà,* little one?"

She did not understand, but it did not matter.

The next afternoon at the studio at the end of the hour's work he told her he would arrange a screen test for her.

She gasped. "When?"

"Perhaps next week."

She hesitated, then threw her arms around his neck. Lightly, rigidly, he held her, then gently drew her arms away from him.

"So we must work."

"I'll do anything."

"Your imagination, my dear child. You must learn how to use it."

Her face had the radiance of a spring morning.

Chapter Fourteen

Despite the languor of a Roman mid-August every table in the dark-walled room was taken. Voices in half a dozen different languages rose, fell, bargained, and transacted. Hands gesticulated and eyes shifted, watched, and appraised. Clavo's—or "The Club" as it was affectionately known among its intimates—was the most exclusive men's club in Rome. It was said that more world business was done at lunch at Clavo's than at any other dining club in Europe. Skin colors ranged through Nordic pallor, asiatic yellow, and equatorial black, but it was a flippancy of the club that as a man's skin color deepened, his chances of a better table improved. The men who lunched at Clavo's knew that the lodestone of wealth and power was moving south and east. They were the traders and guardians of that inevitability.

Clavo's was not a place where Marc Vallon wished to be seen waiting. He had arrived promptly, greeted acquaintances, bowed to the famous, nodded to the not-so-famous, and been escorted to a well-positioned table. His host had not yet arrived. As the minutes passed some of Marc's euphoria began to fade. No one kept Marc Vallon waiting, not even at Clavo's. The man who invited him to lunch was privileged. However, he would retain his own air of gracious, if bored, tolerance.

His host finally arrived, eight minutes late. A short man with enduring black hair, slight features, superb tailoring, and incredibly small feet encased in shining pointed shoes. Ben Orlini crossed the dining room in an aura of relentless energy and visible power. Marc noticed that he looked neither left nor right. Rather the diners broke off conversations to raise a hand in salute or to catch his eye.

Marc himself hid a slight contempt for the little man who needed so much to impress so few. He rose courteously.

"Marc, old man. So sorry. Bad connection with Hong Kong this morning. Had to wait to get the call through. Your phone system needs more than an overhauling."

Having shifted the blame to his guest, Orlini sat down.

"Order anything you like, Marc." He waved a small round hand. "They know what I want."

Gamesmanship. Power play. Marc knew it all. Privately once again he congratulated himself on the genius of talent and on the thread of nobility bequeathed by his Viennese ancestry. It resulted now in the perfection of his manners and his barely concealed contempt. Solveg had locked him and his affairs into this little man but Marc would not bend to him. He knew instinctively that Ben Orlini hated him.

Once through his cold consommé and poached fish Ben Orlini lit a cigar. He came directly to the point.

"I want to buy up the Manon film, Marc."

Marc had expected only a reminder of his debt. "Buy it? What does that mean?"

"I write a check. I own the film. Would you say $500,000?"

"Ben, you don't have to buy it. Your investment is safe. The premiere is September sixth. Then general release. It's going to be a success. It's a masterpiece."

"You geniuses. Masterpiece. Masterpiece. Screw that, Marc. I offer you half a million. My check today. And whatever you need for your next picture with Soli."

Something Marc did not want to see edged into his consciousness.

"I don't seem to understand this. Are you going to handle the distribution yourself?"

Ben Orlini blew a long stream of smoke.

"There isn't going to be any distribution, Marc."

Marc began to understand, but he moved carefully. "I don't think you understand the film business, Ben. I've made a great film. The public's going to see it."

"How much do you want?"

"It's not a question of money."

Ben contemplated his cigar with a mild smile. "That's what every man says until the price is right. All right, we'll deal. That film is not going to be released. I'm willing to pay for it. A half million was my opener."

Marc saw the pattern and the pit at the end. But he would keep his temper and his style. He straightened. It gave him an added three inches of height over the little man.

"I think you should see the film."

"I have seen it."

Marc was caught off balance. "When?"

"Soli arranged it for Julia in Paris. Julia insisted I
see it. I saw why. My God, Marc, that finish. Soli
ought to sue you."

So Soli had betrayed him. He was surprised but
he was not defeated. "I didn't know you were so protective of women."

"Women?" Ben came as close to a snort as his new
veneer would permit. "Who the hell is protective of
women? Sure, Soli looks like a hag at the end, but how
old is she anyhow? As for my wife, she's been vomiting
her feelings all over me for the last year. If you think
a couple of tired broads could get me in here with a
check for half a million to keep that picture out of
circulation, you better think again. I saw what you
did in that picture. I don't like it. It's out. So we'll talk
money."

"I don't think you're a critic, Ben."

"Who said I was? I offered you my house up in
Thatcher to make that picture. Julia thought it would
be a good idea. Since the boy had his accident, she's
got the wobbles over that place. I won't sell it, so she
wants it used. You took a picture of a man walking to
his death. Accident, suicide, murder. I don't care. But
you let it happen. Everybody who sees it is going to
know that it was my place. Ben Orlini's! Used to make
money on a poor slob's finish. The priest says I'm as
guilty as you are."

"The priest?" This was a new side to the little big
dealer.

"Look, Marc. You artsy guys couldn't see your ass if
you backed into a mirror. But where I am now, I'm
not having any weirdos interfere with me. Leonard
Ross is dead and that's all anybody will remember this
picture for. Next month up in Thatcher they're holding
primaries for the November election. I've got a man

up there who's going to win. He's not much. Drinks too much. Sleeps with the wrong women. But he's mine. He's in my pocket. I need that in Washington. I'm in the big league now. I want a man in Congress who'll say 'Yes, *sir*!' to me, Ben Orlini. That's why I've hung on to that monster of a house when Julia wanted to get rid of it. It's my legal residence in Thatcher. I've put enough money into old Harlan Phelps to get him elected pope. That goddamned picture of yours could tear it up! I'm not having it." Ben flicked an overdue ash on the table cloth. "I've been pretty good to you, Vallon."

Pretty good to Soli, Marc translated.

"And I'm going to see you through the next picture with Soli. What the hell's the name of it? That hot dame! Soli gave me a private rehearsal. I guess that's no surprise to you."

"Soli's life is her own, Ben." But Marc breathed easier. Ben was vulnerable too.

"She's a lot of woman. Julia's been frigid since the boy's accident." Ben leaned forward confidentially. "We've always gotten along, Marc. Julia and Soli are old friends. One picture isn't going to ruin you. You had a bad break. But it never was for Soli, to my way of thinking. The next one will be great. Right for her, too. So name your price."

Marc brushed his lips, put down his napkin. The room was clearing. So was his mind. He was still his own man. Ben Orlini was talking about the past, an aging past that he, Marc, had left behind. Forty-two. He was still a young man on the threshold of his best years. He had put some of his finest work into *Manon*. Someday people would say that it was the best of Marc Vallon's early period. His masterpiece was still to come.

Not all of this went through Marc's consciousness, but enough did to make him forget for an instant Ben's narrowed eyes fixed on him, waiting.

"Well, Marc, is it a deal?"

"There is no price, Ben. The picture will be released on schedule. I am starting a new picture next month. In Paris. It will not be the Thaïs. It will not be with Soli."

He rose with a graceful movement, nodded a brief good-bye to Ben and strode from the dining room. He was aware that eyes followed him. He was aware also that he had left Ben Orlini in unaccustomed and furious defeat. And somewhere in his mind lay the realization that he had pulled all security from under his own feet. But Marc Vallon was a man who lived self-images. When a man is young, why should he worry about money?

Marc emerged from the gilt elevator cage on the fourth floor of his apartment building. Claude was sitting in the hall on the top step.

"My dear child!"

"Oh, Marc!" She ran to him.

"I am late. I'm sorry. You shouldn't have to sit out here. I'll give you a key."

"I didn't mind. Honestly. But you keep telling me to practice my imagination and all I could imagine was that something terrible had happened to you!"

He threw back his head, showing his handsome teeth, and laughed. "That wasn't exactly the purpose, dear girl." He put his arm around her and felt her trembling. With one hand he unlocked the door and ushered her inside.

"No work today, Claude. I'll see what messages I have, then we'll go out and celebrate."

"Celebrate what?"

"I've had a marvelous idea for my next picture. I want to share it with you. There is something I want you to see first."

Claude had spent very little time in her life looking at statues or even at pictures of statues. If this had been with Miss Pickett and Art Class 2A, she would not have minded. But with this man who made her so aware of herself, who talked so fascinatingly as if they had known each other forever, and whose light eyes slid over her and left her feeling weak, Claude found herself confused. So many statues, all of them nude. She had grown up with two brothers but that didn't help when Marc pointed out the quality of the marble, the realism of the sculpture. And the women! Marc would touch a thigh or a breast that seemed almost soft, pointing out the beauties that the sculptor had seen, until it seemed to Claude she was walking among them, as naked as any.

She had fallen silent by the time they entered a small corner room of the Galleria. It was flooded with sunlight. In the center lay a life-size statue of a young girl half reclining on a curved couch. Her long hair fell across a tasseled pillow. She was completely nude, so young, so lovely that she seemed to breathe.

"Well, what do you think of her?"

Claude shook her head, "I—I don't know. She's beautiful."

"Isn't she? I call her *La Marchesa*. There is a story behind that sculpture." She hoped, without being able to tell herself why, that he would take her on a walk through the park outside. Or sit beside one of the cool fountains.

"We'll sit here on the bench for a moment. She looks like you, I think. Do you see it?"

"No."

He smiled. "Then let's say you could look like her. Her name is Bianca. She lived three centuries ago in Florence. She was married very young to a very old man. He was deeply in love with her but he was no longer able to love her as she wanted. He could only touch her and look at her. You understand, Claude?"

"Yes, of course."

"She had no idea how much he loved her because the young never think the old are capable of passion. But she accepted her life as it was."

Claude had taken her eyes off the statue.

"Did she love him?"

"In ways she hardly understood. She did what he asked."

"What was that?"

"The old Marchese knew that everything, even as young and lovely as his wife, changes. He wanted to keep her just as she was when he married her. More than that, La Marchesa was full of life. She loved to attend balls and to ride and to dance. The hours when she was away were long for the old Marchese. He wanted her with him. So he ordered a young sculptor to make a statue of her so she would always be there as he liked to think of her. Everyday she posed for the young sculptor. Everyday the old Marchese came to watch. He took great pleasure from it."

He paused, his eyes gravely on her. Claude said nothing. She did not want to admit the story disturbed her.

"But life is composed of the inscrutable and the inevitable. The young sculptor fell madly in love with the beautiful Marchesa."

"And she with him?" The story had reached familiar ground.

"Perhaps. But of course it was impossible. The more the sculptor loved her, the more slowly he worked. But at last it was finished. Then he killed the old Marchese." Claude gasped. "Then what happened?"

"He was caught and executed, I presume."

"And—the Marchesa?"

Marc shrugged. "There she lies, as lovely as life. For the whole world to enjoy."

Claude was silent. She avoided looking at the nude girl. "I don't think that's much of a story."

"Of course not. It's only a beginning. But that's the story I want for my next picture, in Florence where it happened. Today and yesterday. Impressionistic. Eternal. Where even the stones tell stories. You would like Florence, my dear."

"Me?"

"I want you to play La Marchesa. You are young. You are right for it. You could do it, under my guidance. I believe it would make you a great star."

It was dizzying, the strong sunlight; the gleaming marble; the words she could hardly believe; the quiet, persuasive, beautiful voice. Claude said the only thing she could think of.

"What about the screen test?"

"I'm going to Paris tonight to see about the release of the Manon film. I'll arrange it then. I'll come back and get you. But I assure you it will make no difference. I want you for the part."

He rose and took her hand. She looked back once at the statue, then went with him out of the room.

He drove her to her flat. "Think about it, Claude." He pressed a key into her hand. "I shall be gone for three days. Use the studio all you wish. The books, the plays, the clothes. Study hard. When I come back we'll have dinner at the best restaurant in Rome, where I can introduce my new star."

It was happening too fast. "Marc, I—I don't know. I don't even know whether I could do it. I—I just don't."

"Of course you don't, now. But you will. Trust me, Claude. Together we shall make the most beautiful picture ever filmed."

He took both her hands, kissed them, and very gently kissed her lips. Upstairs in the dimness of the flat she plunged her face in cold water and threw herself on the bed.

It was so different from what she had foreseen. So wildly unexpected. Yet it was what she had longed for, what she had wanted. Almost. She wouldn't have to play it nude. Or would she? She tried not to think of her mother and her father. Of John. Of Uncle Willard and Thatcher. Actresses did these things and they were famous. She could be a star.

She fell asleep and woke up to darkness. She heard a distant plane and imagined Marc flying up there, above her. Flying to arrange everything. Whatever everything was.

She was going to be a star.

The travel-poster mirage of a strange city can dissipate overnight into pinched and stark loneliness. Claude discovered this the next morning when she raised the blind on the faceless wall, dark with streaming rain. Marc had gone, and all she knew of the city had gone with him. The day lay ahead like a jagged hole. There was no telephone call to expect. She knew no one else. Except Hutch. She had no idea where to find him. He might not even be in Rome. He might be gone, flying anywhere. He might be seeing someone else. In that case she would be too proud to call him. Claude decided to sidestep this whole train of thought by the simple process of opening the refrigerator door.

There, facing her, lay another problem. Three pears, a crumbling of cheese, the remnants of a sausage, and the same bottle of drinking water she had found when she arrived. She had not bothered to restock. She had not even bothered to count her funds. Once she had taken her screen test, she would never again have to think about money. Meanwhile she would have to remember where she had passed a dingy fruit and sausage store. She made herself strong, black Italian coffee and wished she had paid more attention to Survival in Science I. Somebody had once survived six months on frozen mammoth.

But hunger would make her look more interesting when he returned. Wan and dedicated. Meanwhile he had told her to work and study. The key to his studio lay in her change purse. Would he have given it to her if he had not meant her to use it? By two o'clock she was drawn like a steel filing to the ornate building overlooking the Pincio. There was no lemon light in the sky. There was only the steady, remorseless rain and a tremor of uncertainty as she unlocked the door.

The apartment was dim and chill when she entered. She turned up a lamp, kicked off her shoes, buried her toes in the deep pile rug, and released a sigh of contentment. This, for a little while, was hers. Here she could be anything she wanted. Here she was not alone because Marc was everywhere.

She would go into the dressing room first. She pulled from the closet a glitter of water-green sequins that had already caught her eye. She took off her own dress and, in front of the full mirror, held the column of sequins against her body. With the other hand she drew her hair high on her head, lifted her chin, smiled into the mirror—and gasped. Behind her, watching from the doorway, stood a woman. A tall woman with mahogany hair.

"Marvelous," she said. "It becomes you."

The sequins slid to the floor. Claude whirled. "I'm sorry. I didn't know. . . ." The words chipped from her lips. She reached for her own dress. "I—I came here—to practice. I mean—I had no idea. . . ."

"Don't apologize. Why shouldn't you try it on? You're Marc's new protégée." It was a flat statement.

"I'm Claude Roundtree. I'm studying to have a screen test and Marc—Mr. Vallon—said I might come here. . . ."

"Certainly." The woman smiled. She was strikingly beautiful in lamplight, her teeth very white, her face strong, her eyes luminous. "He would expect it. I am the intruder."

"Oh, no. No. I wasn't sure if I should come when he was away . . ."

"Marc's away?" The woman caught her lip.

Claude was too busy and too flushed, struggling into her own dress, to hear the surprise.

"He went to Paris to see about—what did he call it—releasing the movie he has made."

"Yes. Of course." She looked sharply at Claude. "You don't know me, do you?"

"No." Even as she said it, Claude saw something familiar in the woman. Her voice, the proud way she held her head, her tall, full figure.

"I'm Solveg Traner."

"Oh."

"Solveg Traner the actress. I played the lead in Marc's

film *La Troisième Manon*. You watched some of it being made in that little town of yours."

"You!" Claude knew she was staring. This elegant woman, the wide-eyed old harpy in black on the cliff? "But—you're beautiful!"

"Thank you." Solveg smiled wryly. "Why don't we sit down and talk?"

Claude followed her into the studio, torn between a longing to escape and a curiosity about this woman who commanded the scene as if she had arranged it. Solveg settled into Marc's chair and waved Claude to a seat.

"So you're going to be an actress."

"I'm going to try to be."

"You either are, or you are not. Marc must evidently think so or he wouldn't have gone to so much trouble." If there was irony in the remark, Claude missed it.

"Has he selected a part for you?"

"He's talked about it, if I do all right. In his next picture."

"Really? What is the role to be?"

"I don't really know whether I can do it. But Mr. Vallon thinks I can. It's a young girl and a sculptor falling in love with her. She's a Marchesa or something."

Solveg rose, walked to the window, and flung the long drapes wide. The rain had stopped but a mist pressed against the glass. She stood looking into it, her head turned from Claude. The silence thickened like the mist itself. Claude shifted uncomfortably. Solveg returned and stood looking down at her.

"You're very young, aren't you?"

"I'm eighteen."

"And I'm forty-eight, though I don't expect you could even imagine that age."

There was no answer to that.

"Look at me. I am a beautiful woman, you say. Look closer. Every line you see in my face, every harsh tone you hear in my voice, I have earned. I have worked for them and fought for them and then worked and fought some more. Do you think that overnight you could dare step into a role for Marc Vallon and do it? As he must have it done?" Solveg strode to the drapes and let them fall. "My dear girl! Let me tell you something. You do not learn to become an actress. You live it because there's nothing else you can do. You laugh and cry and live and suffer and finally that is what you give your audience. Not words! You give them yourself, your life, all the happiness you've ever known. And all the wounds!"

She dropped into the chair, her timing perfect, her performance superb.

"And even then you will not be able to do it without help. Would you be surprised if I told you I would like to help you?"

"Help? Me?" Claude sounded stupid in her own ears.

"Yes. You. Marc will be detained in Paris. Those things always take longer than one expects. Meanwhile, I'm here." She smiled, and Claude knew why she was famous. "You don't want to waste time. Tomorrow night I am giving a little party for some very interesting and important people. The kind of people you must know if you want a career because they can be very useful. Let's begin there, shall we?"

Solveg jumped up gaily and clapped her long slender hands together. "Tomorrow night. At nine. Carlo will bring you. It's settled!"

Claude could never remember afterwards how she

found her shoes or reached the street. Nor could she
guess what there had been in the scene that left her
with an indefinable sense of disloyalty. Solveg Traner
was going to help her. Solveg Traner had invited her
to a party. Yet even as she thought it, she was unsure.
A chill touched her excitement.

In Marc's studio Solveg sat without measuring time.
Then she crossed the too-familiar room to a concealed
telephone and dialed quickly.

"Ben, darling, take me to dinner tonight. Alone."

It was well known that Solveg Traner did nothing
without a motive. So those fortunate enough to be invited to one of her "evenings" rarely refused. Or refused only for a deeper motive. Solveg could be
counted on to supply a novelty, a surprise, even a
crise d'intime that would ensure her name in the next
day's papers with full details of another brilliant Solveg Traner evening. As Solveg told herself, one did
not reach the top and then drop the ladder.

Solveg found herself pleased with her plans. An assortment of editors and producers; a couple of best-
selling American authors; a Greek tycoon, who was to
meet his divorced wife with her two lovers, male and
female; the Contessa, who had been the first to wear
a famous designer's bare-breasted evening gown. Ben
Orlini had, she hoped, left for Paris. Just as well. Ben
could show an oddly popish streak of propriety when
he chose. Julia had returned to Zurich. Hutch would
be a useful escort for the hot-blooded daughter of an
oil sheik and an even more useful eyewitness for
Marc. Marc? Solveg smiled to herself. Thanks to Marc
she had her novelty for the evening.

Solveg touched the pavé-diamond butterflies (bor-

rowed on credit) in her hair and moved toward the
mirror in long-sleeved, green chiffon, slit to the thigh.
Her legs were still marvelous, thank God. She had
been assured they would remain so. After all, some
men cared only about legs. The dressing-table clock
struck a delicate eight. It was time to go downstairs to
greet her guests. The night had turned pleasantly cool,
a good omen.

It was five minutes past nine when Claude entered
the wide empty hall, luminous as water in the light of
two torches. Through the glass doors ahead she could
see lanterns like fireflies among a darkness of trees,
and fountains silvered by concealed lights. She had
never, she told herself, in all her life seen nor imagined any place so beautiful. It was the magic that had
begun when Carlo stopped the car at a plain door in a
dark street, said something to a porter, and ushered
her in to become a princess in an enchanted castle.

But she had no time for fantasy. Solveg Traner was
coming toward her. Any image Claude retained of the
aging black-dressed woman on the edge of the cliff in
Thatcher was gone. This was the most beautiful person she had ever seen. She wished she could be a little
taller when she became a star.

"Claude, my dear girl, you're here. I was worried
about you!"

"You said nine. Am I late?"

"Did I? Of course you're not late. Everybody's here,
but we don't dine until ten so you're in plenty of time.
How charming you look!"

"Thank you." But Claude was not entirely reassured. The orange dress already began to feel too
short.

"Would you like to go in and meet people first or

would you rather come upstairs with me and leave
your sweater?"

"I'd rather go upstairs first, thank you."

Solveg led her past wide-open portals leading to a
long, long room. It was filled with people, and the
talk and laughter rose in a wave as they passed.
Claude wondered what she could possibly say to all
those people when the time came. She caught a flash
of jewels, ripples of flowing tumultuous color. Sub-
dued, she followed Solveg through a corridor, up five
marble steps, not nine as she hoped, and into a small
room.

"Here we are. My most-private study." Solveg shut
the door. "Make yourself at home. If you want to pow-
der your nose, it's through that door."

"No, I'm all right, thank you." If Solveg Traner had
only told her. But she would not have had anything
else to wear anyhow.

Solveg looked at her. She recognized the tremor of
uncertainty. She had been there herself once. How
old was this girl? Seventeen? Eighteen? Solveg had
been seventeen the summer she and Julia had gone
off to Atlantic City for an adventure, and Julia had
picked up Ben Orlini on the boardwalk and she, Solveg, had gotten a job as a hula girl in a penny arcade.
"You got legs, girlie," the thick-lipped man had said.
How long ago? Seventeen? Eighteen? It would be easier to tell this untouched girl the truth and send her
home. But compassion had never solved any problems
that Solveg faced. Steel on steel, if you wanted to win.
There was no reason why this girl shouldn't learn as
Solveg had done.

Claude lost herself in the pictures that lined the
windowless, rosy room.

"Are these all of you, Miss Traner?"

"Call me Solveg—or Soli. Please." She laughed. It was easier now that she had not given way to weakness. "Not all of them. Some of them are my friends. Some of them are people I've worked with."

"That's Mr. Vallon!"

"Yes."

"Oh, there are lots of Mr. Vallon. That funny straw hat."

"That was on Capri many years ago."

"You've known him a long time."

"We've made many pictures together."

"That's you, too? Oh, how beautiful!"

"I was eighteen then."

"You were a star already?"

"No." Soli laughed, and her laugh was rich and warm. "But I'd had my first real part. It was a Polish film. I was raped in a convent by a group of soldiers and died. That was in the beginning of the picture."

Claude stared at the silver-framed photograph of a long-haired girl in the ethereal white dress and thought about her being raped in a convent. Reality and make-believe. They were becoming hopelessly mixed. She felt a deep compassion for this tall woman with such a past. She wanted to like her.

"You've done so many things!"

"I'm an actress. When you're that, you're nothing else. At first you do what you're told to do. Later you can choose. But you still do what they tell you. You learn that first." Solveg seemed in no hurry to return to her guests. "You want to be an actress? Why?"

Claude was startled by the question. She had never asked herself that. It had never seemed necessary.

"Why?" Solveg repeated impatiently. "You must have a reason."

"It's—I don't know—it's something I want to do. I'd like it."

"You'd *like* it? What do you think it is? A pretty dress you can put on? A plate of ice cream you like to taste? I saw you look at yourself in the hall mirrors. I saw you look into that mirror over the clock when you came in. I watched you in the mirror at Marc's apartment."

"I know! I'm sorry about that!" Claude found herself shriveling under this sudden intensity.

"Why be sorry? You have a lovely face, a good body. You want to look at it. Good. But is that why you think you can be an actress? Because you're pretty and young and people will want to look at you? Don't you know that before you can act you must forget! Your face, your body, what you like or don't like. You must forget everything that you see in that mirror! Now, go look at it for the last time! Then we'll see what kind of actress you can be. Come!"

To Claude's astonishment Solveg's hand closed over her wrist in a hard grip. She felt herself drawn, unresisting, through the heavy drapes that curtained the end of the room. She was on a small stage above the people. She recognized the long, crowded drawing room.

"My dear friends," Solveg still grasped her wrist. The talk stopped. Faces turned, egglike, toward them. "I intended to announce to you this evening Marc's new picture. Instead we are fortunate to have with us Marc's newest protégée."

Claude heard a murmur of surprise, a suppressed rustle. Then an awful silence.

"She is Claude Roundtree, an American girl he 'found.'" Solveg's accents were exquisite. "She is to star in his next picture. She will be the latest 'Mar-

chesa.'" Solveg released her wrist. "Tell them about
yourself, my dear. Or perhaps you'd like to give them
a reading. Joan to the bishops. Always a favorite of
Marc's." She was gone.

Claude looked wildly out on the room. Were there
hundreds or thousands of people staring at her? She
felt hot in the white light from overhead. She thought
of her absurdly short dress. Of the women in jewels,
with glistening, coiled hair, of men with half-smiles.
Waiting, waiting.

She tried to think of something, anything, but her
throat had closed. No single word that she had ever
learned took shape in the emptiness of her mind. She
felt rooted as if no power on earth could release her
from this spot. She pushed at her throat as if it were a
locked door. She swallowed and heard her voice at
last, high and thin.

"I've been studying. . . ."

There were a few titters.

"Bellissima!" The voice belonged to a man directly
below her. His eyes were on her legs.

"I have been studying with Marc—Mr. Vallon. He
has given me a lot of help. . . ."

A few titters laced the silence. Claude closed her
eyes against a wave of nausea. Then lifted her chin.
Her words sounded far away. "I'm to have a screen
test and I'm very grateful."

A man called in broken English. "You will pass, little sweetheart!" Another voice. "And Marc will play
the old Marchese? Again?"

"But naturally!" A woman called.

Titters rippled across the room. Claude stiffened.
She had not understood. But this was her chance. Her
eyes searched the back wall, the window, anywhere
beyond the faces. In the pillared entranceway, she

saw a sleek, dark-haired girl in cleavaged black. Beside her—Claude caught her breath—the unmistakable shoulders of Hutch. The panic that she had been holding at bay threatened to engulf her. He was here. He had brought another girl. He would be laughing with the others.

It took only a fraction of a second for these images to clear Claude's mind. As so often happened with her panic turned to anger and anger to ice. The effect was a steadying draught. She brought her voice down from the stratosphere and began again. "Miss Traner has kindly asked me, told me, if I would . . ."

"Louder!"

". . . recite something Mr. Vallon taught me."

Laughter started and was hushed. From the corner of her eye she thought she saw Hutch move. But she did not need him now. She would do this for Marc. "It is Joan to the bishops. 'My lords—'" she hesitated. The words were there somewhere, fuzzy, fading. "'My lords—'" she reached for them in a rush. "'My lords, you want to see me burn.'"

A gale of laughter swept the room.

She stepped back as if to ward off a blow. She wanted to run but could not. The faces, the jewels, the colors, seemed to be growing larger, leaning toward her.

Then her mind played a trick. From long ago, from the security of childhood, from a deep leather chair, a familiar comforting voice: "It's only make-believe, Claude." And the words followed, clear and very loud now in her head. "Alice had grown to her full size. 'Who cares about you? You're nothing but a pack of cards!'"

Had she said them aloud? She turned and pushed

her way through the drapes, the pounding in her ears
drowning out all other sound.

There was no one in the small red sitting room, nor
on the five marble steps. She walked cautiously down
into the empty water-green hall, and hesitated. Which
way to the vestibule and the ancient porter? Her over-
charged mind had lost all sense of direction. She wanted
only to disappear.

She hurried across the vast hall, through the dim
loggia, and into the night. She found herself in an alley
of sweet-smelling trees which led to a semicircle of
clipped hedge. There was a low marble bench. She had
made a mistake. She had trapped herself in the villa's
private park.

There must be a gate somewhere; she would find it.

On no condition would she go back through the
house. For the moment, she was hidden. She sat down
to let her head clear. Overhead a few stars shone bright
and small. She wondered if they were the same stars
she saw from her bedroom at home. She wanted to think
that they were.

Hutch pushed his way through the crowded salon
and into the hall. He met Soli at the foot of the staircase.

"Where is she?"

"Where is who, darling?"

"A nice night's work, Madame Traner. Now where
is she?"

"Oh, you mean the girl? Claude." Solveg gave a
nicely modulated, little laugh. "So naive, wasn't she?
But all in all, rather amusing. And quite sweet. In her
way." She had managed to walk him out of her guests'
hearing and into the loggia. "Ask the porter if you're
so concerned. But I rather think she's still upstairs.

She needs a little time after her 'performance.' We always do. Really, Hutch, she's not a child."

"Not after tonight, she isn't. You're a cruel woman, Soli."

"Someday she may realize what a favor I did her." But she was looking beyond him as if alerted to something he could not see. "Do run along, Hutch. Dinner will be served shortly. I must remind you, you are escorting one of my guests."

When Hutch had left her, Solveg walked slowly, rigidly to the end of the loggia. The figure standing there against a pillar did not come toward her. He stood waiting, the glow of a cigarette indicating he was watching her.

"Marc, darling!" She moved close to him, took the cigarette from his mouth, and kissed him. "How marvelous! I didn't expect you!"

"I'm quite sure of that. Where can we talk?"

"Anywhere you like." She put the cigarette between her lips, drew on it, then dropped it into a nearby vase. "Anywhere. But wouldn't you rather dine first? Then we'll have the night."

In the distant light from the salon his face was greenish, his expression stark and unreadable, unlike anything she could remember. She felt a tremor of uneasiness. But she had always been able to handle Marc Vallon.

"I wish to talk now."

In the salon music had begun. A few impatient dancers silhouetted the windows.

"Of course. But you're really quite naughty, Marc, to arrive without telling me. So many people would want to know."

They were moving into the park. She knew every marble flagstone, every turn of the path. As he did.

They had walked them together, mornings and twilights. How long ago? Now they were strangers. Or worse. In the glow of an overhead lantern he looked ill.

Beyond a large acacia tree at the edge of a fountain, he stopped.

"There's no use wasting time, Soli. I saw Ben Orlini last night."

"How nice, darling. Though I do find his gaucheries somewhat tiring. I'm just as pleased he wasn't here tonight. He is rather stuffy at these affairs. By the way, were you in time to see your little protégée? I did want to surprise you with her success. Instead, *quel dommage*! A debacle! I am so sorry. I did so want to help the girl. I had quite a serious talk with her. But of course, absolutely hopeless. No talent at all, as of course you knew. But I forgive your little *fin d'été* dalliance. Now that it's over, you should really thank me. As she will someday."

"Solveg, stop talking! For God's sake!" His forehead glistened. He wiped a hand across it. "Ben Orlini did what you wanted."

The time for subterfuge had passed. She waited.

"He had the Manon film removed from the studios. It's in his possession now. He said it will not be released."

"He owns it, Marc. It was his money. You didn't have a cent in it."

"I had my life in it! My mind! My heart! Everything I felt and imagined and believed. It was the climax of my life's work. That was mine. Not his! Mine! Not for purchase or hire!"

"My poor darling." She laid a light hand on his arm. It was rigid. "Marc, it was a wretched film. Everybody who saw it knew it. Why won't you face it? Ben

did what was best. The critics would have devoured
you. We'll make another. You and I. The Thaïs will be
your masterpiece. I'll be the greatest Thaïs ever seen.
For you, Marc!" She moved against him, her body
warm and full. "Thaïs, Marc. Full of the passion and
luxury your audience loves. Believe me, Marc . . ."

"Believe you?" He seemed to draw inward as if
gathering a secret strength. "Why would any man believe you, Soli? You are a woman who destroys whatever she touches. It was in your face in *Manon*. You
destroyed me. My greatest film—" He hesitated and
let the words fall, dull as stones. "And you destroyed
your lover."

The truth lay between them, not separating but
binding them, the web of dependence they had
woven to hold together the pretense of their lives.

Claude, huddled on a step beyond the tree, dared
not move, dared not match what she was hearing to
the stubborn schoolgirl that had swept her to this moment.

"I never tried to deceive you, Marc." Solveg's arti-
fice now was gone. "Lennie *was* my lover. You knew
that. You accepted him because you had to. He was
gentle and harmless and he loved me with his body.
But you still thought you possessed me. I was an animal you had trained to do exactly what you wanted.
But when you found out that I was something more,
that it was I who was saving your pictures, making
your success, you began to hate me. In the end"—her
voice dropped almost outside Claude's hearing, but
not quite—"you hurt me the only way you could. You
killed Lennie."

"It was an accident!"

"You wanted him dead, Marc. When we got to that
Ridge you found a way. You rewrote the last scene.

You set it on the cliff. You saw to it that he drank too much. You never marked the place for him to turn toward me. And you made sure with that 'prescription' that he was so confused that morning that he would not turn. He was afraid of heights but he would keep going. Because he would not know."

His clenched hands came from his pockets. She was afraid now. But she could not stop. The drama had to be played out here in this place where they had once loved to the scent of lime and acacia.

"That's why, when that foolish girl followed you to Paris, you took her on. You wanted her to fall in love with you. You needed her on your side. Because she had seen Lennie walk over that cliff with his eyes wide open."

He gripped her arms.

"It was an accident, I tell you!"

She had struck the flint of truth. She could afford to be generous or mocking or contemptuous as she chose. "Nothing you have ever done was an accident, Marc. A mistake, perhaps. But not an accident. As it was a mistake to come here tonight to blame me for your failure! Yes, it was a failure. Didn't Orlini tell you? He's a businessman, Marc. He arranged for a few critics to see the film. Privately. Didn't he tell you what happened? They yawned. They got up. They walked out, Marc, on your great masterpiece!"

"It is a masterpiece!"

She smiled. "I did you a favor. . . ."

"My life's best work! I will not let you and Orlini destroy it! From the day I met you, you've consumed me bit by bit with your insatiable demands, your mockery, your lovers. You thought I filmed the 'Manon' only for you. You have never known how I have wanted to be free of you. To live in a world where you didn't exist. Where you couldn't exist."

His voice had dropped to a monotone. What she saw in his light eyes frightened her. It was the total despair of a defeated creature. "I had gifts. My mother knew this, and my father. My grandmother. A first lady of the theater. Vienna. Paris. Berlin. She said—'You will go on for us, Marc. You have the Vallon genius.' She would hold out her beautiful hands as if . . . as if giving me . . . no! His voice rose. "No! I will not let you . . . *bagasa!*"

He reached for her throat. Soli sprang back. Marc stumbled as if dizziness had seized him. His hands dropped, he wavered and caught himself, then slowly he pitched sideways against the rim of the fountain. A trickle of blood blackened the marble.

"Marc!" Soli's scream, harsh and primitive, scarred the night. It was echoed by a half cry. She looked up to see Claude staring at her.

"He's hurt himself. Get help!" Soli dropped to her knees, cradling Marc's head.

Claude turned and ran. Before she reached the alley of trees she saw people pouring toward her from the house. Floodlights suddenly whitened the scene. Abruptly she felt herself being caught and spun around.

"Oh . . . Hutch!"

"What's happened?"

"Marc. And Solveg. He collapsed! He's injured!"

"You saw it?"

"Yes. I was out there. He needs a doctor!"

"They'll get one. Come on!" He was pulling her, almost dragging her off her feet.

"Hutch! What are you doing?"

"You've got to get out of here!"

"But . . ."

"Before this place fills up. Before every newspaperman in Rome . . . for God's sake, will you run? There's a gate in the wall beyond those bushes."

They reached an iron grilling in the wall. He pushed a fold of bills into her hand and yanked the gate open. "There's a guard outside. Pay no attention to him. Go left to the end of the alley. Left! You'll find a cab stand in the square. Get yourself to the flat. And stay there. I'll call you later!"

She did not understand. She had had no part of what happened. She had come a long way this night. She was a spectator, seeing herself and all that had taken place as on a distant, diminishing stage.

Much as she hated Hutch at this moment, she knew she would do what he said. She heard the gate close behind her. She turned left and walked toward the lights of a square ahead.

No city vibrates more willingly than Rome to the alternating currents of notoriety and scandal. Marc Vallon was a fading luminary but death restored his luster. And Solveg's flamboyance was cherished.

Hard on the heels of the police came Rome's legendary freewheeling reporters and photographers, the relentless paparazzi. They swarmed into the narrow streets, overwhelmed the aging porter, and assaulted the little park's encircling wall. With the help of additional police Hutch managed to marshal some kind of order until the last of the guests was dismissed, Marc's body removed, and Solveg retired to sedated seclusion. Hutch gave a carefully restrained statement to the press, knowing that it was only a finger in the dike. But for the time being he had succeeded in keeping Claude's name out of it.

He had called her once to make sure she had arrived at the flat. "Stay where you are; I'll get there when I can." It occurred to him later that she had made no response after the first distant "hello."

It was nearly two in the morning before he had cleared out the last of the paparazzi. With the police in charge he left the still garishly lit villa. News of Marc Vallon's death on the way to hospital, had been broadcast at midnight.

Hutch, who was not given to reluctance, knocked hesitantly on the door of Claude's flat. She must be in an exhausted sleep. He hated to waken her. But he must see her. For her own sake. He smiled wryly at himself. Who was he kidding? He must see her because he must. He knocked again.

The door opened a crack, held narrowly by a chain.

"Who is it?" The voice was as faint as it was cool.

"It's me. Hutch. I have to talk to you, Claude."

"It's too late."

He did not stop to consider the enigma of that statement.

"Claude, open the door. It's important."

"I don't think so."

"Shall I pound?"

A pause. A long pause. The chain slid back. The door opened. She stood in the faint light, in the same orange dress he disliked. Her face was tight and expressionless. She looked as she might look in another ten years, he thought, her prettiness replaced by something deeper, fine-honed and infinitely lovelier to him. He did not think she had been crying.

"I left my sweater there," she said irrelevantly.

"Claude—" He wanted to shield her from all the folly, all her own misplaced trust.

"I heard it. On the radio. So there's nothing to say."

"Good." He snapped on a second light. The room was friendlier. "Have you any coffee?"

"I don't want coffee."

"I do."

She walked to the other side of the room and sat on a single chrome-and-vinyl chair as detached as herself.

"As a matter of fact, there is a good deal to say. And you're going to have to listen."

He went to the kitchenette, rummaged in a small closet, and found what he needed. He returned with two unmatched, steaming mugs. She was sitting as he left her. He might not have been there.

"Here. Drink it. I'd take you out but the jackals are loose and baying for blood."

The flippancy was wasted. So was the coffee. She ignored it. He drank gratefully. Here was what he had longed for all through the tumultuous night. This small warm room. Claude. And relief.

To his surprise she broke the silence.

"What happened?"

"Marc apparently slipped on the wet marble, struck his head and—"

"I *know*."

The silence returned. He emptied his cup.

"Like the other one?"

"What other one?" Wherever she was, he realized she was not here with him.

"The one on the cliff. In Thatcher. The man who fell?"

He set the mug down and went to her. Foolish as it felt he crouched beside her chair and took both her hands. "Claude, you're an exasperating, fascinating, and damnably maddening young woman. You also happen to be pretty. In a moment of weakness I told you I loved you. Unfortunately I still do. I don't know where that squirrel mind of yours is this minute. I can't say I blame you. What Solveg did was unforgivable. We'll get to that later. But I'm here because you're going to be in trouble unless you do exactly as I say."

"As usual?" She slid from him. "You did not answer my question."

"What question?"

"Was it an accident, too—up on that cliff?"

He got up and regained some dignity. "How do I know? Leonard Ross was not much. Marc hired him because he came cheap. It was always Solveg's show. Lennie was on grass and Zen and a lot of oddball stuff. Maybe he wanted to die. Or maybe he thought he was walking into cloud cuckoo-land. How the hell does anybody know? Are you going to sit here all night and brood over that, too? Because I have something to say. Claude—"

She was looking past him.

"Claude, now listen to me. Marc Vallon is dead. To-morrow there will be two-inch headlines, and every maudlin reporter in this city will be probing into his life. You've been a chunk of it lately. I want you to go back to Paris by train. That takes fifteen hours at least and it will give things here time to cool down. You'll be out of it. I'll fly to Paris as soon as I can and—"

She turned to him. "You know her very well, don't you?"

"What?"

"Solveg Traner."

"Claude, haven't you heard me?"

"You admired her?"

He was puzzled. But he would have to humor her. She was tightly encased in a mood he had never seen.

"Sure, I know Solveg. Too well. I admired her. Like a Bengal tiger. What's the matter with you?"

She walked toward the door. "I'm grateful to you, Hutch. I'm always having to be grateful to you. I'm grateful for your answering my questions. You see, I heard it all. The quarrel in the park. Everything they said to each other. So I know. Don't worry about me. I've made my plans. I'm going home tomorrow."

"Of course you're going home. But not from here. From Paris."

"No. Tomorrow. I've called the airport. I have a seat. It's all arranged." She took a quick breath. "So I won't be seeing you again. Good night, Hutch. I mean good-bye—"

She was light-years removed.

"Are you telling me you really cared for that guy?"

"I'm telling you I'm going home."

"And you want me out?"

She hesitated. In that split second Hutch saw his future as a drowning man sees his past. A future without her. He could walk out. Or he could stay.

The telephone improbably shattered the moment. He picked it up, not waiting for her.

"Signorina Roundtree?" The voice was oily, insistent.

"Nobody here by that name." Hutch slammed down the phone. Paris was not far enough.

"You're right, Claude. Go home tomorrow. If you have any trouble, call this number. I'll get the message."

He went to her. He was quite clear now. There was no option. Rigid and distant as she was, he swept her into his arms, kissed her hungrily, deeply, to stifle all protest, and felt her body yield. It was only a fraction but it was enough.

"Darling!"

"Hutch! I—I hate you!"

"I know. Me, too." His arm tightened.

He kissed her again. It would be simple to pick her up, carry her into the bedroom, and overwhelm all the anguish, the hurt, the false words with his own strength. But the night was not over for him. And the future had not begun. With a wrench that tore through him he let her go.

"I'll be here at eight."

She nodded. Or did he only imagine it? He closed the door behind him. There was no sound, no sound at all, except for the sliding of the chain into place. She would cry now, he hoped. And she would sleep. In the morning—he thought of all the mornings ahead, and went down the stairs lightly, as lightly as if they had been carpeted.

In the dark and silent street stood a group of men, leaning against small motorbikes. They were young and stony-eyed. Hutch recognized them. One man stepped forward.

"You are Hutchins?" The voice was oily, insistent.

"You know who I am."

"You lie too easily, Signore Hutchins."

He did not see the blow coming. As he slid to the sidewalk he knew he had been too late. The paparazzi had found Claude.

In the dark flat Claude lay staring at the nothingness her life had so abruptly become. Death had struck with a savagery she had never known. She searched for grief within herself and found it blunted by shock. What she had witnessed had become a part of the larger make-believe through which she had passed, wanting to belong, craving the unreachable, a walk-on player visible only to herself, living only in the intensity of her imagination.

As for Hutch, whenever she had weakened toward him, she had regretted it. His bulk had come between her and the most fragile of her dreams. She would remember that and hate him until the end of her life. Let him call at eight in the morning—or any other time. She would enshrine the last days with Marc in her heart and face the dullness of life as other women had. Other Roundtree women who had carried their secret loves to their graves.

Sleep came at last, a cocoon of safety, threaded only with the dream of a ringing telephone. She did not wake until the dream slid suddenly into a heavy knocking on the door.

A fiery woman in a black dress and a large apron with a bandana around her head, pushed in, pouring out a torrent of furious Italian. Heavy with sleep, Claude stared from her to the young Italian girl beside the woman who tried, in halting English, to stop the flow.

"Signorina, my mother says—the street is blocked! No one can get in. They are crowding the door. They are fighting! The paparazzi. It is because of Signore Vallon . . ." Both women crossed themselves. "Would the American signorina go away. Now! The paparazzi make this a bad house . . . O, Dio, per piacere . . . go! I will show you a back way out!"

Claude dressed, packed her few things, and looked around as if for something left unfinished. Then she tore a blank page from the little book Uncle Willard had given her and wrote rapidly. She signed it with a quick, neat, final *C* and handed the note to the girl who was waiting to lead her out. It was just seven twenty-five.

Hutch abandoned his cab at the end of the street. Two telephone calls had produced no answer. It was now nearly nine. He pushed his way through the crowd, entered an adjacent building, crossed a moldering courtyard, and took the rear steps two at a time.

The door of the flat stood open. Inside, the landlady, her head in a red scarf, her heavy breasts loose beneath her blouse, was sweeping the floor. Her curious-eyed daughter handed him a note.

It was not the familiar block handwriting that closed his throat. Nor the unexpected tearing in his gut of that not-too-firm good-bye. It was the sight of the Italian girl fleshed into Claude's innocently shameless, heart-tugging orange dress.

Part Four

Thatcher
September

Chapter Fifteen

John Roundtree's campaign headquarters on Thatcher's Main Street was a chaos of rolled bunting, straw hats, stickers and poster pictures of an earnest young candidate, all the paraphernalia of enthusiastic, if inexpert, support. But at this moment, 6:10, of a late September afternoon, five days before the primary, John sat alone at the desk and considered the telephone call he had received that morning. It was Ben Orlini, with the extraordinary request that John call on him at his home on the Ridge at eight that evening. Ben had something of importance to them both to discuss.

John tried to guess the subject matter. Newspaper polls had begun to run in his favor. His speeches had been drawing bigger crowds. Old-time Bollington politicians had begun to call Martin Roundtree's son by his last name. And a week ago Harlan Phelps had been arrested for drunken driving. His companion was Belle Blake. The incident itself was not surprising. The arrest was. A young state trooper had evidently thought it safe to test Harlan Phelps's hold on the district.

But these were merely straws in a rough wind. Reason enough to bring Ben Orlini home to bolster his man, but no reason at all to invite John up to the Ridge. It was a summons. John felt his inexperience. He could make a tactical error either way. Now he did not want advice as much as the comfort of discussion. But he could guess that his father would oppose any meeting with Orlini. Willard might not. A family split on the eve of the primary? Unthinkable.

He locked the door to his office, crossed the street, and walked into the deepening twilight of Thatcher's Flagpole Green. He thought of Ariel, a luxury he rarely allowed himself. She had not come to headquarters since the day she had left the Roundtree heraldry on the wall. But she came often to the house and listened with the family to everything he said. Listened so intently that he was almost glad of her growing bodily burden that put the distance of mystery between them. She was married to Duncan Phelps. She was in love with Duncan. She was contentedly, even glowingly, bearing his child. The Sunday after Harlan Phelps's arrest Duncan had preached a sermon, stoic in dignity, searing in honesty, and compassionate of all human weakness, without ever mentioning his father. All of these qualities John admired and knew he must go on admiring. But it had left him oddly isolated and alone.

There was Claude. In answer to a four-word cable from Rome he had met her plane. She had kissed him lightly, without smiling, and said everything was just fine. He had attributed her quietness to jet lag. The next day the *Thatcher Standard* carried a brief, dignified account of Marc Vallon's death with no mention of Claude or the assemblage of curious birds of passage on the Ridge last spring. Claude became overnight a symbol of something slightly mysterious and distant from Thatcher. She had been to Paris. She had briefly touched the orbit of celebrity. And she had come home. It was all somehow satisfying. Thatcher could even extend the tendrils of sympathy. Claude was young, flighty, and a Roundtree, but she was one of them again.

But John sensed a deep change in her. When the primary was over, he might try to find out what it was. Right now, as he crossed into Flagpole Green, he found himself wishing Claude were beside him, to listen, to laugh, to reassure him, with that sparkling rush of irrelevancies, that the world was not quite as normal as he thought and was never to be taken as earnestly as he took it.

To his surprise he saw her sitting on the library steps. She wore an old skirt and sweater, her old loafers; her hair was tied back and although she did not need them she wore shaded glasses. Beside her lay two books, unopened.

"Claude! What the dickens are you doing here?"

"Oh, hi, John. It's nice here at this hour. Sort of quiet."

"Want company?"

"Oh, sure. Why not?" She moved slightly on the step.

"Larry told me he's asked you to the Harvest Square Dance tomorrow night at the gym."

"That's right. But I'm not going."

"What? The best do-si-do girl in town?"

"Maybe. But it's kid stuff. With Larry."

"Did you know he got a scholarship for medical

school while you were away? He's going to be a doctor."

"It's great," she said with enthusiasm.

"It is for him."

They sat in silence until she broke it.

"I'm so glad you're going to win, John."

"Now wait a minute. I'm just keeping my fingers crossed."

"Everybody says it's in the bag. I just wish I had been more help. But you didn't need me, after all."

"Of course I needed you. And you were a help. How many candidates around here have a sister who's been to Paris?" It was the wrong thing to say.

She picked up her books. "I just want you to win, John, more than—than anything in the world." He heard a slight tremor in her voice. There was a great deal he did not know about Claude now. And he suspected none of the others did.

"Come on, I'll walk you home, Sis."

"Okay."

They scuffled through the first fall of yellowed leaves.

"I've got a problem. Would you be interested?"

"John, you don't have to treat me like that. As if I were glass or something. Just because I'm home. Of course I'm interested."

"My problem is Orlini. He's back. Up on the Ridge now."

She gave him a sharp look but said nothing.

"He called me today. He wants me to come up and see him."

"What for?"

"I'm sure it isn't to wish me luck. He's got something on his mind that isn't for my benefit. My problem is do I go up there on command or ignore him?"

"You mean, run away from him?"

"I hadn't thought of it like that. I was thinking about Dad. You know how he feels. I have to consider—"

To his surprise she turned on him. "Consider! Consider! John, are you ever going to think for yourself? You do what you think you should or you forget it. If you don't do it, it's zero. If you do, you win or lose. But at least you've done what you want and not what somebody else tells you. That's what matters doesn't it? What can Ben Orlini do to you? You're going to win. Tell him so."

It was a new Claude. The penalty of time? Or something deeper? As they walked up the familiar street, beneath the giant maples, yellowing for another autumn, John had a sense of something forever lost. For an instant he would rather have heard a giggle: "Race you to the lamppost, John! Last one treats to fireballs!"

He would go to see Ben Orlini. Not that night, as Orlini wanted. That was too much like answering a command. But the next afternoon.

In the days since Claude's return the nightmare at the villa had begun to fade. The villa, the salon, the sensual mocking faces, the dark quarrel in the park, Marc's death. Not that she could ever believe him dead. Not that glowing intensity he could cast over the simplest things, like a picnic with wine. Perhaps she would never believe it. But the rest had taken on the dissolving colors of an impressionist painting. Like impressionism, the farther she stood away, the clearer certain outlines became. With every passing hour she saw Solveg as the real evil, the harsh, hawklike woman of the cliff, hurling false accusations at a man too sensitive to withstand them. Even before her plane had touched down in New York, Claude had convinced herself of Marc's sincerity. She could bear it all now. And forget the rest.

Even Hutch. Especially Hutch. He had not arrived at the flat at eight as he had promised. Earlier her phone had rung three times. The heavily accented voice had asked for an interview. She had no idea why anybody would want to interview her. Yes, she knew Mr. Vallon but she had nothing to say.

To her surprise Claude, in her first few days back, had not found Thatcher dull. Warmth, her own room, familiar objects, long-loved voices, the routine of everyday reached out to enfold her. She had been far. She was discovering the unguessed sweetness of coming home.

Yet there was a difference. She had done something strange and foreign. Fate had returned her to Thatcher but it had also set her apart. She sensed it first when she went down to John's headquarters. Bonnie was in full command. Six girls were lined up in the small room, Phyllis in front in an ungainly crouch. "Let's hear it, girls . . . chumulacka ching! chumalacka chum! you're the one, John . . . you're the. . . ." It stopped abruptly as Claude walked in.

"Claude! Golly, Claude! You look great!"

There was a brief pause. Exclamations. Greetings. But no one handed her a paint roller or asked her to step into the line. Phyllis returned to her crouch. Bonnie picked up the telephone. Activity went on. Claude stayed for a while, then drifted out. No one seemed to notice. She had done nothing. She had simply failed to make contact.

At the library Mrs. Haskell smiled uncertainly. "Claude, my dear. How nice to see you. Are you home

for good now?" Claude started for the Roundtree
Reading Room. "That reminds me. Whatever became
of that nice young man who was here when you took
out that book on acting? He was looking at topographical maps. But mostly at you, dear. Someone
said he was with those dreadful people up on the
Ridge. But he didn't look it to me. . . ." Mrs. Haskell's voice trailed as it always did when her thoughts
were regrettable.

The most unfortunate encounter took place in Slater's Stationery store.

"Claude Roundtree!"

"Oh, hello, Miss Blake."

"So you've been to Paris! You look thin. But that's
always good. Not sporting a Paris frock? Tell me, did
you get a screen test?"

How Belle Blake knew, Claude could not guess. But
Belle knew everything. And Belle was being talked
about these days. As always her defense was direct
attack.

"No, Miss Blake."

"What a pity! You might have, if you had studied
with me instead of giving up. I heard Mr. Vallon
died."

"Yes."

"But you were gone long before that. You know if
they don't see it in you right away and give you a
screen test, you might as well give up. Hanging
around gets you nowhere. I know. I've seen it happen.
Unless, of course, you had another reason."

Claude survived it as she survived the questioning
look in her mother's eyes.

"I'm just not an actress, Mom. I found that out."

"Well, you're home and that's all that matters. Something else will come along."

Her father had been blunter. "Thank heaven, you came to your senses, Claude." Then, softer: "It's good to have you home, little girl."

Yet a curious ache lingered inside her, something deep and unhealed. Something unfinished. She had no name for it. She would live suspended in this void until after the rally for John and the primary. She would do nothing to intrude on what had gone on so splendidly without her.

After his victory there would be time to pull her life together again.

John had not been to the Ridge since the Orlini house was finished. Now, as he parked his car on the wide circular drive, he tried not to think of the havoc Orlini had done. The great oak, the stands of beech and hickory and pine. He loved trees with a passion that would have sent him into forestry had not Michael, his brother—he would not think of that, either. John Roundtree had taught himself discipline. He could not help but expect discipline in others.

Ben Orlini, in an impeccable lounge coat, knife-pressed flannel slacks, and burnished brogues that made his small feet look even smaller, opened the door himself. He was the country gentleman affably at home except that his eyes were gimlet-sharp, his handshake brief.

"Sorry you couldn't come last night, John. We've lost some valuable time."

"Time for what, Mr. Orlini?"

Orlini smiled, ignored the question, and led the way into a small study paneled in redwood. He gestured to a chair.

"You're a very bright young man, John. I like you. I like a man who fights for success. I had to."

John declined a drink and waited. Ben Orlini wasted no time.

"It seems, John, I've backed the wrong horse."

John sat back in his chair. So this was it. Orlini wanted to buy him. John might at last have the opportunity to tell Orlini what he thought of him.

Ben let the statement register, then continued.

"Harlan Phelps is an idiot. I've known it for a long time. If a man can't keep his booze and his sex away from his constituency, he's worse than an idiot. He's a menace. But he's what I've got."

John was by nature taciturn. It was easier to wait this out.

"I'm not going to offer you my support, John. In the first place I don't think you'd take it. You Roundtrees have sat on your asses too long, cutting off your noses to spite your faces. I have no reason to think you'd change now. Besides I don't see you as a winner. You're doing better right now, but not enough better. You don't understand the game. The game is money. Nothing else!"

John's silence was beginning to nettle Ben Orlini. He poured himself a glass of plain soda.

"I'm not a loser. Anything I put money on comes home. I want Harlan Phelps for this district. We won't have any trouble with the election. The only trouble is the primary. That's you."

John uncrossed his long legs. "Mr. Orlini, what are you getting at?"

"I want you out of the primary."

John smiled. He could afford to. "I could have answered that over the telephone."

"But not this!" Ben rose, went to the library table that served as a desk and picked up a pile of folded newspapers.

"Do you read Italian?"

"No."

"French?"

"Some." John was aware of a sudden chill, a warning.

"But you can read English. There's the *Paris Herald*. I brought them all in on the plane yesterday."

John unfolded the newspaper. It took only a glance to understand.

MARK VALLON'S MYSTERY GIRL

The last love of Marc Vallon's free-style life before it ended after a bitter quarrel with his estranged wife and leading woman, Solveg Traner. She is Claude Roundtree, an American girl Vallon brought to Rome and installed in his apartment.

John's eyes shifted to the two-column picture. A long-haired blond girl, leaning against an ancient stone well. She was laughing, she was radiant, she was unmistakably Claude.

Something chilling gripped John's stomach.

"What's that got to do with me?"

"You recognize her?"

"If that's all you have to talk about—"

"Sit down, John, and don't be any more of a damn fool than you can help. Stiff upper lip. Family hanging in. You can shove that, son, because it isn't going to help. These wire photos are as hot as a pistol and you know it. I don't know what went on. But the truth doesn't matter."

"What do you mean the truth doesn't matter? That's all that does matter!"

"It's what people take for the truth that matters.

Hell, son, if you haven't found that out by this time, you better quit politics now. She was at Marc's place in Rome every day. The chauffeur testified to that. She was at his place in Paris. The concierge testified to that. They found at least a dozen snapshots of her around his apartment. As I say, I don't know what went on. The guy's been impotent for years. But that leads to a lot of guesswork, too. Right?"

John managed to keep his hands at his sides. He let the papers drop to the floor. Orlini retrieved them.

"Marc wouldn't listen to anybody. About anything. Even that lousy film he made up here at my place. Well, at least the world won't see that. But you have to feel sorry for the guy. Not because the film was a turkey, but because he didn't know it."

John had a sense that Orlini was talking to fill time. That he had not heard it all yet.

"Makes it tough for everybody. A thing like that." Orlini slapped the newspaper. "Most of all for you, John."

"Me?" John despised the small, shrewd man, but he despised himself more for being there.

"You don't get it, do you?"

"Sure, I get it. I don't know whether it's the truth or not. Claude's her own woman. Maybe she won't have to see it. If she cared for him, it will hurt."

Ben Orlini stared. "God Almighty, I don't believe it. You don't see. Look, John." His voice dropped to a softness his enemies would have recognized. "Look, I don't like to do things this way. I don't like to hit anybody who can't fight back. I got two sons of my own. One's a mental case in a Zurich sanatorium. The other's a Seeker of Light. Yeah, that's what he calls himself. Out in California. He wears sandals and shaves his head. My son, the Seeker of Light. The only time he sees it is when he's broke and writes me for money. No, I don't like to play rough with little guys. Unless I have to." He paused. "You don't have to tell that fancy little sister of yours anything. She can read all about it in the *Thatcher Standard* the day after tomorrow. The day before the primary."

Then John understood.

Ben continued. "Marc Vallon died a has-been. *The New York Times* won't give it much. The local papers may pick it up by next week. But that's too late and I know where Frank McQuade stands on the Round-trees. He'd kill it unless it's put under his nose."

"Which you'll do?"

Ben Orlini's voice was almost gentle. "I've got to win this one, John. I've come too far to miss. So it's up to you."

"Go on, spell it out."

"All you have to do is to announce that you are throwing your support to Harlan Phelps to—what the hell do they say—bind up the wounds in the district."

"You know I won't do that."

"In that case you've lost already, and little Claude—goddammit, John, don't make me do this. It's dirty, and I'm past that. I'm sick of fighting and I've had a bellyful of this town. I sit up here in this spook house and the phone never rings. I walk downtown and nobody talks. So I cut down an old tree. It was rotting, rotting they told me . . . don't you understand that? Now the roots reach out to the cliff, and three times the driveway has buckled." He looked past John. "Oh, get the hell out of here. Take those newspapers. Like I said, we haven't much time. I'll wait until midnight for your answer."

* * *

It was four o'clock when John reached the house. His father would not be in yet. Claude, his mother informed him, was upstairs in her room.

"I think she's getting over her blues, John. She looked quite happy when she came back this afternoon."

John went heavily upstairs carrying his newspaper-choked brief case. It would be kindest, he decided, to let her see them before Martin arrived home.

But kindness was thin solace now.

It would be an early fall. The autumn colors had already begun to fade, and the leaves were drifting, dry and carpetlike, across Thatcher lawns. Claude pulled her jacket closer and headed her bicycle out toward the valley. She regretted her rudeness to John last evening on the Green when he wanted to talk. But she could not lose her feeling of detachment, as if she no longer belonged to this place and this time. Perhaps because there seemed to be no need for her. She had severed herself this summer and life had flowed on full and expectant without her. John would win. They all seemed sure of that now, leaving her with a decision that had been half-made by her own abrupt return home.

She would go to the state university, at least long enough to get her bearings. She would not look back. She would not wonder what might have happened if she had seen Marc once more. But then she did not have to. She had something better in her pocket at this moment. The letter had come a week ago. Luckily that morning she had picked up the mail first. She recognized with a sudden dizziness the elegant foreign handwriting on the thin gray envelope, post-

marked Paris. She stifled an impulse to show it to her
family, as some sort of proof positive of her dreams,
her Destiny. After the primary perhaps. All the events
of life now hung like a new coat on a hook, for use
After the Primary.

But she had read the letter over and over, until the
folds were ragged and the envelope creased. She
would read it again this afternoon, for she knew now
where she would go. Up the slope, overlooking the
valley where she had sat watching Marc for the first
time. She did not have to remember or imagine. She
had only to relive it, the most meaningful hour of her
entire life.

She sat with her back against a tree, steadying the
gray paper against a new rising wind. The letter was
post-marked "Paris," before he went back to Rome.
He had thought of her even then.

My dear little Claude,

I am sitting in my studio tonight, looking at the
pictures we took together at Pompeii and thinking
of those charming hours.

A screen test is not as important as you think.
Your face will film. But you are young, little one,
so young that I must warn you, you must work,
work, work. You must learn discipline, control, and
the art of being someone else and yet remaining
yourself. That is not easy, but it is then that you
become an actress.

I will add one personal thought, and if it dis-
tresses you, I beg your forgiveness. The days we
spent together in Rome were the happiest within
my memory. You have the divine gift, the joy of
life. You shared it with me. I was grateful. What-

ever you become, that is your true essence, little
one. Never forget that. Never lose it.

> Your faithful and admiring friend,
> Marc Vallon

The name was scrawled. Claude reread it and again
the tears came to her eyes. She would never forget, not
as long as she lived. She had glimpsed greatness. She
would always be set apart.

"Good afternoon, young lady."

She gave a start and thrust the letter guiltily into
her pocket, a gesture Willard Roundtree did not miss.

"Hi, Uncle Will."

"I caught sight of you up here from the barn. So
you like the wind, too."

"What do you mean, too?"

"I like to think fresh wind is like new wine. Proves
the seasons roll." He glanced at her closely. There was
a change. Like a growing plant. Invisible, unmarked,
but suddenly a difference. "I haven't heard much
about that trip yet."

"I know. It's sort of frantic at home."

He nodded. "How was it?"

"The trip? Oh, neat."

"Did you make any notes in that book Charlie and I
invented for you?"

"It was just super, Uncle Will, but I didn't. Except I
did write one word. Rome." She smiled, and he was
glad to see it. The smile faded. She looked off into a
space of wide sky above the Ridge.

"One word, eh? That means you were pretty busy."

"Oh, I was." For an instant she longed to show him
the letter, to pour out the magic of those days that lay
like imprisoned light within her. But now now. Not

yet. "And I read that poem you wrote in it. It was neat."

He sighed. Her soul might have expanded but not her vocabulary. "Henrietta wrote one more verse. I'll write it in someday."

"Why not now?"

"Because you've come home."

The wind had turned sharp but she made no move to leave.

"Uncle Willard, that girl who ran away to New York a long time ago. And then came home and died. Chastity Roundtree. Was she a great actress when she came back?"

"I'm not sure what that means. But she was a great woman. The tragedy was that she was too young to know it."

"Too young! At *twenty-two*?"

He swallowed a smile. "Sorry, my dear. I do lose my perspective. Come back with me to the farm. Have some hot cider. Then I'll truck you and your bike home."

She shook her head and jumped up. "A rain check, Uncle Will, please."

"Anytime. Charlie Redwing's been asking for you. So has Clancy." As if in answer a deep, baying bark came from the valley. Willard motioned with his head. "He's got a porcupine down there now. Same old fella he worries at every fall. But he's getting smart. Finally."

She kissed him lightly. "Give that to Clancy for me."

She could not have explained her sudden impatience to leave. It was all so normal, so dear to her, yet it clung like cobwebs that she could not brush away. As if the strong old man, the baying dog, the familiar spread of fields and hills all conspired to imprison her in a childhood she had so completely fled.

She picked up her bicycle on the road, looked back, and waved. Willard lifted his cap in a courtly salute. He stood as if grown from the land, as straight and rooted as a tree.

At the fork in the road, she hesitated. Then slowly, thoughtfully, she headed her bicycle toward Thatcher and home. She passed John's campaign headquarters and abruptly stopped. She owed John more than she could ever repay and she had hardly thought about him. His picture, serious and intent, stood in the window like an accusation. She leaned her bicycle against the building and went in.

John was not there but it seemed to her everybody else in Thatcher was. A crowd of her friends were milling around, talking, answering three telephones, wearing hats that said JOHN ROUNDTREE, and filling the small office to overflow.

"Claude!" It was Bonnie Smith. "Where have you been? You're just the person we need!"

Larry Higgins, home from medical college, clutched her elbow. "Claude, we've been looking everywhere for you! You've got to lead this show!"

"Is John here?" Claude felt like a truant.

"No, he left early. And we're just as glad. For a wonderful guy like that, he is so bashful." It was plump, exuberant Phyllis, daughter of the newspaper publisher. "We've got a lot of ideas for the big rally the night before the election. And we want you up on the stage to lead it. Right?"

Claude caught her breath.

"Look, Claude . . ." Bonnie pulled her to the side of the room. "You've got to do this. Everybody knows

you went to Paris to be an actress. That's sort of glam-
orous. Besides, you're John's sister. You'll lead the
cheering and tell everybody how great John is. We'll
give you the program. Larry'll be up there with you!"
Bonnie swung to the crowd. "She'll do it, everybody!
Right, Claude?"

Claude heard a voice from somewhere. "She'd better! She hasn't done much yet."

She swung around, furious. "Oh, haven't I? Well,
maybe there are other ways of making John famous
besides just wearing a funny hat. Sure, I'll do it!
John's the greatest guy in Thatcher, and I know he's
going to win!" Claude felt all eyes on her. Somebody
began the applause. It was music. She heard her own
voice rise to a cheerleader yell. "Come on, everybody!
Chumlacka chum, chumalacka chow, who's gonna win
the game for us now? ROUNDTREE! JOHN
ROUNDTREE!"

The small office rocked with shouts. Somebody
slapped a campaign hat on her head. She heard yells
and applause.

"All right, everybody." Bonnie Smith was newly
brisk with authority. "Now let's get down to details.
The rally is at seven o'clock, the night before election,
at the school gym. It's up to all of us—you too,
Claude—to get the whole town out. Just hang on the
telephone. We'll distribute lists of names. Now let's
finish the signs."

It was late when Claude reached home. Edythe, in
the kitchen, gave a strained glance at Claude's face.

"Dinner's almost ready, dear."

"Where's John?"

"In the den, talking to your father."

"Right."

"Claude, why don't you wait until after dinner to talk to him?"

"I just want to tell him he's going to win. It's in the bag. But okay." Her mother looked suddenly tired.

The newspaper lay open on her bed. She stared at it, at the black headlines, at the picture of herself and then back again at the letters that broke into little black pieces which she could not seem to pick up and put together. MARC VALLON'S MYSTERY GIRL . . . Claude Roundtree . . . brought to Rome . . . installed . . .

"No! oh, no!" her cry was silent. For the first time in her emotional life Claude found no tears. Only that pounding in an emptiness. She realized there was a knock on the door.

John entered.

"I thought this was the kindest way, princess."

She nodded.

"I'm sorry. Honest to God I am."

She stared at him numbly. Didn't he believe her? Would anybody believe her? Something so precious in her life was being made ugly; sordid. And Marc was gone. No one could help her. No one could explain.

"Sit down, funny face."

She sat robotlike on the bed.

"Look, if you want to talk, okay. If you don't, okay too. If you don't feel like dinner I'll take you out and you can pretend to eat a hamburger."

"I'm all right, John."

"The hell you are. None of us are."

"Has Dad seen it? And Mom?"

"Claude—" he sat down next to her on the bed. "—it's over and done with. It's pretty rotten but it's behind us."

John sighed. And then was saved an answer.

"Dinner, everybody!" It was Edythe from the hall.

Martin was standing at the bottom of the stairs. A glimpse of his face, and the total implication of the lurid newspaper article struck Claude like a laser beam of deepened pain.

It was a tacit rule in the Roundtree household that whatever the crisis, dinner was to be faced, and talk civilized. More than one mouthful had been gulped down in silent anguish. But as often happened, by the time dinner was over, the crisis had been reduced to manageable proportions.

Edythe saw to it on this night that dinner was simple and quick. Claude ate little and said less. Kim's eyes drifted toward her, for suddenly Claude wore an aura of mystery. Martin was concerned lengthily about the situation in Washington. John volunteered that there was talk of a possible nuclear power plant on the site of the factory at Juno's Landing. Martin said he would certainly oppose that. Too many people in the area. Kim, when asked, answered that the pony Milkshake would remain in Jimmie's father's barn.

The name Marc Vallon lay like ghost's writing on the table cloth. To Claude he was a presence as heavy as pain. She glanced once at the oval painting that looked down on the table—Henrietta, with her dark, direct gaze, her masses of tumbled hair, her enigmatic smile—and wondered if that girl had ever sat at this same table in a torment she could not share.

At last it was over. Edythe said Kim would help clean up. John followed Martin into the study. Claude stood uncertainly for a moment in the hall.

"I'm going down to the stationery store. Anybody want anything?"

Martin paused at the study door. "No, thank you, Claude. You'll be back soon?"

"Yes."

Once settled in his black leather chair Martin took up precisely where he had left off before dinner.

"So he was married, too, John."

"If that's what you call it."

Martin adjusted his glasses on the newspaper he held and read: "'Mr. Vallon's friendship with his protégée, Miss Roundtree, was the last of many. He was married to Solveg Traner, the film actress, and despite their well-publicized stormy relations, neither ever sought a divorce, preferring to let their eighteen-year marriage drift into what amounted to secrecy.'" He peered over the paper. "I call that marriage, John, and if you don't, you'd better not let the voters know it."

"If you want the truth, Dad . . ."

"I'd like it from somebody."

". . . at this moment I don't give a damn about the voters. If they want me, they'll vote for me. If they don't, okay. Claude's taken a blow."

"Deservedly."

"She's been foolish. She knows it. Did you watch her tonight? She looked twenty-five. Maybe she cared about Vallon."

Martin slapped the newspaper back onto the table. "I don't wish to discuss that aspect of the matter with you, John. I've asked Claude to talk with me."

"Oh, no, Dad!"

"Are you telling me I haven't the right?"

"I'm asking you, Dad, to let her alone. At least for now. Stay off her back!" He had said too much and he knew it. He saw the old alienation in the fine aris-

tocratic face, the angry bewilderment that surfaced so
frequently since Michael had gone. But he could not
handle his father at a respectful distance forever.
Sometime, somehow, there would have to be a bridge.
An understanding that today was not yesterday, nor
tomorrow.

"That's a pretty ugly phrase, son."

"Let's skip it, Dad. Get on with Orlini."

Martin spoke softly, as if he hadn't heard. "A man
brings children into the world with what he hopes is
forethought. He raises them with what he believes are
principles. Decency. Loyalty. Honor. If you and your
generation think you can get on better without those—
necessities, then you'll try it. But not in my house or
under my roof. When you find you're wrong, I hope
you'll have the courage to come back and say so.
That's all I've ever expected of any of you."

It was more than his father had revealed of himself
in a long time. It was off the point, John thought, but
it was the wall behind which Martin found his security. He had to respect it.

"Sorry, Dad."

Martin was looking beyond him. Looking at Michael, John told himself. No matter what any of us do,
it's Michael he's never forgotten. Not for the first time
John found himself with the curious half-thought,
wherever Michael was, he had taken the wiser course.

"Orlini's deadline is midnight, Dad."

Martin rose. "You know what you want to do about
Orlini better than I do. If you don't give a damn
about the voters, as you say, the decision is even easier. You fight for what you believe in, son. Nothing
else is worth it."

Claude was standing in the doorway. "I changed

my mind about going out. You said you wanted to see me."

Martin sat down again. "Come in, come in."

"What did you want at the stationer's, Claude? I'll go down." John covered his discomfort.

"No, please, John. Anything Dad wants to talk about, I want you to hear."

She looked so vulnerable, so thin, as if drawn on a spindle to a fine thread. Yet father and son sensed, in their separate ways, that the thread had the tensile strength of wire. She was no longer a giddy teen-ager.

"This is not something I want to talk about, Claude. But I must."

She remained standing and nodded.

"Don't you want to sit down?" The question came reluctantly. Martin seemed to be losing already. He smiled thinly. "I dislike sitting in a lady's presence."

Dutifully she perched on a stiff chair. Like a schoolgirl, John thought. But not quite. As if she were filling a space she had already left.

"You saw the Paris papers, Claude?"

"John showed me before dinner."

"Orlini wants to give the story to the *Standard*."

"John told me. I'm sorry."

Martin brushed the words away. "I simply want to ask you, Claude, what happened?"

"What happened? When?"

"With this man—Marc Vallon."

For an instant she looked bewildered. Then her face lit up. What happened? A lie was too small for this, and the truth too big. She could never explain. Not here in this threadbare capsule of a vanished childhood. What happened? She would remember now only the magic, the golden light of Rome, the little trattoria across the river, the garden picnics, the moon-misted slave girl in the Forum, the charioteer in Pompeii, her own imagery of the future. She was even able to smile. And the smile reminded Martin of the oval painting in the dining room.

"Did you know he was married?" demanded Martin.

She shook her head. She had come to terms with that revelation. "You're either married and then you stay with somebody. Or you're not."

"So I must assume . . ."

"You must assume nothing. Because you can't. You don't know. You asked me what happened? How can I tell you? How could I ever describe it. Everything happened!"

Even John turned his head sharply.

"Everything!" Claude had found her release. "Everything that is magic and beautiful and different. Everything I never knew and will never see again. Everything that will never happen again as long as I live. I'm not an actress. I'll never be one. I blew it. The whole thing. I didn't tell you that, did I? It doesn't matter now. But I had my chance. I stood up in front of a lot of people and I couldn't remember anything, not one word that Mr. Vallon taught me. All I could remember were the silly lines from *Alice's Adventures in Wonderland* that you had read me, Dad. *Alice's Adventures in Wonderland!* Of course everybody laughed. But that doesn't matter now, either. You're asking me what *happened*." She stopped abruptly as if seeing Martin's expression for the first time. "But that's not what you really want to know, is it? You're asking me if I had an affair with Marc Vallon. If I—I slept with him."

She caught her breath. She would put it into words

for the first time. Right here at the core of her life and then she would be free of it forever.

"Would it have made so much difference to anybody, if I would have been happy?" She turned the wondering face of a woman to them. "It wasn't like that," she said softly. "It was different. He never asked me. If he had, I—it wasn't like that," she repeated. "And now—now he's gone."

She slipped from the chair, hesitated, and slowly walked past them out of the room, taller than Martin seemed to remember. For a moment he and John sat listening to the silence and the new rising of an autumn wind. Then he rolled up the Paris newspaper and thrust it into the waste basket.

"Tell Orlini," said Martin Roundtree quietly, "nothing."

Chapter Sixteen

Ben Orlini had not underestimated the weight of his attack on the Roundtrees.

Frank McQuade, editor of the *Thatcher Standard*, labeled the story scurrilous and printed a discreet account of Miss Claude Roundtree's return from Europe where she had been studying drama with the late Marc Vallon. It was not enough.

The *Bollington Eagle* repeated in embellished detail the story of Marc Vallon's filming on the Ridge and an imagined meeting of Claude and Marc.

But it was the grass-roots newspapers of the county, a chain owned by Caleb Appleby, Jr., unswerving in loyalty to Harlan Phelps, that gave full tongue to scandal. Front-page pictures of Claude appeared on the newsstands in such unlikely places as Pinebrook, Grantsville, South Forks, and East Canon. Issues were quickly sold out and as quickly found their way to Thatcher.

Martin Roundtree continued to walk to the office, his head high, his greeting courtly. John shook hands, aware that some eyes were more curious than cordial. At Ariel's urging Claude found herself spending more and more time in the shabby little yellow house now so incongruously Ariel's home.

"Claude, it will blow over." Ariel had the far-away look of pregnancy. Claude remembered the bitter gossip when Ariel had married Duncan, after Lowell had broken her engagement to him. There were some in Thatcher who had never forgiven the "French Cousin."

"I wouldn't mind if it was just about me, Ariel. But it's John. If he loses the election—"

"If he does, it wasn't meant for him. I tell Duncan that when he gets so discouraged about his work."

It was an inscrutable answer. And not like Ariel. But then Ariel had grown into herself in an odd way. Claude never felt so alone. All she wanted now was to get through the week ahead and go away. Anywhere.

For the night before the primary John's supporters had scheduled a rally in the high school gym. As the time neared, Claude's name skipped from tongue to tongue. There was talk about the Roundtree blood. It had always been unstable. Some of it downright bad. Older citizens remembered Chastity. She had taken her disgrace over the Ridge with her. No one expected that now, thankfully. Girls took those things less seriously these days, but there was the blood, and it was in young John Roundtree's veins. Decent, forthright, young John was a credit to the town. But when it came to sending a Roundtree to Washington . . . Thatcher's soldier citizens prided themselves on balanced judgment and fairness in their fashion. There was considerable head-shaking.

Claude's defenders were young, some envious, some ogling, but most recognizing her as one of their own.

"She didn't do anything in Paris worse than what goes on any summer in this town." With three pregnancies after Senior Prom, one of them the judge's daughter, and the Haskell boy caught with pot, anyone who listened—and few did not—had to agree!

No one troubled about the truth.

But deeper than truth, deeper than the Roundtree name, lay something troubling to the old town. Something furtive, born of long-ago isolation and ancient guilt, and lodged as firmly as the rocks in its ungentle soil. It was the inherited New England conscience. On its darker side, superstition.

A man had died inexplicably on the Ridge one day last spring. Thatcher had never been easy about the hasty conclusion that Leonard Ross's death was an "accident." Had he been sent to it by human hands that had so far escaped punishment? Or had he been drawn to it through a force beyond human control, true to the phantom-ridden legend that had long ago designated the Ridge "Place of Mighty Anger"? In Marc Vallon's end many in Thatcher saw justice done and their inherited fears realized. The Ridge had struck again at its enemies. And Claude Roundtree had entangled herself with them.

Whatever else was said or left unsaid, few in Thatcher intended to miss John Roundtree's rally the next night. That much, at least, Ben Orlini had guaranteed. One question only remained: Would Claude have the effrontery or courage, depending on the speaker, to be there?

At twenty minutes before seven they stood grouped in the hall. Martin, Edythe, Kim, and John. Claude came down the stairs slowly, a jacket over her arm.

They were unaware, all four of them, that they were looking upward, watching her.

"What are you waiting for?" She had reached the middle step.

"You! Slowpoke!" John was determinedly cheerful. Martin had his pocket watch in his hand. Edythe looked nervous. "Do hurry, dear."

Claude stopped on the third step. "I'm not going with you," she said evenly.

There was a small gasp. The answers came in a volley.

"Claude dear!" "Oh, come on, princess." "Chicken!" said Kim. Martin's was the firmest and the last. "I think you must, Claude. We'll all be together."

She descended to floor level, their level, telling herself she must speak slowly, coolly. She must make them understand. "I am not chicken," she said icily. "I will not be coaxed and coddled like a child. And there is no reason why I *must* go with you. I have thought it all out. And I've called Bonnie and told her I will not lead the cheering. I will not sit on the platform, with you, John. I will not sit in the first row with my family. And they can do anything they want. Without me."

"Right on, everybody!" John moved toward the door.

"I'm not through yet!" A tightness in her voice brought them back. "I'm not afraid to do any of those things. That's what everybody will say, but I can face that. John, you've got to win! I want that more than anything. And I haven't been any help to you." The tightness spread to a tremor. "But I'm not going to hurt you. Any more than I have. If I sit up there on that platform tonight, you know who they'll be looking at! You could talk all night and turn cartwheels and they'd still be looking at me and whispering." She made a mock gesture with her hand concealing her mouth, with a vivid grimace. Kim giggled.

"What's more. . . ." She caught her breath. "I might as well say it all now, Dad. I don't want to be 'all together.' You and Mom want to protect me. You think if you're all around me when I get there, we'll show everybody we're one great, happy family. Dad, I can't be like that. I'm grown up now. I don't want to be protected. I don't want to be safe because you make it so. I want to make my own mistakes even when I know they're mistakes. I went to Paris this summer and made a lot of trouble for everybody. I'm sorry for that. Sorrier than any of you know. But it wasn't a mistake. Maybe there was a lot I didn't understand but it wasn't a mistake," she repeated. "Look!" Her eyes filled and her hand shook as she reached into her skirt pocket and pulled out a crumpled gray envelope. "Mr. Vallon wrote me this. He was going to help me. Now. . . ." She swallowed, and her eyes glittered. She blinked back the tears. "But I can do what he told me. 'Work, work.'" She pocketed the letter. "And that's what I'm going to do. I'm going to the university. They have a drama department. And I'll get a job. And if I don't make it, it's my problem. Isn't it? Don't you—"

A car horn interrupted her and sent Kim to the window. "It's Larry Higgins, Claude. I thought he had a girl."

Claude slipped past them to the door. "He said he'd drive me to the rally," she said quietly. "I wouldn't miss it, John, for anything. I'm just going to sit with everybody else, and if they talk about me, it won't hurt you. I know you're going to win! I just know it!"

"Hasn't Larry a girl?" Kim demanded.

"I'm not going to marry him, silly. I'm just going to the rally." Claude managed a smile. "See you later."

Edythe dimmed the hall light. It was hardly necessary. They were all aware that Claude had taken most of it with her.

"We'd better start, John." Martin returned his watch to his vest pocket and gathered his two remaining children. "We should not be the first. Nor the last."

Chapter Seventeen

Davison L. Hutchins slid his rented car into the rain-soaked traffic leading out of Kennedy Airport and swore softly. The near-hurricane on the Atlantic Coast, so common in early fall, had blown up from the Caribbean to delay his plane three hours, cause him to miss his connection to Hartford, and force him into this creeping traffic. It would be late afternoon at best before he reached Thatcher and that was not the way he had planned it.

In fact he could hardly call it planning. It was gut reaction or instinct or, on a lesser level, stubbornness. The letter she had left for him in Rome was clear. Much less would have sent him flying from any other girl he had ever known. He knew it by heart.

> Dear Hutch,
>   There is no use waiting for you to take me to the airport, because it won't help anything. I do not want to see you again, although you have been very nice about some things. I am going

home and that's that. At least you didn't say I
told you so. There are a lot of reporters or something wanting to get into the flat, because it was
Mr. Vallon's, I suppose. So a girl here will show
me out a back way. Please don't—DON'T—follow
me to the airport because it will only confuse everything. I wish you a lot of good luck and plenty
of soaring, if that's what you really like.

Goodbye,
C.

Under the *C* she had seen the beginning of another
letter that could have been *L*. but he was not sure.

He was too angry to pursue her. In the hectic days
that followed he found it easier and easier to resist
calling or writing her. Besides, he told himself, what
could you convey to a girl like Claude in writing? She
would read it upside down or right to left and make
of it something far from his intention. It was not until
the morning her picture had jumped at him from the
front pages of the Rome newspapers that he knew he
must see her once more. Only once. Her face revealed
her happiness. He recognized the ancient well at Pompeii. So Vallon had taken her there, too. He did not
believe one word of the news story. He knew better.
But he had to see her. Once more.

He wound up Vallon's tangled affairs as best he
could, while admirably enacting public grieving. He
saw Solveg through her stages of hysteria and the
pressures of her creditors. When a new benefactor appeared, he had not been surprised. Solveg retired in
becoming black to Capri. Ben Orlini, he was sure,
would ultimately follow.

At last he belonged to himself. His life had taken
some shape with the arrival of a cable from Denver

offering him a partnership in a new air freight company. He cabled his old flying buddy a fast "Yes."

He would arrive in New York in the early morning, be in Thatcher by midday, then take a midnight plane to Denver. It was no plan at all; it allowed for nothing unforeseen. But he didn't want to call ahead. A phone call could terminate everything. He wanted to see her. Her face. Besides, he had a sweater to deliver.

Traffic lightened on the Connecticut Thruway. By the time he turned northwest at Bridgeport, the skies were beginning to clear. He hardly noticed that September's glory of color had been stripped from the trees by the storm. As the hills appeared and the landscape widened, Hutch was grateful for every intervening mile. What happened in Pompeii would never vibrate to Thatcher.

It was three thirty when he drove into Juno's Landing, nine thirty at night, Rome time. Hutch remembered that he had not eaten in ten hours. Near-starvation was not a condition in which he wished to see Claude Roundtree for the last time. He pulled his car up at Big Moon's Diner.

"Coffee and a hamburger," said Hutch. "Rare. No onions." The big man behind the counter scrutinized him, but Hutch looked away. Okay if he was recognized. He just didn't want to talk about it now.

There was one other customer in the place, youngish, with a tawny beard and a wilderness of long hair to match.

"More coffee, Pete?"

The young man nodded and rested his arms on the counter. "Well, the kid did it, didn't she?"

"Yup." Big Moon slid a cup and saucer to Hutch.

"I thought when that guy stood up at the rally and

hollered out her name, John was going to come right off that platform to mix it up good. Instead she comes walking down the aisle as if she owned the place and could spit on it." Pete grinned. "And she sure did. 'I know what you're thinking, you big dummy, and all of you, and I don't care. You're here for my brother, and he's not me. All I can say is you better vote for John because you'll never find anybody greater in this whole town.'" Pete drained his cup. "I don't say she won for him, but she sure didn't hurt him." He chuckled. "Bet it's the first time Fatso Muller's ever been called a big dummy. In public." He dug for a dollar bill. "Think Johnnie will change when he gets to Washington?"

"Why would he?"

"Sure, they're all proud as hell, that Roundtree tribe. But they know who they are. And I guess that's class." He rose. "Class or whatever it is, the kid's got it." For an instant Pete looked distantly at something he would never possess. "Got to clean up the Rock before the heat turns up. This weather's lousy for business."

Hutch finished his hamburger quickly.

He would have liked to talk with the bearded man. With both men. But he felt oddly alien, out of it. They knew her. They belonged, all of them. He was the stranger. He wondered if it was his own life that had gone awry. Maybe the kindest thing he could do would be to turn around and drive directly back for the Denver plane. She was all right. And the worst was over. *I do not want to see you again,* she had written.

The wind was dying; a lemon light drenched the sky. He scuffled through the dry leaves on the porch and pushed the doorbell. He waited and pushed again. Nothing. No footsteps, no voices. He pushed a third time and listened to the answering silence.

It was the one thing he had not expected. There was nothing unusual about people all being out in late afternoon, he told himself. But he had pursued a wavering mirage of her face, her welcome, of a house always warm with life.

He returned to his rented car and drove aimlessly onto Main Street. He lingered along the Green, looking at the library steps as if she still might be sitting there. In Higgins Pharmacy, a counter boy told him briskly that Larry wasn't working there now. He could not go around town asking for a whole family.

He headed the car out of Thatcher, took a turn he remembered with the clarity of hope, and drew up in front of Willard Roundtree's farmhouse. The great red dog lying in front of the door rose and let a bark dwindle to a growl.

"I believe we've met. Clancy, isn't it?" said Hutch.

The dog's heavy tail wagged but he did not move from the door.

"Is anybody home?" said Hutch.

The dog's tail continued to sway but Clancy stayed where he was.

"Okay. I get it. Mind if I ring the bell?" Hutch leaned across the dog and rang. The same emptiness, the same deadened silence. "I guess not. Where is she, fella? I've got less than three hours in this town. Less than three hours to ask the biggest question in my life. You don't have to ask questions, boy, but I do. And I can't find her. What the hell, I can't find anybody. Where is she? Where's Claude?"

The big dog's tail thumped vigorously. He stretched, barked, and put his huge head in Hutch's hand. Then he lay down again and fixed his eyes on Hutch.

"Right. We're friends. But you aren't telling, are you?"

He stood for an instant looking down the long stretch of empty valley. He had responded to it the first time he had seen it. Now he knew that if he could find her, he would take her from it.

He drove quickly down the road, on an impulse turned at the fork, and went up the Ridge. The heavy chain across the approach was gone. There was no barrier to the spread-eagled, glass house. For a reason he could not explain, except that there seemed nothing else left to do, he continued up, up to the graveled circle of the driveway. He noticed cracks in it. Dead leaves covered the brick path. He skirted the house to the leaf-skimmed pool and remembered Solveg sunning her superb nude body. He walked along the edge and saw Claude again, blue-jeaned and up-ended, trimming grass, her hair a fan of silver across her face. At the end of the pool the satyr still clasped the nymph, but one thick marble hand was missing.

"Looking for someone?"

The voice came from the terrace, thin and hostile as an east wind. Hutch whirled. In a sheltered angle of the terrace a man sat in a wheelchair. A robe was spread over his knees, one hand lay beneath it. Hutch walked rapidly up the steps toward him.

"I'm sorry. I thought there was no one . . ."

"Why did you think that?" The man was neither young nor old. He might have been handsome except for the deathlike pallor of his skin, emphasized by near-black hair and dulled eyes. His mouth slacked at the corners.

"I know the owner, sir," began Hutch.

"I am the owner. Come on, come on. I want to look at you. I thought at first . . ."

A suspicion entered Hutch's mind, interrupted when a tall graying woman, muffled in a bulky gray sweater and scarf, slid open the glass door.

"Who are you talking to, dear?"

Julia Orlini saw Hutch and stared.

"We have a visitor, Mother."

She came toward Hutch. "I know you, don't I?"

"Davison Hutchins, Mrs. Orlini. I apologize for intruding."

She brushed that aside. "Of course. Hutch. Marc Vallon's assistant. We met several times."

"Who is it?" The whine came from the chair.

"It's a friend, darling. Davison Hutchins. He was here last summer with the movie people. Hutch, my son, Nicholas Orlini."

Nick held out his left hand. Hutch shook it. It was limp and dry.

"Ben is still in Rome." Julia bent and adjusted the wheelchair robe. "On business. Nick wanted to come home and so did I. Doctors know so little these days. We haven't really had time to put things in order."

"You're not the preacher-boy," Nick said unexpectedly. "I thought you were. If you had been . . ." He drew his right hand from beneath the lap robe. It held a small black revolver. He took aim at the spot where Hutch had been standing beside the pool. Julia gave an almost imperceptible shake of her head. The gun, she seemed to say, was not loaded.

"Had a bad fight with the deacon once," Nick dropped the revolver in his lap. "Over a girl. A hot wench. I wanted her. She married the preacher-boy instead. What was her name, Mother?"

"It doesn't matter, does it, darling?"

"Ariel. I was even going to marry her. Ariel Round-tree. She'd have given me a bad time. Like all the Roundtrees." He aimed the gun again, this time at one of the life-sized, nude statues flanking the pool.

"We said we'd forget all that, Nick. You promised to be happy here with me." Julia moved nervously to put a quieting hand on the thin shoulder.

"I am happy, Mother. We're up here. They're all down there, the bastards! They beat us this time, but it's going to be Dad's town someday. And mine. Then you'll see."

Julia's eyes pleaded with Hutch. "How long are you going to be here?"

"Just a few hours." A slow horror had begun to uncoil in the pit of Hutch's stomach. He had known about this son. The car accident, over the Ridge. But he could not have guessed the hatred left in that damaged brain. He wondered if that was all that was left.

"You know where the Roundtrees are now?" The revolver waved back and forth. "In church. All of them. I saw them going in when we drove past. On their knees, I hope. But no time to pay my respects then, was it? 'The quality of mercy.' Shakespeare. Ariel liked Shakespeare."

"Nick darling, you're frightening Hutch with that thing. Explain to him, dear, it isn't loaded."

"My mother would like me to explain, Mr. Hutchins, that this revolver is not loaded. She checks on it every once in a while to make sure. And of course Mother is always right. Right? Right."

Julia spoke hurriedly. "If you're in Thatcher again, Mr. Hutchins, do come and see us. We don't have many visitors."

She was urging him to leave. He shook hands and forced himself to walk slowly from the terrace. As he reached the corner of the house, he heard the shot. He spun around. Julia was holding her hands to her eyes. Nick was smiling.

Alongside the pool one of the statues stood headless. At its base lay a shattered marble face.

The September day was fading. Here and there a light appeared as Hutch drove into Thatcher. Had there been any wisdom in that madness? He would not try to guess why the Roundtrees were all in church. But he would drive down the street once more, if only to free his mind of the horror on the Ridge, to find normalcy in the steadfast old house on West Street.

He turned the corner. To his disbelief the windows glowed with light. A wedding? Or what? He felt his heart pound. A line of cars forced him to park away from the house. He loped down the block, caught his breath at the white picket fence, and slowly mounted the worn, painted steps. He first looked through the window.

The room was filled with people. He caught a glimpse of John talking seriously to someone. He looked confident and at ease, the look of a winner. He saw Willard Roundtree seated on a divan, talking to an animated, dark-haired woman he did not know. She had a Roundtree look. There was no sight of Claude.

He rang the bell. The door opened almost at once. He was confronted by a chubby, pigtailed girl.

"Miss Claude Roundtree?" In his own ears he sounded like a schoolboy.

The pigtails bolted. He heard a yell: "CLAUDE!"

And then she was coming toward him, straight, direct, in a honey-colored dress that did something to her skin, and an expression he could not remember

seeing. Not surprise, not uncertainty, but a steadiness
that was a little disconcerting.

"Hutch!"

"I have two hours here. Will you come and have
dinner with me? Now?"

"Who is it, Claude?" Edythe had appeared behind
her.

"It's—It's Hutch. Someone I knew . . ." she was
fumbling. So she still had feelings.

"Davison Hutchins, ma'am. I was here last spring. I
would like your daughter to have dinner with me."

"I can't. The whole family's here. Ariel's baby was
christened and—"

Edythe glanced at her daughter. "I don't see why
not, Claude. It's all over and, goodness . . ."

That put a new focus on the matter. Hutch was
aware that the pigtailed child was surveying him from
the shoes up. Willard Roundtree had come through
the hall.

"Hutchins, my boy!"

"Good evening, Mr. Roundtree." They shook hands
gravely, their eyes meeting. "Saw your Clancy this afternoon, sir."

"Well." The eyes twinkled. "Did you pass?"

"He wagged his tail but he didn't say."

Claude was standing woodenly.

"Well, well. Nice night to go out, Claude. There
ought to be a moon. Calm after storm, you know."

Then they were outside, Claude trailing silently.
Hutch stifled an impulse to help her into the car. She
got in quickly and closed the door. As he started the
motor, he held up his hand.

"Don't say it. Don't say anything. Not for quite a
while. Just sit there. Just—be."

He drove out of Thatcher. He had no idea where he

was going. More of his nonplanning. Besides, he was feeling a certain unaccustomed giddiness in the head. She sat there, small, silent, her hands folded in her lap, looking straight ahead.

As they left the outskirts of the town, the rim of a huge orange disk showed over a distant hill. Suddenly he knew where he wanted to drive.

"I thought you said you had only two hours, Hutch."

"Some two hours are longer than other two hours."

They were on a flat promontory of rock above the floor of the land. She sat with her arms wrapped around her knees gazing into the night. The great golden moon had crested the hills and now was silvering, flooding the valley below with a sea of light. Bright enough, he thought, to see the color of her eyes if she turned them to him, and the lustre of her hair if she had not pinned it high on her head. Bewitching, but different. Too different.

The air had the softness of Indian summer, that autumnal blessing that followed the first hard frost and told man that the earth was at rest and that a brief hour of magic was his.

The silence was complete. But not quite. No country silence ever is. From the distance an owl protested the night's brilliance. Nearer, crickets lifted the strident frenzy of their seasonal dance.

But it was the silence he sought. Silence for two.

She spoke at last. "How did you find this place?"

"Devil's Spy? On a topographical map. I like maps." He wondered if she remembered. But she did not turn her head. "I read this is where the Old Boy watched the town."

She let another pause pass. "It has another name. 'Smoke of Peace.' Indians used to send up signals when their enemies had gone."

He concealed a smile. "Have you been up here lately?"

"No," she said gravely. "Not for a long time. We used to come here with Uncle Willard. It's at the far edge of his property. He has a cabin over there that he keeps for hikers and cross-country skiers. Just as a shelter."

The silence returned. He saw the log cabin now. Twenty yards away, the corner of the roof showed in the moonlight.

"There are lights!"

He turned abruptly, but she was not pointing to the cabin, but far across the valley. In the moonlight he could see the gleam of glass and a few pinpricks of light.

"I thought the house was empty. Mr. Orlini has gone."

It was not what he wanted to talk about. "Mrs. Orlini is there. With the son."

"Nick?"

"Do you know him?"

"Not much. But my sister Lowell does. She was mad for him once. That's why she didn't marry Dunkie. Wait'll she hears he's back. She'll be home for keeps. He must be better now."

That was a road he would not follow. He rose.

"Claude . . ."

She jumped up. "I guess we better be going. Right?"

Had Thatcher totally enfolded her as he once hoped it would? Or had she been so deeply hurt that she had only this capsule, this outer entity, to withdraw into so that nothing would ever hurt again? He had indeed pursued a mirage.

"Hungry?"

"Sure. But I'd like to take a look at Uncle Will's cabin before we go."

He followed her past a group of birches and a thicket of juniper, bark, and berries, silver in the night. She pushed the cabin door open. "Uncle Willard leaves it unlocked. He just trusts people to be neat. He says people who come this far into the valley can be counted on."

The cabin was swept clean. A Franklin stove, a broom, and a bushel basket of kindlings furnished it. The moonlight filled it.

Suddenly they were aware. The stirrings of the night, the closeness, the aloneness, and the mystery within themselves.

"Oh—Hutch!"

"I love you."

"I—I—"

"And you love me, if you weren't too pigheaded to admit it." He kissed her, tightening his arms as if he would never let anything so slight and so tense slip from him again. He felt her soften, saw her shining hair slide over her shoulders.

"I—I must say it! Hutch—" She pulled back. "Hutch, I've never loved anyone before. Not really. Not like this. Not in my whole life. And no one has loved me. Do you understand?"

He understood. "What do you want, Claude?"

Then she knew. As surely as she knew this place, this moment, and the inevitability of all the days ahead.

She slid her arms around his neck and lifted her face. In the silence that was not silence, the moonlight swept over them. The cabin, that was only a shelter, sheltered their first love.

Willard, dozing stubbornly on the divan, heard at last their return. From the lighted window, he watched them leave the car. On the path to the house they stopped. He saw her go into his arms, saw him hold her, confident and strong.

"It'll be a year before I can get established, Claude."

"I'll be at school. And working. It'll be okay."

"Sure?"

"Sure."

He released her and walked rapidly from her. He looked back once. She stood, one arm half raised, her face newly luminous.

The last, faded lines of Henrietta's verse drifted into Willard's mind.

> But know there is a shore where I, too, walk
> Along a wild and darkly beckoning sea,
> Wind-tossed, and body bared in secret flight,
> From hedge-row'd days and night's numbed
>   custody.

Claude—Chastity—Henrietta. Did he know her, this proud young man?

The moon rode small and cold, foretelling winter. Claude turned slowly toward the house.

A time of waiting had begun.

In this first stirring novel in a 4-part series, you will meet:
Henrietta, the exotic New Orleans beauty who became the
matriarch of the Roundtree clan; Lowell, the fiance of Duncan Phelps, whose spirit runs wild with secret shame about
to explode! And Ariel, Lowell's Paris bred cousin and a restless sophisticate, her destiny calls her back to her ancestral
land—and Duncan Phelps. They are proud. Sensual. Commanding. It is in their blood to take what they have to have.

A DELL BOOK $2.50
(17594-1)

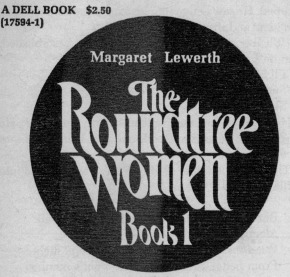

Margaret   Lewerth

The Roundtree Women

Book 1

**The Roundtree Women love
only once. Forevermore!**

At your local bookstore or use this handy coupon for ordering:

Dell	**DELL BOOKS**	THE ROUNDTREE WOMEN: BOOK 1 $2.50
	P.O. BOX 1000, PINEBROOK, N.J. 07058	(17594-1)

Please send me the above title. I am enclosing $_____
(please add 35¢ per copy to cover postage and handling). Send check or money
order—no cash or C.O.D.'s. Please allow up to 8 weeks for shipment.

Mr/Mrs/Miss_____

Address_____

City_____ State/Zip_____